CHUY WINS!

CHARLES ALVARADO

PROLOGUE

His breath was coming back, just like it always did, after all the miles, the practices, the sparring. After all the work, his breath was coming back. Sweat burned his eyes as it always did. His legs screamed for oxygen. There was that familiar weakness and fatigue from the top of his hips to the bottom of his feet. But now there were new feelings, new parts that hurt. His left eye had never been swollen like this. Most of all, his body had never hurt like this before. He had never been hit in the ribs and abs like this. That pain was new, as new as the noise, the lights, huge crowd, and the enormous stadium.

The Land of Lincoln Arena, with its glaring lights and cavernous hallways, was large enough to hold every concert in Central Illinois. Now on Championship Night, with the ring in the middle of the huge venue, all the attention was on Chuy and one of the best middleweights in the nation.

William 'Guns' Gundersen added one more element of unfamiliarity. The guy Chuy had seen in the sports pages and heard about in every boxing gym in Illinois now stood across the ring from him. He was in the blue corner and Gundersen was in the red corner, and now Chuy had a chance to win. 'Pony-boy' Ledesma over 'Guns' Gundersen! Three more minutes and that long shot of long shots could come true!

The minute between this last round was frantic, but time froze for Chuy. All the thoughts that ran through his head: his mother and father, the divorce, literacy class, the first talk with Coach Wolf, sappy Coach Alvarez, tough-ass Coach Sultan, Ms. Kelly and Best Pals Club, Armani and his gang banger wannabe buddies, Billy, and the weed, but most of all, Lucy.

The way Lucy looked after practice, all glowing with sweat, making him feel like he never had before. Her smile made him weak and nervous, and so happy he felt like he would burst. Lucy had fought so well. It had been the fight of the night. At least that's what he thought until the announcer stepped into the ring and jolted him from the thoughts racing through his head. The man with the huge voice and white tuxedo grabbed the mic and announced, "Ladies and Gentlemen, please give it up for these two amazing warriors. *This has truly been the fight of the night!*"

CHAPTER 1

Sophomore year had come and gone as quickly as a summer breeze at West Layden High School. The sprawling, two story, 70's style building, spitting distance from the airport, had made the change from fourth-generation Irish and Italian kids to Mexican youth, whose parents had made their way to the working-class suburb of Chicago. Parents had struggled North from Mexico to the westside of Chicago, and somehow, someway got their families to a small suburban town, surrounded by many other suburban towns. Some of these towns were big, some small, some rich, some very rich and some were battlefields for gangs and drugs. Yet all were within a ten-mile bike ride of each other.

Chuy lived in Northlake and went to school in Northlake, and at seventeen years of age, he did not really know many other places. Sure, he would visit family in Pilsen, the Mexican area on the near south side. He sometimes rode his bike through River Forest where the Chicago gangsters used to live in their mansions with big iron fences and lawns that looked like golf courses. Gangsters had been replaced by surgeons, financial advisors and owners of big companies, but they were still not places where Chuy and his family belonged.

That is, everyone except his *Tio* Eduardo, who was the foreman for Garcia's landscaping. *Tio* Ed worked at the mansions once every two weeks. One time, when he was ten years old, Chuy had gone with him and got a taste of hard, hot work. Chuy liked it. He liked to sweat and work. He liked the large clean lawns, but the huge mansions made him nervous. They were too much for anyone he had thought.

No, living in his little house in Northlake was just fine for Chuy. Layden High School was just fine, too. Layden had its own neatly trimmed grounds, green manicured fields far as the eye could see, fields for football, soccer and of course, baseball. There were two baseball diamonds, a small one for the freshman-sophomore team and a larger, newer, fancier one for the varsity.

This was tryout day. Today was the day when Chuy passed the frosh-soph field and stepped onto the varsity field for real. He had been on the field all summer for summer ball. He had shown Coach Wolf what he could do. He made it a point to be the first one on the field every summer afternoon. He took extra batting practice after every practice. Chuy played the game of baseball like he did everything: steady, solid, hardworking. And Coach Wolf knew it. So now it was tryouts. His time to be steady, solid and the hardest worker.

Chuy knew where he stood in the program, on the team and with Coach Wolf. Star of the team (and Chuy's boyhood friend) Ricky Ramirez, a senior, would start at shortstop. Chuy would back him up, play utility infield this year. Next year he would step into the starting shortstop position. He would not be the star that Ricky was, but not many Layden athletes could achieve that.

The only guy Chuy needed to beat out was Victor Giordano. However, Chuy wasn't worried. Victor was one of the few guys slower than he was and his bat was not nearly as good. Chuy took the field with confidence. At one hundred and forty-five pounds, Chuy was not big and not fast, but he was solid in the field and if he got hot, he could hit as well as anyone.

Now that Varsity tryouts were finally here, Chuy took a minute to take it all in. It was a bright, crisp spring day. The old rusty Layden water tower cast a long shadow across the field. Ricky's girlfriend had brought her friends to cheer on the star, and a few third-shift working fathers had set up their lawn chairs along the third base line.

Chuy surveyed the field, thinking how much he had missed all of it. He loved wearing his cleats and the glove he had been using ever since he could remember. The bat he got last year was slung over his shoulder and it was working for him. He was ready for things to turn out just like he had planned. He was ready to play his part on the team. Ready for this year and the next. What he was not ready for was one of the great facts of life: Complications can get in the way of plans. This time that complication was a freshman named Manny Ochoa.

Two easy laps, warm-ups and time to take some infield practice. Just like freshman and sophomore years. For Chuy it was as easy a routine as waking up in the morning. He loved to take infield practice. Coach Wolf hit grounders, first to Ricky, then to Chuy. Then came the new kid, Manny. *What was this new freshman doing here?* This kid didn't look like any freshman Chuy had ever seen. Manny looked more like a senior. He played like a senior as well, like a guy that had been in the game and playing the game well for more than a few years. A weird feeling was growing in Chuy's gut. The same feeling he had had freshman year during tryouts. His confidence started to diminish. It was disappearing like a grounder into Ricky's glove.

Coach Wolf was popping grounders to the three shortstops: first to Ricky (scoot, gather and fire the ball to first base). Then it was Manny's turn to scoot, gather and fire to first. Finally Chuy, who scooted (not as fast, not as far) gathered (not as smoothly) fired (not as accurately and not with the same "pop" as the freshman). Chuy could feel it. Coach Wolf could see it. Everyone could. Some of the outfielders standing in line were watching Ochoa. Other coaches working with the outfielders took extra seconds between hitting fly balls to watch this over-sized freshman field and throw. The other infielders were getting excited watching Ricky and Manny. Ricky was starring. Manny was shining. Chuy was fading.

I've got to hit! thought Chuy. *I've got to get on track with my bat.*

The pressure weighed down on him from the outside and squeezed him from the inside.

My bat has got to come through today. It's got to come through!

Ramirez stepped to the plate and peppered shots all over the field, smoothly and effortlessly. The word "tryout" did not apply to him. It was just the first and easiest day of practice. Ricky hadn't tried out since freshman year when, even back then, he had been the best player on the team. He cracked line drives and screaming grounders down the lines. When a curveball hung, it sailed over the left field fence. Guys watched more than they fielded as Ricky finished the show and tossed away the bat. It was just another day of being Ricky Ramirez. As they passed each other, Ricky gave Chuy a wink and a smack on the back. For a moment Chuy wondered what it would be like to be a star. To be that good, to make it seem so effortless. No time for that; he needed to concentrate. His bat needed to come through. Chuy needed to keep his spot. Time for Chuy to show Coach Wolf what he could do.

He gripped his bat, ignoring his stomach that churned from nerves. He willed himself into a state of denial. He was going to show that freshman what a varsity infielder could do. The first pitch was a swing and a miss, but that was the only pitch he would miss. Chuy hit steady line drives, a few right to a waiting fielder, but most found their way to the outfield for base hits. Nothing flashy, but steady, consistent, solid. Crack! Crack! Crack! His bat was hot and with each shot Chuy felt loose and more confident.

He glanced over to Coach Wolf who was watching intently. His brow was furrowed with concentration. Next to him stood Ricky, with a big smile on his face. Chuy cracked his last line drive into right center over the mitt of the leaping second baseman. He was feeling unusually cocky, for a guy who didn't like show-offs. He prided himself on not being "that guy." He didn't think it was classy. In the summer, after a win, a big play, or a big hit Coach Wolf would say, "Act like you have been there before." But in truth Chuy had never been there before. He had never been this hot at exactly the right time. On his way back to the bench he walked past Manny. "Beat that, kid!" Chuy said with a smirk.

Then it was Ochoa's turn to bat. The freshman did not look rattled. He looked pissed. Chuy began to wonder if this kid was really a kid. How could he be a freshman? He seemed more like a semi-pro coming back to high school, like the plot in some worn-out movie. All Chuy could do was hope for the best. He hoped for Manny's worst. For a moment he thought he had gotten his wish. Manny swung at the first pitch so hard that he almost fell. Swing and a miss! Chuy was feeling better. He glanced to his left. Coach Wolf was still concentrating. Ricky was still easy-breezy, with a big smile on his face. Chuy suddenly felt another twinge of envy. What would it be like to be Ricky? A star would never have to worry about an overgrown freshman, but Chuy would never know that feeling. Ewe

He pulled his attention back to the freshman. Manny was set; the pitch came, followed by another swing. Way too hard, but this time wood hit ball. A line shot went scorching down the left field line. Foul! What a relief. The next pitch became a towering fly to left, over the fence, but once again foul. Each pitch Manny connected with but pulled foul. Chuy's shoulders loosened and his breath became more regular. Then this kid in a man's body did something that caused Chuy, Coach Wolf, and Ricky to shake their heads all at the same time. Manny switched to the other side of the plate. He was a switch hitter! He could hit right and left-handed! The only thing that made Chuy feel better was that Manny was having the same result on the left side as he had on the right side. There were screaming line drives, several towering fly balls, but almost all were foul. His hope to beat out this freshman was still alive.

Tryouts ended with a short inter-squad game. Coach Wolf put Chuy and Manny on opposite teams, of course, and of course, Ricky did not play. He was involved, though, as a coach against Coach Wolf. Wolf vs Ramirez, Layden vs. Eagles, Gold vs. Blue. But in Chuy's mind, it was him versus the freshman phenom. The game turned out to be pretty great for Chuy, who hit the winning run, with two outs in the bottom of the sixth. A sharp hit up the middle. The final score was two to one, with Chuy's and Ricky's team over Manny and Coach Wolf's team.

Now all that was left was "the list." Chuy had played all summer to make the list. From hitting the weight room through the fall and early winter to showing up the earliest for pre-season workouts every morning, he'd been physically prepared. He had fielded grounders in the gym and spent hours in the batting cage. He was determined to make the list. He'd worked too hard. He was too steady. There was no way he would not make the list. There was no chance, or was there?

The list for the varsity overshadowed every other thought. Ricky had never had to worry about the list. Chuy was sure Ricky had walked in to tryouts his freshman year and his name had been the first. Chuy felt a touch of that familiar envy for guys like Ricky, and for kids like this freshman. Why should it be so easy for this kid? He had three more years to make it. Chuy had been thinking about making the list since he first walked through the doors of West Layden High School. This freshman probably didn't even know there was a varsity list.

One piece of good news: the list would be posted on Monday morning. It saved the guys the torture of thinking about it all day, wondering if they had made it. It saved the guys who didn't make the cut the embarrassment of showing up at practice just to get sent home. Chuy tried to play it cool on Monday morning, so he did the usual: he hung out with Billy.

Chuy's slightly-built best friend since freshman year was Bedros 'Billy' Karamitos, a blonde, big-mouthed kid who Chuy had met in first period gym class during their freshman year. It was as if Billy had found the quietest kid in class and decided, *this guy will be my best friend*. At first, Chuy ignored him, then he began to listen and laugh as Billy agitated the other kids with rambling stories that led nowhere. Finally, they began to talk and hang out, and somehow the crazy little Greek kid with the big mouth became Chuy's friend. You would think with a name like Bedros, Billy would never make fun of anyone else's name, but he was at it again.

"Hey Chuy, where's Han Solo? You always usin' your HANDS SOLO right?" Billy screamed down the hall!

"How many times are you going to use that played out line and still think you're fresh, BEDROS?" Chuy shot back.

"It's Billy, bitch!" Billy puffed up his chest and looked hard at Chuy. The fact that he was 5'2" and 95 pounds soaking wet did not stop him from trying to look like a badass, which made him even more silly.

"Oh! Don't hurt me, bro. I have my first practice today, at least I think I do," Chuy responded with mock fear.

"Watch yourself, *vato*," said Billy with a smile that made him look like a misbehaving second grader. "And quit worrying, you know you made the team. You've been at this since freshman year."

"Keep it down, man." Chuy didn't mind if Billy knew he was nervous, but he didn't want the whole school to know.

"If you are so worried about it," Billy whispered, "go to Coach Wolf's room and check."

Chuy hesitated.

"Don't be a puss. Come on, *senorita*; I'll hold your hand."

Billy grabbed at Chuy's hand. Chuy meant to playfully push him away, but he nearly sent his friend crashing into the cafeteria tables.

"Let's go, Eminem," Chuy ordered, when Billy finally recovered his balance.

Coach Wolf was a great baseball coach, who would one day end up in the Illinois High School Baseball Hall of Fame. As a man, he was even greater. Chuy felt that every time he went by Coach Wolf's classroom and saw "Wolfy's Kids." The students who hung outside room 250 were silly, sweet and funny. A big reason for their joy was Coach Wolf. He made his classroom fun, while still fostering respect and hard work. In the classroom and on the field Wolfy was one of a kind.

The special needs students in Coach Wolf's "Bridge Program" knew that they were loved and protected. When Wofly's kids walked down the hallway, they were met with shouts and high-fives. Their spring talent show, held in the teacher's cafeteria, was standing room only. Additionally, the combination of the steady stream of "jocks" and "cool kids" that came to visit Coach Wolf and were impressed by the effervescent personalities of these students, enabled Wolfy's Kids to be some of the most recognized and popular kids in school.

Chuy and Billy had been stopping by Coach's room every morning for the last two years, so when they turned the corner into the 250 wing Tavo, Lynnie, Missy and Michael ran down the hall to greet them.

"Oh! Oh! Oh!" said Tavo in a full sprint. He was so short he made Billy look tall, but his voice was deep and raspy. "Oh! Oh! Oh!" Tavo was too excited to talk.

Big Mike, who was the size of a large varsity football player, wore his familiar ear-to-ear grin, as he displayed two big thumbs up.

Next up, vying for the boys attention were Missy and Lynnie, the two tiny stars of the class. Missy was always upbeat and cheerful. Lynnie, her best friend, was a fragile, blondie who seemed constantly aggravated by everyone except Chuy. They both stood by Coach Wolf's door, pointing.

"I'm gonna guess you got some good news," said Billy, as Big Mike and Tavo pulled Chuy toward the door.

When he was a freshman Chuy had dreamed about making the list, but he never dreamed he'd have a crew to help him read the list. The curly-haired Missy now took Chuy's hand. Although she was nearly eighteen, and two years older than Chuy, her round face and apple cheeks gave her the look of a ten-year-old. Missy was also the best reader in Coach Wolf's special ed class, though she had a slight stutter which increased when she got excited.

"L-l-l- look, Chh -uuu -y, itsss you!!!"

And it was. The first name on the list: Jesus LeDesma.

CHAPTER 2

High School can be a weird, confusing place. Anyone who is going, or who has ever gone, knows that you can be taking a tough geometry test and twenty minutes later find yourself climbing a rope in P.E. You could be giving a presentation in your best suit in the morning and later trying to flick peas into your friend's hair, hoping he will leave the cafe without noticing and you can laugh your butt off. So Chuy was about to experience his own high and low for the day. High from the thrill of seeing his name on the list and dozens of high fives from Wolfy's Kids, he turned the corner only to run straight into a steaming pile of high school b.s., courtesy of the number one gangster wannabe, jerk of the school, Armani Rivera!

One of Coach's kids, Salim, had wandered away from the safety of the 250 wing and into the stairwell of the main hall. This area was the exclusive hangout of the Kings and their leader, Armani Rivera. Salim, although one of the largest of Wolfy's kids, was by far one of the most childlike and innocent. Whether Armani and his "gang bangers" knew this or not, they had begun throwing crumpled up paper and other garbage along with profanity-filled insults at the flustered special needs kid.

"Hey!" yelled Chuy, as he approached and recognized the situation. At the same time, Armani, and Salim both turned in the direction of the shout. Salim instantly ran toward Chuy.

"Chuy, Billy, they're not being kind to me! They're not being kind to me!" Salim fought back tears.

Chuy put his arm around Salim. "Come on buddy, you don't want to hang out here. Coach is looking for you," Chuy lied.

He knew Armani would back off if he thought a teacher was near. No way was Chuy afraid of Armani, but he didn't need the hassle of a fight in school and getting kicked off the team.

"Chuy, Billy! They are not being kind to me. They are not being kind to me!" Salim repeated.

"Don't worry, Salim, let's go."

"That's right, LeDesma, go back to your retard class," shouted Armani. Strangely, that line made Chuy grin. Armani and Chuy had been in the same literacy class freshman year. The class was specifically for any and all struggling readers, but if you were in literacy you got labelled "special ed," whether it was technically true or not! Now here was Armani calling other kids retarded. Chuy shook his head and continued to walk Salim to room 250.

Chuy had always had a reading disability. He'd dealt with it since he was in first grade and was pulled out with two or three of the other "slow kids." When he was young it bothered him that he struggled with reading. He used to get so frustrated that he would cry himself to sleep, asking God, *"Why me?"* He was ashamed, and thought his mother, father and older brother would be ashamed, too. The memory of his father and mother talking to him at the kitchen table gave Chuy comfort.

"Mi hijo, you have a reading disability. It's not your fault reading is hard for you, harder than it should be," his mother explained in her quiet voice.

"Si, Jesus," said his father. "Mrs. Gonzales explained it to us, but she also said that you can keep practicing and working, and you will be fine. You will be able to go to college like Raul. Chuy, my son, I don't read so good either, but I took those classes at the junior college, and I got my Heating and Cooling Certification, and I know you are smarter than me, hijo." He smiled reassuringly at his son.

Chuy's mother had rubbed her son's back. "You are a respectful, kind young man, and you are a hard worker. Just keep at it, son!"

Chuy remembered his older brother, Raul walking in to join the conversation in his usual cocky way.

"*Qué es eso*? Damn, bro, quit crying and start working. English wasn't even your first language; what do you expect? So you have a reading disability, boo hoo. I knew a ton of kids in school who were like that. The hard workers are doing fine. The lazy assholes are unemployed and living in their parents' basement."

"Language, Raul!" Chuy's mother scolded. "And where are you living right now, big shot?"

"Here for now, *mi vida*." Raul called his mother "my life" in his sarcastic, cocky style. "But after I graduate college you all will be living in my basement."

"*Y recuerdas, mi vida,* and you remember, too, bro." Raul spoke in "Spanglish" with a fake, heavy Mexican country accent. "Some people are born handsome, and some are born smart; I just happen to be both."

Raul grabbed his plate of food and turned towards his family, now speaking in an equally terrible English accent. "If you need me, I will be in the king's suite."

Chuy, his mother, and father roared with laughter.

"*Payaso*, you are such a clown!" shouted his father.

Life did start to change that year. Chuy decided not to be embarrassed about his reading difficulties. He read often, usually Sports Illustrated. Raul helped him sound out the larger words without judging. In fact, Raul seemed to enjoy the reading time they had together. In the long run, it brought the brothers closer. It was also the year when Chuy dominated in baseball. Between his hard work in the classroom and his talent on the field, school wasn't a drag anymore. In truth, Chuy liked it. Sadly, that memory of his junior high years, also marked a change in his mom and dad. An older Chuy could see that they had not gotten along so well. He remembered stories from his dad and advice from his mom, but he had no memory of them laughing and working together like a family.

Billy's voice pulled Chuy back to the present.

"If you are such a badass, Rivera, why ya gotta have all these guys around you?"

"Shut your little ass up," Armani shot back.

"Who *you* callin' little?" Billy demanded.

Actually, Armani wasn't much taller than Billy, but he was thicker, for sure. He always had been. Chuy and Armani had gone to school together since third grade. Chuy recalled when Armani first arrived from Puerto Rico. He had been one of the tallest kids in the class. But now the other kids had caught up and surpassed him. Regardless, from day one Armani always seemed angry, like he had something to prove.

Thinking back to grade school when they both had been called out of class to go with the reading specialist, Chuy had been glad to have Armani with him. No one was going to make fun of Armani and get away with it. Chuy remembered thinking that he might be friends with the new, tough kid, but even back then Armani was on the defensive. That made Chuy uncomfortable, for no one ever knew what to expect from the angry boy. Armani never talked much in school and left everyday with his brother and several other big kids as soon as school was out, cementing the separation between him and the other kids in his class.

Chuy figured out pretty quickly that he and Armani weren't going to be "buds." As time went on, the divide between the two got wider. As they went into junior high, and then high school they became rivals. Chuy grew bigger, better at sports and more popular. Armani got thicker and meaner. He also got involved in the gangs, following in his older brothers' footsteps.

Chuy tried to follow the advice of his own older brother as well. Raul told Chuy he would find plenty of *vatos* in high school and even in junior high, those "wannabes" who would waste their time trying to be bad asses and gang bangers.

"It's all b.s.," said Raul. "It gets you nowhere. They all grow up and realize you don't make a life—a real life you can be proud of—gang banging and selling weed. In the long run, it's chump change."

"Hey, have you ever seen a gang banger with a 401K?" Raul would say, cracking up at his own joke. "Get a real life, a real purpose and real pride in who you become, *hermano*."

Raul was leading by example. He was doing well and ready to get his associate degree from the junior college and head to Illinois State University by next fall.

In Chuy's mind, life always seemed easy for Raul, but not for him. Now slowly, but surely, school was finally going well, and he didn't need some hotshot freshman stealing his spot on the baseball team—and he sure didn't need a hassle with Armani.

Walk away, bro! Chuy heard Raul in his head and now he repeated those same words to Billy, putting one hand on his friend's shoulder and the other on Salim's.

Chuy guided the pair away from Armani and his crew and headed back to the safety of the 250 hallway. They were still looking back when Chuy directed the boys right into Lucy Quinones. *Damn!* thought Chuy, *What else?*

Lucy Quinones was on her way to hang with Armani and his boys. Lucy and Armani were on-and-off boyfriend-girlfriend since junior high. One more reason for Chuy not to like Armani, and it was the only thing about Armani that made him jealous.

Lucy and Armani did share a lot in common. Both had parents who worked all the time, so much so that they had a hard time keeping tabs on their junior high kids who were hanging out with the wrong crowd. Unlike Armani, however, Lucy was very good at academics. She loved to read, and she created and performed spoken word poetry that showed obvious insight, thoughtfulness and talent. Chuy heard her once at an afterschool poetry jam. He was amazed how strong and powerful her words were, as she told the story of a little girl who came to the United States from Mexico when she was in second grade. She told the tale of coming to a strange land to live with people whom she had never met but was told to call them family. They spoke a strange Spanish with a funny accent and some of the young ones didn't really speak Spanish at all.

Lucy had spoken with such flow and rhythm, not afraid to bare her soul:

Who are these people,
Where will we stay,
How can they be family?
Can't understand a word they say
Trade in my friends, my little town by the sea

They want to start a new life
But what about me?

Chuy recalled how her curly, black hair shook in ringlets and her brown eyes flashed as she faced the crowd and spit her rhymes without blinking—fearless!

Now, as Chuy guided his friends away from Armani and the gangbangers, for a split second he was face-to-face with Lucy Quinones. Inches away from those flashing brown eyes. For an instant, Chuy stood mesmerized. He shook his head, as if to snap out of a dream, while unwittingly his hands squeezed the shoulders of his two friends.

"Hey! Take it easy there, turbo," Billy protested.

"Chuyyyyyy!" squealed Salim. "*You* are not being kind to me!"

Chuy jerked his hands up as if they had landed on a hot stove. "Oops," he muttered, embarrassed.

Billy began laughing at Chuy's reaction to his crush, causing Salim to laugh as well, breaking the tension. For a brief moment, Lucy looked into Chuy's eyes and smiled. It took a moment or two before Chuy remembered to breathe.

Standing in front of Coach Wolf's door, having safely delivered Salim, Chuy had had enough excitement for one morning. The list, Salim on the run, Armani and his boys, a smile from Lucy. It was a lot of emotion to handle for one morning.

"Dude," said Chuy to Billy, "I think I'm actually ready to go to class after all this!"

"Yeah? 'Cause I think we should go back and mess up Armani and his punk friends."

"Good call, tough guy. You're gonna get me kicked out of school after finally making the list? No thanks!"

Chuy walked over to verify his team status one more time just for good measure. He paused and looked again. While they had been gone Coach Wolf had written - '*See me*' - beside his name. *What the hell does that mean?* thought Chuy. *What a morning!*

CHAPTER 3

It was a good thing that Chuy was doing well in school. If today was the only example of his ability to concentrate and his quality of work, Chuy would not have to worry about seeing Coach Wolf after practice. He would not be on any team; in fact, he would not be in school at all. He was getting nothing done. Every time he tried to work or listen to the teacher he kept seeing the list and the *"See me"* next to his name. By the time eighth period rolled around, he was very grateful that it was study hall, and that he had a quiet seat in the corner. He could just put his head down and try to think of nothing.

As the bell rang and everyone took their seats, Chuy took a deep breath and closed his eyes. The morning's events went racing through his head again: Armani, Billy, Salim, the list and Lucy; her long, curly hair, brown eyes and the way she looked at him. It seemed that maybe she wanted to talk, or was it just his imagination? He shook off the image of Lucy as his thoughts darted back to the "See me." Maybe it wasn't bad news; maybe Coach Wolf wanted Chuy for something good. Maybe he wanted Chuy to be a Captain? As a junior? No way! His mind raced, but stumbled when he was startled by a tap on the shoulder and a familiar voice.

"Wakey, wakey eggs and ham."

"Ugh," replied Chuy, playing along. "I think you mean wakey, wakey eggs and bakey."

"Is that how it goes?" asked Mrs. Eldridge, in her usual up-beat manner, spouting her corny lines.

"Really?" Chuy hadn't meant to say it quite that loud, and shifted to a whisper. "I forgot you were coming today."

"Well, it's so good to see you, too," joked Mrs. Eldridge. "Is this any way to treat the most awesome teacher that ever walked the earth?"

"I'm not sure; I'll ask Coach Wolf," retorted Chuy with a smirk.

"OWWWW!" Mrs. Eldridge grabbed at her heart, and pretended to pass out.

"Mrs. E," announced Chuy soberly, "I'm really not up to work today. I just wanted a little silence."

"Well, I've got good news and bad news: the bad news: me, there will be no silence. Good news," she continued, looking more serious, "I can listen, too. No work today; it looks like you need someone to talk to. Truthfully, I came to tell you that you are making the honor roll for the third straight quarter. Chuy, you have been on the honor roll your whole junior year! So I'm pretty sure it's not school or reading that is bothering you."

She pointed her thumb toward the tiny classroom in the corner. "Step into my office, young man. Let's get to the bottom of this," she commanded with a weird accent somewhere between British and Australian.

They moved to Mrs. Eldridge's classroom, and she quietly shut the door.

"Okay, let's dish, let's rap, who got beef?"

"Oh my God, Eldridge, please stop!" begged Chuy, rolling his eyes. "You sound so white when you do that."

"Whatever, homie," she continued to tease, "but seriously, what's going on? I know grades are excellent, so is it something at home…is Raul okay? Are you getting to see your dad?"

"Whoa, slow down, Mrs. E! Raul is doing great. He's ready to go to ISU next fall, and I see Dad every Wednesday and every other weekend. Mom and Dad are learning to get along apart. It's all good. I'm good!"

"Chuy, really? This is the end of our third year together. Do we really have to play this?"

It was true; Chuy had met Mrs. Eldridge on the first day of his freshman year: The white lady with big jewelry, big hair and a big laugh. She had helped him practice reading, for sure, but she had helped him with so much more. She taught him techniques in reading: skimming and scanning the page for the most important terms. She showed him that he didn't need to read every word on the page to fully understand it. Her instruction helped him keep up with other kids who read much faster. He learned how to study, when to work and when to take a break. She taught him to succeed and what to do when he wasn't succeeding. She taught him the key to success in school and life: Work hard, do good, be all you should. Chuy had this written in many private places: his school and baseball locker, his Chromebook case, and even a scribbled note that rested on his nightstand. He thought that one day he would have this mantra tattooed on his right shoulder.

Mrs. Eldridge's other favorite saying was "don't sweat the small stuff." In spite of all that he hesitated to tell her about the *"See me"* and about the "freshman phenom" and even about Armani, but finally, he did.

"Chuy," she said, "I know how hard you have been working for varsity baseball. I know you want everything to go perfectly, but that's just not the way things go all the time. Face it, Chuy, every day you tackle a reading disability, and you are succeeding in school—not just succeeding, you are kicking butt! And you've had to deal with your parent's divorce. You are getting pretty good at taking on whatever life sends you. As for young men who have lost their way (I won't mention any names) the universe has a way of working things out. Everyone eventually gets what they deserve, my young friend. You may want to send good thoughts to any kids who aren't as strong and hardworking as you."

"That is teacher-speak for say a prayer for your enemies, right? I'm not sure I'm there yet, Eldridge," admitted Chuy, but talking about it did make him feel better.

"Remember, Chuy, don't sweat the small stuff!"

"And it's all small stuff!" Chuy jumped in to finish for Mrs. Eldridge. "Mrs. E, you need some new material!"

"Are you calling me old, LeDesma? Out! Out! Out of my room! Nowwww is my suggestion, no—my order!"

"Saved by the bell!" laughed Chuy, as the bell rang right on cue. "Thanks Eldridge."

"Go get 'em, champ!" encouraged Eldridge, stopping Chuy in his tracks.

He turned and grimaced at her. "Why are you sooo corny, Eldridge, why?"

In spite of the time spent worrying, Chuy got through the school day and headed to practice, like he had done for the last two years. He snickered to himself as he thought, *Alright, genius, after all this worry about "See me," do I see Wolfy before practice or after?*

The question answered itself when Coach Wolf stepped into the locker room. "Okay, ladies, let's go!" That was his way of saying hello to his players.

Chuy approached Coach Wolf, but before he got a word out Wolfy answered the unasked question. "After practice is fine, Jesus. Alright, let's go sweethearts, we're burning daylight."

The first day of practice was always fairly easy: stretching, then on to 'stations' where the team worked in small groups on fielding and hitting fundamentals. Infielders took grounders, throwing to first, second for the double play, and finally making the out at home plate. Guys took batting practice in the batting cage as well as on the field. This was followed by an inter-squad scrimmage for a few innings, sprints for conditioning and finally meeting in the dugout with Coach Wolf and his assistant, Coach Hamilton.

"Good start, men," said Coach Hamilton, a tall, lanky former pitcher for Wolf, who was now finishing his fifth year as a science teacher and varsity pitching coach. "I see talent on the field, but that means nothing if you are not gonna work! That means working in the classroom, too. Bad grades mean you cannot help us, and more importantly, you can't help yourself. Be a good player, teammate, student, and person. You dig? That's me trying to be hip," he concluded with a silly grin.

"We dig, Coach," Ricky answered for the team, while his teammates groaned.

Coach Wolf stepped into the circle of players. "Yes, we *all* dig. Thanks, Coach." He continued, "Day one, fellas, of your varsity year. Day one of your last year of high school ball for you seniors. For some of you, this will be the last year you will play competitive sports. It all goes fast, believe me. I remember Coach Hamilton's first year on varsity, he had his spikes on the wrong feet. He was wearing his underwear on the outside of his uniform."

"Na, na," protested the young coach. "Lies, all lies!"

"Gentlemen," Coach Wolf's tone grew serious. "We are lucky to play this sport. Know how lucky you are; treat the game, your team, and your school with the respect they deserve. Love it while you can. Sooner or later *all* of us will hear that the game is over for us."

Chuy felt shivers down his spine. *Was Coach Wolfy looking at me when he said that?* The team jumped up and put their gloves together. The seniors shouted in unison. "Eagles on three!"

"One, two, three, EAGLES!"

After practice Chuy waited patiently for Coach Wolf in the coach's office. Just as he thought he might go crazy, Wolfy walked in and closed the door. *Uh-oh, this is going to get serious, Chuy thought.*

Coach Wolf motioned to the chair next to his. "Take a seat. I heard you had to wrangle in Salim again this morning, huh? Let me guess, someone was not being kind to him," Coach Wolf joked, using Salim's famous line.

Chuy grinned at Wolf's impression. "Something like that."

"Chuy," continued the coach. "You are an excellent young man. The kids in my room love you and they are always good judges of character. I've been a special ed teacher my whole career and though I work with a different group of students, I know how difficult it is to have a reading disability. From what I hear from Eldridge and your other teachers, you are the poster boy for working hard and being successful. It doesn't surprise me one bit. You have done the same thing on the ball field. You have turned yourself into a solid, steady player."

Chuy could sense that Coach Wolf was trying to tell him something. He seemed to be struggling to find the words. "Coach," he interrupted, "what do you want to tell me?"

Coach Wolf looked up from the floor and into Chuy's eyes.

"Yeah, this is tough," Wolfy mumbled. He collected himself, sat up and put his hand on Chuy's shoulder. "I know how much you love baseball. You definitely made the team, and I am glad to have you. If it were any other guy I might not say a word and let things play out, but it's you, so here goes: the freshman kid, Manny, is going to be my starting third baseman. I've been around a long time, and you don't see a natural talent like him very often. That moves Pete to second and Jose to back up. Ricky will start at shortstop, of course. Then I got Will, who is a senior, Joe and Andrew.

We are loaded with position players, not just for this year but for the next couple of years. This is a great problem for a coach to have, but not so good for a hard-working scrapper with an inconsistent bat." He paused for a moment, then continued, "Chuy, I'm taking a long time to say that you are on my team, but the chances of you getting playing time over the next two years...well, the chance seems pretty low. I'm just being straight with you, Jesus. You will be a great practice player, a great teammate and always a great kid, but you will not play much—if at all."

Chuy's heart sank. Anger, sadness, and confusion all hit him at once. He wanted to hit something, and scream, and cry and hide. Instead, he just sat in the chair next to Coach Wolf. He stared at the floor for what seemed an endless amount of time, then turned his gaze upward to see Wolf still looking at the floor. He knew his coach felt horrible. Instinctively, Chuy patted Coach Wolf on the shoulder.

"Don't worry Coach, everything will work out."

Coach Wolf looked up quickly. Their eyes met and they both cracked up when they realized they had just experienced a sudden role reversal.

"Yeah, thanks Chuy, this was really tough! Are you going to buy me ice cream now?" Wolf asked, making fun of the situation. "Listen, Jesus, you are one of a kind. You'll still come by class and see me and the kids tomorrow morning?"

"Sure, Coach," said Chuy. "You know I gotta check on Salim."

"Good, make sure you do! I may have something else up my sleeve for you, LeDesma."

"Another 'see me', Coach?" questioned Chuy, opening the office door. "Can't wait!" he added with exaggerated sarcasm.

"You'll see." Coach Wolf offered him a sly grin, "You'll see."

Chuy walked home with mixed feelings charging from his head through his chest and into his gut. *Is baseball really over? Should I just hang in there hoping for a break? Do I spend a season hoping for two or three of my teammates to get injured or fail classes? Could I pretend to be a good teammate while secretly hoping bad things will happen to one of the guys?* Agonizing thoughts and feelings churned within him.

I guess I was never going to make a living playing ball, Chuy concluded. *Maybe I should just get a job?* Chuy had worked all summer so he could concentrate on school and sports during the school year. He liked working at the recycling center near his house, but they only hired high school kids in the summer. He'd have to find something else if he was going to trade work for baseball.

His mind was still racing when he got home. He plowed through the backdoor, almost running into his mother, Maria Luiza. She was a petite, pretty woman with jet black hair, pulled back in a bun. She could be mistaken for a young girl and often was. When she saw her youngest son she immediately sensed that something was wrong.

"*Que pasa, mi hijo?*" asked Chuy's mother, with concern.

Before he could reply, Chuy's older brother, Raul, a shorter, heavier version of Chuy, strolled into the kitchen and opened the fridge, looking for nothing in particular. "Yeah; *que* paso, *senorito?* What's your lamo *problemo?*"

Chuy suddenly felt his throat start to tighten and his eyes start to burn. Emotions welled up in his chest so strongly that it felt as if they were going to punch their way to the outside. He was surprised and embarrassed at the same time. He dropped his head. Chuy was not a crier; that job was left to Raul who cried at the end of his favorite book—"Of Mice and Men" (even though he had read it ten times) and at the end of "Coco" even though he had seen it thirty times. In the middle of a touching dog food commercial Chuy had seen tears in his eyes. The younger brother would point and laugh, and Raul would tell him to shut up and punch him in the shoulder. That was a common event at the casa de LeDesma. Now the tables were turned.

The last time Chuy had cried had been when his father had finally left the house to move into his apartment. Even then Chuy only cried privately that night, softly into his pillow so no one would know. He could not remember a time before that. Most Latino men never cried, unless they were a romantic like Raul. The singing caballero *could* cry, but only for the sadness or joy of others, never for his own fear, pain or disappointment. Nonetheless, Chuy's shame grew as he began to sob. He had lost control, unprepared for his own reaction.

Raul and his mother sat up straight, shocked by what they were seeing. Time stood quietly still while Chuy wept. He released all his emotions at the kitchen table as disappointment engulfed him. Nothing was held back. Gradually, he felt relieved; he felt lighter and, as tears rolled down his face, Chuy felt the weight lift from his shoulders, replaced by the hands of his mother and brother.

Just as quickly as it had come the heavy emotion left him, to be replaced with an embarrassed grin. He looked left into the concerned eyes of his mother, then right to see the scrunched-up face of Raul, all tears and snot!

"Oh my god, Raul! Really?" Chuy blurted out at the unexpected sight.

"Screw you, *cabron*!" Raul punched Chuy on the shoulder. Chuy and Raul burst into laughter and soon their mother joined in. When the laughter faded the little family caught their breath for a moment, but Raul wasn't about to let it go.

"Okay, *digame, vato*," he ordered, "what the hell is going on with you?"

"It's stupid," insisted Chuy, but he went on to explain. "I didn't make the baseball team. Well, I did, but I'm not gonna play. Wolfy said there is a good chance I'll ride the bench for the next couple of years. This freshman superstar showed up and now we are overloaded with talent...It's just not what I expected."

"Hey, man, baseball means a lot to you. You worked hard at it. Chuy, whatever you feel, however you react, it's okay, it all makes sense."

Chuy stared at Raul, his face growing serious. "It's just..."

"Yeah, what is it, bro?" Implored Raul.

"It's just...I never...well...I never thought..." Chuy looked as if he were going to break down again, "I'd be a big cry baby like you!"

Bad acting earned Chuy another punch in the shoulder from Raul.

"The one time I'm trying to be a concerned brother and I get this bullsh..."

"Raul!" Mrs. LeDesma stopped her oldest son.

The three laughed again.

Later, when they sat down for dinner. Maria Luiza LeDesma watched as her sons joked and laughed as usual. She was a little sad for Chuy, but very proud of her boys. She knew that some rain fell into every life, and she was confident that both of her sons could weather the storm and become stronger for it.

CHAPTER 4

The next morning Chuy felt a weird sense of relief as he approached the 250 hallway. He heard the much too loud voice of Billy repeating his familiar played out joke. "Chewbacca, it's me—Han Solo."

"Really, dude?" Chuy faked disgust. "Wow, still funny and not at all lame." In truth, he didn't mind a little "familiar" today. He heard his mother's voice in his head: *This too will pass, Chuy. You will always be fine because you will always be you.*

He smiled to himself. She was pretty great and he was very lucky. With Billy by his side, he turned into the hallway for more "familiar": Lynnie, Missy, Big Mike, Paris and Tavo. Even Salim was where he was supposed to be for once, as the whole crew came running toward him like he was the MVP at an all-star game, all noisily vying for his attention. Tavo got there first, wearing an oversized, hand-me-down school homecoming shirt he had been given by his older brother. "Heeeeeey!" he shouted, pointing proudly at his tee-shirt.

Lynnie was close behind, pointing to a large pink bow in her hair, "See, see, see, Chuy!"

Missy was next and, being her usual sweet self, she asked, "Chuy, how was practice?"

Chuy addressed them one by one. "Hey, love the old school tee, Tav. Lynnie, your bow looks so nice. Missy, you are too much," he reached down to give her a quick squeeze.

He and Billy went on to greet and high-five all the students.

"C-c-chuy!" Missy shouted to get his attention again. "L-l- -look!" She grabbed Chuy's hand. "C-c-coach A and Ms. K-k-kelly, l-l-look!"

Missy opened the classroom door before Chuy could knock, catching Coach Alvarez right in the middle of a typically long-winded performance for his "audience," Wolf and Kelly. His hands were on an imaginary steering wheel, and he was looking up at an imaginary police officer.

"I swear this cop looked like he was in Junior High!"

Ms. Kelly, equally as demonstrative, grabbed her face with hands on each cheek and pulled down giving her the appearance of a bored zombie.

"Omgosh, Alvarez, this is the world's longest story. Is there a point?"

Alvarez continued his tale without skipping a beat. "Then I turn, and he says, 'hey, got any I.D. that says ya work there?' I'm like, dude—it's 7:30 in the morning and I'm wearing a Layden shirt that says Coach Alvarez. Does that count?"

"You have been here for years, and you have no Layden I.D.? I got mine the first day I was hired!" chimed in Ms. Kelly, trying to match his volume.

"Look at you, you're soooooooo cooooooool! I'm *the* Chuck Alvarez, dammit! I need no I.D. This is my I.D." Alvarez folded his hands under his chin like a bad prom picture. "Who doesn't know me?"

"If you did that pose, he should have thrown you in jail," Coach Wolf said, rolling his eyes.

Chuy stood quietly, not wanting to interrupt the party. These teachers, who he had seen around the school, but had not met before, were obviously having a good time making fun of each other. Wolf finally noticed Chuy.

"Jesus! I'm so sorry you had to witness that, but just think: someday you will graduate. I'm stuck with these two knuckleheads for the next twenty years."

Coach Wolf thanked Missy for delivering the boys, then began introductions. "This loud person is Ms. Kelly. Jess, this is Chuy LeDesma and his friend Billy. These two are regular visitors to our class here."

"Hi, guys," said Ms. Kelly, lowering her voice only slightly.

"And this is…" continued Coach Wolf.

"Stop!" interrupted Alvarez. "They know who I am, right fellas? Go ahead, tell Wolfy."

"Coach Alvarez," Chuy replied.

"You know who I am, too; right, buddy?" Alvarez pointed to Billy.

"Sure," answered Billy.

"See, everyone knows me, Wolfy. You aren't the only future 'hall of famer' around here! And just how do you guys know me, talent show director? Football coach? Handsomest teacher at Layden?"

"None of those," Chuy volunteered. "I just heard Ms. Kelly say your name."

Wolfy and Kelly cracked up while Alvarez shook his head in feigned disgust.

"Well, Chuy," Coach Wolf began. "I didn't invite these two crazies over for entertainment, as you can probably guess, after what you just saw. They actually have real value."

"Watch out, Wolfy, that's how rumors get started," joked Alvarez.

"Listen, Chuck," Coach Wolf replied, "I know *you* get to do whatever you want around here, but I actually have to teach in a few minutes, and Chuy and Billy need to get to class."

"All the more reason for me to take over," Alvarez announced, stepping in front of Wolf. "Chuy, I know the baseball season is not starting the way you wanted it to, and I also know you have worked your tail off. Actually, I have been where you are. Ya see, my love was football and the guy who started ahead of me was the coach's kid. But truthfully, I wasn't ever going to be a big-time football player. I was just too small and too slow, and no matter how hard I worked that wasn't going to change. Sound familiar?"

"Yeah, too familiar," Chuy concurred.

"After a year of being on the punt team and cheering from the sidelines, I could see my high school football career wasn't going the way I hoped it would be. So I moped and pouted for a week or two, but then my break came from an article in our local paper, when I saw two guys featured on the sports page. They had just boxed at a tournament in Rockford. It got me thinking *I can do that*. Then, when I started boxing, turns out it was one of the few things that came naturally to me." He paused to grab a breath, and then continued, "You may have heard that we have a few guys going to the Maywood Boxing Club—not too far from here. Wolfy said you and your old man are big boxing fans."

Chuy glanced at Coach Wolf and thought back to a brief conversation they had had when Mayweather fought McGregor. Coach Wolf was truly full of surprises, to remember that trivial little talk.

"We go Monday through Friday, after I finish supervising the weight room. Bring this character with you," Alvarez suggested, indicating Billy with a nod in his direction.

Billy threw his hands up in the air. "Whoa! I'm a lover, not a fighter," he objected.

The group let out a big laugh, just as the bell rang, and Wolf's kids came spilling into the classroom.

"Typical!" shouted Ms. Kelly over the raucous laughter and chatter that now filled the space. "Alvarez talks so much I missed my turn!"

"Snooze ya lose... Aaaaa LLOOOSSSER," taunted Alvarez, preparing to dart out of the classroom. "See you in the weight room on Wednesday, fellas. Don't need a thing except yourselves." Then to the students still getting to their seats: "Hey, guys, let's hear it for the most handsome teacher in the whole world... Me!"

Some students booed, some cheered, but they all made noise.

"Thanks for that," Coach Wolf shouted after him as Alvarez performed an exaggerated bow and finally exited.

Out in the hallway, Ms. Kelly walked with the boys. "Well, Chuy, I guess I lost my chance for a chat right now, but I could definitely use your help. Can we talk later? You have a study hall with Eldridge, right? Eighth period?"

Chuy nodded.

"Okay, I'll find you there," Kelly promised.

The next day Chuy's life was back on solid ground. His concentration and work had shifted back to normal without his teachers even noticing the tough time he had had the day before. Chuy was happy with his classes, his teachers, and his classmates, and so the morning flew by. Soon it was time for lunch and crazy Billy again.

"So is it going to be Rocky or Star Wars now, Chewbacca?" joked Billy as they sat down to eat.

"Ugggh" protested Chuy. "Now two lame movies for you to make lame jokes about."

"Lame? Ya mean two of the greatest movie franchises ever made? And you can be like Chewbacca—Aaaahhhh." Billy did a pretty good Chewbacca impression. "And like Rocky—Aaadriaaann!"

"Please tell me again why we are friends," teased Chuy.

Their joking was interrupted by a push on Chuy's hand that sent his food and his fork sailing. Billy, who got most of the mess on his shirt, jumped to his feet.

"What the f...? You asshole!" Billy screeched, looking past Chuy to the three guys behind him.

At the same time, Chuy sprang up and turned to face Armani, with two of his crew. Hands reached out to grab Chuy. Snarls and shoves were exchanged in the blink of an eye. Billy started to leap across the table, but was stopped by Mr. Norris and Mr. Jefferson, the two most popular security officers at Layden. They always seemed to be at the right place at the right time. They may have been the only two who could stop any fight dead in its tracks. It was no coincidence that Jefferson and Norris often stuck close to Armani and his boys. Wherever they were, trouble was always nearby.

"Alright, fellas, let's keep it together. Armani, keep walking! Take a seat, Karamitos!" barked Norris, quickly positioning himself between the group of boys. "We don't want to visit the dean and the police officer today, do we fellas?"

Jefferson moved quickly to block Armani, who was still obviously itching to fight. "No reason to ruin a beautiful day. Right, guys?"

The five boys exchanged hard looks, but gradually, Armani and his boys started walking away.

"You're lucky, LeDesma," Armani hissed under his breath.

"Get to steppin'!" Billy waved them off, full of bravery with the security officers backing.

Armani flipped his middle finger and scowled as he walked away.

"What assholes!" Billy scoffed as he wiped at his food-covered shirt with a handful of napkins. "You should box his punk ass, Rocky."

Chuy shrugged off the hassle and headed toward his next class. He remembered what Raul would say about the gang banger wannabes, just wasting their time trying to be tough. He was currently completing a project in graphic design class, and the satisfaction that was bringing him pushed the anger right out of his mind.

Finally, it was eighth period study hall, and the day was almost done. He settled into his desk, closed his eyes, and took a deep breath. Before long he received a familiar tap on the shoulder. Chuy turned, expecting to see only Mrs. Eldridge, but was surprised to see Ms. Kelly was with her. The two women led Chuy into Mrs. Eldridge's office. The group made themselves comfortable in the cozy, quiet room.

"Finally!" exclaimed Ms. Kelly, "It's my turn!" She looked around and joked, "Chuck Alvarez isn't coming, is he? He'll take up all my time again with some long-winded story."

"He's not allowed in here," Mrs. Eldridge assured her, "otherwise we'd never get any work done!"

"Good call! That's a veteran teacher at work," Ms. Kelly said approvingly, then faced Chuy. "What I want to talk to you about, Jesus, has nothing to do with baseball or boxing. It doesn't have anything to do with class work, but it has everything to do with you." She paused for a moment, to build drama. "Chuy, I'm starting a new program also. For it to succeed I need good leaders and kind people, and your name has been coming up a lot."

Chuy sat up a little straighter, his interest piqued.

"Don't look so surprised, Jesus. You don't know how much Wolfy's kids love you."

Chuy listened intently and silently as the young teacher continued. "I'm sure you know there are quite a few special needs students here at West; in fact, so many that we thought a club where they could connect with our regular ed kids could really be amazing."

"Wait a second, I'm in a special ed class," Chuy reminded her.

Ms. Kelly smiled reassuringly, "Chuy, you have a learning disability. You are getting help from Mrs. Eldridge to strengthen your reading skills. What I'm talking about is connecting with students like Salim, Lynnie and Missy, and even some other students who may have more challenges than most of Wolfy's kids. We have some students who don't have the ability to walk, talk, or even see. Those kids could really use some fun activities with students like you. I mean, you are kind of doing it anyway. You spend time with Wolfy's kids. Coach told me you went on their holiday field trip to the mall. He also told me how you watch out for Salim, and you come to see Missy, Lynnie, Tavo and all the kids pretty much every morning."

Chuy started to relax. This was beginning to sound like something he could not only do but enjoy doing.

"The club is called Best Pals. Schools all over the state are starting these clubs. I think you would be perfect as a member and as a junior class officer."

Out of the corner of his eye he saw Mrs. Eldridge's face beaming, as she reached for tissue then dabbed away a tear or two.

"Really, Eldridge?" he teased, busting her for her excessive emotion.

"You have just come such a long way, Chuy." She smiled through her tears.

"Really?" Chuy repeated.

"You know, Jesus, Raul isn't the only cry baby. You'll see Alvarez is the worst, but...I'm...I'm," (now totally *fake* crying,) "I'm so proud!" She fanned her eyes with her fingers, pretending to dry the tears.

Ms. Kelly cleared her throat and brought them back to the topic at hand. "Say 'yes' Chuy," she encouraged, closing her eyes, crossing her fingers and waiting for his response.

"Yes!" exclaimed Chuy without hesitation. "Sounds great!"

CHAPTER 5

Lucy was the oldest of the Quinones sisters. There was also an older brother, Eddie, who had moved out long ago and was almost ready to start his own family. That left Lucy, Jasmine, Alexandra, and Journey, the youngest, still at home. The Quinones girls were all beautiful young ladies who looked like versions of each other. If Jasmine, who was fourteen, wanted to know what she would look like at seventeen, she just had to look across her bedroom to her oldest sister. If she wanted to remember what she looked like at eleven, she had only to look into the top bunk above her at Alex. The youngest one, Journey, who slept between their mom and dad, looked like a little doll version of her sisters. She had just turned seven but the family treated her as if she were age four, and Journey liked that just fine. She played the baby role beautifully. In fact, without even knowing it, all the girls played their parts in the Quinones family to a tee.

Lucy, as the oldest, was without question the boss. She was tough, but no matter how hard she was on her younger siblings she always demonstrated absolute warmth and love for them. She watched out for them, overly protective even though she tried not to show it. Lucy was a mother hen with a cool, hard street edge that made the other girls fall in line without question. Like most kids, they would argue and whine when it came to directions and chores from Mom and Dad, but when Lucy talked they knew she meant business. Jasmine and Alex idolized Lucy and though they were very different from each other, they both wanted to be pretty and popular just like her. Journey, on the other hand, had the whole family—including Lucy— wrapped around her little finger.

It was springtime, and the Quinones family was entrenched in their morning routine. Journey heard Lucy, who was always the first to wake up and had already claimed the only bathroom in the house. She scrambled out of bed, as she never missed the opportunity to get attention from her older sister, even if it meant leaving the warm nest between Mom and Dad.

"I have to go nowww!" She whined outside the bathroom door.

If one of the other girls had dared to break into Lucy's routine there would have been trouble, but Lucy just grinned.

"Then go, *munequita. Rapido*, little doll."

Journey, capitalizing on her cutest move, hugged Lucy's legs.

"Okay, *mi jefa,* you're the boss," she said, skipping in front of Lucy into the coveted bathroom.

"And make sure you flush!"

Lucy went back into the bedroom to check on her other sisters, still fast asleep. She would have to get them going soon enough, but for now she let them sleep. She heard a flush and little bare feet pat their way back to the front bedroom.

"Next time wear your *chanklas*," she hissed, not wanting to wake up everyone else, but needing to correct her little sister. After all, correction had always been her job. Lucy chuckled to herself at her own bossiness. It almost cost her this time, as her younger sisters stirred in their beds. She did not want to wake anyone. It was five in the morning, and her private time, what she called 'Lucy time.' She would have the house to herself for another hour. That was precious to Lucy; it gave her a chance to organize, to plan, to reflect, and most importantly in the small two-bedroom, one bath home, to use the bathroom! She could take her time showering as well as drying her long, curly hair. Her and her sisters' clothes had been laid out the night before. Lucy always made sure of that. This gave her more precious time, her only easy time.

As she sat before her mirrored vanity and observed her sleeping sisters, she was suddenly struck by the idea that most high school students felt that time was a slow-moving vehicle toward adulthood and freedom. They wanted to grow up fast. But Lucy wanted to freeze time, at least this moment in time. Her parents were gradually becoming financially successful, so the pressure of taking care of the girls was lifting off Lucy's shoulders. She felt happier and more at peace than she ever had.

As she continued drying her hair, she watched her sleeping sisters through the mirror. She marveled at the sisters' physical resemblance to each other, yet how different they all were! Jasmine was studious and shy, a girl who loved school, but unlike her older sister, she made no secret of it. She loved tests, huge projects and numbers. She was a self-proclaimed nerd, who took pride in being one. She thought shopping for "cool clothes" was a waste of time, when *really* cool kids wore vintage, so the hand-me-downs that Lucy provided worked out just right for everyone: cheaper for parents, less work for Lucy, no time-wasting for Jasmine.

Alex rustled in her bed and opened her eyes slightly to catch her oldest sister looking at her lovingly.

"What are you looking at, loser?" she grumbled.

"Time to get up, lazy," lied Lucy.

"Ugggh," she replied and pulled the covers over her face.

Alex loved school, too, but not at all for the same reasons as Jasmine. She loved to laugh and talk with her friends. She loved sports and clubs, drama and excitement, especially when she was the cause of it. In Alex's mind, if it wasn't for that silly schoolwork, and tests, and learning stuff, school would be the perfect place to expand her socialization. Through hard work on Lucy's part, and a lot of lost privileges, Alex was finally doing fairly well in school. She was a hard-head, but she was beginning to realize that the right way was the easiest way.

Lucy recalled going to the parent/teacher conferences to translate for her parents. It was always the same. Jasmine is such a great student; Alex can be…ah …challenging. Jasmine is such a hard worker; Alex is ah… very social. Jasmine is so well behaved; Alex is ah…spirited. At the last conference, however, Alex's grades had been solid, and Jasmine seemed to have been spending time in other activities aside from Math Club. Now she was involved in the Make-A-Difference Club. In typical Jasmine fashion (of being uber-prepared) she had already begun her campaign for student council for next year.

Lucy, in a moment of clarity, realized that not only were her sisters growing and evolving, but the school also was evolving. There were plenty of translators available now. Older brothers and sisters, like her, were no longer doing that job. Now a lot of the teachers spoke Spanish, though they weren't fluent by any stretch. They could, however, communicate. Additionally, watching the teachers struggle with a second language made parents feel better about their own struggle with communication. Yes, Washington Junior High was good and getting better.

As the sun began to rise, Lucy combed her damp hair and stared deeply into the mirror, sinking deeper into her own thoughts. *Was everything getting better?* In her home good things were happening. Her father and mother were both home at night. Not so long ago even the suggestion of that had been silly, as her father had worked as a cook and her mother as a waitress for so long that no one in the family could remember a different life. The two had met when Lucy's dad, Eduardo, met the beautiful Catalina when he first came to this country and started working as a busboy. They had both worked at Catalina's Uncle Ignacio's restaurant and somehow they had managed to save enough to buy a house and raise their boy, Eddie, and the girls.

Restaurant work not only meant low pay, it meant being gone on nights and weekends. Lucy had no idea how desperate her parents had been when they left her to take care of her sisters when she had been only ten years old. Eddie had checked in on them when he could and thankfully, the restaurant was only a block and a half away from their home. But her parents did what they had to do, and Lucy let her nature as the little mother take over. She did the job better than many older kids would ever do and the family made it work. Lucy remembered her mother coming home smelling like tortillas and carne asada. Catalina had held her so hard that Lucy could still feel it today, getting kisses as her mother whispered a sorrowful thank you for her help.

"Mi hija, te amo mi hija, gracias, mi amor, gracias por todo." Catalina Quinones voice would tremble as she held her oldest daughter. "I love you my daughter, thank you, thank you for everything."

"No hay nada, it's nothing, Mama, don't worry," Lucy would whisper, always making her mom cry. She could still feel her mother's warm, salty

tears transferring onto her cheeks and lips as her mother squeezed her tightly.

Only now did Lucy understand how frightening it was to leave a child in charge of babies. How guilty her mother must have felt, how worried she was each day and how relieved she would be every night when nothing major had gone wrong during her absence.

No matter how competent Lucy was, her mother had felt ashamed. Shame for the chances she herself had to take and shame for the carefree childhood she was forced to take away from her oldest daughter. Those days of heavy responsibility faded into the past as the girls grew older and Lucy understood the seriousness of what could have happened. But she realized there had not been any other option. Lucy tried to imagine Journey, the *munequita*—the little doll, taking care of younger ones. All Journey had to take care of was her own dolls.

Things were now so much better. Her father, Eduardo, living on four hours of sleep, had somehow gone to Northwest Tech, the nearby junior college, to get his mechanics certification. The family was no longer desperate for money, so Catalina got a job in the cafeteria at Journey's school, spoiling her even more by driving her to and from school every day. No common school bus for the little princess. *Yes, things are good. I should get her that t-shirt,* Lucy thought, picturing her sister with *"NO BUS FOR THE LITTLE PRINCESS"* written across her chest.

Lucy noticed the time and snapped out of her pleasant morning gratefulness as the real world came back with a jolt. "Get up girls!" Come on, lazies, *con prisa,* let's go! Get up! Get Up! Get Up!"

Jasmine popped out of bed and swiftly collected her things for her turn in the bathroom.

"Ugh, shut up," Alex whined, pulling the covers further over her head. "Is it Saturday yet?"

"Yeah, you wish. Okay, miss the bus—you can walk," Lucy declared as she finished dressing. *Life is pretty good,* she almost said out loud.

"Oh, by the way, you two need to hear something very important," Lucy announced a few moments later.

Jasmine stopped collecting clothes and toiletries and Alex removed the covers from her face to give their big sister their attention.

"You all are looosssers!"

Pillows flew as Lucy ducked out of the room. Things were pretty good.

That same morning for Billy was just another repeat of his own personal "Groundhog Day." Every morning was the same. Alarm-snooze! Alarm-snooze!

Mom screams, "Billy! Goddamn it, get up!"

"Alright! Alright! I'm up, I've been up," Billy would lie.

Ten more minutes would pass.

Mom at the door. "BILLY GODDAMN IT, GET UP!"

"OKAYYY, MAAAAAA!"

Out of bed; water on face, and then—*Why did I play Fortnite so late last night?*

Now looking at himself in the mirror, water still dripping down his face, it was time for his morning pledge: "No more Fortnite!" he said sternly to his reflection. "This time I mean it!"

Next, he hit some Eminem, his favorite since he was a kid and had heard it blasting from his big sister's room. On Billy's playlist was every branch of the Eminem musical tree: Dre, of course, NWA, old school Snoop, all the way back to Slick Rick and Big Daddy Kane. Shower on, blast music. Wait for it…mom at the door:

"Hurry up! You're gonna miss the bus. Breakfast is ready!"

Wait for it one second; two seconds:

"AND TURN DOWN THAT RACKET!"

"There it is." Billy smirked into the mirror.

He had stuck to his routine solidly, and it was only Thursday! Thursday is a good day; one more day to the weekend. Springtime was finally approaching and if Billy could admit it, he liked school with its routine, its comfort, and its safety. Sure, there were gang bangers at Layden, but for the most part they kept to themselves. For the most part—except for that asshole Armani. He did one last check in the mirror as he heard the bus rounding the corner and coming to a halt steps from Billy's front stoop. Josie, the driver, knew to wait for him. That was a traditional part of the routine. Billy struck a boxer's stance in the full-length mirror by the front door. Maybe he would go with Chuy to the boxing club. Maybe something besides hanging out and playing Fortnite wouldn't be so bad. He threw a jab with the wrong hand and pictured himself standing in front of Armani and his boys.

"I don't think you want this, fellas," he snarled. (Jab, jab.) "No, you don't!"

Two honks from Josie.

"Billy!" From Mom. Out the door. Yep, all part of the routine.

Armani woke before the alarm went off. That's just the way he was. The house was dark, as always. Without turning on the light, out of fear of waking his older brothers, he began the morning pick up: beer cans, Hennessy bottles and ashtrays. He worked quickly and silently, almost glad that the living space was only one room with a tiny galley kitchen. At least it was quick to clean. He picked up, swept, and then mopped with his favorite—the good old Swiffer. The house almost felt clean. He noticed a few clumps of dust and some dog hair along with dirt from the boots of his brothers' homies. One more swipe with a clean Swiffer sheet and the cramped two bedroom rowhouse at least smelled better, less like cigarettes, weed, stale beer and dog.

The dog was Diablo, sitting patiently at the door. The grizzled pit bull, once the toughest fighting dog on the northwest side of the city, was getting old. He whined and limped a little as he got up to go outside. Diablo was smart, and he knew that his masters would be passed out until noon so this was his only chance to get outside to do his business. He also knew that Armani would have a delicious can of dog food waiting for him when he was done, and perhaps a few minutes of affection. It was the only affection the old warrior would receive until Armani and his little brother, Joey, returned in the afternoon.

Armani dropped the empty dog food can into the garbage. That would be the final can for this bag. He took the overflowing garbage to the outside can, petted Diablo and sucked in fresh spring air.

"Hah!" he remarked to the old dog. "A difference between real spring and Swiffer spring, right boy?"

The grateful dog looked up with his kind old eyes. It was hard to believe that Diablo had been in more than fifty fights, though the many scars he bore were proof.

"Come on, boy."

Diablo jumped like a puppy with his tail wagging as Armani roughly rubbed his neck. The two walked back into the house. Diablo did his hobbled version of a run to his bowl, which Armani had already filled. Armani stopped for a moment to look around. *Not so bad,* he thought, feeling the satisfaction he always received from his work. Trying not to think of how the place would look when he got home that evening, he took a deep breath, then went back to work making Joey's breakfast and lunch. Armani grabbed a step ladder to get to a higher cabinet, one that his older brothers or their friends wouldn't bother with. It was the place where he stashed a loaf of bread and an extra-large jar of peanut butter, hidden behind containers of Swiffer sheets. If his brothers or their homies ever did look up there Armani was certain the cleaning supplies would scare them away.

He pulled out five pieces of bread. He covered the first slice with peanut butter and shoved it in his mouth. Two more went in the toaster; the others were for a sandwich. Peanut butter toast for breakfast, peanut butter sandwich for lunch. It's a good thing Joey loved peanut butter—it made Armani's job a lot easier. He went to the fridge to get milk for Joey. Empty milk container again! Tap water would have to do.

With lunch made and breakfast ready, Armani headed back to his room, first pausing to glance across the tiny living room to check on whether or not his older brothers' door was closed. Seeing they were still asleep, he stepped quietly back into his own room, careful not to wake Joey just yet. He scrambled under his bed and reached up into a torn corner of the box spring. Armani's fingers searched until he found what he was looking for. He pulled out a wad of cash, mostly ones and fives. He would stop at Oscar's, the convenience store near the school, this afternoon as per usual. He would get deli sandwiches, chips and bottles of pop for himself and his little brother. He also made a mental note to pick up milk and do a better job of hiding it in the back of the fridge. He looked at the wad of cash in his hand and separated out four fives and ten ones. He looked at the remaining cash, toying with the idea of buying a mini-fridge and sneaking it in on a Friday night when his brothers were gone. But that could cause all kinds of trouble. His brothers would think he had too much money and that might screw up everything. It would definitely screw up "The Plan."

Armani woke Joey up and sat down to daydream while he waited for his younger brother to get ready. His mom had been gone a lot ever since Armani was Joey's age, and he had never known his father. Rita Rivera had gone back to Puerto Rico for weeks at a time, then months. Eventually she stopped coming back at all, or even calling. Maybe she figured that the brothers, Daniel, and Xavier, were old enough to take care of Armani and Joey. Maybe she thought Armani was old enough to take care of himself. After all, by the time his mom had been his age she had two sons. But none of that mattered because Armani made it work, and he had formulated his own plans. When he turned eighteen he would get an apartment in the Kitchenettes, the rundown apartment complex off Mannheim Avenue. He would sell weed and he would take care of Joey and Diablo. He would be an important member of the Kings and he would be treated that way— especially by Daniel and Xavier, not like some little kid mascot they could push around and make fun of when they were drunk.

By the time Armani finished reliving his dream for the future, it was time to go. He didn't need to look at the clock. "Get your coat, *cabron!*" he ordered Joey.

He gave Diablo a last rough rub on his neck. Joey went out to wait on the front stoop. Armani grabbed his coat and then, with well-practiced stealth, he crept into his brothers' room. He reached into the bottom drawer of the nightstand between the two snoring men. Ever so quietly he pulled out three quarter bags of weed. Usually the move was to close the drawer and out the door. This time, however, Armani paused and looked to the foot of the bed where a pair of jeans hung. He quickly snagged the twenty dollar bill that peeked out of the front pocket.

"You can never have enough Swiffer sweeps," Armani joked to himself, feeling cocky. He stuffed the weed and the twenty into his jacket pocket.

"Let's go, JoJo," he said to his patient little brother.

CHAPTER 6

Chuy suspected that boxing was going to be a whole different kind of animal. First of all, this was the first day of baseball practice and Chuy would be missing out. He had not missed a baseball practice for years. He thought longingly about the familiar routine: stretching, fielding, batting cage, conditioning. *What would boxing practice be like?* He wondered with more than a little trepidation, and then he sighed. *Too late to change my mind,* he reminded himself.

Raul had driven Chuy and Billy to the gym, an old railroad station which had been converted into a small community center, with a daycare facility on the first floor and a boxing gym on the second. Chuy was the first to reach the entrance, where he paused for a moment at the bottom of a dark staircase.

"Well, Rocky, we're going in, or what?" Billy teased. "Out of the way—this place doesn't scare me!"

"Of course not," Chuy teased back. "You're too dumb to be scared. But I'm going first; if you go first they may kick us out before we get started."

His initial hesitation dissolved, and Chuy bounded up the stairs, stopping at the gym entrance to take it all in.

There were two big rooms visible. The furthest room contained all the boxing equipment. Four heavy bags nearly the size of human bodies hung on heavy chains suspended from huge hooks in the ceiling. Speed bags, supported on wooden bases and metal braces, hung on a swivel, lined up neatly on one wall. The bags were smaller than a volleyball. On the other side wall was positioned a two-handled bag, the same type of bag as the speed bags, but this one was attached by two rubber lines, one coming from the floor and one from the ceiling. Chuy had seen bags like these on television, but he had never seen them before in person. All this stuff was the real thing! Also stationed in the room were dumbbells and kettlebells, neatly stored from lightest weight to heaviest on racks. Two football blocking dummies and a big pad mounted on the wall completed the array of equipment, strange to both Billy and Chuy.

In the front room, to the left as the boys stood in the entrance, was a long, thin blue mat lined up parallel to a mirrored wall. Seven boys and three girls stood on the mat in lines facing the mirror. The fighters were all different heights, sizes, and colors, but they all had ropes in hand, and they all looked like they knew what they were doing.

Coach Alvarez was there chatting with a young athletic African-American man and a large, heavily-tattooed Latino with a shaved head. The big man could have been twenty or forty years old; it was difficult to tell without staring. The two men nodded their goodbyes to Alvarez and stepped in front of the line of fighters, their backs to the mirror. Assuming this was where they needed to be, Billy and Chuy headed to the far left and took their place in line. To Billy's right stood a pretty African-American girl. She was perhaps four inches taller than him, but it did not stop Billy from nodding to her.

"Hey, how you doin'?" Billy took no time to begin flirting.

Chuy shook his head and chuckled at his little friend's arrogance.

An African-American gentleman with wide shoulders and heavily muscled arms, along with a proud pronounced belly, left his stool in the middle of the gym and strolled down the line, then back again before turning to the fighters. Judging by his silver hair and beard, he appeared to be in his late sixties. He had a limp and walked with a cane, but it seemed to Chuy that he could probably drop the cane and throw a knockout punch whenever he chose. He began addressing the fighters in a deep voice that had a hint of a southern drawl, not heard very often in Chicago. Chuy liked the way he sounded, and he wanted to hear him talk more. He got his wish when the man turned to him and Billy.

"I see Alvarez recruited a couple of new guys. Fellas, just follow along, play a little follow-the-leader. Y'all will get the hang of this before you know it. I'm Coach Sultan, by the way. You can call me Coach Sultan, but that's all you can call me. Call me something else and you are giving me full permission to knock you out!"

The other fighters smirked and giggled at the same introduction that they heard every time new kids showed up to the gym. Chuy smiled too, but immediately knew Coach Sultan was not a man to be messed with.

Coach Sultan finished his opening speech. "I laugh and I joke, but I generally do not play. So GET TO WORK!"

With that the two men in the front led the group through a series of exercises: squat-thrusts, mountain climbers, sets of ab work and push-ups. Chuy had no idea that there were so many stomach exercises, or so many ways to do a push-up.

Squat-thrusts, mountain climbers, scissor kicks, wide hand push-ups Squat-thrusts, mountain climbers, crunches, narrow-hands-under-the shoulder push-ups. Squat-thrusts, mountain climbers, V-ups, hands form a diamond, stick your nose in the diamond push-ups. And so it went for seven sets in nearly twenty minutes.

Chuy struggled to keep up, but he hung in until the end. By the end of the second set, however, Billy's workout consisted of standing up, laying on his back and laying on his stomach. The pretty girl at his side knocked out the work in a steady rhythm which proved that she had been coming to the gym for a while. She grinned at Billy as she went smoothly from one set to the next.

Chuy kept thinking, *If this is warm-ups, I think I'm in trouble!* He had never been physically pushed this hard in his life. Mercifully, the team finished their last set right before he gave up.

"Grab a rope; you guys know the drill! *Con Prisa!*' shouted the Latino man. His voice did not match his fierce look. He sounded much happier and gentler than Chuy had expected. Still, he hustled like the rest of the team to grab a jump rope from the forty or so that hung on the front wall on either side of the mirror. Most of the fighters had their own ropes which they had snatched from their bags, giving Chuy and Billy a lot to pick from—too many! Chuy quickly took a handful of ropes and began sorting through them for one, but not knowing what to look for. Meanwhile, Billy was still laying on his back on the floor.

"Billy!" Chuy hissed, like a mother scolding her son in church.

"Here, Chuy!"

Startled, Chuy turned to see Coach Alvarez offering him a plastic rope.

"This should work for you to start. Here's one for your boy, if we can get him off the floor."

Chuy's thanks was interrupted.

"TIME!" The Latino man's voice rang out to signify the beginning of the round. Now his voice was far from gentle.

A buzzer sounded and hip-hop music blared, but it did not drown out the tap, tap, tap of ropes on the floor. The team had spread out throughout the front room, all facing the mirrored wall. Chuy and Billy did the same. The mirror provided visual proof as to how skillfully the rest of the team could jump and how Billy and Chuy could not. Ropes created a whizzing sound as they were crossed over and double-jumped. With the music pounding, each boxer performed his or her own dance. Some were smooth and steady, going on one foot then the other, some moved with more speed crossing the rope over and over as they jumped through the "X" created by their own arms, doubling the jump by spinning the rope twice as they jumped straight and high. Some pumped high knees as they moved back and forth in their own area.

Billy and Chuy stood close to the wall, jumping the rope once, swinging it toward their feet where it would hit their toes, stinging painfully. Attempting to ignore the pain, they would step over the rope and repeat. It was as painful to watch as it was to perform.

The pretty girl, still on Billy's right, shot her knees up and down like pistons as she moved back and forth. She hit some doubles, then crossed over, then settled into a skilled rhythmic skip. She looked over at Billy. "Don't worry, you'll get it. I was like you when I started; all it takes is practice." Without skipping a beat, she returned to her double and cross over jumps.

Billy grinned at Chuy way too confidently, taking the girl's kindness as a sign that she was "into him." Chuy chuckled at his cocky little buddy.

Inspired by the attention, Billy whipped the rope down faster, performing his one jump at a time with renewed vigor. Fifteen minutes of rope seemed like a lifetime to Chuy, but the other fighters seemed to love this part of practice as they completed their rhythmic dance.

"Stations," someone yelled when the music stopped, and the athletes scurried to different parts of the gym. Coach Alvarez headed to a heavy bag. Chuy and Billy started toward his familiar face, but the large Latino man blocked them.

"Newbie's with me," he informed them.

The boys appeared terrified, as they looked yearningly toward Coach Alvarez, who smiled encouragement at them. The Latino coach guided them into the second room and Chuy saw that the gym contained a third room that he had not seen from the front. It was the "ring" room. A boxing ring took up the center, with standing room only around it.

"You need to pay attention or you'll never get in that room, *vato*."

Chuy snapped his attention back to the big man.

"Hey, it's all good, fellas. Relax!" said the coach, sensing the boys' apprehension.

"I actually get to teach today. I'll work the stations with you guys. I'm Coach Herida, but you can call me Cesar."

"Big Ces!" chorused the nearby fighters.

Cesar acknowledged his fans with a wave. He suddenly seemed much younger and not at all scary.

"I'm gonna take you *vatos* through each piece of equipment. There are right ways to hit these bags and wrong ways. I'm gonna teach you two characters how to do things right. That clock on the wall will buzz every three minutes with a thirty second rest time between rounds. We will move through each piece of equipment, from one station to another. You newbies get it?"

"Got it!" Chuy and Billy answered in unison.

"We're gonna start at the shadow boxing station, all we need is a mirror." Big Ces positioned the proper boxing stance.

"You fellas are both right handers, so let's get the left foot forward, right foot back, on the toes, bend the knees, turn the body so the other guy is seeing more shoulder than chest." He paused to study his students. He adjusted their foot placement then, satisfied with what he saw, continued,

"Okay, fellas, your front hand—your left—is your jab hand. That's your stick. Now let's keep that right hand tucked against your jaw; that's it, tuck the elbow." He again adjusted the boys' stance. When he was satisfied, he kept going. "Jab, or left hand, is your stick; the right hand is your club. Let's say there's a big, old dog tryin' to get ya. Use that stick to keep him away. Stick, stick, stick…" The coach modeled the jab, shooting out his left hand and bringing it back to the starting position. The boys followed along as best they could.

"Stick! Stick! Stick! Now that dog ain't going nowhere, so ya hit 'em with the club—boom!" He punctuated by throwing the right hand. "Now you are good to go, unless that was my dog, then I would have to knock *you* out." The patient young coach continued to correct, and the two new students continued to learn how to throw punches correctly.

"Jab left! Jab left! Jab left! Right hand, boom! Jab! Jab! Jab! Right hand." Cesar kept the cadence going. Three minutes seemed like ten. Though their coach maintained a slower pace, after three rounds of shadow boxing Chuy and Billy were tired.

On to the heavy bag and more of the same. "Jab! Jab! Jab! Straight right!" Chuy kept the pace the best he could, throwing punches to Big Cesar's cadence, while Billy resembled a sleepwalking zombie. The newbies stood out from the fighters on the other bags, who moved with a quick steady rhythm, moving, crouching, popping jabs, straight hands, hooks and uppercuts.

"Thirty!" shouted Big Ces when there was thirty seconds left in the round. Fighters threw punches as fast as they could, pounding the bag until the buzzer went off. Ces read the disheartened look on Chuy's face and noted the puddle of sweat that used to be Billy.

"Don't worry, guys, you'll get there. Like Alvarez always says, anything good takes time."

"Is that what he says?" Billy managed to croak out between huffing and puffing, unable to lift his head.

"Oh, yeah." Ces covered Billy's scrawny shoulder with his big paw. "Like he told me back in the day: 'no matter what happens today, fellas, your job is to hang in and come back tomorrow.' Ya feel me?"

Billy and Chuy nodded weakly and did just that. They hung in through each round—three rounds on the heavy bag, then three more rounds hitting the pads mounted on the wall. Just when the boys thought they could take no more, Cesar returned them to the shadow boxing station. This time he picked up the pace, shadow boxing alongside of them as he barked out instructions.

"Correct stance, *vatos*! You remember; on the toes, stand in an imaginary box—right foot front corner, back foot left corner. Knees bent, right hand tucked under the chin, left hand out, shoulders turned so you don't give the other guy a target in the middle of your chest. Aim your punches to the middle of the other guy's chest and to his chin. The jab is your stick, so stick and move to your right. Stay on them toes, Billy! The right hand is your club, your knockout punch. Throw it straight and hard to the targets. Okay guys, you gotta turn and stretch on the hips, bring it back to starting stance as quick as possible. Jab, jab, jab, right hand! Jab, jab, jab, right hand! Now add foot movement, up and back. Jab, slide up, jab, slide up, jab, slide up, boom! Right hand. Boom! Now let's move backward the same way: jab, jab, jab, straight right!" The big man talked and moved as if he had taught these techniques a hundred times; perhaps he had.

"Keep your form, elbows in. Let's throw punches high now. High punches are harder to do, but they make you stronger. On the toes, Billy! Bend the knees, snap it back."

With Chuy on the right and Billy on the left, the three moved in an athletic dance—same punches, same steps, same time. However, it was short lived. Billy faded quickly, Chuy hung in longer and Cesar continued to snap punches and move with a graceful rhythm. As the music blared, a hip hop boxing ballet was led by this scary-looking, heavily-muscled, tattooed Latino man with a heart of gold.

When the buzzer sounded Cesar stopped to observe the boys, a broad smile lighting up his face as he suddenly appeared youthful and carefree in front of their eyes.

"Listen, homies, you're doin' just fine! You should've seen me the first day Alvarez brought me here...didn't even make it through warm-ups. Hard part is over; just hang in there, it's all good."

Hang in there, thought Chuy, *how many times have I heard that today?*

"Speed bag, two-handled bag and that's all for you boys," Big Cesar announced encouragingly.

Hang in there, Chuy's thought process kept repeating.

Cesar escorted the boys over to the side wall to demonstrate the speed bag. His hands held high, he hit the little ball of a bag against the wooden base with his right, then again with the left when it bounced back. Of course, Cesar did it with ease, creating another of the many rhythmic tat-tat-tat sounds of the gym: speed bag, jump rope, heavy bag, and now the speed bag. All sounding their distant tat-tat-tats: the orchestra of the boxing gym. Chuy took it all in and for a time, forgot how tired, uncoordinated and dumb he felt as he enjoyed the symphony.

I could get used to this, he thought. It was like a cool movie that he now felt part of, even if he wasn't the star.

Cesar stepped away. "It's all you Jesus, take a turn, *vato*."

Snapped back to attention, Chuy sighed and stepped up as ordered. Tap and miss. Steady the bag with both hands. Tap, clunk, deep breath. The rhythm of the new kid on the speed bag added somewhat clumsily to the orchestra. When the buzzer sounded it was Billy's turn to clunk, tap, miss. With the next buzzer the first practice was finished.

Cesar put his big hands on the shoulders of the boys, gave the two a wide grin that made him look like a twelve year old boy who had just pulled a prank. "Okay homies, just remember to..."

"Hang in there," the boys chanted in unison, beating Cesar to it and giving him a hearty laugh.

Coach Alvarez appeared out of nowhere to wrap sweaty arms around the boys necks, his hair and shirt also drenched with sweat. "Easy-peasy; right, fellas?"

"They did great, Coach A. Now, will they be back?" Big Ces wanted to know.

"We'll see you tomorrow," Chuy insisted.

"Yeah, that's what this guy told me," Alvarez said, flipping his thumb at Big Ces. "He was so sore the next day he didn't even come to school!"

"Whoa, I'm the one that got you involved in this club in the first place, remember, Coach?" said Big Ces, now with his huge paws on Alvarez's shoulders.

"Because you needed good coaching," responded Alvarez.

"Because I needed a ride!" joked Cesar, and they both cracked up laughing. "Okay, *vatos*, some of us have to work for a living. Peace and chicken grease," he said in parting, as he slung his bag over his shoulder. "See you tomorrow."

Raul was late as usual, so Billy and Chuy stood waiting outside the gym.

Alvarez exited the gym and saw them leaning against the building. "Lemme guess, you are waiting for Raul."

"Wait, you know Raul?" asked Chuy, a little stunned.

"Hello! I know everyone, remember? Well, correction—everyone knows me. I've been doing this for a while, man! I know you guys and your brother and sisters. I even know your oldest sister, Bill."

"Yeah, I know," Billy replied with a smirk. "She said you used to be hot."

"Used to be? You little son of a ..." Alvarez threw a pretend jab at Billy as the boys laughed.

"Well, fellas, in the old days I could give you a ride, but that's not allowed now."

"No sweat, Coach A, here he is." Chuy recognized the car heading in their direction.

"Hey, Alvarez!" Raul hollered out the window.

"What up, LeDesma?" the coach returned. "When we gonna get you here?"

"Come on, Coach, I'm a lover not a fighter."

"Hey, that's my line." Billy protested.

"Well, Big Billy Karamitos, after what I saw today, I hope that's true."

"Says the guy that used to be hot," Billy shot back as quick as a jab.

"Owwwww!" Alvarez took a big step back, pretending to take the shot to the chin. "The knockout punch!"

Outside the old railroad station, the teacher, the graduate and the two students shared a good laugh after a long day. Boxing life had begun for Chuy LeDesma, and although he was tired to the bone he felt peaceful and content.

CHAPTER 7

The next morning Billy and Chuy dutifully followed their routine, feeling immensely sore after the previous evening's practice. That same morning Lucy entered Layden High School and immediately relapsed into her Jekyll and Hyde identity. She did not like it, but she had played the role since her freshman year. Back then, she did whatever she had to do to fit in and gain respect from her peers. Now, as her junior year was coming to a close, her alternate identity was ingrained within her, and she could not see what she could do to change.

Lucy had always been a good student, but many teachers throughout the years had misjudged her abilities and her drive. Initially she had appeared to be the tough girl wearing too much make-up, sweatshirts, and baggy, ripped jeans. Teachers often judged her immediately when she first walked into the classroom as the Latin gang girl, only to discover that she was quiet, but insightful, introspective, and driven. She worked not only for A's, but for the highest grade in the class. As the weeks wore on each semester, Lucy surprised her instructors, especially those who had judged her by looks alone. She surprised them with her competitive fire, but also with her willingness to help others in the class. As teachers recognized her gift for helping Lucy was often teamed with students who were shy, or apathetic, or just less skilled.

The "'tough gang girl'" finished each semester with instructors happy to have met her, but so sorry to see her go. She had been nominated for Student of the Month honors for leadership and excellence more times than she could count. Lucy was unaware that at least once a semester a young teacher had burst into the teacher's cafeteria announcing that he or she had discovered this "diamond in the rough."

"You mean Lucy Quinones? Yeah, she's a good one," the veteran teachers would respond, stealing the rookie's thunder.

Once more, as her junior year was coming to an end, Lucy was being recognized by the faculty for the excellent student that she was. She had just received word the day before that she was nominated for the "We Are Excellence" award as the outstanding student in the Junior Class, which would be given at the end of the year. An award that many students would give anything for, Lucy's sense of self-preservation screamed at her to decline it. And it was all because of a strange, familiar feeling that made no sense and yet, it made perfect sense.

Lucy knew why she harbored such a mixed-up, nonsensical dread of public admiration, but she still felt helpless against it. It was the same thing she experienced outside the safety of the classroom—in the lunchroom, in the hallways, at the bus stop, outside Oscar's on Friday night. The thing that drove her to play a part was fear. As Lucy had aged, she had perfected the act. Her role had become stronger and bigger and way too familiar. Outside the classroom her clothes, make-up, hair and walk defined her. They surrounded her and buried her under the tough-girl facade. She was now in so very deep that she had no idea how to escape.

It had started in the sixth grade, on her first day of junior high. She had been the first girl in her family to experience growing up in Northwest Chicago and, although she never showed it, she had been scared. Her first interaction had been with Nancy Robles, who was by far the biggest, meanest- looking sixth grader at Washington Junior High. Lucy had played it tough, too, and soon enough they had become friends. Like many friendships, things started with a natural unspoken agreement to help each other. Lucy helped Nancy with her studies. Nancy, who was the youngest of five siblings, helped Lucy to understand how to be "cool." That meant no one was going to push her around. It also meant she had to be in good standing with the local gangs. Lucy had played it smart and learned quickly.

She was also smart enough *not* to play her tough girl role at home. Her parents would not like it and she knew things were difficult enough for them already. Slowly, but surely, she traded out the clothes her mother had bought for clothes she picked out for herself. Makeup hidden in her purse was applied while riding the bus to school. As Lucy did with everything, she took on her new part meticulously, with an eye for detail.

Lucy's parents were too busy and too tired to take much notice. In those junior high days she left for school before they were awake and was in bed at night before they got home. Weekdays or weekends were the same; her parents were working and Lucy was on her own. As long as she took care of her sisters and her grades, all was well. Her hardworking parents learned to be satisfied with brief conversations and mumbled replies from their eldest daughter. They did not have time nor energy for more than that.

Nancy often came home with Lucy after school. They would do the required chores and schoolwork together. Life was easy for Lucy, as schoolwork was not challenging and her sisters were even more frightened of Nancy than they were of their big sister. Thus they did chores without a fight.

With the responsibilities taken care of, Lucy and Nancy turned their attention to their favorite topic: boys. They talked to boys on the phone for hours throughout the week, but Saturday nights were when Lucy would play her part to perfection, and the feeling of being bad grew like a cancer within her.

On Saturday nights *Tia* Beatrice often came to watch the younger girls, so Lucy was free to escape. By the eighth grade Lucy fell into her part as easily as falling into a stream and floating with the current. Beatrice was happy to sit on the sofa and watch a movie with the younger girls. Lucy would even make the popcorn, followed with a kiss on the cheek to *Tia*, a warning to her little sisters not to stay up too late and to listen to their aunt, and she was off into the night. A pause outside the house under the streetlight to put on eyeliner, a flannel shirt tied around her to emphasize her tiny waist, the tight, black tank top and jeans pulled down just enough. There she was—a tough Latina gang-banger with a touch of little girl playing dress up thrown in.

She joined up with Nancy and the night began. They were young girls roaming the streets, feeling the sense of adventure and the excitement of potential danger. Now the familiar rapid heartbeat with senses heightened and breathe a little quicker, and something else—an ever-so-slight, sick feeling in the pit of her stomach. There it was: the strange and the familiar.

After nearly four years there were still mixed feelings she could not ignore no matter how hard she tried. One minute Lucy and Nancy were smoking weed, feeling silly. The next thing they were involved in a gang fight over something that never really mattered. There was the shameful feeling of being too young to be kissed and touched by boys who were too old. The feeling was bad, awful, sick, but it came as a package deal with the role that Lucy played.

When she finally met Armani, he was cool and dangerous, but at least he was her age. She became his girl and she took her place as royalty, a princess in the highest Latin King family in the neighborhood. Nancy, on the other hand, had fallen for an older guy who bought her beer and weed. Unfortunately, He was a Cobra, a sworn enemy to the Kings. That was enough to break up their relationship and by freshman year, they were no longer friends, but, in fact, rivals.

Now, as her junior year was winding down and as she approached the main school entrance, Lucy was drowning in the mixture of feelings once again. She stopped for a moment, blew out a deep breath and then entered the building to go to her spot, the place she hated, but belonged. It was 7:15 a.m., only fifteen minutes until her first class—American Literature. Fifteen minutes and she would be in her classroom, where she could come up for air and float in a sea of Steinbeck and Hemingway. She would discard the disguise and be herself, in just fifteen minutes!

Lucy moved down the hall to the main stairwell, to take her spot next to Armani. He and his boys seemed especially wild.

"Babe!" He called out to Lucy, with excitement in his eyes. "The shit is going down!"

Not today, thought Lucy. *Spring break is almost here.*

Suddenly, without warning even to herself, she had had enough. Lucy struggled against the current as a thought screamed through her head. *I don't want anything to do with this, Armani! I don't want to be part of this!*

To Lucy's surprise, her mask began to crumble.

Armani was shocked by the negative expression on her face, "Babe, it's the Cobras! It's gonna happen, in the lunchroom TODAY!"

The current tugged at Lucy, and again she fought it, but this time words came pouring out. "No, Armani, I've got better things to do than deal with you and your gang bullshit!"

Armani's excitement switched to anger. "What the f…?" he cornered her against the locker. "This is *my* bullshit? You the one that has beef with that bitch, Nancy. And this is *my* bullshit?!"

It was true. From their freshman year, when Nancy had become the girlfriend of the Cobra, the girls had never exchanged a civil word; in fact, they had viciously fought each other twice outside Oscar's, both time stopped by the police and Oscar himself. The last time they had fought Lucy had taken two punches from the larger Nancy that had left her bruised. Lucy's proud, competitive nature had filled her with a desire for revenge, which sucked her back into the dark waters of anger, fueling the latest bad blood between the two rival gangs. Now, as Armani reminded Lucy of the pointless battle between Nancy and herself, the sick feeling returned. She pushed him away and sat on the bench below the windows of the hallway. Armani went back to his boys, fired up and ready to fight. Lucy dropped her head in her hands. *Ten minutes to class. Only ten minutes more and she could breathe again.*

That morning Chuy headed toward 250, but something was missing. *Where is Karamitos with his big mouth and lame jokes?* Chuy wondered.

"Wait up!" He heard, but before he could add to his thought the words were followed by a weak moan. He turned to see Billy staggering toward him.

"Dude, what's wrong with you? Fall off your skateboard, or get hit by a truck?"

"You and your damn boxing is what happened to me! I'm dying over here.

"You'll feel better after practice," suggested Chuy, patting Billy on the back. Billy winced.

"We will get the soreness out," Chuy declared encouragingly.

"Whatcha mean we? You and the mouse in your pocket?"

"You can't expect to be ready to fight without going to practice," Chuy responded.

"Wait! You think I'm going to do this whole thing with you? One practice was enough for me. Besides, I've got a busy schedule," Billy whined.

"Correct! You will be busy going to boxing with me," Chuy insisted, reaching the 250 wing. "And we are busy right now, seeing Ms. Kelly about Wolfy's kids."

"Dude, I don't have time for all this jock, do-gooder stuff."

Chuy stopped short. Suddenly he was not smiling. "Then don't, Bill. Play video games all day for all I care."

Billy stood, mouth open, surprised by Chuy's serious tone. "Okay, Chewbacca, okay! Don't get all Darth Vader on me! I'm afraid of the dark side."

"Just come on," Chuy shouted over his shoulder, as he strode purposely toward the classroom.

Billy hurried to catch-up, dodging Wolfy's kids who were running forward with their morning greeting. Chuy and Billy turned into the room across from Coach Wolf's where Ms. Kelly, four senior students, and a stack of Best Pals program binders were waiting. Chuy stopped for a moment to survey the scene. *Best Pals, boxing, and Billy, Who would have thought it!*

CHAPTER 8

Life can be stranger than fiction, and so it was on that Tuesday afternoon in the Layden cafeteria. The Illinois winter had slowly and begrudgingly started to blossom into spring. The days were, at last, getting longer, so slowly that it was painful, but spring break was just around the corner! Spring break by no means signals beautiful warm days, but it does mean a week away from school. The rich kids head to Cancun and will return with ridiculous tans, while the poor kids are left with plenty of time to seek out trouble. But most importantly it marks the beginning of the end of the school year. It's a time when students should be relaxed, more than halfway done with the final semester of the school year. They should be settled into their classes, understanding all rules and expectations. Any initial headbutting should be long over with. Teachers traditionally have already completed the most difficult projects of the class, and ever so slightly begun lightening the load. The class ship should smoothly sail toward the end of the year and that sweet summer that lay so enticingly ahead.

As any teacher knows, however, (especially teachers in the midwest) that is far from the case. Winter brings cabin fever. It has been cold and dark for months. The spirit of joy and the good will of Christmas has long since been replaced by slush and drudgery. Cabin fever is a plague upon

57

students desperate for change. Two weeks before Spring break is when that desperation peaks.

In the cafeteria on that Tuesday Mr. Norris and Mr. Jefferson could feel it, the student's desperation preparing to break out. The two security officers moved between tables and scanned the students. Most kids were laughing, clowning, or in deep conversation, but the word was out that the Kings and Cobras had beef to be settled.

In addition to the security guards, two teachers patrolled the cafeteria. One of the teachers was Chuck Alvarez, who always requested cafeteria duty because it was the best way to interact with kids, especially for a special education teacher with small classes. Most teachers hated cafe duty and preferred to sit in a lonely hallway or a quiet study hall. Alvarez hated to sit, and he loved to talk and to steal French fries from kids' trays. This Tuesday, there was an addition to the usual staff members who were working in the cafeteria. The group had been joined by Mr. Rudy, the dean.

As Alvarez joked with students and stole fries, the other professionals appeared hypervigilant. Dean Rudy and his security staff had been around long enough to take the rumors seriously. Something was going down and they were prepared to stop whatever it was before it became dangerous.

Boys in groups of two and three were heading out of the cafeteria to the adjacent hallways, where students lounged as they waited for the bell to ring. Dean Rudy noted how groups of Kings exited through one door, while Cobras went through another on the opposite side of the eating area. He knew an unspoken choreography would lead them to meet face to face, in the hallway, with groups of ten to fifteen on both sides. Norris had also noticed the activity and he had elected to follow three Cobras. Dean Rudy and Jefferson exchanged looks when Norris' voice sounded over the walkie-talkie. He had stopped a kid for throwing up gang signs and had pulled him away from his crew. Rudy signaled Mr. Jefferson to follow him, and they hurried over to where Alvarez was joking with a table of students.

"Chuck, we have a problem in the hallway; can you handle it in here?"

Alvarez nodded his head and looked around the room. The majority of students seemed unaware of what was going on. He made his way over to the table where Lucy was sitting. He recalled that Armani had been one of the first to leave the cafeteria. Alvarez anticipated that a call would surely be coming from security to keep the kids in the cafeteria. He was fairly certain that these girls would be the first to make a break for the hall if there was a fight.

"Ladies, you need to smarten these boys up; they are gonna get themselves booted out of here with all this kid stuff. Such a waste!"

In her mind Lucy agreed, but instinctively began to get up to join in the action. The students started to surge for the hallway. Alvarez had been in these situations before, and he knew he could not wait for Dean Rudy's call.

"OK, EVERYBODY, STAY AT YOUR TABLE! WE ARE GOING TO STAY IN HERE TODAY!" His voice boomed.

Then to the teacher on the other side of the room:

"MR. ARNONI, PLEASE STAND IN FRONT OF THE DOOR, NO ONE IS LEAVING."

Dean Rudy's voice finally came over the walkie-talkie, "Coach keep them in the cafeteria."

The excited lunch crowd surged again, paying no attention to Alvarez's orders. The girls sitting with Lucy were raising from the table. Gang wannabes and regular students, excited for all the action, were ready to abandon their lunches in favor of the potential action. Chaos threatened!

Alvarez' voice bellowed again. This time he looked angry. "I SAID SIT THE HELL DOWN! I SWEAR, THIS STUFF IS SO LAME! I GOT KIDS FROM THIS SCHOOL THAT FIGHT REAL FIGHTS IN THE RING. I NEVER SEE ANY OF YOU AT THOSE FIGHTS. NOW THESE PUNKS WITH THEIR LITTLE PUSHIN' AND SHOVIN' AND YOU ALL GOTTA WATCH??!! TOTAL BULLSH … Alvarez stopped himself when he noticed the students were staring back at him wide-eyed. They were clearly shocked by the angry teacher.

The man who always smiled was not smiling now. He looked down and shook his head, trying to control his rage. Students, shocked by the display of emotion from the usually happy-go-lucky teacher, returned to their seats immediately. Alvarez's side of the lunchroom was completely silent, stunned by his rant.

Suddenly, out of nowhere, a tidal wave of movement came from the other side of the cafeteria. Arnoni had lost control and students were spilling out the far door into the outer hallway. Alvarez turned and ran to aid Arnoni. With that, his spell was broken. All the students went to the far door as if the near door still maintained an imaginary force field, but Arnoni's force field had been ripped wide open.

On the other side of the doors the fight had been stopped before it had begun, and Armani and two of his boys were being escorted up to the dean's office by Dean Rudy himself. Jefferson and Norris had three other boys under control and were following at a safe distance. Fortunately, the bell sounded to end the lunch period, and the first students rushing the far door realized that the excitement was over, and the brawl was a dud! Much ado about nothing! The word quickly spread among the mass of students and the current slowed and ebbed.

Lucy was relieved. She would be in class in minutes and her breath flowed smoothly and steadily once more. Suddenly she felt a nudge to her shoulder. It was a girl she recognized as a friend of Nancy. Nancy's face appeared over the girl's shoulder, but Lucy did not see Nancy's fist that caught her on the side of her head.

A whirlpool of angry fists exploded in the midst of the river of students, taking shape and expanding to a crescendo of noise and fury. Lucy swung a short compact punch that connected with the face of a girl who was pulling her hair. The girl fell, taking out chunks of Lucy's hair as she landed on her butt in a sitting position, stunned by the blow. Lucy's eyes teared up from pain, but she could still see two hands shooting to her throat. It was Nancy, who grabbed Lucy and squeezed, attempting to choke her former friend. Lucy swung both hands up to break the grip, then she threw a hard overhand right just as Nancy did the same. Both girls were simultaneously rocked off balance and reached for each other to stop themselves from falling. They wrestled for a few long seconds, then Nancy, the larger of the two girls, fell on top of Lucy and they banged into a table and fell to the ground.

The smooth stream of students now turned and churned again. Calm to chaos in less than a few seconds. The tide turned once more at the back of the cafeteria, which had erupted into a girl gang fight. Alvarez doubled back, fighting the raging current of students as he made his way toward the action. He saw Lucy and Nancy wrestling on the floor. As soon as he could reach them he pulled the girls up. The force of his pull, however, sent him and the girls off balance, toppling back onto the lunch tables. All three landed on their butts. For a moment everything stopped as they looked at each other. In a blink, the girls went back to wrestling and throwing punches.

Alvarez had witnessed many fights over the years, but this one had a ferocity he had never before seen. The two girls, who were once friends, now fought like animals, not out of hatred, but out of frustration. Somewhere hidden in the back of their minds they remembered their friendship. The betrayal of that friendship fueled their anger. They had grown apart because of boys and gangs, and now in this battle they wrestled and pummeled and kicked and scratched at the girl who used to be the other's best friend. The rage was a geyser that exploded, witnessed by a crowd of students who were stunned into statues, as the two girls went at each other.

"ENOUGH!" Alvarez, who was seconds late to the scene, screamed in a voice he seldom used, but had used twice within the last ten minutes.

"ENOUGH, DAMMIT!" He repeated. The girls stopped, not because of the furious teacher, but from pure exhaustion.

"Enough!" One last time.

The three sat on the floor, the girls' bodies heaving from their heavy breathing. Lucy looked at Nancy, and Nancy looked at Lucy. For the first time since junior high the two girls truly saw each other.

"Enough," Alvarez whispered to himself, sad and himself exhausted.

CHAPTER 9

In the fitness center that afternoon Chuy and Billy did their best to prepare for boxing practice by hitting the ropes, or more accurately, the ropes were hitting the boys. Coach Alvarez noticed their struggles and stepped away from spotting and correcting the form of some kids doing squats. He hustled over to where Chuy and Billy were and offered the boys a few pointers on the ropes.

"Two feet first, fellas. Get the rhythm, no hop in between. You aren't doing one-potato-two-potato like your little sister at the playground. After that, you can do one foot at a time, then progress to the skip, but that will come later."

Off he went to the squat racks, after assuring himself that the boys were on the right track.

"Lower, Virginia, and keep the back flat," he instructed a tall blonde girl. She adjusted her stance and slowly squatted again, this time deeper and more deliberately.

"Now you're working!" Alvarez shouted over the clanging of weights and hip-hop blasting from large speakers above the entrance.

Alvarez stopped for a brief moment and drank it all in. The gym had always been his sanctuary, throughout high school, the military, then college. No matter where he was, he had always found a gym where he could find his own special kind of peace.

He had begun his teaching career at Provo High not far from Layden. It was a rough school with an extremely high dropout rate. Alvarez had started an after-school weightlifting program, as much for himself as for the kids. Before his father had passed away, Alvarez had gone to his hometown to teach and be near his family. He had enjoyed lifting weights with the students, even though the room was "staffed" by veteran teachers who sat reading the newspaper while they got paid for "supervision." They had been Alvarez's old coaches. He held no hard feelings for doing their job for them. In fact, he enjoyed lifting with the kids with no sense of forced responsibility, just for the pure joy of training.

It was there he first began to funnel kids from high school into boxing, to his old boxing gym and into the realm of one of his true heros, Coach Louie Rios. The man had been family to Alvarez, and had taken the shy, skinny fifteen-year-old with pretty boy looks and turned him into a champ, respected in the community and around the state. Alvarez was one of Louie's first fighters, but he was far from his last. Coach Rios had, over the years since Alvarez had fought under his tutelage, grown the team from a few kids in the basement of a drug store in tiny Depue, Illinois into a two-story building near the school. Now, fighters from all over the area filled the gym from opening until closing time each day. Alvarez had loved the place almost as much as he loved "Uncle Lou," as he affectionately called his coach and mentor.

He had spent most of his evenings in that smelly, sweaty, wonderful place, pounding the heavy bags and sparring for hours, leaving the anxiety of every high school kid he worked with at the door. The gym was way more to him than a place to train. It was a place to hide, to run away from a world of hard knocks and harsh reality. An Alcoholic father had made Alvarez's childhood home sad and uncertain. He had never known what he would walk into when he came home from school.

Generally, things were quiet, if not tense. He would never know, however, when he and his brother would come home to "Drunk Dad." "Drunk Dad" was unpredictable. Drunk happy dad, drunk angry dad, drunk apologetic dad, drunk furious dad. But the gym was always the same, safe, and predictable. A shelter where he could unwind and relax.

After hours of practice Alvarez had gone home stronger and renewed, ready to face anything including "Drunk Dad."

Now he had moved on to Layden. He hoped it would be his forever school, his forever weight room at Layden High, and Maywood Boxing Club his forever boxing gym. He had first met the head man at Maywood, Coach Sultan, when he had been a kid fighting against a boxer from Sultan's club. Louis Rios' Boxing Club and Maywood had both become known for tough kids who were well-conditioned and never quit. When the members of the teams would fight each other at tournaments it was always a battle between equally well-trained athletes. Sometimes the Maywood fighter won; sometimes the Rios boxer won. But in five fights, Alvarez had never lost to one of Sultan's middleweights. When he began working at Layden he was happy to discover that the gym with the tough old coach was only a mere five miles away. He had to stop by. He had never been there, since the gym itself was too small to host events, but it looked exactly the way he expected it would. Sultan did not look a bit different, either. He was still old and mean.

When Sultan had recognized Alvarez, who was wandering around his gym, the old, gravelly voice came thundering out, bringing back memories. "Lookie, look, it's Chuckie Alvarez, the 'Pony Express' himself! Louie told me you were teaching in the hood. You gonna bring me some of those Latino fighters from Layden? We gonna make ourselves a super team!"

Alvarez had protested; he had wanted to get his feet on the ground with classes. He was already coaching freshman football, but he had promised Sultan that he would come back and see him when the season ended, secretly hoping Sultan would forget about the promise. That hope disappeared when the day after the football season ended, a huge Hispanic kid with a baby face and a sly smirk had appeared at his classroom door. Backing him up were four guys, including a boy who didn't look old enough to be in high school. The other three hadn't seemed much older.

"Coooaaacch," came the greeting from the man-child, that made it sound like the two had known each other for years.

Still new to Layden, Alvarez—so far— had no run in with the gangs, but his initial reaction had been one of caution.

"Yeah, what's up?"

"Cooooach, someone sent us for you!"

Alvarez instinctually stepped into his boxing stance. "Really?" He replied, still smiling back at the huge baby face beaming at him. *Okay,* he thought, *I've got the biggest kid in the school with the littlest shrimp they could find.*

"What do you fellas need?" asked Alvarez, losing the smile.

"Sultan sent us. He told us all about you. He said you were going to start a boxing club here."

Alvarez had let out a relieved sigh, realizing in that moment that these guys were no threat; however, Sultan was a dog with a bone.

The big kid just kept grinning. "Coooach, I'm Cesar, but you can call me Big Ces, and these are my boys: Yoshi, Juan, Carl and Yoshi's little brother, Ulises. Coach, We know all about you. When you going to get this boxing thing started?"

"Sounds like you already got it goin'. What do you need me for?" Alvarez teased, trying to look stern.

Then it had been Big Ces' turn to drop the wide grin in favor of a serious demeanor. "It's not something I can do, Coach Alvarez, but if you help us, you won't regret it."

Alvarez had been surprised by Big Cesar's sudden change to a serious side.

He had clearly recalled when he had been as green as these kids standing in his classroom, looking hopeful. The young coach had remembered back to when he had been just a kid from the tiny town of Utica, Illinois. He had talked his friend Gio into driving him to the gym on a Monday in the summer. There, he had met Louie and went through his first practice for a couple of hours. Louie had told them to come back on Wednesday to spar with Joe Moreno, the toughest light-middleweight in the gym. That had been Chuck Alvarez's first time in a ring. His only other experience up until then had been back yard and garage fights with neighbor kids. That first sparring session Alvarez had barely made five rounds of boxing, thanks to good wind capacity from running the 800 meters in track. He had recalled that he also had copied a stance he had picked up from watching Sugar Ray Leonard on television, along with a jab and straight right he had picked up from all the backyard fights. The chin that he had inherited from his father had been put to the test often against Moreno, who easily whipped the novice. However, when the session was over Louie had told the new kid to show up at 5:00 p.m. on Saturday and he would have a fight in Mendota, a nearby city in Illinois.

Saturday had been a big day for Chuck. By seven that evening the sixteen-year-old had beaten a twenty-three-year-old, part-time police officer with a TKO in the second round. Alvarez had soon become the best middleweight in the gym, then in the state when he won his first Gloves tournament.

He had honed his boxing skills even further when he joined the Army, serving in the demilitarized zone of Korea. He had won the Second Division Championship and finally the Korean Championship, finishing undefeated after two years of service.

When he had returned from the service he had had dreams of fighting in the Olympics. With the dream of winning a gold medal, then becoming a special education teacher, the young veteran had enrolled at Illinois State University, financed by the GI Bill. Alvarez had spent most of his time boxing and learning how to teach special needs kids, which became his two favorite things to do, though meeting girls had been a close third. As Alvarez had begun his climb into national competition it became evident to him, and to Louie, that he was going to be a teacher for a living, not a boxer. Alvarez quickly learned the difference between really good fighters and great fighters and he was firmly in the first category. He fought good, tough fights, but never made it out of the quarter finals. Alvarez would always remember the day when Louie and he were driving home from Indianapolis after an early exit from the Midwest Regionals of the Gloves.

"Chuck, time to work with kids. That's what you do best," Coach Louie had bluntly announced.

Alvarez had had no argument. Without regret, he switched from fighting to teaching and coaching. Just as he was finishing up with college, he led practices at a local boxing club. He had gone on to help Louie coach at the same time he had been teaching back at LaSalle-Peru.

Then a few years later, at his "forever" school, he had been confronted by the big, baby-faced kid with pleading eyes. Alvarez had planned to settle in for a year or two before he took on anything else. Big Cesar and his boys had changed all the careful planning.

Alvarez had stalled, but in his heart he knew he had been hooked.

"Let me think about it, fellas. Gimme me a week."

"Coooach!" Cesar's smile lit up his face, telling Alvarez that this kid had his number. It was only a matter of time!

Alvarez had gone to the go-to-guy, Dean Rudy, and found out that Cesar was an ex-hardcore gang banger—not a wannabe, but a legit gang member! But he had fought his way out of the gangs, and by his senior year turned his life around. He may or may not have known it, but Big Ces Heredia was also turning the school around.

When Dean Rudy found out that the young man had approached Alvarez, he hadn't been able to contain his joy. "Yes!" he declared, with a fist pump for emphasis.

"Why didn't he just go to the club on his own? That's what I did," Alvarez questioned.

"First Avenue is Blackstone Nation and Cesar was a Latin King," Rudy had explained. "Heredia is a big guy, but he's still a kid. I'm guessing he feels insecure; he wants those boxing coaches to know he is legit. He may be showing up at the Maywood Club, but he needed something to show them that he is really invested, that he and his guys are done with the life—out of the gangs. Looks like that thing is you, Charlie Alvarez," Rudy had said, with a hearty handshake and a toothy grin. "Congratulations, Coach, I got a feeling this is the start of something big!"

So boxing had drawn Alvarez in again.

In the months that had followed two cars full of kids ran from West Layden High to the gym, making the trek down North Avenue, hanging a left on First Avenue and on to the club. Monday through Friday, every week, and so it had gone.

Ulises, the little, skinny grade-schooler, who had tagged along with Big Ces was now tall and muscular, a poster boy for what hard work could do for a body. He now offered Chuy and Billy jump ropes. "Saw you fellas at the gym. So Alvarez hooked ya in, huh?"

Chuy recognized him from the hallways at school, but things had been too much of a blur for him to have noticed Ulises from the gym.

"Well, one of us anyway." Chuy took the rope from Ulises. Billy had already melted into the floor.

Alvarez took notice of the conversation between Ulises and Chuy and walked over to join them. At least one good thing had happened that day. The fight in the school cafeteria had left Alvarez shaken and still a little angry. He had received an invitation, or more accurately, an order to attend a meeting tomorrow with Dean Rudy and the parents of the girls in the fight. He hoped to try to do something to help the situation. If it worked it would be wonderful for the school and for the two girls.

Thinking too much again, Alvarez scolded himself.

"So this is the next champ, huh, Coach?" Ulises interrupted his thoughts.

"We'll see," replied Alvarez. "We'll see. We may have a few new fighters coming our way, Ulises. We are going to need guys to replace you, since you're going to be working and going to college full time next fall. Now quit talking and show these boys how to use those ropes!"

CHAPTER 10

Alvarez silently cursed himself for not being able to speak better Spanish. His father always said, "I married a white girl so you kids could speak English," but even as a teen Chuck had known that he should speak Spanish to get along in a bilingual world. He regretted having not spoken Spanish more with his father, even though his father would get angry with his mispronunciation and underwhelming vocabulary. *I need to practice with my students,* thought Alvarez, *and study more. I need to take classes.* Yet here he was, unable to speak fluently to these Latino families.

Dean Rudy's small conference room was full: two sets of parents, the dean, the liaison police officer, a counselor, Lucy, and Nancy. Additionally, the person Alvarez was most happy to see: Carla Flores, the school translator.

"*Mucho Gusto, Soy* Chuck Alvarez," the young coach said, introducing himself to the families. *Ha,* he chuckled to himself, *could I have a more white first name?*

"Mr. Alvarez is the teacher who broke up the fight in the cafeteria. I would like him to be part of the meeting." Dean Rudy spoke slowly and clearly to the parents, pausing frequently as Mrs. Flores translated. "As I explained to you earlier, fighting means a three-day suspension. Gang fighting means five days and a final warning. If after today, these girls are involved in, or found to be part of ANY GANG ACTIVITY they will be expelled from this school. Obviously, this is a very serious situation!"

After a lengthy pause to give the families time to recognize the importance of the meeting, Dean Rudy continued. "I have been part of too many meetings like this." He stopped, shaking his head in sadness at the truth of his statement. "This situation is especially difficult because I know what good students and good kids these two are." He paused as Mrs. Flores finished translating.

He looked to Nancy's parents. "Mr. and Mrs. Robles, we met too often when Nancy first came here. She did not have a good start and even last year we had some problems, but I have seen Nancy come such a long way. Her grades are good, she has had no problems in class or in the halls for months, but more than that, I have seen her grow and mature as a young person. She doesn't walk these halls angry; she stops by to see me and Officer Palma just to say hello. I actually catch her smiling!"

He shifted his eyes to Nancy and spoke to her directly. "Nancy, whatever things were going on outside of school, you kept it outside. I know that, that's why I'm so disappointed."

Nancy lowered her head, her long hair covering her face. She leaned over, her arms in her lap. Several teardrops escaped to the floor. Mrs. Flores handed both Nancy and her mom a tissue as they both wept quietly.

Next, Dean Rudy turned to Lucy. "And you, Lucy. I know who you are only through your teachers and counselor. I know you are a top student. I know your teachers think you should start applying to top colleges. I know this is a waste of my time, your time and your parents' time."

Lucy had walked into the meeting ashamed, but she was not going to let anyone know it. She had not apologized to her parents because she had convinced herself there was no need to do so. This whole thing was a stupid, ridiculous kid-stuff screw-up. She had already promised herself that she would never be so stupid again. The second the fight ended, and she had been escorted to the dean's office by security, she had decided Armani was out of her life. She had been completely ashamed that she had lost control and put herself in this situation. *Stupid, stupid, stupid!* she kept repeating in her head. She had decided that she would attend the meeting. She would not say a word. She would go back to work. Armani and his bullshit would be out of her life! She did not need these people to "fix" her; she would deal with the punishment and get back on track.

Lucy had been all bravado before the meeting, but now she was surrounded with tears, sadness, and disappointment and all she wanted to do was dig a huge hole, kiss her mom and hug her father, scream goodbye and jump in!

Dean Rudy paused. Many years of experience with young people had instinctually let him know that he had said enough. The room grew painfully silent except for the sniffling of the mothers.

"Any student involved in fighting has to take part in our after-school intervention program," continued Rudy, "but I feel like this situation could use a different spin. Sometimes the right person is in the right spot at the right time. Mr. Alvarez was the teacher who broke up the fight, but he also has a proposition I think you might find interesting. Mr. Alvarez, the floor is all yours."

"Mucho gusto," Alvarez began. *"Yo soy Senior Alvarado, soy un maestro aquí a West Layden,"* Alvarez introduced himself, with a Tex-Mex accent he had copied from his father. "But if we don't want this meeting to last three hours I'm going to have to continue in English."

The tension dissolved as the parents understood and laughed softly.

Mr. Quinones spoke first. "I speak English, but I also speak Spanish and I have no idea what you were trying to say!"

The other Latino parents nodded their agreement, causing all to laugh. Perhaps Alvarez's accent wasn't as good as he had thought.

"Fair enough," he replied, happy to break the tension. "As Dean Rudy said, I was the teacher on cafeteria duty during the altercation, but that's not why I asked to attend this meeting. Mr. and Mrs. Quinones, Mr. and Mrs. Robles, a couple years back a young man approached me because he knew I had a certain expertise. He also knew, more than anyone, that he was heading down the wrong path. He knew his life had to change. He got me and quite a few kids involved in an afterschool program."

"Is this the gang intervention program?" asked Mr. Quinones.

"No, let's call this a different intervention. You see, your daughter has an association with gang kids, but she has been a model student for almost three years. Nancy has also made great improvements. I'm not sure they know it, but a lot of young ladies look up to them. They could be great examples, and not only help themselves, but help the school." Alvarez paused, allowing Mrs. Flores to catch up. For the next sentence, he did not wait for translation. *"Esta programa es una programa por boxeadores*—a boxing program!"

The parents were taken aback. This is not what they had expected!

"NO!" said both fathers simultaneously, then looked at each other. They each blamed the others' daughter for this fight, but now their eyes met in agreement, and it made them feel correct in their immediate reaction.

Mr. Quinones spoke, "This is the intervention program? Really? Is this what all students do?"

Dean Rudy explained. "Officer Palma and I have developed a program that all suspended or expelled students must attend before they are allowed back in school. It's a good program, but I feel—actually I know—that your daughters and this entire school could benefit from thinking outside the box. I am urging you both to give Coach Alvarez's program a chance."

Mr. Robles spoke sharply to the translator in Spanish after the dean finished his persuasive argument.

"Mr. Robles does not want his daughter fighting," stated Mrs. Flores. "He does not want her getting hurt or hurting anyone else."

Robles spoke again in rapid Spanish.

"If we are here because of her fighting, why would we encourage more fighting? It makes no sense," Flores translated.

Alvarez was ready for the objection from the fathers. "I know on the surface, this suggestion may seem the opposite of what the girls need, so please let me explain. First, let me say that this program is to strengthen the body and the mind. We emphasize discipline and honor through team building and training. When it comes to actually competing, even sparring, no one is ever forced to step into the ring!" Chuck paused for Mrs. Flores to explain to the parents, then he continued. "We have students who have not—and never will—actually get in the ring. What the students do get from the program is a place to belong, a place to test and grow their will in a positive atmosphere and, yes—a safe place to release their aggressions." After another pause he went on. "The girls could go through the standard program, complete it and be done. From what I have seen they are both smart enough to learn from this incident. But, if you decide they can go in a different direction, if everyone buys in, especially the girls, we can achieve something much greater! Perhaps we can even influence a whole school!"

Alvarez halted once again, feeling emotion welling up inside him. "Parents, Lucy, Nancy, this school is a wonderful place filled with amazing kids, but it could be better, much better. My father came to this country with nothing, but he raised three sons who now have everything. I am one of those sons. Layden has been my home for several years now, and I am proud of my home. But there is a dark cloud that hangs over this school, a black mark, a cancer, and *we* can do something to stop it. It's these damn gangs; they are cockroaches! They would infest the whole school if it weren't for people like Dean Rudy. They get a hold of the low-functioning kids, or lonely kids, or the kids who think it's cool to be bad because of some crap they saw on TV." (Now Alvarez had everyone's attention.) "It's passed down through families from older kid to younger kid, from father to son, like a bad disease, no different than alcoholism."

Alvarez stopped, sensing anger and sadness were getting the best of him. He took a deep breath, exhaled, and went with a deliberate softer, in-control voice.

"I am proud to be here. I am proud of my students who are part of making this place better. I just feel sorry for the others, and I want to help make a change." He focused on the girls. "Kids talk to other kids; they tell their parents; the word gets out. 'Did you hear about West Layden? Did you hear about the gang fight in the cafe? Did you hear about those Mexicans, or Puerto Ricans or whatever gang? Did you hear about the fighting? I can't send my kid there.' That talk spreads and it grows and It's bull sh…," Alvarez caught himself breathing too hard again.

Dean Rudy was half out of his chair. Chuck looked at him, assuring him with his eyes that he was under control. Even so, everyone in the room could feel his passion.

"Your daughters, through their actions," Alvarez continued in almost a whisper, "put another black mark on my school. Let's do something to erase it."

He sat down, spent. Mrs. Flores finished translating. Alvarez's message was sent, and the room was silent.

After a moment, Dean Rudy broke the silence, pleased to know that he had brought in the right man for the job. He had done all he could do.

"Mr. Alvarez made it very clear how he feels, and I agree, but you have options: the standard intervention program, or Mr. Alvarez's option. Both young ladies are suspended for two more days. I will need your choice before they are allowed back in school."

As everyone began to get up from their seats, Lucy's father spoke up, "You can have my answer now."

Dean Rudy was caught off guard. "Excuse me, Mr. Quinones?"

"She will be expected to train, but she will not fight in the ring. Q Is that correct, Mr. Alvarez?"

"Yes, that is correct," answered Alvarez. "She will be expected to train after school five to seven, Monday through Friday."

"What about schoolwork?"

"I'm glad you asked. Students usually stay at school and do their homework before practice. When they finish they come to the fitness center with me. You can pick them up and drive them to the boxing club from there, though many students carpool or ride their bikes—which is how I'm getting there these days; it's a great warm-up before practice. Our coaches do monitor the students' grades, but from what I know of your daughter, she does a pretty good job of that on her own."

"No fight, only train?" Nancy's dad asked in a thick accent.

"Well, ultimately that's between you and your daughter, but like I said, many kids go for the training only. The girls will never be required to even step into the ring."

Mrs. Flores began to interpret, but Mr. Robles signaled his understanding. "Nancy, too," he said. "Yes."

Alvarez's smile lit up the room, but he stopped himself to look at the girls.

"Now the most important question, ladies. Are you two in?"

"Yes!" Nancy and Lucy answered as one. They glanced at each other for a moment, forgetting they were on opposite sides, forgetting they were supposed to be tough, avenging enemies. Embarrassed, they both studied the floor.

"Good," pronounced Alvarez. "See you Monday; come ready to work!"

Meanwhile, on Rhodes street, Armani was late picking up his little brother, but Joey was used to it. He had played with friends after school until they had left. Now he sat on the front steps of the school making imaginary pictures on the cement with a stick. He pretended it was a paint brush and he painted the giant tree across the street, a stallion leading a wild herd of horses across the prairie, and the moon as it lit up the back alley behind Oscar's.

Past experience told him that Armani would be there no later than six, but when he was this late it meant there probably had been trouble at school. Usually, Armani would take Joey home right after classes ended. He would make sure that Joey finished his homework, had dinner, and was ready for school the next day. Then, and only then, would Armani go back out to do his business. Armani was only late when there was trouble at school.

Joey didn't understand his big brother's problem. Joey loved school, learning, his teachers, his friends, even the ones that wasted class time clowning around. He loved the hot lunches, his classroom and how the teacher decorated it for every season and holiday. There was always something new.

"I never have trouble in school," Joey muttered to himself. Then aloud he added, "if I did, Armani would kill me!"

"You crazy? Who ya talking to?" Armani surprised him when he approached from behind. Joey jumped up and silently began following his brother toward home. He knew better than to ask his older brother why he was late. Knifing through the silence, Armani surprised him with a question.

"How was school, JoJo?"

Joey answered with a sideways look at his older brother, "Ummh... fine."

They fell back into silence for a block.

"Joey, you are good in school. That's good, you like school, that's good, too. Being a good, smart kid is the best way to be, don't let anyone tell you different."

"Who are you and what have you done with my brother?" Joey joked.

"Hey!" Armani stopped and grabbed his brother by his collar. "I'm not playin'! You are doing the right things now, but that can change. One bad choice, one friend you follow, one day when you decide you don't care about school or doing the right thing! It can all change! Do you understand?"

"Okay, okay, Armani!" Joey was shocked. Other than play-wrestling, he could not remember a time when Armani had ever laid a hand on him. "I promise, I promise."

Armani let out a breath and let his brother go, fixing his collar and adjusting the zipper on Joey's coat. "Yeah, alright then, just remember that."

They turned and fell into step again. Eventually they could see the light on their front porch in the distance.

"Is everything alright, Armani?" Joey asked in almost a whisper, afraid he would make his brother angry.

"I got kicked out of school today."

"What? Okay You got kicked out?"

"No big deal," Armani said, as if he were trying to convince himself. "I was on final warning; they want to send me to some bullshit place. I gotta take a bus there, but don't worry about it."

"Don't worry? Bus?" Joey was not ready for this.

"Yeah, don't worry, nothing's going to change. I'm not even sure I'm going." He paused, then added, "I think I'm done with school."

Sudden anger exploded from Joey, no longer afraid of his brother's wrath.

"That's bullshit, Armani! You tell me to do good in school. You tell me to make good decisions, but you are dropping out. That's total bullshit!"

He braced himself for Armani's anger, certain that this time it would be for real.

Instead Armani stopped and looked down. "I know" was all he said. He resumed walking toward the lighted porch, leaving Joey at a standstill. After four steps Armani motioned to his little brother,

"Come on, *cabron*, we need to get you dinner."

CHAPTER 11

After all the action and tension there had been throughout the week, the weekend was a welcome break. It was a bright, warm day, picture perfect for a stroll through the zoo. A crowd was already gathering at Brookfield Zoo, but Ms. Kelly was easy to spot, wearing a bright yellow Layden 'Best Pals hoodie.

"Okay, Layden over here! Whoop! Whoop! Layden in the house!" She was louder than any coach Chuy had ever heard, and when she saw Chuy she got even louder. "HEY! The Chewster!"

"Really?" he grimaced, while Billy roared with laughter.

"Yes! The Chewster...love it!" Billy matched Kelly's volume.

"Sorry about that, Chuy." Ms. Kelly fake-apologized. "Glad to have you two. Are you ready to have some fun?"

"Sure," answered Chuy. "What do we do?"

"Well, we call it 'Best Pals Zoo Stroll' because that's what it is. You find some kids to hang out with and you walk with them through the zoo," Ms. Kelly informed them. "Of course, you won't have to look very hard; all of Wolfy's kids will want to walk with you." Then in a whisper loud enough for anyone to hear, "Now your buddy on the other hand, we may have to bribe some kids."

"What? These kids love me." Billy's objection was interrupted by Missy, Lynnie, Salim and the whole gang clamoring around Chuy. Seeing him outside of school, and at the zoo (no less) had Wolfy's kids acting even more excitable than usual.

Missy was the first to chime in. "Chuy, d-d-do you like my s-s-shirt?"

"Hi, Chuy, Hi Billy, Hi Chuy, Hi Billy!" Salim repeated, desperately trying to step in front of Lynnie and Big Mike.

"Salim!" Protested Lynnie, stomping her foot and scowling.

Big Mike was unperturbed as he continued to smile serenely and wave like a beauty queen on a float.

"Well, I see you have the 'find kids to hang out with' part covered," Ms. Kelly chuckled. "After the walk, pizza, and dance party. Right, guys? Whoop, whoop!'"

The kids pulled Chuy and Billy with them down the path toward the first stop of their walk.

"Where are we headin', Missy?" Chuy asked.

"First stop, lion house!" The kids screamed in unison.

The "stroll" was more like a ride on the famous Chicago "L" train, stopping and starting, fast and slow. Missy and Salim running ahead to the next exhibit, while Big Mike, Paris and the rest of the gang ambled down the wide pathways, distracted by everything and anything.

Slightly after twelve noon the group met at the food court for pizza. Chuy, Billy, and the other sponsors sat down to enjoy a slice, but as soon as music began blasting from a set of portable speakers that Ms. Kelly had set-up, relaxation time was over. Hoodies and jackets were discarded, and the dance party was raging. Mercifully, for the adults and sponsors, within the hour parents began arriving to pick up their child. Best Pals Zoo Stroll would go down as a huge success.

"Dude!" Billy sat on a picnic table. "Wolfy's kids can party! I'm more tired now than I am after practice."

"That's because you worked harder today than you do at practice," Chuy teased. "But, to tell you the truth, I'm spent too. Can't wait to hit the couch."

"Hey, man," Billy squinted in the sunlight as he looked at his friend, "thanks, Chuy; this is really good stuff. Thanks for getting me involved."

"Billy-boy," Chuy wrapped his diminutive friend in a head-lock. "Stick with me and you'll do alright, but you must remember one thing, my friend,"

"Yeah, what's that?"

"Just this...I get shotgun, ha!" Chuy turned and sprinted toward Raul's car he had just spotted entering the parking lot.

"Aww! You suck!" Billy shouted, lagging five steps behind.

After spending a Saturday morning with some very special friends, the boys were feeling satisfied, proud and exhausted as they jumped into Raul's car.

For Lucy Monday could not come soon enough. Most people hated Monday mornings because it meant going back to work, but for Lucy it meant the hardest work of the week was over: taking care of her sisters, being the good daughter, and (worst of all) being a gangster's girlfriend. She usually hid her sense of relief—if not full blown happiness—from her friends on the bus because no one is supposed to like school. However, this past weekend had been one of the best that she could recall. Before the meeting she had felt shame and regret, but afterward she had felt a tremendous relief that she had never before experienced. The weight of pretending to be the perfect daughter had been shattered and had fallen off her shoulders. It had been an emotional weight, and she had never even realized it was so immense. The talk with her father after the meeting had been difficult, but Lucy had promised him that her days with Armani were done. She had already promised herself that, the minute that last punch had been thrown in the fight. When she had been escorted to Dean Rudy's office, shame had washed over her. Now her need to portray perfection, that had begun with the adoration that always shined from her father's eyes, had been washed away also.

More importantly, Armani was out of school, maybe for good. She didn't know for certain, for she had ignored his calls and texts, but they were over with, and he should have gotten that message by now.

She completed her morning duties, relief mixed with excitement as she packed a gym bag for the after-school workout and boxing practice. It would be a long day, but Lucy was ready. Ready for the change, ready for the work, and thankful for the relief.

The day went by quickly, with only two differences in her usual routine. Instead of going to the stairway where the gang-bangers hung out, Lucy went to the media center before school, and then to avoid the cafeteria she returned during lunch, sneaking in a sandwich, and noticing that no one seemed to mind. Mrs. Asmus, the librarian, was one of the happiest teachers in a school full of happy teachers. She appeared joyful that another student chose to come by during lunch, so when Lucy came back a third time to do homework before going to the fitness center Mrs. Asmus almost burst with giddiness.

"Lucy! OMGOSH! We are going to have to get you a job here!" The librarian wrapped Lucy into an embarrassing hug.

Why not? thought Lucy, sitting down in her now familiar spot. She let the peace of the place fill her and took a giant breath.

I could get used to this, she thought. She finished her homework quickly, then headed to the fitness center.

"Hey, there's my girl!" It was the unmistakable voice of Coach Alvarez, dressed in workout gear and sounding almost as bubbly as Mrs. Asmus.

What is with these teachers? Lucy thought.

"Look at this, I get to work out in a great gym, get to see amazing young people get better every day, and the best part, I get paid to do it! Ha! What could be better?" Alvarez's voice rang out over the clang of the weights and the booming hip hop music.

Okay, I guess that answers my question, Lucy thought to herself, bringing a smile to her face.

"Now, you're supposed to say: Hey, Coach A., how are you?"

"Hey, Coach A., how are you?" repeated Lucy, unable to stifle a giggle.

"Wow! Thanks for asking; that's very nice of you, Lucy. Well, let's see...I've got this pain in my shoulder and my internet is a little slow, but overall I can't complain."

Lucy was still grinning when her eyes met Nancy's, who looked as if she had already been there a while, judging by the amount of sweat soaked into her shirt. The girls immediately shifted their eyes away from each other.

Although it appeared that Alvarez had ignored the uncomfortable moment, he took note of it. "Do you know what you want to do in here, Lucy?" he asked.

Lucy did know a standard workout from gym class and nodded her head.

"Now you can say—yes, Coach Alvarez, I know what workout I'm doing," Alvarez teased, trying to get Lucy to interact.

"Yes, Coach Alvarez, I know what I'm doing."

"See, you used your words," he continued to joke with her. "Now, don't overdo it; I want you semi-fresh for boxing practice."

"Yes, Coach Alvarez."

"See how easy that was! Alright, GO TO WORK! "Oh, and Lucy,"

Alvarez's voice lowered as his tone became serious. "We are really glad to have you. You're in the right place."

"Yes, Coach Alvarez," Lucy repeated, this time making Alvarez chuckle, then matching his seriousness she affirmed, "I am in the right place."

Later that evening, at the Maywood Boxing Club Chuy was in his groove. His rope would tat-tat-tat under his feet, the exercise having become a familiar dance, and although he would occasionally miss a beat, fifteen minutes on the rope was a sweet warm-up. The dancer in Chuy took over as he gave himself up to the music, the rhythm, the tat-tat-tat. His cross-over was coming along, as was his double jump. Working on the double cross-over, he performed those moves first, then found his rhythm with the rope, smooth and steady, lifting one foot at a time (ever so slightly) the rope blurring with the tat-tat-tat. The rhythm, the routine—he was into it. He loved it!

Chuy looked over his right shoulder to see Billy struggling with the rope, putting more energy into offering the tall, pretty girl one of his winning smiles as she jumped. Concentrating on her own rhythm, Chuy figured that she didn't even notice her admirer.

"You look like a pro, Karamitos." Poking fun at Billy was becoming part of Chuy's routine as well.

It was only the start of week four for the boys, but Chuy was learning quickly, mostly because he knew how to work hard. He practiced six days a week, twice a day. Chuy had learned that all real fighters did road work in the morning so that's what he did. Up at five a.m., he ran, shadow boxing as he went, throwing punches in the air like he had seen Rocky do in the movies. When he had first begun, he made it for about fifteen minutes before he could throw no more. That was his sign to turn around and head home in an old-fashioned run.

Each day he tried to last longer throwing punches. Already he was up to forty-five minutes, with an extra few minutes of shadow boxing at his turn around point and again before he ended each session on the patio behind his house. His wind was increasing. He especially felt it in the gym. The running, the rope, the push-ups, the stations, he was definitely getting stronger. He noticed it and Coach Sultan noticed it as well.

Billy and Chuy were still working with Big Ces. More accurately, Chuy was working with Big Ces, while Billy was doing a lot of watching. As with everything he did, Chuy put his heart into his new sport, and it was paying off. He remembered how hard it had been to learn to field and hit a baseball. Hour after hour, he had practiced, but, good as he had become, he had never felt the pride in himself that he was feeling now. For some reason boxing was different; it was like he had been doing this his whole life. His stance came easy and it felt good. Just like Big Ces taught him. Right hand up by his cheek bone (that was his club), left hand poised in front of him, (that was his stick). On the toes, light on his feet, just like when he jumped rope. On the heavy bag: Stick the jab, move, pound the right, pop and move! With Big Ces holding the big bag and maneuvering to keep it between him and his young, promising fighter, Chuy worked relentlessly to increase his skill and endurance.

"Pop, Chuy, pop! Two jabs then right hand, three jabs, right!" Big Ces barked out instructions. "Stick! Stick! Stick! Club! Jab! Jab! Jab! Right hand!"

Three rounds, five rounds, on to the next station, then the next. Chuy pushed himself as the sweat poured, each day getting stronger. Each day the punches popped a little louder off the bags. Big Ces grabbed the paddle gloves.

"Yesss!" Chuy celebrated under his breath.

Paddle gloves were the flat mitts that were used as both targets and weapons by a coach. It was the closest thing a coach could do to simulate real sparring and Chuy loved it. It also meant he would be allowed to work in the ring. There was only one ring and a lot of fighters, so when a boxer got ring time it was special. Chuy swelled with pride. This was the second week in a row he had been honored with the privilege.

"Watchya waiting for, *primo*, get in the ring."

Before Ces got the last word out of his mouth Chuy was inside the ring and had taken his stance. The big man couldn't hide the twinkle in his eye. He liked this kid.

Big Ces took a stance with one flat mitt up. That one mitt signified the opponent's head, the target Chuy would hit with a pop. Big Ces would use the other mitt when he wanted Chuy to hook to the body, or uppercut, depending on how he positioned the glove. That same hand would also be used to pop Chuy on the side of the head, as a not-so-gentle reminder, if his right hand dropped. The first time Chuy had felt the pop on the side of his head—the pop that made his ears ring—had been his last. After that, he had learned to bend his knees, to duck the blow, or lift his hand to block it. The mitts had also taught him to keep the right elbow close to his body when Ces went low, and to move slightly right or left when the mitt, simulating a jab, came directly at him. Now, Chuy could move his head to one side or the other to "slip" the jab and fire back.

Slip! Jab! Jab! Ces turned the mitt sideways, Chuy's cue to throw a hook. Jab! Jab! Ces raised the mitts next to each other directly in front of his face. Chuy threw double jabs, straight right, then immediately ducked the swinging mitt that he knew was coming at his head. Jab! Jab! Straight right, duck, fire back two jabs and another straight hand, tighten the elbow for the body punch from Big Ces. Jab! Jab! Slip! Hook, hook, block, fire, fire, fire again!"

When Chuy had first begun an almost painfully slow version of this dance with the coach they had worked outside the ring, big Ces calling out every punch and block slowly and patiently.

"Stick, Chuy! Okay, remember what holding the mitt parallel with the floor means?"

"Uppercut," Chuy replied.

"Sideways?"

"Hook!"

"Good," encouraged the patient coach.

"Block the lower shots, Jesus. Don't try and duck 'em! You only duck the hooks coming to the head. Now right back to the jab! Jab! Jab! Right hand, duck! Jab! Jab! Hook! Block there; that's it, Chuy!" Ces called out each punch and each move.

Since Chuy had graduated to working in the ring, Ces listened to the pop of the mitt with only an occasional instruction needed. "Keep the knees bent, elbows tight, kid!"

Pop! Pop! Pop!

Chuy was almost in a trance as he danced around the ring, while the coach manipulated the gloves to keep his athlete guessing.

"Put your power at the end of your punches! Wait! Wait! Wait a minute."

Chuy was suddenly aware of a new voice.

"Give me those things." It was Sultan! Despite his limp, he threw down his cane, expertly climbing into the ring with Chuy. "Ya movin' good, boy, ya doin' good, but you need to get your power at the end of your punches! Step back just a hair."

Sultan grabbed the gloves out of Cesar's hands. "Give me a jab, jab, right."

Chuy popped the gloves extra hard, striving with quick, hard jabs, to impress the old coach.

"You crowdin' yourself, son. Step back an inch or two."

Sultan held up the mitt in the same position, signaling Chuy to throw the jab once more.

Chuy popped the gloves again. This time the sound could be heard throughout the gym.

"Feel that? That's where your power comes from, boy! Next, make sure ya turnin' your hips on the hook. Ya doin' good, boy, but you got the tendency to arm punch. Got to throw from your hips and turn on the hips. Ya got it?"

Chuy nodded, "Yes, sir!"

"Don't never call me sir, young man! Ya see, I was a staff sergeant in the United States Army; I worked for a livin'," Sultan said with a wink.

"Yes, Coach!" Chuy corrected himself.

"That's better, young man, oh and ah, one more thing..."

"Yes, Coach!" Chuy barked back military style.

"I like this kid," the old coach informed Ces. "He needs to spar this week." He turned to Chuy as he stepped out of the ring. "You best get ready, boy. You got your first fight in two weeks."

As Chuy received the surprising and exciting news, in a different area of the gym, Ulises was working with one of the new recruits. "You don't jump rope here like on the playground," he pointed out.

Nancy glared at him. "This sucks!" She declared, throwing down the rope.

"Whoaaa! Slow it down, girl. You are doing better than most who come in here. Let me tell you how it's gonna go. It will take you at least two weeks to get this rope moving right, and that's if you practice on your own. So every practice for the next two weeks you get to feel like a dork."

Nancy laughed in spite of herself.

"After the rope we'll do warm-ups, and you will be lucky to get a quarter of the way through. Two weeks—if you practice every day—if you get through it like everybody else, but just when they start to get easy we'll add more. I'll take you through the bags and you will suck, but..."

"I know" interrupted Nancy, "two weeks."

"Yep, except..."

"Except?"

"Except the speed bag takes longer, usually a lot longer."

Nancy groaned.

Ulises snickered.

Nancy looked sideways over toward Lucy. The two still hadn't spoken, even though they had arrived at the same time and had made an uncomfortable walk up the steps together.

"What about her?" Nancy motioned with her head.

Lucy was moving the rope smoothly and steadily. No fancy moves, but the rope was whirring under her feet, while her knees were pumping as she ran in place, five steps up, five steps back.

"I guess she was at a different playground," observed Ulises with eyebrows raised. "Hey, don't worry about anyone else. It's like Alvarez always says: '*it's not where you start, it's where you finish*,' and I'll give you one more secret."

"What's that?" Nancy asked, leaning in to hear better.

"Don't spend so much time talking," Ulysses advised, giving her a wink. "Now, hit it!"

Nancy was correct about her former friend. Lucy could handle a rope. In fact, this was not the first time she had been to a gym or even seen a practice. Lucy had been around boxing, if only a couple times a year, since she had been old enough to walk. The smells and the sounds of the place made her nostalgic as she remembered how she used to go with her father to Uncle Robbie's practices, at his old west side gym, that looked very much like the place she was working out in now. While she jumped rope she recalled attending his fights. The smell of cigar smoke, stale beer, and the sight of old men with young women, wearing too much jewelry and too much make-up came back to her. It had been special when she spent time with her dad, not sharing him with anyone else.

Robbie had been a very good welterweight, who had dominated the Chicago Gloves tournaments, easily winning first place for several years. However, after a short-lived professional career he had hung it up for a family and a steady job.

Lucy remembered her father, moving and ducking while he watched his younger brother fight, throwing punches in the air, then ducking imaginary punches. Watching her father have fun had been fun for Lucy, too. As she recalled, it was the only time her father hadn't been serious, or tired, or both. Back then Lucy would jump rope on the playground or in the backyard just like her uncle had done in the gym. She had shadow boxed and pretended that she had a speed bag and a heavy bag to hit. While babysitting her little sisters, as they played with their dolls, she had jumped in front of the mirror and shadow boxed, pretending that she was in the twelfth round of a WBC championship fight. She had imagined one eye swollen almost closed, but always she had been battling, on her way to winning the belt.

When Lucy had been eight years old, her father had sat at the kitchen table, holding up his hands for targets, while she threw the jab and right, sticking and moving, ducking, and bobbing, imitating her uncle's style. Eduardo Quinones would let out a loud, "Ouch!" shake his hands and give his little fighter a bear hug. At almost every family party Lucy had been called over to the group of uncles to show her skills.

"*Miras*, Robbie! This is how a real fighter moves!" Her father would joke as Uncle Robbie had lifted her on his shoulders. "*Campeon*! Lucy's the champ!" her uncle had shouted.

But those days were gone now. Uncle Robbie had ended his career and Lucy had grown into a teenager, confused, and struggling to understand the world in which she lived. The special time with her father had become a faded memory. This first practice at the Maywood Boxing Club, however, was bringing back all those good memories. In fact, Lucy had not felt this good about herself for the past several years.

Eduardo Quinones was a wise man. He had not talked to his daughter for the entire weekend following the meeting at the school. He had allowed her to go from embarrassed to defensive, to angry, to sorry, and back again. By Sunday evening, well after family dinner, her father had called Lucy back to the kitchen table. She had entered the room to see her mom washing dishes while her father sat in his chair at the head of the table. With a gesture, Lucy was summoned to his side. She came defiantly, matching his gaze, eye-to-eye, until she could no longer handle it and dropped her head. The silence between the two lasted forever.

Finally, her father had spoken. *"Mi hija*, your mother and I want to thank you for all that you have done for this family. We are very proud of what you have done in school, and we know you are going to do great things in this world. I want to tell you... I want to say," her father took in a deep breath, "We are sorry, *hija*. I am...I'm sorry."

Lucy's head shot up. She had not expected that from her father. Guilt and regret welled up inside her.

"Sorry? Why are *you* sorry?"

"You have taken care of your sisters when we could not. It was not fair to you, that you could not be part of so many things after school because you had to be here to help us."

Lucy dropped her head again. She could not look any longer into her father's eyes. She tried to speak.

"No Lucy," he stopped her. "Listen, I have more to say. After you finish with this boxing nonsense, you do any activity you want after school—dance, music, art, whatever you choose. Your mother and I have been at our new jobs for almost a year, the girls are getting older, you don't need to take care of everyone else anymore. We should have had this conversation long ago. It took something like this for us to realize you need to be free from duties that a young girl should not have."

Her mother stopped washing dishes and turned to Lucy, placing her hand on her husband's shoulder. *"Lo siento, mi vida*, we are sorry," she said in her kindest voice. "This will be a new time for all of us, my love."

Lucy was shocked by these unexpected sentiments from her parents.

No "I told you so!"

No "You were sneaking around behind our backs."

No "We are ashamed of you."

Nothing that Lucy had expected and felt that she deserved had been said. Instead love and understanding hit her like an arrow and exploded in her heart! In the tiny kitchen that still smelled of fresh tortillas, Lucy, her mother, and her father had cried and hugged and clung together. It had felt so good that no one wanted to stop, but eventually the spell was broken when they heard the other girls arguing over a brush. They had all laughed as they separated.

"So," concluded her father, "finish this month and choose what you want to do next."

Now at her first practice, Lucy jumped rope and went through warm-ups. She hit a "real" heavy bag, as opposed to the imaginary one of her childhood. She cursed herself when she whiffed on a "real" speed bag, missing it entirely and pawing the air. Lucy took a breather and looked up into the ring and noticed a boy from school. She didn't know anything about him except that his name was Jesus, and he was nice to the special needs kids—and she had always thought he was cute. Lucy postponed her struggles with the speed bag to watch him expertly hit the paddle gloves. She smelled and listened and marveled at all the activity of this gym. Suddenly Lucy knew what she wanted to do next. This was next!

CHAPTER 12

The alarm rang, Chuy instinctively grabbed his clothes and threw them on, still half asleep. Without missing a beat, on went socks, shoes, sweatpants, and a hoodie. It was an exceptionally warm spring morning for Chicago, but Chuy wore an old, black pair of mittens that reminded him of mini-boxing gloves. He liked throwing punches into the dark morning air wearing those gloves.

Minutes later he began his roadwork. The young man's footsteps were the only sound on the street. He was blocks from Mannheim and North Avenue, where cars were already humming up and down as suburban traffic picked up, but in his part of the world, tucked off of 25th and Diversey, things were still quiet and asleep. After a month of working out, Chuy had the routine down to a science: out the door before he had time to think or get lazy, then run his miles through the neighborhood, throwing punches with each step. The sound of his gym shoes hitting pavement, his heavy breathing and an occasional barking dog accompanied him. The run was a peaceful way for Chuy to begin his day. It gave him time to think, and right now he was thinking of a girl.

He had seen Lucy Quinones at the gym yesterday. She was so pretty, even in old gym clothes. At one point during practice he thought he had caught her looking at him. He smiled as he remembered hitting the mitts extra quick and hard, only to look back and see her concentrating on the speed bag.

Is she actually coming to the gym or was it a one time thing? Does that mean Armani will be coming, too? Chuy frowned and unknowingly threw punches faster and harder. Thoughts continued to assault him. *What was that other girl from the Lady Cobras doing there? Is she friends with Lucy? They didn't seem to talk much, and wasn't there a fight in the cafe with all of them?*

Chuy frowned again. *I don't want that shit in my club,* his thoughts continued. *My club? I've been there a month and it's my club.* He chuckled at his own arrogance. *No time for that; let Sultan and Alvarez worry about that, I got a fight to get ready for.*

All this thinking made his run go by very quickly. He suddenly found himself in his own backyard.

"Need to work harder," he said out loud. He ran ten hard sprints in his backyard, then went into a corner of the patio. "Ladies and gentlemen!" he whispered. (No need to wake the family.)

"In the blue corner, wearing the blue and white, from the Maywood Boxing Club—Jesus "Chuy" LeDesma! Ding! Ding!"

Chuy stepped to the center of the concrete square, throwing lefts, rights, hooks, uppercuts, ducking, bobbing, blocking and slipping. He jabbed his imaginary opponent into the far corner and then let rip his arsenal of punches, moving in and out, throwing to the body until he found imaginary openings in his imaginary opponent's defense.

"Bam! Bam! Hook, and straight to the head, and down he goes! First round knockout!" Chuy raised his hands in victory and danced around the make-believe ring.

"Who in the hell you talking to? You crazy, *cabron!*" Raul stood at the door rubbing his eyes. Chuy smiled an embarrassed smile, startled by his brother.

Raul motioned him inside. "Come on in, Rocky. You can make me breakfast."

The week rushed by and soon it was Friday. Fridays were always a little bit easier than the other school days. Everyone seemed more relaxed. Spring in Illinois was always unpredictable. This year had been warm, although often overcast, but that could change from day to day, even hour to hour. This particular Friday morning was bright, crisp, and fresh. Spring break was one week away, which often caused tension in school, as students and teachers were anxious for the break, but on this Friday morning all was relaxed and well.

Three Layden students, who were riding on their school buses, were feeling better than they ever had, after a solid week of workouts. Chuy had increased his roadwork over the past few weeks. Lucy, being Lucy, had put in an hour a day of road work as well. She knew fighters ran in the morning, and if she was going to work out with fighters she would train just as hard as they did.

Nancy, also, had begun training in the morning, but only for a couple of days. She had come to the conclusion that it was better to be frustrated in private than at the gym, so she got up early to jump rope, or at least try to jump rope. After fifteen minutes of jumping and mostly missing, she dropped the rope and practiced shadow boxing, watching herself in the reflection of a nearby window. On this, her third morning, she had managed to get a few good minutes of jumps in before she became discouraged. The shadow boxing felt good, however, and when she was done she had noticed that she felt less anxious. Now, after a shower, she sat on the bus and felt peaceful, even happy. She concluded that boxing practice and morning workouts were working for her. Nancy's body and spirit felt great for a change. She would never admit it to Rudy or Alvarez, but she was looking forward to school and practice. *I still need to conquer that damn rope,* she reminded herself.

Missy, Lynnie, Salim and the whole crew surrounded Chuy and Billy, who had just arrived at the 250 hallway. Pandemonium broke out as each of the special needs kids vied for attention. Chuy high-fived as many of them as he could get to before he was interrupted.

"Super Star!" came Ms. Kelly's ultra-loud voice.

Chuy noted that for a wisp of a woman she could sure belt it out. She looked like a young bag lady as she struggled up the back steps from the teacher's parking lot, arms full of books and tote bags, keys in hand. She still managed to beat Chuy to her classroom door.

"Say hi to your fans, Chuy, while I put my stuff down." She directed. "You are the first one here, as usual."

"L-l-look, Chuy!" said Missy, pointing to her shirt. "It s-s-ays f-f-frozen!"

"Hi, Billy! Hi, Billy! Hi, Billy!" Salim bounced up and down.

"You all look great, guys. Did you have fun at the zoo walk? I didn't know you were all such great dancers," Chuy called out over the ruckus.

Immediately, the kids all broke into dance. Billy began to beatbox in accompaniment. Ms. Kelly returned from desk to door, flipped on her lights and saw the dance party in the hallway. Without missing a beat, she jumped into the impromptu celebration.

"It's your birthday, it's your birthday, gonna party like it's your birthday!" She sang out.

Salim scooted over to Ms. Kelly. "Ms. Kelly, Ms. Kelly, my birthday is August 10th!"

"Whoop! Whoop!" Shouted Ms. Kelly, still singing. "August 10th is Salim's birthday!"

The dance party ended as quickly as it had started when all the kids began shouting out their birth dates.

"Mine's June 22nd; don't forget to buy me something nice," Kelly called out to the crew. After several years with Wolfy's kids she knew how to go with their flow. "Okay, Chuy, let's go. Meeting time."

The students meandered back to their usual spots, sitting in the hallway as though the dance party-birthday shout out had never happened.

Billy followed Chuy, who followed Ms. Kelly into room 250. The other officers of Best Pals gradually filed into the meeting. Within minutes everyone was seated and ready to get down to the business at hand.

Ms. Kelly began. "Guys, first let me say the zoo walk was awesome. The kids loved it, but as you know, we've got another big event coming up."

"What's that, Kelly?" interrupted Billy.

"Well, new member, Billy Karamitos, who has apparently elected himself as an officer, I will let one of the *real* officers give you that information. Joanna, would you care to explain?"

Joanna Gomez, a senior and the acting vice-president of Best Pals stood up and smiled at Billy. "Guys, before you know it, it will be prom. As you may know, we ask the officers from the junior class to take part of their evening to make sure all the Best Pals are participating, fitting in and enjoying themselves."

"So what you're doing is asking me to prom, but I'm sorry, Joanna, there's a hottie at boxing practice I got my eye on," Billy informed her.

"Umm, first before you go to prom with someone, you might want to know their name, as opposed to a 'hottie' at boxing practice," Ms. Kelly shot back with an eye roll. "But since it's the last year for our seniors," she continued, "we ask our junior officers to take the lead. So Chuy, Julie, Katie, Brandon and—I guess you, Billy—are you up for this? Are you willing to give some of your time that evening?"

"I really wasn't planning to go to prom," mumbled Chuy. "I mean, I don't even have a date."

After covering several other topics, the bell rang and Ms. Kelly ended the meeting by opening the door. Wolfy's kids were already gathered on the other side waiting for Chuy.

"Remember what you said about no date for prom, Chuy?" teased Ms. Kelly, "Looks to me like you have plenty of dates!"

It was an exceptional Friday morning for Lucy. She presented a PowerPoint on Greek philosophers in her World History class. She loved presenting. It meant the hard work was over, and though she would never admit it, Lucy loved presentations. She always signed up to go first, confident that her's was A-plus work. The rest of the hour she relaxed and observed as the rest of her class presented less impressive projects. After that her morning was easy, with mostly fun classroom activities, perfect for pre-spring break. She also loved her late lunch because it meant the day was almost over, but as that time rolled around her luck changed. She approached the media center with a lunch hidden in her bag. Lucy was looking forward to a quiet half-hour when she spotted a sign from several steps away:

- Media Center Closed During Lunch Periods Due to Testing -

"Ugh!" She took a deep, annoyed breath and turned back down the steps toward the cafeteria. She contemplated sitting on one of the benches in the hallway but knew that area would soon fill up with students clowning and playing. Better to find a quiet table inside and hang there until the bell.

The cafeteria was already filled on both sides closest to the double doors. However, the middle of the room was always available, so she opened her book and her lunch bag, feeling isolated enough to be comfortable.

Across the cafeteria, Nancy may have been the only one to spot Lucy. Since their fight they had only seen each other at practice. Nancy was eating with her usual group of friends but sitting among them she realized her feelings had changed. She had changed. Nancy had always been proud of her tough girl (the baddest Lady Cobra) reputation, but since the fight she had no feelings of pride, only the anguish of embarrassment.

She was ashamed that her parents had been forced to come to school because of her. And the look on Dean Rudy's face had been almost too much to bear, when he discovered that not only had she been in a fight, but—much worse—it had been gang motivated. She felt every teacher who had been proud of her was now disappointed. They had lost faith in her and, even though it had been several weeks since the fight, she wondered if she would ever regain that trust.

Nancy looked around at the girls at her table. These were supposed to be her friends, yet other than dating a Cobra, she had nothing in common with them. Now, since breaking up with the last gang banger in a string of gang bangers, she did not even have that. Nancy could not help but compare these so-called friends to the relationship she had had with Lucy. They had been together in junior high, had passed notes in class and giggled at the same silly stuff. Nancy had her first sleepover at Lucy's house and recalled with a smile how they always hid from her little sisters and ate popcorn and stayed up way too late talking about boys. That had been their pattern every weekend for almost two years.

Without any more thinking, Nancy picked up her tray and walked over to Lucy's table. At first the girls she had been sitting with did not notice, but as she walked to the "no man's land" in the middle of the cafeteria, they stopped talking and craned their necks to see where she was going. As Nancy approached Lucy's table the noise level dropped, and even more students stopped talking and turned, standing, or crouching to get a better view. They anticipated a rematch between the two girls who had fought so savagely just a week before.

Lucy, who was lost in her book, was startled by the sound of Nancy's tray at the other end of the table. Nancy did not make eye contact as she sat down and began eating. The volume of voices and silverware clanging soon returned to normal when students realized there would be no brawl that day. Lucy warily returned to her lunch and book. The two girls ate silently. The lunchroom began to clear as the period approached its end and Nancy finally looked up from her food.

"Hey," she said so quietly that Lucy did not hear her.

"Hey!" She repeated much louder than she had intended.

Lucy looked up, again startled.

"Can you um…" Nancy looked down and took the last bite of her lunch, "Can you um…do you think you can umm… help me out on the rope today?" she asked, eyes finally making contact.

"Sure," came the reply.

With that settled, the girls got up together and walked to the trash cans. Standing nearby was a smiling Coach Alvarez.

"Hey girls! Happy Friday!" He quickly looked away.

Nancy nudged Lucy's elbow. "This guy…I think he's going to cry!"

"He's so weird." Lucy rolled her eyes and the girls shared a laugh.

"Later," Nancy nodded.

"Yeah, later," Lucy nodded back.

Alvarez looked up briefly, then looked down again.

"This guy, ha!" repeated Nancy, as the girls headed in different directions, still sharing the same laugh.

CHAPTER 13

With Spring break just around the corner, the teachers seemed to be taking their foot off the gas and the workload was lightening up in most classes, but it was quite the opposite at the gym. That Friday afternoon Sultan pushed the team hard. Lucy and Nancy had gotten there early to work on the rope. They knew that once practice started there would be no time for talk, even for newbies like themselves.

"No jump in between," instructed Lucy. "Get that thing around! Speed, speed, stay on your toes, good!"

Nancy was getting the hang of it and soon found a rhythm that worked for her. When she appeared to be more confident, Lucy added more moves.

"Now lift one foot just a little. Wait! Don't try and switch yet. Just on one foot; lower it toward the ground."

Nancy missed and let out a sigh of disappointment.

"Hey, I've been doing this since I was eight years old; you're doing awesome," Lucy encouraged, sensing the other girl's frustration. Nancy shook her head, half-smiled and began again. This time she succeeded.

"That's it! Two feet first; now lift one foot, stay on it—that's it! Now switch feet. You got it! See!"

Nancy hit the groove and switched from foot to foot. She kept a smooth steady motion as the tap, tap, tap, echoed through the nearly empty gym.

"Hey!" she exclaimed, with a broad grin. "I got it! Thanks! Now what about double and crossover?"

"Damn, girl, slow down! We'll get to that!" Lucy patted her old friend on the shoulder.

Guys and girls had been trickling into the gym, and the two old/new friends had not noticed that Coach Alvarez had also arrived and was watching them from across the ring. He walked by the girls, nodding to them, but not making eye contact. The girls lined up next to him, but he moved a few steps away while still looking down.

"What up, Al-Varrr-ezzzzz?" shouted Nancy. "You don't want to be next to us? We don't got cooties!"

Alvarez raised his head, looking straight into the mirror. The girls fell into each other, hysterical with laughter when they noticed his wet eyes.

"Dude! How is anyone such a cry baby?" Nancy teased, pointing and roaring.

"Shut it!" returned Alvarez out of the side of his mouth. "I got somethin' in my eye, that's all."

"Yeah, that's all," echoed Lucy sarcastically. "I bet you cry at dog food commercials, Alvarez. You know, when 'Old Blue' can't get up the steps anymore."

"Maybe…yeah, so, I'm proud of you guys, okay? Now shut your faces and go to work; stop making fun of my allergies."

The girls howled.

"Allergies!" They both shouted at the same time, then roared louder. Now even Alvarez couldn't help but crack-up along with the girls. They were only interrupted by the voice of Sultan.

"Okay, ladies, the party's over. Time to work!"

The buzzer sounded and the familiar sound of forty jump ropes began.

As practice wore on Chuy felt strong and Billy…was being Billy. Punching, looking around, doing push-ups, checking himself in the mirror, jumping rope, fixing his hair. Billy's lack of dedication and focus was not setting him up to be the next flyweight champ. The two boys approached the heavy bag station when Big Cesar gave out a shout.

"Jesus, *ven!*" he barked. "Get over here!"

Chuy hustled over, while Billy shuffled slowly, five steps behind.

"You go back to the bags, killer," Cesar instructed Billy. "Chuy, come up here; get those bag gloves off."

Chuy jumped into the ring and stood in front of big Cesar, waiting.

"You got your mouthpiece in?"

Chuy pulled back his lips to show his mouthpiece. Sultan made it a rule to train with a mouthpiece in.

"Good, just making sure," said Big Ces. "Okay, get the hands out."

Big Ces checked Chuy's hand wraps. He had shown Chuy how to wrap his hands before the first practice and Chuy had followed instructions well. The long cloth bands had been wrapped tightly and neatly around his hands to support his wrist and thumb.

"Good," Big Ces said again when he observed that the wraps more than met his standards. He began giving Chuy instructions as he gloved him up.

"Listen, *primo*, this is your first time in the ring for real. Don't forget what ya learned. Remember how you work the paddle gloves?"

Chuy shook his head and tried to clear the butterflies that suddenly invaded his stomach. He knew he would be sparring, but he assumed it would be next week. He tried to mentally prepare himself.

"Hey," Big Ces tapped him on the head, sensing that Chuy was not listening. "Concentrate! Hands up, throw punches in bunches, and ..."

Chuy looked Big Ces in the eyes.

"Have fun!" finished Cesar with an encouraging smile.

Big Ces stepped out of the ring at the same time that Chuy caught sight of his opponent, who was just stepping between the ropes. Juan Calderon was the number one lightweight at the gym, a fighter ready to turn pro. Chuy's butterflies exploded in a dozen different directions. This guy was good, and everyone knew it.

Big Ces, standing on the floor with his head up under the bottom rope, pounded on the ring mat. "Hey! Ledesma, hands up, remember your training and relax, it's just sparring, not the WBC championship."

Chuy nodded. *Tell the butterflies*, he thought. Before any more thoughts could run through his head the bell sounded and the two fighters hustled to the center of the ring. Chuy knew that sparring was the best way to prepare for a real fight. He knew sparring meant giving it your all, backing off only if you hurt the other guy, never going in for the knockout. That was the only difference between sparring and an actual fight. He had already seen some real wars in the short time he had been coming to the gym, and he knew one guy would walk out of the ring an unofficial winner.

Of course Calderon knew it, too. Having had many fights, and far more rounds of sparring under his belt, he was the most experienced fighter in the gym and he wanted this new kid to know it. The veteran came out throwing punches, bouncing back Chuy's head with a double jab. Not only had Chuy never seen a double jab, he had never been hit in the face before and it opened his eyes wide.

"Move and throw, *primo!*" Cesar's voice boomed out.

Chuy did just that. He threw his jab and moved to his right, away from Calderon's power. Calderon responded by chasing Chuy into the corner, trapping him. Chuy tried to wriggle out and throw back punches, but Calderon overwhelmed him, landing an uppercut right on Chuy's nose that made his eyes water.

"Get out of there, Jesus!" yelled Big Ces. "Time!"

The bell sounded. Calderon headed to his corner.

"Was that three minutes?" asked a bewildered Chuy.

"No, bro, it was more like forty-five seconds." The coach snickered. "Three minutes and he would have killed you! Listen up, *primo!* First: keep moving right. Don't let him back you into a corner. Fight to the center before you get caught in there. If you do get stuck, throw the hook to either side and step out."

Moving expertly, he showed Chuy what he meant. "Step hard to his left away from his power. You can't do that, tie him up! Keep your hand up, shoot your chin into his shoulder, wrap your arms around the top of his arms." Cesar demonstrated by bear hugging Chuy, who almost disappeared in the embrace.

"Hey, we gonna get my guy any work?" Sultan shouted across the ring. "Do I need to get someone else?" That was the ultimate insult to a sparring partner.

"You're gonna go three minutes," Ces whispered to Chuy. "I can't stop this again. See you between rounds, *primo.*"

The bell rang and Chuy sprinted back to the center of the ring. He needed to stay with this guy!

Throw and move, throw, and move, throw and move.

That's exactly what he did. Coach Cesar's words had revitalized him. Calderon landed far more clean punches, but Chuy held his own. He used his jab well to keep the charging Calderon off of him, and he even landed a few clean straight rights, to Calderon's surprise. Chuy did not get caught in a corner, as he used the techniques that Big Ces had just shown him.

"Yes that's it, *primo!*" a delighted Cesar shouted when the second round ended.

Chuy returned to his corner. In sparring, the fighters do not sit down between rounds, so Chuy stood as Ces poured water over his head, took out his mouthpiece and gave him a drink, then leaned in to talk in his ear.

"You're looking good, young man. The right hand is working; now how 'bout you mix it up? Throw hooks and uppercuts. You saw the double jab from him. Maybe it's your turn, *primo.*"

Chuy said nothing, breathing hard.

"You feeling it, Jesus?" asked Ces.

Chuy could only nod his head.

"Supposed to," laughed Ces, pushing him back in the middle of the ring for round three.

Chuy landed the double jab immediately and Big Ces let out a yell.

"It's on, young man!" he called out to Chuy—and it was on!

The double jab stung, and angered Calderon. He immediately returned fire. The veteran fighter threw shots from every angle. Chuy instinctively ducked, bobbed, and threw his jab, sidestepping to his right, but before he realized it, he was trapped in a corner. Chuy threw a hook and moved left, but his sly opponent read his move and beat him to the step. Chuy tried to tie up the more experienced fighter but caught a wicked uppercut.

From across the ring Sultan motioned Cesar to end the bout, but Cesar put up a finger. "One more minute," he mouthed the words.

In a sudden burst, Chuy fired back! Right! Left! Right! A quick step right and a right hook to Calderon's body seemed to slow down the veteran. Chuy had fought his way out of the corner! Ces threw a silent fist pump. The two boxers were now in the center of the ring exchanging blows. Chuy caught a hook to the head that sent him spinning just as the bell sounded.

He shook off the blow and noticed that the gym was silent. Everyone had stopped what they were doing to watch the battle.

Calderon tapped Chuy playfully on the side of the head. "What's your name, kid?" He asked through his mouthpiece.

"Jesus," Chuy answered. "Umm...Chuy, you can call me Chuy."

"Okay, Chuy, you can work with me anytime."

"Yeah? Thanks; thank you!"

Big Ces met Chuy in the middle of the ring. "Good job, *primo*, did you have some fun?"

"Yeah, but why did you end it?"

"The bell rang, homes; that was the full three minutes. Why, you want to go some more?"

"Not this time." Chuy was more fatigued than he had ever been in his life. The weight of the gloves and sparring helmet seemed to be draining his energy and stifling his breath and he couldn't wait to get them off. "I got my ass kicked!"

"No way, Jesus, you did good. You got a lot to learn, for sure, but Calderon has been doing this since he was a kid and he's twenty now. He's got a couple more amateur fights, then he's turning pro."

"But he's smaller...you know, lighter than me."

"Well, you see how that don't always make a difference," Ces pointed out. "Speed is power, bro. Check it, the first two rounds, they were ready to kick you out of the ring cause you weren't givin' him no work. But that third round, *primo*! Yeah, yeah, bro!"

Chuy tried not to look too satisfied with his performance. The sound and action of the gym were back to flowing now. As he stepped down from the ring, fighters were giving him a glance and a nod. He nodded back at them as he headed to the bags.

"Good work, kid." He heard a voice from behind; it was Sultan.

"Now get yo ass back to work, son!"

"Yes, sir! I mean—yes, Coach!" Chuy replied. *I guess my moment is over,* he thought to himself. It had been short, but sweet and he would remember that rush of pride for a long time. He went to work on the heavy bag, hitting harder and moving quicker, thanks to the ego boost from his new experience.

Practice ended; Chuy still felt high from his sparring session. When the team gathered up their things and headed toward the door, he passed Lucy and Nancy, who were headed toward the speed bag to get in some extra work before the gym closed.

"Hey," Nancy called, "you're Chuy LeDesma, right?"

"Yeah," Chuy tried to answer casually, not daring to look at Lucy.

"You did good in there. How long you been comin' here?" Nancy inquired.

"Been about a month," replied Chuy, not feeling casual at all.

"Yeah? Cool! How ya feeling?"

"Spent!" Chuy grinned shyly. "Hi, Lucy," he added, feeling awkward.

"Hello," Lucy responded, feeling equally awkward.

The two had known of each other since junior high. More accurately, they had watched each other since junior high. They had never been in the same classes, and they certainly had not hung out with the same crowd. Lucy had always thought Chuy was a gentleman, especially when compared with Armani and his gang. Very polite, very kind and a bit shy. She had noticed that he had become close with the special needs students, and she liked that. But he was a jock, a guy that was only into sports, and that meant he was not her kind of guy.

Chuy had noticed Lucy the first day of junior high and had instantly formed a tremendous, unwavering crush on her. However, this was the first time he had actually talked to her, and a pitiful hello was all he could muster. He hoped she thought his red face was from the hard practice and not the embarrassment of actually meeting her. Lack of knowing what else to say caused him to drop his head and scurry toward Billy, who was of course bothering the tall, pretty, girl.

Nancy looked at Lucy with raised eyebrows.

"What?" Lucy asked innocently.

Nancy expertly lifted one eyebrow even higher.

"Shut up!"

The two girls giggled. They turned to see Alvarez wearing a goofy look.

"Really?" Lucy gave Alvarez a teenage smirk.

"Alvarez, you are so weird," Nancy called out over her shoulder as the girls headed for the door.

"What?" Alvarez shot back. "Can't a guy smile around here? You two knuckleheads are here a week and ya think ya own the place."

"Weirdo!" Nancy called again as the two girls descended the steps.

Alvarez could still hear the girls chuckling after the door shut behind them.

The gym was quiet. He picked up ropes and straightened equipment. Another Friday had come and gone with its usual chaos and hustle, laughs and hassles, triumphs and failures. Now, in this quiet gym, he sat down to change out of his boxing shoes. His mind raced back to his own youth:

alcoholic father, tiny little mom, the rock of the family. He remembered the first time he walked into Louis Rios' gym and the first time he stepped into the ring. He recalled his first fight at age sixteen, all the fights in Korea while he was in the military. Now, watching Chuy in the ring, and watching Big Ces working hard to make the boy into a fighter made him proud for the part he had in their lives. Those two girls making fun of him, coming to the gym together and cracking-up together made him teary. It had only been a couple of weeks ago that they were trying to tear each other apart. Alvarez sat for a while in the silent gym. He gazed across the floor to the big mirror to see himself with tears streaming down his face, pride bursting from him.

"Weirdo!" he said out loud to no one. "They got that right, weirdo."

Shaking his head in disbelief at his own crybaby emotions, he got up and turned off the lights. Darkness washed over the gym as the silhouettes of hanging bags, lit by only the moonlight shining in through the windows bounced off the mirrors like the beam of a lighthouse off the ocean. In the peace and silence no one could guess the number of young lives that had worked, struggled, succeeded, failed, who had lost and won in this old smelly gym. Now the darkness and silence flooded the place. In the morning light fighters would return to the task of being just a little better than the day before.

CHAPTER 14

C huy woke up the next day so sore that every single muscle seemed to be screaming in anger at him. It was going to be a sunny, not-so-cold Saturday, only one more week until spring break and he had completed three good rounds with Juan "Combat" Calderon. Life was good, no—it was great! He began his morning run at seven, two hours later than usual, but his neighborhood was still sleeping. He loved running on Saturday; the streets, even the air were still and quiet. With the sun already beaming down, he warmed up rapidly. It was a beautiful morning by Illinois standards. The last remnants of winter snow remained, from what had been huge snow drifts along the sides of shoveled-out driveways, and from the shaded corners of yards. Today's sun meant they would disappear by the afternoon.

Chuy ran, throwing punches, a satisfied look on his face, while he replayed the sparring session in his head. He threw rights, lefts, and uppercuts at an imaginary Calderon, but this time they all landed. He slipped and bobbed under every punch.

"Ha!" he exclaimed aloud, punctuating every punch. By the time he reached his back patio he was circling the now dazed "Combat" Caldron in his mind, with his body following suit.

"Jab, double-jab, double left hook to the body! The veteran fighter is hurt!" Chuy provided the play-by-play aloud. "There's the straight right, now left, right, left. What is keeping Calderon up? Ledesma is a buzz saw! Devastating right hook! Down goes Calderon! Calderon is down! The champion, Juan "Combat" Calderon has been defeated by the winner and new champion, Jesus "Chuy" Ledesma!"

Chuy instantly stopped the action. *What kind of nickname is Chuy?* he thought, frowning. 'Rocky' had been his favorite movie. He was the Italian Stallion. *Why couldn't I be the Mexican Stallion? Maybe it doesn't have quite the same ring, but it sounds pretty good to me.*

he called out from the backyard patio. "The winner and new Welterweight Champion of the World, Jesus 'The Mexican Stallion' LeDesma!" Then looking into the distant reflection of the garage window he continued talking to himself, feeling especially cocky. "Stallion, you are one bad mutha f…"

"Jesus!"

Chuy was surprised by his mother's voice. He was unaware that she had cracked open the kitchen window and could hear everything!

"Ha, ha, ha! Classic! Way to go, Stallion? Maybe you should try Pony instead," Raul cackled from behind the screen of the sliding glass door. Chuy turned away quickly, trying to hide his embarrassment from his older brother.

"Come on, Pony," said Raul. "Come in and face your mother, It's time to…"

"Yeah, I know, time to make you breakfast," Chuy interrupted. "One question—when do you make me breakfast?"

"Really, dude? You making breakfast is pouring cereal," Raul pointed out, opening the door to escort the boxing champ into the cramped kitchen.

"And getting out the bowls," Chuy added.

"When you become champ of something besides the backyard, I'll make you breakfast. Now get in here."

Chuy dropped his head and stepped into the kitchen wishing he were facing 'Combat' instead of his perturbed mother and smart-ass brother.

A few blocks away, and a few hours later, Lucy walked toward the sun enjoying the crisp spring morning. The late morning sun felt good on Lucy's face, but her apprehension over going to Nancy's house after such a long time kept her from complete enjoyment. However, Nancy had insisted. Lucy knew enough not to fight her on that. Ever since Nancy had been a kid, if she had her mind set on something, it was going to happen. Lucy sighed in resignation.

Approaching the house, she was delighted to see Nancy outside practicing with her rope.

"You're gettin' good, girl," Lucy called out, unfurling her own rope.

"Shut up," replied Nancy with a frustrated smile.

"I keep telling you, I've been around boxing stuff since I was a kid."

"Yeah, I remember your uncle was kind of famous around here," acknowledged Nancy. "How is he doing?"

"Good; he has twins. He's got a good job, too."

"Hey, maybe we can get him to coach us," Nancy suggested.

"I don't know; he's pretty busy, but I'm sure he'll give us some pointers."

"Let me reset this." Nancy walked over to an old egg timer she had placed on the back stoop.

"Ten minutes?" asked Nancy hopefully.

"Twenty," replied Lucy sternly.

"Awwww, alright. Time!" Nancy yelled, and the girls commenced jumping. Lucy went into her normal, almost trance-like rhythm. Nancy kept pace for the most part, missing a few crosses, but clearly beginning to master the rope.

"Shadow box for a few?" Nancy suggested after the timer went off with a "ting."

"Sounds good," Lucy replied, throwing her rope to the side.

While Nancy was setting the timer for three minutes the back door opened and Mrs. Robles, dressed in her waitress uniform, stepped out.

"Lucy? *Que bueno, como estas?*"

"Senora Robles!" acknowledged Lucy with a sheepish smile.

Mrs. Robles gave Lucy a long, warm hug, "You see! This is the way it should be with you two! *Que bueno! Que bueno.*"

Both girls chuckled at the sweet woman's excitement.

"I missed seeing you here," said Mrs. Robles.

"Yeah, I missed being here—more than I knew." Lucy finished almost to herself.

"Um, Mom, aren't you going to be late?" Nancy reminded her mother.

"Oh yes, I've got to go," agreed Mrs. Robles, still beaming. "Okay, one more hug!" She squeezed Lucy tight, then turned to her daughter

"Now it's your turn, *mi muneca*."

"Ah, Mom," protested Nancy weakly.

"Never too old for kisses and hugs, *mi vida*."

"Ma, we're training here."

"*Si, si*." Mrs. Robles turned the corner, still throwing kisses at the girl.

"Your mom's still a trip, Nancy." Lucy had missed her huge hugs.

"Oh yeah, she sure is." Nancy finished setting the egg timer. "Time!" she yelled.

The two girls completed their workout, finishing with stretches, settling back into friendship as though no time, or boyfriends, or fights had ever come between them. After they finished the morning workout Nancy invited Lucy in for breakfast. When she entered the home she instantly remembered the look and feel and smell of the cozy house.

"I love Saturdays," Lucy announced.

"Yeah, me too," Nancy agreed, getting out bowls and cereal.

On Monday Chuy woke up to the welcome surprise of a warm wind. *It's going to be a beautiful week,* he thought. *Next week it will probably be cold or rainy, or both for Spring break.*

Of course, the kids from other schools and even a few of the rich kids from Layden would be going to Cancun for the week, but Chuy didn't mind. He would be happy just to go to the gym early, be done early and chill out the rest of the day. At home in the cold and rain would be just fine for him; no school for a week was all the break he needed. He nodded happily at the thought as he rode the school bus, eager to get Monday going and over with. He did a mental checklist on how the day would go: horse around with Billy, visit with Wolfy's kids, maybe a quick check in with Ms. Kelly, classes and finally the gym. All good.

Chuy was grinning when he stepped off the bus. He turned too quickly to avoid a crowd and smack! He smashed into the back of a girl.

"Ouch!" he heard a familiar voice exclaim. Nancy and Lucy stood in front of him.

"Hey! I jab with that arm." Lucy rubbed her shoulder and gave him a frown.

Chuy stood motionless with a stunned look on his face. "I, I..." he stammered.

"Damn, Chuy, you don't gotta run the girl over." Billy's voice came from behind.

"I.... um," Chuy was still stuck in the moment.

"Come on, Chewbacca. Do I have to teach you everything? Don't just stand there like a cardboard cutout. Say: 'Hi Lucy'."

Chuy, yet to say a word, tried to relax. "Hi, Lucy," he managed to stammer out.

Billy, now at Chuy's shoulder, said, "Good job! Now repeat after me, excuse me for bumping into you."

"Excuse me for bumping into you," Chuy repeated.

"See you at practice," Billy prompted.

"See you at practice," Chuy repeated again.

"Would you go to prom with me?"

"Would you...Shut up, Billy!" Chuy poked Billy in the ribs, then too embarrassed to say anything else, turned and started taking long strides down the hall.

Giggling, the girls headed in the opposite direction.

"That boy has a thing for you," Nancy whispered into Lucy's ear.

"Well, he did look mighty fine sparring the other day," Lucy replied, moving her eyebrows up and down, making her friend crack up again.

"Dude, really?" Chuy snarled at Billy.

"What? I just helped you out, bro. You gotta get some game. Watch this," Billy said.

"Watch what?"

"Chewbacca, don't you ever watch the movies? She's gonna turn and look at you. That means you got something going. Wait for it...wait for it."

The boys stopped walking. Almost to the end of the hall, Lucy glanced back as predicted. The two girls continued walking shoulder-to-shoulder still giggling. As they disappeared around the corner Billy put his hand up for a high five.

"Whatever." Chuy shrugged it off, but inside he was glowing.

"Are you serious? I called it! Chuy's got a girlfriend; Chuy's got a girlfriend!" Billy sang.

"Dude, there is something seriously wrong with you," Chuy growled. He pushed Billy and sent the smaller boy flying. Chuy's heartbeat faster as warm feelings rushed through him. In spite of Billy's antics, he couldn't help but grin like a jack-o-lantern.

Billy, still not letting it go, continued to sing. "Chewbacca's in love, yeah yeah, Chewbacca's in love, yeah, yeah!"

"Let's go, Eminem, Wolfy's kids are waiting," Chuy said, putting Billy in a headlock. *It's gonna be a good week,* he thought one more time.

CHAPTER 15

Armani had not grown any less bitter over the past weeks. At Layden, he had been placed on final warning, but the very real possibility of getting kicked out of school took a while to set in. He had been suspended before, twice, in fact. First for two days, then a week. It had never been a big deal; he would return to school after suspension and within hours it was as if he had never been gone at all. This time started out the same as the others had. Armani still maintained his morning routine, waking his little brother, making sure he was ready for school and walking him there. He would return home and clean, then watch TV. When he heard his other brothers starting to get up, he would dart out of the house, not wanting any questions about why he wasn't in school. A couple of times he got caught, but he just told them he was sick. Now the house had never been so clean, and Armani was confident that all would be good; after all it was only for five days.

This time, however, was different from the past suspensions. This time, after the five-day suspension, a little yellow bus came to his house to take him to PROVE, the "school" for students who had been expelled from schools in the surrounding area. There, students mainly worked from computers, minimizing the interaction with instructors and other students.

The purpose of PROVE was to allow students kicked out of their home school to keep up their credits for a semester. They were then required to complete an after-school program at their home school. Only then, would they be admitted back to their regular classes. Any missteps after that and it was right back to PROVE.

Armani had been told about the program when he first entered Layden. He had been warned by teachers, counselors, Dean Rudy and even by other students. He never dreamed he'd actually have to go there. Armani always thought he could play the game just right, just enough to stay at Layden. Now at the end of his junior year, he had walked the line for what felt to him like a long time. One little fight would not put him in PROVE, or so he had thought. Anger kept welling up inside him over his own stupidity. He should have waited to fight until after school, at Oscar's like usual. Better to run from the police, even get busted, than to get kicked out of school.

Armani would never say he liked Layden, but now after walking Joey to his school, anger gave way to a sick, empty feeling in the pit of his stomach. As he approached his house he saw the little yellow bus waiting for him. Without thinking about the consequences, Armani pulled his hood over his head and walked quickly to his fenced-in front yard. With one hand he opened the gate, with the other he stuck out his middle finger to the driver. There was a momentary sense of elation at blowing off school, then he went inside his house. He should have at least four hours to decide what to do, as his brothers seldom got up before noon. He closed the front door behind him and headed to the cabinet containing the cleaning supplies.

Outside, the bus driver waited to see the door close, shrugged his shoulders and pulled away. If the driver had a dollar for every time a kid flipped him off, he wouldn't be driving a bus. Armani's house was now part of the driver's route for the semester. If the kid wanted to ride, that was fine. If he didn't, that was fine, too. It made no difference to the driver.

Inside, Armani silently cleaned. It made him feel a little better. It made him feel a little less lost.

In the past, for Chuy, Spring break had meant baseball games and practice for the entire week, so he was used to focusing his energies on sports. Even if he had had the money to go somewhere for the holiday, baseball had kept him home—and that hadn't bothered Chuy a bit! He would pretend he was in the big leagues, or at least working his way through the minors, playing ball, practicing, lifting weights. He would go home, eat, sleep and do it all over again the next day. Chuy had always wished Spring break could last forever, not because he wanted to lay around or party, but because he loved to focus on one thing and get better at it. Boxing intensified that desire even more. His imagination now had him being an up-and-coming young fighter, training for his first championship bout. Chuy was in his element. Even though he tried to sleep for an extra hour (because he could) he woke at five a.m. He upped his amount of road work, and shadow boxing sessions in the backyard were also extended. He pictured himself, 'the Stallion', working his way through a long list of tough opponents. Utilizing lefts, rights, upper cuts and hooks Chuy ducked, bobbed, blocked and slipped his way to numerous impressive mental victories. By the end of the twelve round bout both fighters were bloodied and exhausted, but Chuy would muster a final assault, taking down the champ.

"Ladies and Gentlemen, the new Welterweight Champion of the World: Chuy "The Mexican Stallion" LeDesma!" Chuy would say it loud and proud, knowing that Raul, also on Spring break from Triton Junior College, was staying up way too late at night and sleeping way too long in the morning, and wouldn't be around to make fun of him. Chuy performed his scenario every day with reckless glee. Afterward, he ate his breakfast and watched television until the gym opened at noon. It was the schedule of his dreams, and he was loving every minute. However, he did miss Wolfy's kids which surprised him. *Maybe I'll bring them to the gym one day*, he mused, but that aside he did not miss school at all.

Yes, this was a great week, but the very best part of the very best week—the part that made it the best of all—was Lucy. He saw Lucy every day. He got to see her workout, he got to hear her voice, her laugh and admire the long ringlets of hair drenched in sweat, which unfurled as she took out her braids after practice. He actually had worked up enough nerve to talk to her and, though he wasn't very good at making small talk, they managed to find something to discuss every day. Her smile was his reward and all that he hoped for, the smile that made his head spin like a left hook to the temple. Now it was already Wednesday. More than once

Chuy found himself wondering, *why does the school week drag, but Spring break go by in a blink?* Regardless, today meant one more day when Chuy could hit the bags, spar and see Lucy. Another perfect day made even better because the gym was only half full in the morning, with just the students on Spring break present.

"Ledesma, Quinones, you two rookies up in front!" shouted Sultan. "Time to be leaders. Run the warm-ups!"

Chuy and Lucy were quick to follow orders. Ropes first, then calisthenics. Both fighters had not been there long, but the extra work they had each done on their own gave them the ability to breeze through warm-up as if they had been doing it for years. Some kids who had been in the gym much longer still struggled with warm-ups, but Lucy and Chuy kept a good pace and shouted words of guidance and encouragement.

Next they moved to the stations. As the team rotated from bag to bag and from one area to the next, Sultan barked out instructions, his voice sounding even more intimidating than usual.

"Ledesma, Quinones, let's go, you two." Sultan stood in the middle of the ring with paddle mitts ready.

The pair stopped mid-round and headed toward him.

"Since Big Ces ain't here, you gonna have to work with me, son. Workin' the mitts is the next best thing to sparring."

Chuy nodded and took his stance.

"Oh, no, young man! You gettin ready for a fight, put on the headgear. Where the hell is your mouthpiece? We got to get your butt ready! You goin' Saturday after next, son. Now move!"

Chuy scurried to his bag for his mouthpiece, while Lucy stood in the blue corner.

"Whatcha waitin' on, girl? I ain't standin' here for my health. I've seen you hit those bags; let's see what you got up in here!" He motioned for her to meet him in the middle of the ring.

It was the first time Lucy had worked in the ring, but she was not intimidated. She quickly assumed a stance. Sultan flashed the paddle gloves, giving her a target for her jab, and Lucy popped it, immediately bobbing and popping it again. Sultan stepped back, eyebrows up in mild surprise. He moved to his right, flashing the mitt and Lucy moved with him, popping the target, first with jabs and straight rights, then with hooks and uppercuts, each followed with a bobbing head motion style made famous by such fighting greats as Joe Frazier, Boom-Boom Mancini, and Mike Tyson. Lucy maintained the movement and pressure throughout the round, landing combinations, ducking, and bobbing to avoid becoming a target herself. By the end of the round the old man was almost giddy with what he had witnessed.

"Girl, where in the *hell* did you learn to move like that?"

Lucy, breathing hard from exertion, thought for a moment. "Umm, I guess from watching my uncle."

"Who is your Uncle? Joe Frazier?"

"Robbie Quinones."

"Robbie "Rockem" Quinones? Well, I'll be! Small world! You tell him old Sultan said 'hey'. Robbie's a good boy. A tough-ass little fighter. He's your uncle, you say?"

Lucy nodded her head.

"That explains a whole bunch." Sultan, let out a huge belly laugh. "Girl, you come from good boxing stock. To tell you the truth," he lowered his voice as if he were telling Lucy a secret, "I think you hit harder than old Robbie. Great fighter, but never much of a knockout punch. I think you can Rockem *and* Sockem!" Sultan's voice boomed through the gym with a new proclamation: "Ladies and Gentlemen, we got ourselves a new fighter right here: Lucy 'Rockem, Sockem' Quinones!"

As Spring break flew by Lucy, Chuy, Nancy, and Billy worked hard and loved it. Well, three out of four worked hard. Billy, of course, just talked hard.

Sultan became even more involved with these younger athletes. He passed by the bag station as Billy was doing more talking than hitting, bothering the same girl he had been bothering since day one.

"Billy Boy," announced Sultan, "if we had an all-talking team, you would be a champ for sure! You ain't never have to worry about gettin' knocked out. With that thick head and strong jaw from all that talkin', they have to hit you with a brick to get you down."

Billy smiled at what he took as a compliment and concentrated on hitting the bag, for all of thirty seconds before he began talking again.

During that same time, Ulises was preparing for a final fight. He had decided to keep coaching, but his boxing career was coming to an end. With that in mind, before and after practice he worked with Nancy. Though Ulises seemed much older, he was only one year ahead of her in school. He had followed his older brother on the path to joining the Kings when he was only in the sixth grade but had also followed his brother out of the gangs. He was the little guy who had been there when Big Ces recruited Alvarez and had been part of the Layden-Maywood Boxing Club ever since. He had been a solid member, never winning a championship, but perpetuating the reputation of tough, hard-nosed fighters from the club. Now as his senior year of high school was coming to an end, Ulises was becoming a very good coach. He had also been an effective, helpful teacher's aide for Alvarez. Ulises had not yet decided what he would do for a living, but through his experience in the classroom with special needs students and at the gym, he did know he was going to work with young people for the rest of his life.

Although he and Nancy had been in the same school for several years they had never met. Now, thanks to boxing, they were heading into a budding romance that their teammates had begun to notice.

The buzzer sounded, signaling that it was time for the girls to move on to the speed bags, which was the only piece of equipment Nancy had not yet mastered.

"Ugh," she complained to her friend. "I still can't hit this little ball."

"Don't worry, your boyfriend will teach you," replied Lucy, trying to hide a grin.

"Shut up!" Nancy hissed out of the side of her mouth. "He's not my boyfriend."

Lucy began a whispered sing-song; "Nancy's got a boyfriend; Nancy's got a boyfriend."

The buzzer rang, ending the round and the teasing that Nancy was barely enduring. Lucy instantly tapped the bag into an easy rhythm. First one hand, then the other, then both as she moved lightly on her toes reaching up to the bag. Nancy took over again and struggled, getting in two decent jabs before the third missed a perfect landing and sent the tiny bag off in the wrong direction. She let out a deep breath of frustration, grabbed the bag with both hands to center it, and then began again. As the buzzer sounded to end the round, Alvarez approached

"What am I doing wrong, Alvarez?" Nancy demanded to know.

"You're doing it correctly, Nance; it just takes practice."

Nancy exhaled in disgust.

"You know…like your boyfriend showed you." Alvarez wore an angelic expression.

"Shut up! He's not my…" realizing how loud she was talking, a red-faced Nancy waved her glove at Alvarez. "Forget you!"

The round ended and Lucy took her turn at the speed bag.

Alvarez continued his innocent act. "Not everyone can grow up with boxing like Lucy; I mean *she* had to show *her boyfriend* how to hit this thing."

Lucy's head shot around. "Chuy's not my boyfriend," she protested without thinking.

"Who said anything about Chuy?" Alvarez asked with a wink to Nancy.

Nancy's face lit up as the buzzer sounded.

"Lucy's got a boyfriend! Lucy's got a boyfriend!"

The rhythm of the speed bag was briefly interrupted as Lucy stopped to push her friend, but an amused look stayed on her face the rest of the round.

Maybe I do have a boyfriend, she thought to herself.

CHAPTER 16

Saturday mornings meant a morning run and a trip to the gym for Chuy. He had given Billy a call and, although Billy had answered, all Chuy heard from the other end was mumbles. *Okay, no Billy. No biggie: Lucy will be there.* That realization sent a warm feeling through him. Chuy had developed a deep, extreme crush that resulted in having Lucy on his mind most of the time. Since the morning was warm and sunny, he decided to ride his bike to the gym. Boxing and Lucy. He was a very lucky guy.

The ride to the gym was a breeze. Chuy hoped the weather would stay like this, though Illinois weather could change daily, even hourly! Regardless, he enjoyed the ride so much he decided to add it to his routine from this day on. He was planning his future rides as he arrived at the front door of the gym. Chuy looked up to see another cyclist arriving. It was Lucy!

"Hey, Jesus! Great minds think alike!" She shouted as she coasted toward him.

He was taken by surprise and all he could manage was, "Ha, yeah."

"You know, Chuy, you don't have to be scared of me. We aren't even in the same weight class."

"Ha, yeah."

"Good thing you box better than you carry on a conversation."

"Ummm...ha...yeah?" Chuy repeated, this time taking part in the joke.

His line got a chuckle from his crush as she stepped into the doorway ahead of him, missing the delighted look on his face.

"So, how was your ride this morning?" he blurted out, way too quickly to sound cool.

Lucy stopped at the door, turning her head sideways. "You trying to have a real conversation? See, that isn't so hard. My ride was good. I go down Diversey to 25th. The 25th bridge is steep, but I kind of like it. How about you?"

"I'm straight down 25th all the way to Lawrence. Yeah, I wasn't ready for the bridge. I should have got a running start!"

The two started up the narrow stairs, Lucy in front.

"Oh, we could meet on Diversey and ride in together sometime," she suggested over her shoulder.

"Yeah, except…"

"Except what?" Lucy asked, stopping at the top of the stairs and giving Chuy a surprised look.

"Except I'm in great shape and you probably couldn't keep up."

Lucy busted out in giggles at the teasing and punched him in the shoulder. "Right, try the other way around."

"Hey," Chuy protested, rubbing his shoulder. "That's my jab hand and I got a fight coming up."

"Yes you do!" interrupted Sultan, who had come up behind them. "If I might invite you two to get practice started any time in the near future that would be lovely. LET'S GO PEOPLE!"

The booming voice of the old coach ended the first real conversation between the two as quickly as it had started. However, their brief exchange left both Chuy and Lucy with a little extra energy and the practice flew by.

On the bike ride home they talked about school, family and nothing at all. The quiet side streets and the leisurely pace made the ride perfect for getting to know each other. When they got to the busy intersection of Grand and Mannheim they stopped to lean on their bikes and talk. Ten minutes later, after the green light had come and gone countless times, Lucy finally took measure of the imposing steep climb of the bridge.

"Ledesma, you've been stalling. It's go time!"

Lucy hopped on her bike and headed up the incline. She had gotten the jump on Chuy, who almost fell getting back on his bike, to the glee of his challenger. The two pumped the pedals up the bridge and flew down the other side without pedaling. Chuy's route kept him in a straight line, while Lucy took the first right toward her house, catching the light perfectly.

"I WON!" they shouted simultaneously upon passing an imaginary finish line.

"See you Monday," Chuy called out over his shoulder.

Lucy, boxing and Saturday morning had Chuy in the clouds, where he stayed for the rest of the weekend as the best Spring break of his young life came to an end.

Beautiful spring weather made the sting of going back to school a little more tolerable for the students and teachers. A few of the more wealthy students returned with dark tans and haggard faces, souvenirs from time spent in Cancun. Others looked just as tired, though far more pale, from staying up every night playing video games for a solid week. Now, like the shock from a springtime jump into Lake Michigan, Monday arrived, and they were forced back to early mornings and school work.

Of course not all students played the break away. Some had been working early morning shifts at their after-school jobs, while others had been involved in the Spring play, or other school activities. Coach Wolfy's baseball team returned exhausted following a week of non-stop baseball, having played seven games, including two double headers. Freshman sensation Manny Ochoa and his teammates had been competing for the conference championship.

Salim, Lynnie, Missy and the rest of Wolfy's kids had enjoyed the break from classes and even added some outings with their Best Pal partner to places like the mall and roller rink. Alvarez and his small band of fighters, with the exception of Billy, had stuck to a strict practice schedule that made the return to school relatively painless.

It was business as usual, even more so for Chuy who had his first fight on the coming Saturday. He not only sparred more frequently at the gym, but he also sped up his morning run, moving, ducking, throwing more lefts, rights, hooks, and uppercuts each day. He shadow-boxed for five full rounds on his back deck, moving and throwing as fast and hard as he could. He strove to do everything necessary to be ready. Now, as he got off the Monday morning bus, he could already feel the beginning of nerves bubbling like a little stream inside him. He tried to picture what fight night was going to look like, smell like, be like when he was pulled out of thought by that big familiar voice:

"Chewbacca!"

"Yeah, nice to see you at practice, Billy," Chuy said, lightly jabbing his friend. He didn't wait for Billy's lame excuse but headed quickly to the 250 wing. Salim was out by the main staircase, where he typically would have been harassed by Armani and his crew. However, since Armani had been kicked out, the group of wannabes had disbanded, leaving Salim to wander around the stairs, hearing only an occasional, "Hi, Salim," but mostly being ignored altogether. Seeing this, Chuy couldn't help but wonder to himself, *could my school be changing, right in front of my eyes?*

The boys guided Salim back to the safety of the 250 hallway. Salim chattered all the way about his adventure at the mall. When the boys turned the corner they ran into the rest of the kids. Missy greeted them, brimming with excitement.

"Ch-ch-chuy, guess wh-wh-what! I went r-r-roller s-s-skating!"

"Me, too!" shouted Lynnie.

"Me, too!" echoed Big Mike.

"You did not, Mike," Lynnie protested.

"Did, too! I went with Sarah Erl; she took me with her sister!"

"We didn't see you!"

Chuy stepped into referee. "Okay, guys, I bet you all had fun, right?"

"YESSS!!!" The students cheered.

"Okay, guys, my turn to talk to Jesus."

Ms. Kelly stood by Coach Wolf's open door and motioned Chuy inside. Typically, Alvarez and Wolf were laughing and poking fun at each other.

"Hey, champ! I'm hearing good things," Wolf exclaimed.

"Not yet," Chuy modestly protested, "I'm a long way from being champ."

"Yeah, he's got to win the first one first," said Alvarez.

"Saturday's the big day, huh? Where?" asked Coach Wolf.

Chuy was confused; he wasn't really sure. The location of the fight hadn't come up yet.

Alvarez noticed and bailed him out. "Good old Morris, Illinois. The Morris Armory, seven o'clock. Be there or be square."

"Well, I'll be square," Wolfy snickered, "'cause I sure ain't driving out to Morris after a double-header at Downers Grove High. I will be there in spirit. How about that?"

"Playing for the conference lead, right Coach?" asked Chuy.

"Ahhh, you have been paying attention, I see," Wolfy confirmed.

"Yeah, I know Ricky is tearing it up, but Manny may be the best hitter on the team right now."

"Yep, the freshman has managed to straighten a few out since tryouts," replied Wolf. "And now you're on your way to the Olympics. I know how to call 'em, don't I?"

"Whoa! Slow your roll, Wolfy. Let's get the first win before we send him off to the Olympics," Alvarez said, with a wink to Chuy.

"Don't listen to Alvarez, Jesus. I know a champion fighter when I see one." Wolf's enthusiasm was unstoppable.

"Wolfy, before I came around you thought boxing meant putting things in boxes," Alvarez replied, faking disgust.

Ms. Kelly interrupted, "Um, hello, I know you two bozos have nothing better to do than fight over who's the coolest, but I've got business with this young man." She pointed a finger in Chuy's direction.

"Dammmn!" objected Alvarez. "Bozos?"

"Harsh," added Wolfy. "Please, your highness, continue if you will."

"Thank you, bozos." Kelly gave an innocent smile. "Now, Chuy, I'm sure the kids told you they took part in activities with their Pals over Spring break."

"Oh yeah, I heard all about it."

"You need to record those events on the website and download some pics, if you would."

"I'm on it," Chuy assured her. "I also wrote up the information for the parents about prom and I sent it to you. Did you get it yet?"

"Yep; I tweaked it a bit, but it was well done. We can send that out at the beginning of next week."

"Also, next week after my fight I'm inviting the kids to my gym," Chuy added.

"Oh, they'll love that!" Kelly exclaimed, clapping her hands together.

"Um...I gotta go now. I need to run up to the library," Chuy informed the teachers, after allowing them a few more moments of idle chatter.

"Sure, go ahead," answered Kelly. "Sounds like you have things lined out."

"So what's going on in the library?" Alvarez asked, pretending not to know. "Overdue book or somethin'?"

"Oh, I'm going to study," Chuy replied vaguely, moving quickly for the door.

"Got a big test the first day back, do ya? You better hurry, you may not get enough 'study' time." Alvarez made air quotes, not even trying to hide a smirk.

Kelly and Wolfy exchanged knowing glances as Chuy hurried out. Behind him he could hear Alvarez begin a quiet chant:

"Chuy's got a girlfriend; Chuy's got a girlfriend."

"Man! That must be people's favorite song around here," Chuy grumbled, not caring if anyone heard him.

The week leading up to Chuy's fight passed with supersonic speed. His attention was focused on practice, Lucy, sparring, Lucy, school, Lucy, a visit from Mrs. Eldridge, Lucy, Best Pals and of course, Lucy! Friday practice came, seemingly in a blink. After the usual warm-ups and ropes, Sultan called Chuy over to his side.

"Okay, son, in the ring with the mitts. I wanna see five good rounds, then finish with the bags. Tomorrow do your road work, then rest. Be here by three 'cause we leave at one minute after three with or without you. Understand, boy?"

"Got it," Chuy said through his mouthpiece.

"Ledesma, you've done good work in the gym. You're ready, and I been around long enough to know what ready is all about."

Chuy swelled with pride. That was the biggest compliment Sultan had given him since he had walked into the gym almost two months ago. If Sultan thought he was ready, then he was ready. Now all he had to do was make it through those brutal hours of waiting before his fight. Saturday night could not come quickly enough!

As promised, one sleepless night and restless morning later, three o'clock finally arrived and two cars proceeded from the Maywood Boxing

Club down 17th to the Eisenhower Expressway, and on down the highway west to Morris, Illinois. Everyone was happy for the light Saturday traffic. In the back seat were Chuy, Billy and a young junior gloves fighter, twelve years of age, named Angel. Cesar was behind the wheel of his SUV chatting with Alvarez, who was seated up next to him.

"Everyone okay back there?" asked Big Ces after some time had passed. "You all are pretty quiet."

The fighters were preparing for their fights in silence. Waves of nerves assaulted Chuy's stomach. Billy noticed and knew to keep his mouth shut, answering Cesar only with a thumbs up. The more experienced fighters, including "Combat" Calderon and a light-heavyweight by the name of Justin "the Quiet Riot" Roberts, rode with Sultan in his beat up station wagon. Other fighters from the club had talked about making the trip west to watch the matches and cheer for their teammates, but Chuy was glad that hadn't happened. Billy was crowd enough for him. He was really happy that Lucy had not come. He did not need the added pressure of performing in front of her. Certainly not his first fight, anyway.

Big Ces again broke into the silence of the back seat.

"Angel, how many fights is this for you?"

"Twenty-seven," answered Angel.

"Yeah, boy," Alvarez commented. "You been doing it for a while."

"When did you start fighting," Billy quietly asked the boy.

"I was eight," replied Angel.

"Yeah, he's just waiting to turn sixteen and move out of the junior division," Cesar explained.

Kids could begin competitive boxing at eight years old, but there were exhibitions for children as young as six. They gradually moved up from one-minute rounds to two minutes, as Angel was doing now, finally enduring three, three minute rounds at age sixteen and over, like Chuy. Chuy was the only fighter from Maywood who would be fighting in the novice division, meaning he had fewer than fifteen fights under his belt. Since the age limit for Gloves was twenty-five, there was a good chance he would be going against a grown man with some experience. The thought crossed his mind, bringing on another wave of nerves.

"Do you remember your first fight, Angel?" Chuy asked.

The boy just smiled and shook his head no.

"I bet Big Ces remembers his," Alvarez called out to the back seat. "I know I do."

Cesar chuckled at the memory. "Hell, yes! By the third round I was bent over with my hands on my knees."

"He was bent over trying to catch his breath, but still throwing a jab to keep the other guy away!" Alvarez roared with laughter.

"Hey, a win is a win, right, Chuy?" Big Ces checked the rear-view mirror to see how his boy was doing.

The cars were moving smoothly across Interstate 80 West. Cornfields began to appear on both sides of the highway.

"Damn, WE in the COUNTRY!" Billy announced loudly and unnecessarily, then sat back after a stern look from Chuy.

Big Ces had noticed a worried expression on Chuy's face. "Jesus don't think so hard, *primo*. This is an armory in the middle of nowhere; it ain't the Olympic trials. If you win, you'll learn; if you lose, you'll learn more."

"What the hell is the armory?" blurted out Billy. "Is that where they have tanks and stuff?"

This time Chuy was secretly grateful for Billy's big mouth. He had no idea what an armory was either.

"*Payaso!*" Ces glanced up in the rear-view mirror as he spoke.

"That means clown," Chuy whispered to his friend, "but don't take it too personally; I'm sure he meant it in the nicest way."

Ces continued his explanation, undeterred by Billy's silliness. "You know our big gym at Layden? The Armory basically looks like that with a ring set up in the middle. There will be seats on the floor and maybe even a few people sitting on the bleachers if we get a good crowd. That's it; it ain't Madison Square Freaking Garden, *primo*."

Chuy was thankful for the description. Fear of the unknown had wreaked havoc on his nerves. The more Ces explained, the more he relaxed.

Cesar continued, "When we get there the place will be pretty empty, and they have an area where you go for your physical and weigh-ins."

"So have you been here before?' asked Billy.

"So long ago I don't even remember but trust me they are all the same."

Chuy said a silent thank you that Billy asked so many questions. Being able to visualize helped to relieve some nerves. Each answered question helped Chuy relax just a little more.

Why didn't I ask these questions myself at least a week ago? I need to remember the things that will help me prepare mentally, Chuy noted to himself. He took a deep breath and exhaled, making a physical effort to relax his body. The nerves were still coming in waves, but the waves were small and gentle for now.

"Who is Chuy gonna fight?" Billy continued, probably just to hear his own voice.

"Don't know yet. After weigh-ins Sultan will match you up with a novice welterweight. Could be anybody from anywhere, Rockford or Aurora, maybe. Jack Whittinghill and 2nd Avenue guys may be here. *Vamos a ver.* We will see."

"There is always a chance you won't match up with anyone," added Alvarez.

That news sent a new feeling of dread running through Chuy. Maybe he wasn't ready. Maybe he needed more time to train. Maybe he could get out of this thing. On the other hand, he wanted to fight. He'd come all this way. All this tension and no fight? That would be worse than losing.

Ces was regularly checking the rear-view mirror as the long straight highway stretched out in front of them. Still miles of cornfields spread to the left and right, dotted with the occasional farmhouse. The big man read Chuy's face.

"So, don't get all crazy, Jesus. You come ready for anything. You fight your fight. Trust me, you wouldn't be here if you weren't ready. It's all good, homes! Check it, here's our exit."

Momentarily a tsunami of nerves threatened to come crashing in again. Chuy quietly inhaled and exhaled. He pictured himself going to the weigh-in, waiting, warming up and facing an opponent. In his mind, his imaginary opponent looked very much like "Combat" Calderon. He gave himself a silent pep talk. Gradually he stilled the nerves down to a slight trickle in his gut.

You got this, Stallion, he thought with a measure of confidence.

"Here we are boys!" Ces announced a short time later.

The two-car caravan turned into a huge parking lot off route 23, two miles outside of the sleepy little river town of Morris. Big Ces parked, opened his door, and turned toward the boys.

"An hour, twenty-five minutes! Record time, fellas. You ready, Angel?"

Angel nodded confidently.

"Chuy?"

Chuy did the same.

"You're always ready right, Billy?"

"Damn right, Big Ces!" shouted Billy much too loudly, "Let's get those mutha …"

"Whoooa, turbo!" Ces mocked. "The only thing you're gonna be knocking out is hot dogs!"

Chuy burst into much needed laughter, which broke the tension for a moment.

"Let's do this, fellas!" exclaimed Big Cesar, leading the way.

As the small group from Maywood Boxing Club walked into the gym, Chuy could see that it was much the way he had pictured it on the car ride. Just as Cesar had described it, it looked like any other gym.

"Go change in the locker room, but bring your stuff back with you," Alvarez instructed his fighters.

The four boxers did just that; in fact, the three veteran fighters had already started heading there when Chuy realized the instructions were mainly for him, the only novice in the group.

"Where're those hot dogs?" asked Billy. "I'm ready to eat!"

"First go find us a place on the bleachers where we can make camp," Alvarez told him.

The team was one of the first to arrive, so Billy had his choice. He picked a spot near the section where weigh-ins and physicals were taking place. Chuy, who had changed quickly, easily spotted the group and headed toward the area.

"Alright, boy. You got ready fast," observed Sultan, slapping him on the back. "I like that. No waiting—just step to that young lady sitting right over there." He pointed toward a corner of the gym where tables and a scale were set up.

Chuy approached the check-in table and gave the woman his name. She passed him off to a nurse stationed next to her, who took his blood pressure and pulse, checked his heart, and asked him a few basic questions on how he was feeling this afternoon.

"Have you been knocked out at any time over the last six months?" She inquired.

"No, this is my first fight," replied Chuy.

"Oh!" She smiled broadly. "Well, good luck; I'm sure you'll do great."

She directed him to the next station. "Head to the scales for weigh-in, please."

The weigh-in station was relatively quiet. An older man with a tiny pair of glasses sitting on the end of his nose stood behind the scale and another younger man sat at a small card table, ready to record. Not far from the scale, a few fighters were in plastic suits, jumping rope and doing jumping jacks, trying to sweat off the last few pounds of water. Chuy had no such worries. He removed his tank top and white Chuck Taylor gym shoes, wearing only his Layden PE shorts as he stepped onto the scale.

"Name and club," demanded the man at the table.

"Jesus LeDesma, Maywood Boxing Club."

The man moved the weights for a second or two, "145 and 3/4 pounds."

"145 and 3/4 pounds," repeated the man at the table, carefully noting the weight next to Chuy's name on his roster.

Chuy thanked the men and put his shirt and shoes back on. Now all that was left was the fight itself. He looked at the clock. *Three more hours until fight time*, he thought, wondering how he could make the time go by faster. Next time he'd bring a book.

Chuy had no choice but to pass the time laying around on the bleachers. Billy had given up trying to talk to him, but he had already eaten a hot dog, the first of many that afternoon. The armory slowly filled as people claimed the seats surrounding the ring. When no more of the choice seats were left, the crowd began to fill the bleachers. Cesar and Alvarez, who had been talking with the other coaches, joined the boys.

"Got good news, good news, and more good news," Ces told Chuy.

"Got you a fight. He's green as you, older though. Just got out of the Navy and he's about 6'4"."

"What's the good news?" Billy interjected.

"You gotta fight, young man!" Alvarez clapped Chuy's shoulder. "That's the great news! And he's from Morris! They've just restarted the club here, which means everybody's green, so he probably doesn't get good sparring like you get."

"And more good news, *primo*!" Ces chimed in. "You're up early. There are only five junior glove fights, then it's all you, CHUY TIME!"

Chuy felt a few butterflies start to stir in his gut. "Should I warm up?"

"Give it a few minutes," suggested Ces. "When they start the first little kid bout, that will be your signal: stretches and shadow box. We'll work up a good sweat."

The crowd had settled in their seats and a man in a suit entered the ring. "Ladies and gentlemen, please rise and join us in our National Anthem." The crowd stood as two pretty young African-American girls stood in the center ring and sang the familiar words. Billy elbowed Chuy and nodded at the stage, raising his eyebrows. Chuy just rolled his eyes at his cocky friend. With the anthem completed Sultan left his spot sitting with the older fighters, to talk with his novice.

"How ya feel, boy?" he asked.

"Ready," Chuy assured him.

"Yes you are! Guarantee you had better training and better sparring than anyone you're gonna fight tonight. Remember that, boy! This guy didn't have "Combat" Calderon to spar with; you know that—right, boy?"

Chuy nodded yes.

"They didn't have me training 'em either, you feel me, boy?" Sultan added with a slight grin, "Now go warm-up and get a win."

"Yes, sir! I mean yes, Coach!"

Chuy felt strong. Fear gave way to a new swell of confidence. What Sultan had just said was right. No matter what his opponent had going for himself, he had not worked harder nor had he been trained by better coaches. Chuy retreated to the rear of the gym to warm-up with Big Ces.

Meanwhile, the junior glove bouts flew by as judges and ring personnel moved the fight card along quickly. Chuy was stretching just outside the circle of chairs surrounding the ring when the announcer introduced the next fight.

"Ladies and Gentlemen, wearing red shorts with a silver stripe, in the red corner, from Maywood boxing Club... Angel...Ortiz!"

Angel placed his gloved hands at his chin and bowed to scattered applause. He looked every bit as experienced as a kid should, who had been in the ring since he was eight years old. The bell sounded and the two boys met in the middle of the ring and began expertly throwing and blocking punches. The twelve-year-old looked as if they had been in the ring their entire lives.

When the bell rang ending the first round, Alvarez gave Angel water and instructions. He had been intently watching his fighter's opponent and had noticed a couple of weaknesses that Angel could take advantage of. Sultan stood outside the ring near the corner but said nothing.

The coaches cleared their corners. The fighters stood as the bell sounded for the second round. Angel came out firing combinations of punches and within seconds it became apparent that the other fighter could not match him. The referee stopped the action, stepping in front of Angel's opponent and counting slowly to eight. A standing eight count is meant to give a fighter a chance to recover before he takes on further damage, or is knocked out, but in this case, it could not help the outclassed young opponent. Angel unleashed a ferocious attack, forcing the referee to stop the fight in the middle of the second round.

"Way to go, Angel!" bellowed Ces, so loud that everyone in the gym heard him. He beckoned to his next fighter. "Okay, Chuy, we're up."

"Let's knock this son of a bitch, the F OUT!" came a voice from behind.

Cesar turned to see Billy making his way toward the ring. "Where in the hell do you think you're going?"

"Chuy's corner," answered Billy.

"No, no, you stay there with the hotdogs; just me and Sultan are in the ring."

"But Sultan doesn't even talk."

"One fight and ten hotdogs and you think you're an expert, *vato*? Go sit down!"

With that Chuy and Big Ces headed down the aisle to the red corner.

"Good job, Angel," Chuy praised the boy who was climbing out of the ring.

"Your turn, Chuy," replied Angel. "I know you can do it, too!"

The teammates touched gloves. Alvarez stepped over the bottom rope on the way out, standing on the edge of the ring and lifting the rope for Chuy to enter. Ces rinsed the mouthpiece for Chuy while giving him last minute instructions. "Fight your fight, *primo*. Remember, you have already been in the ring with better fighters than this guy."

The announcer's voice echoed out of the speakers: "Ladies and Gentlemen, this bout features two novice welterweight fighters. In the red corner, from the Maywood Boxing Club, in his first amateur fight, Jesus "Chuy" Ledesma."

"Take a bow, homes." Ces gave Chuy a shove toward the center of the ring.

Chuy took another step forward and awkwardly bent at the waist to a smattering of polite applause, plus a loud shout from Billy.

"We got to work on that bow, *primo*," Ces chuckled into his fighter's ear when Chuy stepped back into the corner.

"And in the blue corner, also in his first amateur fight, from our own Morris Boxing Club, by way of the United States Navy, Jake ''The Snake'' Summerville."

When Chuy had been visualizing his first fight, this was not the picture he had formed in his head. He had seen a young, Hispanic kid, like himself. No way would he have guessed he was fighting a six foot, four inch, lanky beanpole of a grown man, who just happened to also be a Navy vet.

Sultan stood on the floor below Chuy's corner, sensing the young fighter's apprehension.

"Yo, boy! Listen here! He ain't ready for anybody like you. Just get inside that long reach and take care of this kid."

Is Sultan nuts? This ain't no kid. He's at least twenty-four and looks even older, but before Chuy could do any more thinking the bell mercifully rang and his training kicked in. He quickly found his range, throwing jabs and straight rights. The long arms of the opponent were working in Chuy's favor as he was well inside his opponent's reach. He easily landed punches without much threat of retaliation. At mid-point of the first round Chuy hurt the lanky fighter with a solid left. The referee stopped the action, stepping in front of the dazed Summerville, slowly counting to eight. Chuy's confidence grew. He *was* much faster and better trained than his gangly, plodding opponent. Summerville was on wobbly legs by the time the first round neared its end. Chuy had his opponent pinned against the ropes, throwing punches to the shoulders of Summerville, whose greater height meant that he could stretch his head over the ropes outside the ring. The older fighter couldn't throw punches in that position, but he could avoid receiving any strong blows to the head. Chuy was scoring points and dominating the fight, but not causing any real damage to his outclassed opponent. The referee soon brought the fighters back to the middle of the ring. Unexpectedly, Summerville let go with a long right hand that seemed to unfurl like a rope. The blow caught Chuy flat-footed. His head spun, but luckily the bell sounded almost simultaneously with the punch. Chuy turned to his corner and tried not to wobble as he made his way back.

Ces stood waiting with a knowing grin. "Caught you sleeping, *primo*. You gonna let that happen again?"

Ces squirted water in his fighter's face, removed his mouthpiece and shot more cold water down the back of Chuy's neck. The water snapped Chuy back to his senses. He sat on his stool and realized how tired he was after only one round.

"Straighten the legs, deep breaths." Big Ces grabbed the band of Chuy's shorts and pulled them slightly out from the waist so the fighter could breathe easier.

"You know where your range is, *vato*?" Ces asked quietly.

Chuy nodded his head.

"You know where his range is?"

Chuy nodded yes again.

"Okay, then pay attention and DON'T GET YOUR DUMB ASS CAUGHT AGAIN!"

Chuy couldn't help but smile as he continued to take deep breaths.

Suddenly Sultan spoke from the floor. "When he stretches his head out of the ring, step hard to the left and throw the left. If he gives you the body, TAKE THE BODY. You got it, boy!"

Ces sprayed water one more time. "Drink! Spit!"

Without speaking, Chuy did as he was told. Big Ces popped the mouthpiece back into place.

"Coaches, clear," came the instruction from the referee.

Fighters stood and faced each other again. Summerville was still breathing heavily, and his right eye was swelling. Chuy knew how to capitalize on those weaknesses. At the sound of the bell he moved quickly past the center of the ring and met his weary opponent in his own corner. Immediately Chuy was in his own range and well inside the range of Summerville. He was in the pocket, the sweet spot, where he could land shots without fear of receiving them. His opponent automatically returned to an awkward defensive stance.

"Step left; throw left!" Sultan screamed from the corner, and much to his delight Chuy was already doing just that. He *knew* he liked this kid!

Chuy took a big step to the left and threw a vicious left hook to the body, which brought an "Oooooo" from the crowd. In the gym the fighters trained with sixteen-ounce gloves, but here, in his first competition, the ten-ounce gloves on Chuy's hands felt like mittens. He could feel the cheek bone of Summerville on his knuckles, and it felt both savage and sweet, like he had hit a home run. The skinny fighter crumpled from the blow, but Chuy threw an uppercut that made Summerville's head bounce back up. The referee stepped in to end the fight the moment that the punch was thrown, and he got there in time to keep the beaten fighter from falling to the mat.

Chuy turned slightly to see Ces rushing up the steps of the ring cheering and fist-pumping. Meeting his trainer in his corner, Chuy dropped onto the stool. Now that the action was over Chuy realized how spent he really was. His legs ached from the top of his hips to the soles of his feet. Big Ces took his mind off his pain for a short time by dumping water on Chuy's head. "*Como esta, primo?*"

"Tired," mumbled Chuy, barely able to speak.

Sparring rounds in the gym had not prepared him for how much energy an actual fight took. *This was only a round and a half. I need more training!* he thought, not allowing himself to bask in the win.

Gradually, Chuy's breath returned to him and the referee signaled both fighters to the center of the ring. The two combatants embraced in the middle of the ring then took a stance on each side of the referee. The ref grabbed each fighter by his wrists.

"Winner with a TKO at 35 seconds of the second round. From Maywood Boxing Club, Jesus "The Stallion" Ledesma." The ref lifted Chuy's hand high in victory.

Stallion? How did..." Chuy looked down in his corner to see Billy's goofy look of pure pleasure and he knew at once who had informed the announcer of the nickname.

Okay, Stallion it is!

CHAPTER 17

W hen Chuy awoke the next day after sleeping very late, (especially for him) he opened his curtains and saw what looked like the return of winter.

"Well, Spring didn't last very long," he grumbled with a sigh. In Illinois, it was no surprise that winter held on like a hurt fighter grabbing his opponent, squeezing hard and trying to last the round. Usually, the prospect of another cold, dreary day would bring Chuy down a bit, but after last night nothing could take away the exhilaration that flowed through him. The tidal wave of butterflies from the day before had been replaced with calm relief and a sense of pride.

He studied himself in the mirror, examining his right eye, which was slightly bruised and discolored. He kind of liked it. It was a reminder of the night before, a badge of honor that recalled what success felt like. He took his boxing stance and began throwing a few punches, but quickly realized how sore he was. He knew it wasn't from the fight; he had trained too hard to be sore after a round or two. It was the nerves. He needed to handle them better. Now that he knew what it was like, he could prepare. He couldn't wait for his next fight. He would be more than ready the next time.

Chuy walked into the kitchen to see his small trophy still sitting in the middle of the table where he'd left it. Chuy had gotten home late. His mother had already been asleep, and Raul was still out, so he'd put it where they would notice it first thing in the morning.

"What happened, champ? Win one fight and you sleep all day?" Raul joked from his seat at the table.

"Congratulations, *hijo*," Chuy's mother scraped her chair back and rushed over to give him a huge hug.

"Tell us about it, champ," Raul demanded with a jab to Chuy's shoulder.

They spent most of the morning eating and listening to Chuy. He described his fight in glorious detail, and also the fights of his teammates, all of whom had won their matches.

"Did you call your father yet?" Chuy's mom eventually asked.

"Yeah, he called here last night," added Raul. "He said to call him first thing."

"You should go see him," suggested his mother.

"Yeah, I will; I'm gonna stop and see Dad, then I'm going to the library," Chuy informed them.

"The library?" Raul and his mother asked simultaneously. It was not like Chuy to spend a Sunday afternoon studying.

"I need to get some studying in...I have a few tests next week..."

"My amazing son!" gushed Margarita LeDesma. "You are such a good boy! Always caring about your schoolwork!"

Chuy's face turned slightly red at the undeserved praise.

When their mother left the room, Raul stepped closer to Chuy. "Studying, huh?" He arched his eyebrows in disbelief.

Chuy nodded as innocently as he could.

"Okay, champ, make sure to tell your girl I said hi."

Chuy couldn't prevent the sheepish grin that took over his face.

He bundled up against the biting cold and rode his bike the short distance to his father's. The memory of yesterday's fight and the anticipation of seeing Lucy kept him warm all the way there. Hustling from his quiet street for two blocks, Chuy pedaled up to Grand Avenue—the four-lane street that was never quiet. He made a quick left and braced himself against the bitter Chicago wind, which made him extra glad to arrive at his dad's home.

It was a small row house, one of many in the neighborhood. The house faced the back of a large shopping plaza on the corner. This morning the smell of doughnuts from the local bakery was blowing around in the wind. In the early afternoon, that smell would be replaced by that of carnitas, prepared at the restaurant in the same plaza. Chuy dropped his bike at the side door, did a quick knock and walked in.

"Surprise!" came the shout of two little girls.

Lilliana and Isabel, the daughters of his father's girlfriend, squealed with delight at having a breakfast party. The girls were little carbon copies of their mother, Sonia Ruiz, a thin, light-skinned latina with long, thick hair who was working at the stove. With her back turned she called out, "Sit down, champ, we have something for you."

Sonia turned to present Chuy with a stack of pancakes. 'Way to Go, Chuy!' was written in chocolate shaky, uneven writing atop four steaming hot cakes.

"I wrote that for you!" Six-year-old Lilliana exclaimed, jumping with glee.

"Look! Look, Chuy!" Four-year-old Isabel called out, trying to be louder than her sister. She waved a large, white paper covered with glops of blue, red, and green paint. "Look!" she insisted, "It's you, Chuy, it's you!"

"I did one, too!" Lilliana elbowed her way in front of the smaller girl.

Chuy took a seat and the girls jumped to either side still vying for his attention.

The girls' mother finally had to intervene. "Girls! Girls! Settle down! Give Chuy room! Go wash your hands now; we are going to eat."

"I'm first," announced Lilliana as she raced to the bathroom, her little sister screaming behind her.

"NO, ME!"

"They are very excited, in case you couldn't tell," laughed Chuy's father, Ignacio. "They've been up since seven, getting ready for the fiesta!"

"How did you even know I was coming?" asked Chuy, a bit confused.

"Raul said he would get you here. He must have seen your trophy because he left a message late last night. So, you won! Tell us about it."

The girls came racing back to the table, fighting over which one got back to the table first.

Chuy added syrup to the chocolate writing. "If I ate like this all the time, I would be in a different weight class," he proclaimed.

139

Details of the fight were related between bites of the sweet cakes and the girls' constant interruptions.

"Son, listen, I am proud of you," began Ignacio LeDesma when Chuy had finished his story. "You know I love boxing, but …I'm not sure I love my son boxing."

Chuy, concerned, looked up from his almost empty plate. He didn't like where this conversation was going.

"When your mom and I talked about it...well...there are many bad, scary things a sixteen-year-old boy in this neighborhood could be doing. I think baseball always kept you out of trouble, but I know it wasn't playing out like you hoped it would, so I decided, or I guess we decided, not to stand in your way when you wanted to get involved with boxing. Should I be worried? Did we make the right decision?"

Chuy thought for a minute before he replied. "I always appreciate how you and Mom work together, Dad, but please don't worry. I've got good trainers. We spar the right way; we get physicals before each fight. I know, Dad, it's not the safest sport, but I will always train hard and be the best I can be. But I do like it, Dad. I mean—I like it a lot—maybe even more than baseball. And I'm good at it. I think boxing and school keep me on the right track."

"You mean school and boxing, don't you, son? School better come first," Ignacio corrected him.

"It has to, Dad," agreed Chuy. "One of the teachers, Mr. Alvarez, is a coach at the club. If you're failing, or even near to failing classes, the coaches will not let you fight, or even come to practice."

"Well, I like that," said Chuy's father, finishing his last bite.

"When's the next fight?" asked Sonia.

"Well, we always have to wait two weeks for safety between fights, but to tell you the truth, I'm not sure when or where the next fight is taking place."

"You will let us know, right?" she asked.

"For sure," he assured her, shoveling the final bite of pancake into his mouth. "Listen, I got to go." He took his plate to the sink, hugged the girls and their mother, and started for the door.

"Way to go, Chuy!" chanted the girls, clinging to his legs.

"You guys know it was just one fight, right?" Chuy chuckled, patting their heads.

"Hey *hijo*, you can't win them all if you don't win the first one. Now get out of here! Raul said you were meeting your girlfriend at the library."

"She's not my... aw, forget it. Bye, and thanks again."

As Chuy closed the door behind him and jumped on his bike he heard the girls arguing over the last "championship" pancake. *Everyone made such a big deal. If I win a tournament they may throw a parade,* he thought as he rode off.

The trip from his father's house to the library was brief, just across a large parking lot. Chuy arrived before there was time to feel the cold again. He spotted Lucy immediately upon entering the building, sitting at a middle table, wearing an old hoodie and sweats. Ringlets of hair ran down her shoulders, taking Chuy's breath away. The butterflies that had faded away after the fight came flooding back in force. He pulled out the chair across from Lucy and stood there a moment, marveling at her concentration. Lucy was writing so intensely that she hadn't even noticed his arrival. A long minute passed before she looked up.

"Hey," she greeted him softly with smiling eyes.

"Hey," he echoed back.

"Where's your book bag?" she asked.

"I didn't have any homework, so I thought I'd get a start on my junior research paper."

"No paper, no pen?" Lucy observed. "You call yourself a study partner?"

"Yeah, um..." Chuy stammered, unable to come up with a reply.

She laughed. "I'm just messing with you!"

When she laughed, her whole face lit up and Chuy noticed, for the first time, the cutest dimples at the sides of her mouth. He was frozen, completely entranced.

"Tell me about the fight. What happened? What was it like? How was the guy you fought?"

Chuy shook himself out of his trance and shared the details of his fight, from the long drive in Ces' car to the weigh-ins and finally, the knockout victory. As he talked he began to relax, allowing himself to be himself. Lucy paid attention to every detail so she could be more prepared, if and when she ever fought. They talked about that, then about Chuy's win and Lucy's fears. About their families and their homes. About their hopes and aspirations.

Outside the windy city weather fought to take back the Spring, but inside the Franklin Park Library the two young friends talked and laughed and dreamed.

"Chewbacca is the champ! Chewbacca is the champ!" Chuy heard, stepping off the bus. His fellow passengers looked back at Chuy and smiled. No one bothered to ask what Billy was talking about. They were used to Billy Karamitos making noise.

"Dude, so loud on a Monday morning?" Chuy protested.

"Chewbacca, you da champ, son!"

"It was one fight, Billy," Chuy modestly reminded him.

"Yeah, and you knocked out the mutha f..." Billy stopped short, seeing Mrs. Eldridge coming their way.

"Hey, Jesus, I heard you had a good weekend." Mrs. Eldridge beamed at Chuy. "Congratulations."

"How did you …?"

Mrs. Eldridge cut Chuy off. "News travels fast around here. Officer for Best Pals, honor roll last quarter, now a win in the ring! This is the year of LeDesma. Gosh, can't wait for next year!"

Chuy thanked her, and the two boys continued on to room 250. After visiting with Wolfy's kids, Chuy poked his head into Coach's room to find the ever-present trio of Alvarez, Kelly and, of course, Wolfy.

"Hey, there he is!" exclaimed Coach Wolf from behind his desk. "Big win this weekend."

"You, too, Coach! You guys beat Hinsdale." Chuy was happy to return the praise, feeling a little embarrassed by all the attention coming his way.

Ms. Kelly did not let him off the hook. "Hey Chuy, it's your birthday! Gonna party like it's your birthday." She sang, doing a little dance with her hands over her head.

"Really?" asked Alvarez, arching his eyebrows.

Kelly scrunched up her face and thought for a moment. "Well, I don't know any 'you won your first fight' songs, but here goes... hey Chuy, you won your first fight, gonna party like you won your fight."

Alvarez rolled his eyes. "Don't you have lesson plans to do?"

"I want to hear about it," Ms. Kelly continued, ignoring Alvarez.

Chuy just grinned, always unsure how to respond to the constant pretend bickering between the two teachers.

"Well," Alvarez took over, "if you are going to see him fight, you better get there early. Jesus is quite the knockout artist. Early second round TKO against a Navy vet, who was a lot older and a foot taller."

Chuy raised his arm straight over his head, "Yeah," he agreed, "like this; I almost couldn't reach him."

"So cool, Chuy, but now I need to talk business," said Ms. Kelly.

"Sure," Chuy replied, happy for a change of subject.

"Are you getting any parent permission slips back for the prom?"

"Yep, almost all of them. The kids seem really excited. The parents all have the schedules, and each kid's buddy is calling their home just to make sure everything is good. I've got a checklist ready on-line, and I gave you and the other officers access. That is the only thing the senior buddies are responsible for. After that, the junior officers will meet the kids at the prom and make sure they have a good time. Is there anything I missed?"

The three teachers stood quietly, looking expectantly at Chuy.

Chuy had no idea what they were waiting for. "Isn't that alright?"

"Yeah...um ...that's perfect," answered Ms. Kelly.

The teachers were still quiet, and now they all had strange smiles on their faces.

Chuy was puzzled. "Is that okay?" he repeated.

"It's just that we..." started Wolfy.

"Never heard you talk that much," Alvarez finished, and the three adults burst out in belly laughter.

Chuy laughed with them. A red tinge of embarrassment brightened his cheeks while a warm feeling of pride filled him up.

"Okay, I gotta go," he said, still smiling.

Ms. Kelly stopped him with a hand to his shoulder. "Oh, Chuy, one more thing..."

"Yes?"

"Don't forget to get *your* date for prom."

Chuy just shook his head and left the three still howling behind him as he walked out the door.

CHAPTER 18

W hile the school days seemed to drag on forever, in the blink of an eye the weeks somehow flew by. Chuy and Lucy met every morning in the Media Center and every afternoon on the corner of Diversey and 25th to ride their bikes to practice, no matter how dreary or cold the day was. Some days the afternoon was warm and sunny. Other days the cold breeze from Lake Michigan would flow all the way to their northwest suburb. Regardless, Chuy always looked forward to the ride, especially on the way home, when the two rode leisurely up quiet 24th Avenue, talking all the way.

"Big Ces said there aren't too many more fights this spring. Everything is kind of finishing up until summer, then it gets busy again," Chuy remarked as the two pedaled side by side on one of those days. "I really want to get some more fights," he added.

"Yeah, I bet. You want to get more attention," teased Lucy.

"Jelly?" joked Chuy, "When you gonna fight? I know you're ready."

"Well, they got to let me spar first."

"I would bet anything that happens this week. I'm guessing tomorrow," Chuy assured her.

"I think so, too," agreed Lucy, "but that's part of the problem."

"I don't get it."

"Well, ..." Lucy's voice trailed off.

"Well what?" inquired Chuy.

"The thing is ... my dad... I mean, he loved when my uncle boxed, and Alvarez talked him into letting me train. You know, because I was a big gang banger."

"Yeah, ya were," Chuy teased.

"Shut up! Anyway, my dad and mom are glad I'm doing something besides school and babysitting, but they don't want me to stay in boxing. Getting them to let me actually fight—that's gonna be tough."

Chuy protested, "But Lucy, you're so good and you love it."

"Don't tell me that; tell my Dad."

"I will," said Chuy with resolve.

"Ha!" Lucy scoffed, as they approached her corner, "Listen to you! Until a couple of weeks ago I didn't know if you could talk at all. Now you're gonna tell everybody what's up, right?"

Chuy smiled. "Well I would, for you, if you thought that would help."

Lucy shook her head, "No, this is my job. Besides, I'm not even ready. I need to spar first, but you're very sweet, Jesus." With that, she leaned over and kissed him on the cheek, then rode off.

"See you tomorrow," she hollered over her shoulder.

Chuy stood, frozen in place from what had just happened. He was going to yell goodbye, but she was already gone.

He jumped on his bike and pedaled as hard as he could up the street, feeling like his heart was a geyser ready to explode. When he got home he completed his chores and homework, the last task being to set out his workout clothes and school clothes for the next day. Later that night when Chuy was lying in bed, the warm feeling from that one little kiss still ran through him. He smiled as he replayed that moment in his head, savoring the memory of Lucy's warm lips on his cheek. It sure was better than a straight right from Jake the Snake, he grinned to himself as he drifted off to sleep.

The next day, Nancy and Lucy decided to eat in the school cafeteria. Spending time in the morning with Chuy and now lunch with Nancy made for a nice day with a little less drudgery and a lot more fun. Now that gangs, tension and fighting were behind her she could simply enjoy her day. There was a noticeable change in the school as well. There were still kids that identified with the gangs, but they were not the 'cool, badass' kids anymore. With Armani and other gang leaders gone, the school moved along like an old slow river, flowing surely and steadily, no longer menacing, or dangerous. The gangs had been discarded like trash along it's shores. They were not thought of as bad; they were not thought of as cool; they were simply not thought of at all. Students had become more concerned with their own lives: grades, sports, part-time jobs, status, friends and music claimed their attention and energy. Accumulating friends, status, or drugs through gang affiliation became passé, thus a slow, but certain death for them at Layden High School. Two obvious examples of the change sat together talking in the cafeteria.

"Hey, Luc, have you ever been a Student of the Month?" Nancy asked, out of the blue.

"Yep," answered Lucy. "What about you?"

"Well, Ms. Foss just nominated me for my fashion design class."

"Fashion design?" Lucy almost shouted, though her voice just blended into the din of the cafeteria. "Ha! All you ever wear are jeans and hoodies."

"I design, *cabrona*. That doesn't make me a model. What? You want me to walk around high school like a fashion show?"

"Sorry, *mi hija*, I just didn't expect it."

"What you think—I'm only good in gym class and lunch?"

"Okay, guurrrl, my bad! Congrats! How come I haven't seen any of your designs?"

"You never asked," replied Nancy, throwing a french fry at her best friend. Now tell me, what do you gotta do for Student of the Month?"

Lucy shrugged. "Nothing, they have breakfast for you and your parents. You stand up when Ms. Foss calls your name. She will say something nice about you. That's it. Alvarez will be there."

As if he had heard his name Alvarez suddenly appeared, strolling through the cafeteria, talking to students, and stealing French fries.

"Hey, Alvarez!" Lucy stood up and motioned him over to the table.

"What up girls?" greeted Alvarez, "You got some fries you want me to test for you, or need some tips?" Alvarez began shadow boxing a la Muhammad Ali, complete with the Ali shuffle.

"What the...?" The girls laughed in unison. "Could you just stop!"

Alvarez reluctantly stopped the show.

"Nancy got Student of the Month for fashion," Lucy announced.

"Cool!" Alvarez offered a high five to Nancy. "I'll see you at the breakfast this Thursday."

"Did you nominate a student?" asked Nancy.

"Not this month."

"Well, do you run the program or something?" Nancy wore a puzzled look.

Lucy turned to her friend to explain. "Nothing like that; Alvarez has first period off and comes for the free breakfast and to cry."

"And I'm starting already," Alvarez added, dabbing a napkin to his eye.

"Oh he's playing now," said Lucy, "but you'll see!"

Alvarez tried his best to make an angelic face, "I'm considered one of the highlights of the program. I bring the emotion."

"Yeah, and you eat for free," quipped Nancy.

With that, the bell rang, and students scrambled for the doors.

"Throw away your garbage!" Alvarez's voice bellowed through the room. More than a few tables were still littered with leftover debris.

"Ugh," groaned Alvarez to the girls. "Is this why I got my Master's degree? To clean up after you lazy little sons a ... Hey! How 'bout some help?"

"Bye, bye," the girls cackled, as they ran toward the doors.

"Uggggghhhh!" Alvarez responded even louder, "Oh! And congratulations, Nancy!"

The girls waved goodbye and disappeared down the hall to complete their afternoon classes.

Lucy asked, "Hey, since you are so good at design, did you ever think about designing prom dresses?"

Nancy grinned. "You going to prom, gurrrl?"

"I'm just asking, and how about you? You'll need a dress when you ask Ulises."

"Shut up," protested Nancy.

"I'm just saying,'" Lucy smiled as they parted ways.

Nancy turned toward the home ec wing, stopping to admire the prom dress display that she had helped set up. She took a minute to think of the events that had taken place over the last month. *Hummm,* she thought almost out loud, *friends with Lucy again, boxing, Ulises, Student of the*

Month. I guess you never know. She smiled at the reflection of herself in the mirrored display case. *I guess you never know.*

Practice throughout the week saw everyone in a good place. The team and Chuy had had an excellent showing at the Morris' fights. Lucy and Nancy were well into the routine of practicing to perfect every boxing skill. And Billy? Well…Billy practiced being Billy. Mostly he was working his jaw muscle, but he, too, was part of the boxing family.

"Billy Boy, it's too bad they don't give a trophy for jaw flappin' cause you would be the champ!" Sultan's big voice resounded through the gym. "I keep sayin' boy, you the number one on the all-talkin' team."

Billy paused his very mild workout to flex his scrawny biceps and shout out, "Yeaaah boyyyy!" To which Sultan simply shook his head.

Other than Billy the team was working hard. Various sounds from the gym echoed through the old building, punctuated by the buzz of the timer, only to be replaced by the quieter sound of heavy breathing. One minute of rest, then the pops, taps, thuds, and grunts would echo again. Such was the refrain that played throughout the busy hours.

"Hey, Rockem, Sockem," Sultan shouted out between rounds one day in the middle of the week.

Lucy hustled over to face the gruff old coach.

"You been here plenty of time now, girl. Hell, I think you could have sparred the first week you were here! So, you got your mouthpiece, let's hit some mitts first, then I think it's time for you to mix it up a bit."

Without any questions, Lucy quickly jumped into the ring. She was finally going to spar! As she quickly put on the boxing gloves the feeling that she was doing something wrong began to eat at her mind. Her parents had supported her in boxing as an after-school activity and a way to get in shape. She knew, however, that her father did not want her to actually get in the ring and fight. He had never said that; he didn't have to. Lucy knew what her father and mother wanted, and she surely knew what they did not want. They had surprised her by letting her get involved in boxing in the first place, but that had more to do with the fight in the cafeteria and the guilt they had felt over Lucy's necessary supervision of her little sisters. Her dad would not want her in the ring for any other reason than to hit gloves that did not hit back. Sparring would be out of the question.

She pushed those thoughts out of her head. She needed to focus on the task at hand. She concentrated only on the mitts, moving and striking expertly as if she had been doing it her whole life, as to some extent she had.

Jabs, double jabs, hooks, double hooks, right and left, ducking Sultan's swinging hand and answering back almost too quickly for the old coach to set up a target.

"Wooey, gurl...Rockem Sockem, you are a natural."

The coach called out to Lucy's friend after he caught his breath, "Nancy girl, you gonna do some sparin?"

Nancy approached. "Na, Coach, I'm just coming for the workout; been fightin' my whole life. I would like to get in the ring and hit those mitts, though."

"Why, sure," said Sultan. "Ain't nothing wrong with that. You take a break, Rockem, while I work with your girl. Don't worry though, we'll find you somebody to spar."

Nancy put on the gloves and began to hit the mitts the old coach held for her. Sultan moved her slowly and gave pointers on her punches and stance.

Lucy watched her friend with admiration, not for her boxing skills, but for how she simply said what she wanted with no care for what anyone thought. Lucy did want to fight, but if she hadn't would she tell her coach as casually as her friend had? *If I were more like Nancy,* Lucy thought, while she shadow-boxed in the corner to keep loose, *I would tell my dad how I feel, tell him that I love boxing and I want to compete. I would ask him why he supported his brother in boxing. Ask him if it would be different if I were a boy.*

Lucy's thoughts were interrupted by Sultan who called to Juan Calderon from the ring, "Combat, you sparred yet today?"

Without answering, the lightweight came to the ring and began putting gloves on. Lucy knew he was the best fighter in the gym, and the same guy who had broken Chuy in a few weeks back. She was determined not to let that intimidate her.

"Work on the jab, Combat," Sultan instructed, "and watch out for this girl; that's Rockem Sockem right there!"

The two fighters met in the middle of the ring and Calderon immediately began popping his jab into the Everlast logo on the front of Lucy's sparring helmet. Instinctively, Lucy ducked and bobbed, avoiding the piston-like jab.

She threw a hook to his body, inducing a slight grunt from the lightweight. Calderon stepped back and grinned, happy for the competition. He was not going to take this new fighter lightly. She had skills.

Calderon used his jab and movement to keep away from the solid hooks thrown by this tough new kid. She actually caught him in the corner a couple of times, forcing Calderon to use his superior strength to tie her up. As the end of the first round approached Lucy threw a hard hook to Combat's body. He blocked it, countering with a right to Lucy's jaw. Even though he had pulled the punch, Lucy could feel its sting.

"Got to mix up your punches, and don't let that right hand drop," the veteran fighter advised through his mouthpiece.

Lucy acknowledged the advice with a nod of her head. She would remember that.

Through the next two rounds Lucy worked her punches as Calderon expertly moved around the ring, throwing almost exclusively jabs, but mixing in a right now and then to keep Lucy guessing. As the third round ended Lucy felt a mixture of satisfaction, adrenaline, and fatigue from her first sparring session. It was a good start, she judged.

Sultan echoed her feelings. "Not too bad for your first time, Rockem, but we're gonna need to find you some good sparring partners. You'll be ready for your first fight in no time!"

His words snapped Lucy back to the looming problem with her father. He would be angry if he knew she was sparring. He would never allow her to become a real fighter.

"Not many fights left until summer, then we'll get real busy." Sultan continued. "You'll have the Gloves tourney sneaking up on you before you know it. We can use us our first female champ around here. You ready for that, gurl?"

"Sure, Coach." Lucy tried to sound positive, but she was already dreading the conversation that must take place between her and her father.

As she came down from the ring, Lucy's friends met her at the bottom of the steps.

"Hey, you did great!" Nancy gave Lucy a big hug.

Billy offered her a high five. "Rockem Sockem, how ya feelin'?"

"Exhausted!" Lucy admitted, exhaling.

Chuy hugged her, even though she was wet with sweat. Her hair hung in the familiar ringlets that brushed against his face, leaving a trace of wetness and the aroma of her shampoo. He tried to act casual and hoped his face was not turning red.

Lucy put out both hands so Chuy could take off her gloves. "You get way more tired sparring than hitting the bags or doing anything else," she told him, "But I like it. I like it a lot!"

"Yeah," agreed Chuy. "Wait 'til you get your first fight. For me it was crazy; I thought my legs were gonna fall off."

Lucy's gaze jolted Chuy, as though she had landed a straight right to his chin.

Damn! this girl is pretty, he thought, averting his eyes, hoping she did not know what he was thinking. He untied the last knot in her gloves.

Lucy was too deep in worried thought to notice the effect she was having on Chuy. "Maybe I can get your advice about that. There's no way my dad is going to let me fight."

"Why not? I'm sure he knows how hard you've been working at this." He helped Lucy get her hands out of the gloves, then set them aside.

"For one thing, they think I'm just doing this to get in shape, and for another because of the fight at school."

"Yeah, but didn't your uncle fight?"

"Chuy, you know how Mexican fathers are, at least my Mexican father. He doesn't want his "little girl" in a ring, throwing punches and getting hit."

"Well, you are a delicate flower." Chuy grinned.

"Chuy!" Lucy gave him a quick punch to the shoulder.

"Ouch! Okay, you're no delicate flower," Chuy conceded, then added, "Sultan said we may not even get a chance to fight 'til summer, which would suck, but at least it would give you time to talk to your dad."

"I guess." Lucy didn't sound as though she felt any better. "It's just everything's going so well at home and school that I don't want to stir up any bad vibes by arguing with him."

The two gathered their backpacks and walked down the steps to their bikes. On the leisurely ride home they talked and laughed, then as they approached Lucy's street her tone became more serious once again.

"You know, Chuy, when I was with Armani I always felt like I was leading a secret life. I took care of school and my sisters, but I would sneak out and hang out on the streets. It's not like I really did anything bad, and at first I thought it was cool—thought I was cool. You know." she said, somewhat embarrassed at her own admission. "I played the badass, but as time went on I just felt stupid, and kind of...you know... trapped. And now, boxing and being with Nancy again, and this freedom and getting to know you, this has been the best. I don't want to hide things from my family anymore. I'm proud of me, of every part of me. I want them to be proud, too. And I want to be a real fighter. Really spar and fight, you know—like you."

"Hey, I've only had one fight," Chuy protested modestly.

"Yeah, but you've at least started, and it's not something you have to hide."

Chuy thought for a minute, then responded. "You know, Luc, we have time until the next fight. I know your mom and dad are getting home earlier to see you and your sisters a lot more. They have to know how serious you are about boxing. I mean, you look great!" Chuy paused; a bit embarrassed by what he had just said. "I mean...you know what I mean; you've been taking good care of your sisters. Your dad knows that. Think about it, a year ago if someone told you that your dad would let you go to a boxing gym every day after school, what would you have said?"

"I'd have told 'em they were crazy," Lucy admitted.

"You don't have to deal with this today and worrying never helps. Enjoy your first sparring session. Enjoy the good times at home, and the good times at school. Things will work themselves out. Lucy, you aren't doing anything wrong," Chuy reminded her.

"Okay, Jesus!" Lucy sighed. "I will take your advice. But you forgot one thing I'm really enjoying."

"What's that?" asked Chuy.

"I really enjoy spending time with you." With that Lucy put both hands on Chuy's face and looked up into his eyes. He lowered his lips to meet hers.

The evening was chilly, but the two felt only warmth as they shared their first real kiss on the corner of Diversey and 25th. Lucy slowly dropped her hands from Chuy's face to the handlebars of her bike and stepped on the pedals. She was off!

"Ride safe!" she shouted, speeding down the street. Chuy stood for a second, still reeling from the kiss.

"Yeah, yeah, ride…safe," he managed to croak out.

"LeDesma. You're a dork!" Lucy teased over her shoulder. She turned the corner and disappeared into the spring night.

Chuy shook his head and smiled at his own awkwardness. "Yes, LeDesma, you are a dork," he said out loud. He jumped back on his bike and covered the three blocks to his house in record time. Thoughts of Lucy and the kiss kept him company all the way.

As school slowly, but steadily moved to its yearly conclusion, Spring slowly, but steadily, warmed the earth. The sun would peek out from the clouds only to soon disappear, resulting in more bitter wind and gloomy skies. While Chuy, Lucy, and their classmates trudged through the final days, they were motivated by routine, the calendar and friendship, all of which warmed them as much as the sporadic, sunny days.

Armani, on the other hand, was falling deeper into dark gang life. Loyalty to his younger brother and dedication to his own habitual ways kept him waking in the morning and getting Joey off to school, but now he would immediately walk back home and go back to bed. The house was showing signs of neglect, deteriorating like Armani's spirit. The first few weeks after his suspension Armani had tried to hold on to as much of his old life as he could. He had called and texted Lucy several times a day, but she had never responded.

For a while he had stuck to his old cleaning habit, and didn't go back to bed, even though he had nothing else to do but watch TV. He had even thought about taking the little bus to the other school, but midway through the second week it stopped coming; the driver had done his duty. Before too long, Armani's grip on his old life had withered away. He began to smoke weed and drink with his brothers. He hung out on the streets and sold pot and other drugs like a good soldier. All of his time was spent with his brothers and other members of the Kings.

Now on a cold, but sunny day Armani was hanging outside Oscar's Deli and Convenience Store. A few guys from school had skipped out early to hang with him, and Armani had rewarded them with joints and beers.

They all smoked and drank in Armani's brother's car, which was parked near the back of the store. They took quick hits off the joints and forty-ounce bottles, so as not to get caught by the cops, or hassled by Oscar, if he should come out back to throw out trash. It didn't take long to catch a quick buzz, and two of the younger guys were sent in to buy sandwiches and sodas. The sandwiches were not only excellent tasting, especially after smoking weed, but the purchase kept old Oscar off their backs. As long as they spent money and were relatively quiet, they could hang around without getting hassled for loitering. Beer, weed and a sunny afternoon made the small group of gangbangers feel invincible.

School let out and a steady stream of kids headed to Oscar's for their afternoon junk food. A few more of Armani's wannabe buddies showed up and joined the guys in the car, hoping there was still some smoke and beer left, but they were too late. The late-comers didn't mind that nothing was left; at that point it was more about appearance, trying to impress a few girls that had come along. Now there was a group of eight, grown braver and bolder with its increased number. Armani knew it was only a matter of time until old Oscar came out to shoo them away, the whole thing possibly ending with a phone call to the cops. Too many now to sit in the car, the group migrated to the street corner.

"Go clean the car, *cabron*, before the cops come," Armani ordered one of the newcomers. "And make sure you get rid of those little-ass roaches."

The younger boy responded immediately, taking the keys and jogging toward the car.

Armani was preparing to take off before the cops could arrive when two small freshman boys walked out of the store, holding several bags of hot Cheetos and two cans of Coke. Not paying any attention, the boys walked right into the group of gang bangers.

"Hey! Check it out, these two *vatos* brought us snacks," hissed one of Armani's boys, nudging the guy next to him.

The two young boys (one Hispanic, one blonde) had turned the corner smiling and laughing, but now their faces reflected pure fear.

"Good deal, I got the munchies, homes!" announced Jorge, a heavy-set teen, sporting the beginnings of a mustache.

Two of the other gang bangers snatched the chips from the frightened boys.

"Hey, what the hell's wrong with you?" Armani grabbed one of the bags and threw it back to the scared freshmen. He took a drag from his cigarette. "Get lost, ya little punks!" He waved the two off as he exhaled a cloud of smoke.

The two boys sprinted away while the gang laughed and broke into the stolen bags.

Armani just shook his head, "What real bad assess you guys are."

"Hey, come on, *jefe*, we're just having a little fun," protested Julio, one of the few wannabe's brave enough to speak up.

Armani didn't answer. He took another drag from his smoke as he watched the two young boys hustling down the street. When they were at what they judged to be a safe distance, they foolishly began yelling curse words and throwing up Cobra gang signs. Armani dropped his smoke and ran after them, his whole group following closely. Armani motioned the group to head on down the street, but he veered off through the backyards of the row houses and into the alley.

The two Cobra wannabe's turned the corner and shot down the street, with a group of seven angry boys well behind, but not giving up. They had not counted on Armani taking a shortcut. He had sprinted through the alley, knowing he could cut off the two. The boys were laughing at their daring, sure of their safety when all of a sudden they were facing Armani, who had sprung from the alley and now loomed menacingly in their path. They halted, frozen by terror as they faced the high school leader of the Kings, the most dangerous guy around, whose brothers were actual killers. Armani sneered, observing their fear. They looked like babies, standing there clutching their cans of soda. Although they were freshmen at Layden, they looked younger than his little brother. One of the boys began to cry. Armani grabbed them both by their collars.

He growled out between clenched teeth, "Never throw gang signs!"

The boys looked up. Tears streamed down the faces of both.

"YOU HEAR ME?"

The boys nodded their heads vigorously. They could not speak, but pathetic, indecipherable whimpers left their lips.

"That shit will get you killed; you get me?"

Pleading, tear-filled eyes looked up at Armani, but they were still unable to speak.

Armani sighed. "Get outta here!" He released them.

Still whimpering, they sprinted away before he changed his mind.

Armani lit up another cigarette and strolled up the street to meet his boys. The gang slowed as he approached them. All of them were breathing hard, some with hands on hips, some with hands on knees. Two were laying in the grass, panting like overheated dogs.

Armani couldn't help but smile. "Bad asses! You losers got beat up by the air," he sneered as he continued past them.

"Ain't we gonna kick their little asses?" Julio winced trying to catch his breath.

"I'm outta here," Armani called out over his shoulder. He continued up the street alone, back to the car, feeling like he was going nowhere.

CHAPTER 19

Thursday rolled around and Chuy and Billy made their daily walk to room 250, having to stop to talk to each of Wolfy's kids before they could reach the classroom door. They had grown to love all of Coach Wolf's students, and the attention and adulation they received in return made them feel like celebrities.

"The Three Amigos," Billy shouted out even before turning the corner, expecting to see only Alvarez, Wolfy and Kelly.

This morning, however, they had a couple of visitors. Lucy and Nancy stood in front of Coach Wolf's desk. The talking stopped as the boys were mesmerized into silence at the sight of the two young ladies in business attire. Lucy wore a navy pantsuit with black heels, her hair pulled back to reveal tiny stud earrings. Nancy was in a blue knee-length skirt with a pressed white blouse, her long black hair in a ponytail that reached halfway down her back. The conference at the desk halted momentarily because of the puzzled looks on Billy's and Chuy's faces. Ms. Kelly decided to break the silence.

"What ya lookin' at, fellas?" she asked, over the background giggles coming from the two girls.

"We are going to the Student of the Month breakfast," Nancy answered the unasked question from the boys. "My parents can't make it, so Lucy is coming with me. We came to get Alvarez to join us for his monthly free breakfast and crying session."

"I don't cry at *every* Student of the Month," Alvarez protested.

"Must be nice—having first period off. I like to cry." Wolfy did a fake whimper, grabbing a tissue from a box on his desk.

"Yeah," Ms. Kelly chimed in, "and I like to eat!"

"It's because I work so hard in the afternoon, unlike you bums, that they have to give me the morning off," Alvarez replied.

"I knew that's why you are all dressed up," Billy interjected. "It's just that Chuy said Nancy would never wear a dress."

"It's a skirt, you idiot." Nancy punctuated her words by giving Billy a punch on the shoulder as she headed out the door.

"Damn, girl, be more ladylike! See you can dress them up, but…" Billy's voice trailed off as Nancy reloaded another punch. He backed up a step, with hands up in mock surrender. "Okay, okay, just joking. You look great; tnice skirt!"

Chuy remained motionless at the door, watching as Lucy followed her friend. She passed by him with a smile. He managed an awkward, "You look pretty."

He noticed Billy's goofy grin and punched him in the same shoulder that Nancy had attacked.

"Owwwh!! What was that for?" Billy rubbed his shoulder, exaggerating his pain with a grimace. "I won't be able to be at practice because of you guys," he whined.

"That's such a shame," said Nancy, her voice full of fake sympathy. "The gym will finally be quiet without all your yappin'. You coming, Alvarez? It's eat and cry time," she reminded him.

Alvarez had been unusually silent as he observed the friendly squabble between the students. The change in these kids over the last nine weeks had been nothing short of amazing, and he said a silent thanks to the Universe for letting him be a part of all this—the school, these kids, his friends and colleagues, and his job. A feeling of gratitude washed over him (as it often had lately) but even though he tried, he couldn't keep the feelings bottled up. His best friend, and veteran teacher, had grown used to Alvarez and his heart-on-his-sleeve emotions. Wolf sighed and picked up the square tissue box from the corner of his desk and tossed it to Alvarez. "Here, looks like you need this already."

Students and teachers alike burst into laughter at the expense of the emotional teacher.

"Keep it, Wolfy; they always have a box down there for me."

The room vibrated with laughter and exaggerated groaning as the students joined in to tease Alvarez mercilessly.

"Alright girls let's get going! Student of the Month and...eggs, coffee, cry," Alvarez started to chant as he hustled out with the girls.

"Eggs, coffee, cry! Eggs, coffee, cry!"

Billy led Wolfy's kids in the chant which followed the sappy teacher and the two smartly dressed young ladies.

"Eggs, coffee, cry!" They sang, "Eggs, coffee, cry!"

Practice that day began like any other, but Sultan had given Lucy and Chuy a hint when they first entered the building that some surprise was waiting for them.

"Let's work hard, you two; I've got some good things up my sleeve for you newbies. Today will be fun, but tomorrow, Wooooooo-eeeee!"

Lucy and Chuy looked at each other apprehensively, then the buzzer sounded and they began their rope work. Sultan called the two over after observing that the rest of the team had hit their stations and were all busily working out.

"Glove up you two" ordered Big Ces, standing next to the coach. He had missed a few days, due to his work schedule and was eager to get back to his volunteer coaching duties. He quickly got gloves and headgear on both fighters. Chuy and Lucy stood outside the ring, each looking around for their competition. They finally looked at each other with the situation dawning on them at the same moment.

"That's right," Sultan grinned. "You two love birds gonna go at it. Now don't worry, I'm gonna teach today; save the battlin' til ya married a couple years."

"Oh, snap!" Cesar whooped.

"Come on, Coach!" Both fighters protested through their mouthpieces.

"In the ring," Sultan continued. "This is called controlled sparring. You can work this a couple times a week; it's more effective than the mitts."

The fighters slipped through the ropes, followed by big Ces, who climbed onto the apron and stood in the blue corner. Sultan instructed from his tall stool outside the ring.

"Okay, one fighter on the offense, one on the defense. We're gonna throw all body punches, five quick shots—start out easy, but let 'em pop. After five shots, I'll call 'switch.' Remember, keep 'em to the body! Block with the elbows tight to your body, but keep those hands up!" When Sultan had finished with the instructions he pointed to Cesar.

Cesar set the clock. "Time!" he shouted.

The fighters met in the middle of the ring.

"Chuy—offense!" Sultan barked out.

Chuy instinctively pulled his punches, throwing far too lightly at his female counterpart.

Sultan noticed and corrected him. "Okay, boy, this girl ain't no cupcake. Put a little pop in those punches." Chuy threw a straight right and left, and then stepped in with a left, right, left hook. Lucy kept her arms tight to her body, moving with each punch to block Chuy's shots.

"SWITCH!" roared Sultan.

Lucy complied with a ferocious double hook that made a loud pop when it connected with Chuy's shoulder.

"Whoooaaaa, guurrl! Pull it back, Rockem Sockem. We just gettin' in work now, killer."

"Sorry," Lucy apologized through her mouthpiece.

Before Chuy could respond, Sultan yelled out "Switch," and Chuy took his turn once more.

Soon the "Switch" was back to Lucy who continued her offense with stinging blows. Chuy rolled his body away from the punches to minimize the power behind them.

"She teachin' ya somethin', LeDesma," Sultan howled.

"Yeah, boy! Chuy, good job trying to move away from those shots," Big Ces added.

Chuy was grateful when the bell gave him a break from Lucy's powerful hooks.

"Ya'll gettin' the feel of this?" Sultan inquired.

Both fighters nodded.

"Good! Now, learn somethin' from each other. Lucy, you see how he bends his knees, but keeps the shoulders high when he throws those straight lefts and rights to the solar plexus? Right here!" Sultan pointed to the middle of his chest.

Lucy signaled her understanding.

"And Jesus, you see Lucy doublin' up on them hooks. You need to do the same, you dig?"

Chuy acknowledged his understanding as well.

"Time!" yelled Big Cesar. "Chuy, up first!"

Once again the fighters met in the middle. Chuy immediately threw a double-right hook to Lucy's shoulder, throwing her off balance.

"Oh, sorry," he said without thinking.

Sultan wagged a finger at him. "Don't be sorry, son. That's what it's supposed to look like."

Lucy gave Chuy a playful jab to the head and motioned with her hands to keep it coming.

Chuy took her at her word, throwing a straight left-right, then he took a quick step left and threw a smooth double hook.

"Now ya cookin'!" yelled Sultan. "Switch."

Lucy immediately bent at the knees and threw a straight left-right combination between Chuy's elbows, landing both shots sharply into his stomach. Without a pause she continued with a left double hook and a wicked right hook to the shoulder that knocked Chuy off balance.

"Ahh, sorry," she said sarcastically, her grin showing the white of her mouthpiece.

Both coaches roared with appreciation.

In his excitement Sultan jumped up from his stool. "Yeahhh, Gurl! That's what I'm talking about!"

Chuy and Lucy continued, giving the coaches a smooth, steady, impressive sparring session, falling in sync with five or six punches, then switching attackers without a prompt. By the fourth round the whole gym had begun to take notice. Alvarez, Billy and Nancy had even left their stations to stand near the ring to watch the fluid dance taking place in the ring.

When the bell rang after five rounds of controlled sparring the spectators erupted into applause and whistles. Unaware that they were entertaining all the other athletes, Chuy and Lucy looked out in surprise at the sea of approval surrounding them.

Sultan cut the celebration short with his booming voice. "Okay y'all, show's over! Anybody else gonna get some work done around here? This ain't the Wide World of Sports." Although his words were harsh, the delighted look on his face gave a different message.

Billy and Nancy returned to the speed bags. Alvarez hastened to the heavy bags where he had left some of the younger kids waiting, but not before he let out a whistle and called out, "Well done, you two! Better watch it, you're gonna turn yourselves into real fighters!"

The tired duo stood in the blue corner while Big Ces removed their gloves and headgear. They were still breathing hard and drenched in sweat.

Sultan met the fighters in the ring. "Now remember, that's called controlled sparring. Y'all did it just right. Next time we can add a jab." He tapped the Everlast insignia on Chuy's headgear. "Ya just gonna aim for right here. That means we go hard to the body, pop the jab, but save the big shots for the fight. Remember—this is important—if you ever hurt a guy sparrin', y'all pull back. You get me?"

Both fighters nodded.

Sultan continued, "Now that we got the gear off, we got one more thing we gonna work on here in the ring. A lot of fatigue during a fight comes from when you wrestlin' around in there. I'm gonna show you two a way to get them legs stronger. Okay, lean forward. Now, put your head on the other one's shoulder."

The novice fighters looked at each other hesitantly.

"Come on now; you just whipped each other for five rounds, this here's the easy part." Sultan pushed them together and gave instructions. "Head on a shoulder, both hands up, grab the back of the head, that's right; both hands now, lean forward just like you see those pro wrestlers do on TV. Lucy, you push Chuy forward. Chuy, you give ground, but make her work for it."

The two formed an upside down "V" as Lucy pushed forward and her body became almost parallel with the mat. Chuy gave ground until his back was against the rope.

"Now it's your turn, Chuy."

Lucy did her best to offer resistance while Chuy pushed her back to the ropes.

"That's the way! Back and forth now," Sultan encouraged. "Don't make it easy on 'em. Now, Lucy, push to your left and Chuy, you push to the right. You see what we're doin?" Give me a couple more rounds," Sultan ordered, climbing out of the ring. "I gotta see what else is goin' on in this place—can't spend all day with you two. Come on, Ces, you got young ones to work with."

The coaches cleared the ring area and Chuy and Lucy were left alone in the ring to complete their task. When the second round began Chuy couldn't help but get lost in Lucy's thick ringlets of hair. He wondered how it could still smell like shampoo after all this sweat and work. A couple of not-so-gentle pushes from her got him back on track. They took turns pushing and resisting without conversation.

"I thought we would have a few dates before we got this close," Lucy confided between heavy breaths after the session ended.

They laughed together, feeling spent and happy.

"This was a good practice; thanks," Chuy remarked.

Lucy responded with a smile and a high five.

"Oh, Sultan's got more for you two tomorrow," Big Ces shouted out, making his way back toward the ring, picking up gear from the practice along the way.

"What's that?" Lucy shouted back.

"You'll see," Sultan interjected, slowly walking back to his stool. "Yeah! Yeah! You two just gettin' started! See you tomorrow!"

It didn't take long to figure out Sultan's surprise when Chuy and Lucy entered the gym on Friday afternoon. On the near wall, not too far past the doorway, a group of five fighters, both boys and girls, were taking off sweatshirts and putting on wraps. An unfamiliar coach stood next to Sultan's stool, talking, and laughing with the old coach. Since there were few boxing competitions in the spring, Sultan had apparently brought the fight to them.

Practice started as always with fifteen minutes of jump rope, with the visiting fighters taking over the prime spot in front of the mirror. Lucy and Chuy jumped side by side into a spot slightly off to the right. They scanned the mirror to size up their competition but tried not to be too obvious about it. At the opposite end of the line were a young man and woman older than Chuy and Lucy, but appearing to be about the same weight, maybe slightly heavier. The mystery of who they were was revealed minutes later when Sultan called his pair over to where he and Big Ces were conferring in the blue corner. Alvarez stayed in the red corner to help the visiting coach and fighters with headgear and gloves.

Sultan yelled out so all the participants and coaches could hear. "My guys, I got you some experienced fighters here. You're gonna make them work. Those two you were lookin' at are two of the best in the state, Jamal Willard and Shantel Burns. They're top division, and they're both up a weight class from y'all, but that don't make no never-mind, especially for sparrin'." Sultan turned to the red corner. "Coach McSherry, like I told ya, my kids are green, but they're pretty tough. Keep 'em off the canvas, we'll be alright."

McSherry nodded. "Who we startin' with?"

"Let's start with the fellas. We'll be switchin' every round ladies, so be ready."

With that Lucy and the visiting fighter, a tall, thin African-American woman with sinewy long arms, stepped out to the ring apron. They already had gloves and headgear on, mouthpieces in. They were ready to go the first round without hesitation.

Chuy's opponent was also African-American. He was light-skinned, and heavily-muscled, slightly shorter than Chuy, but at least ten pounds heavier. He stood in the red corner and the two faced each other until the bell sounded.

The fighters touched gloves in the middle of the ring and immediately Chuy's opponent began firing jabs. The speed and direction of the jabs caught Chuy by surprise. He instinctively moved to his right. Pow! He was caught by a straight left that shocked his system. The older fighter stepped back, giving Chuy time to gather his bearings. Chuy heard two things: a ringing in his ears, and the laughter of his coach. This was not starting out well.

"He's a southpaw, Chuy. Ya gotta move to your left, away from his power."

Sultan had set him up with a bigger, stronger, more experienced fighter, who was also a left hander! He had to move in a different direction than he was used to, away from his opponent's punishing left arm.

This is going to be a long afternoon, thought Chuy. It certainly turned into a long round. The younger fighter looked uncomfortable and out-classed. Everyone could see it. And worse, Chuy knew they could feel it.

"Go light this round, Jamal," Coach McSherry shouted from his corner, making Chuy feel even worse. He was taking a beating, both physically and mentally.

"You got to throw punches, Chuy, or Jamal came here for nothin,'" Sultan yelled, adding insult to injury.

Near the end of the round Chuy threw two straight rights that caught Jamal on the insignia of the headgear. He nodded to Chuy, happy to finally get some fight out of the kid.

With the sound of the bell, Chuy gratefully retreated to the corner as Lucy slipped in between the ropes to face her opponent. Chuy passed her, so embarrassed that he couldn't meet her eyes.

Alvarez was waiting for him at the base of the ring. "Come on. Step down here."

Chuy looked back to see Lucy and her opponent in the middle of the ring, touching gloves.

"Nah, Jesus, no time for watching; we got three minutes to get you right. Stop thinking and start moving!" Alvarez, a southpaw himself, took Chuy to the side.

He had seen the problem, and if Chuy did not get some coaching the whole session would be a waste. It was going to seem unnatural for Chuy, but now he needed to move smoothly to his left, utilize his jab and step hard with the left-right combination. Chuy was dying to watch Lucy, but that would have to wait for another time. His honor was on the line, increasing his attention and determination to represent the gym to the fullest.

Unfortunately for Chuy he was missing a good battle. The girls had touched gloves, then stepped back and began throwing punches. They came in a barrage, with neither fighter giving an inch. In Lucy's familiar style she ducked and bobbed, unleashing a body attack on her taller, slimmer opponent. For her part, the veteran shot back lightning-quick jabs and straight rights, moving around the ring, never allowing her back to reach the ropes. Lucy ducked and slipped, but several punches caught her flush; however, they failed to slow her forward movement, or her punches to the other woman's arms and body.

"Whooa, whoa!" Came the bellowing voice of Sultan, stopping both fighters for a moment. "This ain't the Olympic trials, ladies! Y'all need to take it easy." Both girls nodded to Sultan as if they agreed, then faced each other and resumed throwing punches, not missing a beat.

"Well," Sultan shrugged to the visiting coach, "I guess we got Ali-Frazier all over again."

True enough, as in the classic heavyweight battles, the determined young boxers moved at a furious pace, Lucy—taking the role of Smolin' Joe Frazier—ducking, bobbing, and landing right hooks over the relentless, punishing jabs coming at her, to connect with the chin of the veteran. Shantel Burns had the long, snapping jab and the graceful footwork of Muhammad Ali, as she danced away from Lucy, flicking the jab, but getting caught with vicious—almost jumping—right hooks to her jaw by her tough-as-nails opponent. After three minutes of non-stop action they went to opposing corners, both breathing heavily and grateful for the extra-long break. Chuy stepped back into the ring for his second round and Alvarez opened the ropes for Lucy, hitting her with water. When she reached the stool he patted her approvingly on the shoulder, and they turned their attention to the ring.

Alvarez called out, "Chuy! Remember: move, don't think, step hard, throw the right hook to head and body, then come back with the left-right."

Chuy raised a gloved fist to signify he understood the plan.

He turned to Lucy. "Now you! Let me show ya how to cut off the ring so you can catch this kid in a corner."

The bell rang and Chuy and Jamal touched gloves for the second time. Jamal came out expecting an easy round and was surprised by a left jab, then a hook, followed by a straight right, all landing with loud pops.

"Woooo, boy!" his coach hollered. "Jamal, I knew I brought you here for a reason!"

"Okay...alright," Jamal muttered to Chuy, "let's do this, youngblood."

Jamal threw a lightning quick jab. Chuy blocked and answered with a jab of his own, and the two fighters went to work. Jamal was bigger and stronger, but with every minute Chuy gained confidence. His double jab-straight-hand-right combination landed successfully. Then he mixed it up with body shots, keeping his experienced opponent off guard. Jamal may have been an excellent fighter, but Chuy counted on his own will and conditioning to give the veteran a run. As the round wore on Chuy grew even stronger and more confident. If not winning the fight, at least it felt like he belonged in the same ring.

Lucy and Shantel's next round, on the other hand, continued to be an all-out battle. Lucy had dealt with everything the stylish, experienced champ could dish out and was giving back equal measure. The gym was eerily silent as everyone, including all the coaches, watched the two face-off for the final round. The ring was surrounded by other fighters, including Jesus and Jamal—now spectators—as the bell rang and the two young women moved together, both hands out to touch both gloves of the opponent, the ultimate sign of respect. Back in their stances, the battle that had gone from sparring to an all-out fight commenced. Not coaches, not anyone on Earth was going to stop these two combatants from seeing who was the superior fighter. Everyone in the gym knew they were witness to a memorable show.

The girls began somewhat slowly, this time feeling each other out. Lucy was bobbing and moving left, well outside the reach of the more experienced fighter. Shantel danced, pawing the left jab in the air. Both were looking for openings before engaging another sign of respect for the speed and power of each opponent. It was Lucy who stepped in first, catching a snapping jab to her forehead, but still managing to deliver a sharp hook, though it was blocked by Shantel's arm. The thud it created upon landing was a testament to its power. The silence in the gym was broken by the blow, as if a dam had burst. The fight was on!

Shantel threw a double hook; Lucy ducked the first, but ate the second blow, which, though powerful, failed to slow the tough novice. She answered with a double-left hook to Shantel's body, then a left hook to her head, sending her reeling backward. Lucy was on the hunt and the experienced fighter was answering back with jabs but was unable to land a solid right.

"Punches in bunches!" called out Big Ces. "Come back with the right."

"Cut off the ring like I showed you, Lucy! Get her in the corner!" Alvarez instructed.

The coaches continued to shout out advice over the cheers from the small crowd. Lucy may, or may not, have heard the instructions, but she did "cut off" the ring by stepping hard left, leaving Shantel no path of escape, and finding herself caught in the red corner. Lucy didn't give up her advantage. She threw the left hook, followed by a right. The punches sent Shantel's back against the ropes. The crowd roared. Though she was rocked by the blow, Shantel was adept at handling a good shot. She instinctively bounced off the ropes, using forward momentum to catch Lucy with a spectacular right hand. Lucy was dazed and took a backward step for the first time. She shook her head to clear the cobwebs. Alvarez started toward the ring, but Sultan put his hand out. "Let'em go, Coach."

The two dazed fighters took a split second to clear their heads then re-engaged. Lucy continued her vicious body attack, while Shantel replied by raining down shots, some that missed and some that landed. The pace was furious, but towards the end it was Shantel who finally seemed to slow. Lucy's body attack had taken its toll. The veteran fighter knew that the round was coming to a close and unleashed her final assault on this tough, new kid. With a crafty veteran move, she faked toward Lucy's right, tucking her chin into her shoulder to avoid the right hook she knew was coming. She put her jab hand behind Lucy's head and pulled down, putting Lucy in a bear hug. It was the first clinch of the match between these two and it caught Lucy by total surprise. Shantel then spun her around.

Now it was Lucy who was in the corner with her back against the ropes. Shantel followed with a solid right that caught Lucy flush on the chin and snapped her head back. The blow would have stopped any other opponent, but Lucy bounced off the ropes, almost as if she were going to the floor. Instead, she stepped right, throwing one more powerful right hook to Shantel's ribs, folding her, and leaving her gasping for air. She fell into Lucy, trying for a desperate clinch as the bell sounded. The warriors remained in an embrace in the red corner as the crowd exploded in appreciative cheers for the battle they had just witnessed.

Shantel, eventually able to talk and breathe, stepped back, resting her hands on Lucy's shoulders.

"Damn, gurl! I ain't never been hit to the body like that."

Lucy touched her rapidly swelling left eye with her glove. "Well, if it makes you feel any better, I think you left me with a souvenir."

The two girls chuckled in the middle of the ring until the respective coaches entered to remove gloves and headgear.

"Hey, Big Ces," said the visiting Coach. "I thought you said your girl was a novice."

"First real sparring session," Ces confirmed.

"Damn! I think that's the best fight Shantel ever got. And that includes the gloves tournament last year. Is she lightweight?

"Yep."

Coach McSherry whistled in approval. "Okay girl, keep working and we will see you at Gloves. I say we got the lightweight and welterweight champs standing in the ring right now. What do you all think?" he shouted to the gym crowd, raising both girls' hands.

Everyone at the gym apparently agreed, judging by the resounding applause, whistles, and cheers.

Chuy was waiting at the bottom of the steps. When Lucy descended she nearly knocked him over with an unexpected bear hug. She clung to him and squeezed hard, feeling a high she had never felt before. Chuy hugged back, holding her close. He smelled her damp hair and sighed.

"You did so great," he said when she finally loosened her grip.

"You, too." She pointed to his eye.

"Hey," he observed with a grin, "looks like we've got matching shiners."

After the sparring session the two teams joined together again for a warm-down, ten minutes of jump rope and stretches. Finally fighters were unwrapping hands and gathering jackets and bags. Nancy came over to Lucy and Chuy, pulling Ulises along with her.

"What's all this about?" Ulises was drenched in sweat from his workout and looked perplexed.

Nancy began in an unusually loud voice, as though she were making an announcement. She caught the attention of the coaches and other fighters who stopped talking to listen.

"Ulises, I know you're getting really busy with work and everything..."

"And, Chuy, I know you are going with Wolfy's kids," Lucy chimed in, equally as loud.

"But...!" the girls said in unison.

"But what?" Ulises still looked puzzled.

"Maybe...!" both girls paused.

Chuy noticed that Alvarez and Billy had their phones out and pointed in his direction. Meanwhile, the girls grabbed two large poster boards that had been hidden in the corner and turned them to face the boys. The word "PROM?" in huge, glittery letters was written on both boards.

Everyone who was still milling about, including visiting coaches and fighters, hooted and hollered.

"Nah, I can't make it," teased Ulises, giving Nancy a sweaty hug.

"You better say 'yes' or I'll knock you out," Nancy teased back, over the jeers of the bystanders.

Chuy just nodded his head, appearing more shocked than if he had taken a surprise right hook. Lucy gave him his second amazing hug of the evening. It sent tingles through him.

"How in the hell did you sneak these posters in here?" Ulises inquired, still a little amazed by the girls' performance and props.

"That was easy. I went down to the car and grabbed them while you were hitting the bag; you never pay attention to anything else when you're working out." Nancy playfully pushed her boyfriend. "I didn't know these two would be battling like Rocky lll!" She pointed a thumb at the other couple.

"Yeah, that could have been bad, especially after my first round," Chuy admitted with a smirk. "Hey, now we can have matching black eyes for pictures."

Lucy giggled, but immediately took on a serious expression.

"Hey, don't worry," Chuy was concerned by Lucy's reaction. "I'm sure they will be gone by next Saturday."

"No, it's not that," she assured him. "It's just...well, I'll tell you on the ride home."

When the two rode their bikes home after that amazing practice, they agreed that it was good to be alone at last on the quiet, dark side streets.

"What was bothering you back at the gym?" Chuy asked with concern.

"Well, you know, I forgot all about this eye."

"Just put ice on it; I think it's cool as hell."

"No, Chuy, it's not how it looks. It's that my dad is gonna know that I've been sparring for real. He's not gonna be happy."

They stopped at a well-lit street corner to rest and talk.

"Oh, now I totally get it!" exclaimed Chuy. "It was okay when you were training."

"Right," said Lucy, "but I know him. It was hard enough for Alvarez to convince him to let me train. He thought I would do this for a month or two, then I was going to get involved in something else. I'm sure he would rather have me in dance class, or something like that."

"Dancing hummm...?"

"Come on, Chuy, be serious!"

"Okay, okay, you really don't think you can convince him. I mean you love it and you're really, really good at it, Lucy."

"He's a Mexican dad. How do you think your dad would feel if his little girls wanted to start boxing?"

"My dad's two girls need boxing!" Chuy declared, rolling his eyes.

"I'm serious, this whole thing sucks!"

"I know, Lucy. I know you're serious, but all you can do is talk to him. He may surprise you; I mean, his brother was a big-time boxer; he's doing really well now, right?"

"Yeah, *Tio* Roberto just got transferred to Indiana. They bought a big house and everything."

"Boxing didn't hurt him. Probably kept him out of trouble. Lucy, you have got to tell your father! Can I help?"

"Chuy, I lov..." Lucy stopped herself, embarrassed for almost saying the "L" word.

"Chuy you're the best," she began again. "Talking to you is already the best help ever."

"You can talk to me about anything, or nothing; I just like being with you."

All at once they found themselves in the middle of a kiss on the street corner of 24th, one block away from the loud and constant traffic of Mannheim. Chuy and Lucy kissed and kissed and kissed some more. Lost in time, and safe in the warmth of each other against the cool Chicago spring evening. For that moment there were no cars, no cares, no concerns, only deep warm emotions, as if they had waded into a warm pool.

Eventually, they separated slightly, and Lucy nestled into Chuy's neck. They held each other for a while until Lucy raised her hands to cup Chuy's face. Then they spent several more minutes looking deeply into each other's soul. Lucy lightly touched Chuy's swollen eye.

"Does it hurt?"

"A little," he admitted, gently touching her swollen eye in return. "Does it hurt?"

"A little."

For a few more seconds, they gazed into each other's eyes, saying more than words ever could.

Finally, Lucy broke the spell by grabbing the handle bars of her bike and jumping on.

"Okay, dork, race ya' home!"

"Please! I always win," Chuy shouted, already twenty feet behind.

They sped off into the chilly night, one of those rare, wonderful nights, the kind that they would remember for the rest of their lives.

Later, at home, Lucy slept the peaceful sleep of a young person in love. She was in love with school, in love with the way she and Nancy had become friends again, in love with her new activity-filled life (including the freedom from responsibilities at home). Although she respected the words too much to say them aloud, she loved Chuy most of all. The way he made her feel. The way they were friends first and foremost. How he was so innocent and kind. He only wanted to talk with her, hold her and give her gentle kisses. He made Lucy feel safe with no pressure to do anything else but be together. No wonder she loved the way she felt when she was with Chuy. At that moment there was no happier girl anywhere than Lucy Quinones.

CHAPTER 20

Early morning sunshine poured through her bedroom window as she lay smiling, inwardly still contemplating her amazing life, returning her thoughts to where they had been interrupted by a good night's sleep. Allowing herself to be lazy, she would begin her Saturday morning run whenever she felt like getting out of bed. She took in a deep breath of happiness and satisfaction, stretching her whole body as much as soreness would allow. Lucy twisted her body and dropped her feet to the floor, sitting up and stretching one last time. When she ran her fingers through her tangled hair, the heel of her hand brushed against her cheek bone. Like a dropped rock sending ripples through the stream, waves of pain shot through her. Automatically her eyes opened wide, the right eye at least—the left stayed slightly closed. Lucy ran to her mirror, hand on her left cheek. She let out a gasp when she saw herself.

"Nooooo!" She whispered.

When she had arrived home last night her parents had already been in their room. She had been so exhausted from all the action and excitement; she hadn't even thought about icing her eye before going to sleep. Now she cursed herself, thinking that at least she should have brought down the swelling. In truth, the swelling was not so bad, but the distinct patch of blue under her eye was unmistakable. Lucy didn't own much makeup, so in a panic she scurried down the hall to the bathroom, silently praying that it was unoccupied. She sent out an equally silent thank you upon finding the bathroom available. She applied cold water for a minute, then grabbed her mom's concealer, dabbed it heavily under the swollen eye, then headed out the door for her run. The longer she could avoid her parents, the better.

As Lucy began her run the panic started to subside, and her mind flowed back to the events of the night before. She replayed the battle with Shantel. Unconsciously she ducked and bobbed as she ran, slipping Shantel's imaginary punches and firing back solid hooks in return. She finished her run thinking of Chuy, remembering his kiss. Suddenly, she felt a slight burning in her left eye. Without thinking, she wiped it with her arm. She looked down to see the concealer smudged on the sleeve of her shirt. She scoffed at her own absentmindedness.

So much for make-up, she thought, approaching the backdoor. She peeked into the kitchen through the glass panes, unhappy to see it full of family activity. *Just what I need*, she thought glumly. *Naturally, the whole family is there.* She took a deep breath and walked inside keeping her head down. The plan was to slip into the bathroom to reapply the smudged makeup, but that didn't work out well.

"Lucy!" Journey intercepted her with a hug to her middle. "Lucy!" she squealed again.

"I'm all sweaty, *monaquita*," Lucy protested.

"EWWWWW! Yes you are!" Journey exclaimed, jumping back, but it was too late. Lucy's beeline to the bathroom had been interrupted, leaving her vulnerable to more attention.

"How many eggs do you want, *hija?*" asked Lucy's mother without turning away from the stove.

Lucy's dad was studying soccer scores and had his face buried in the paper. Her parents' inattention gave Lucy a glimmer of hope. She still had a chance.

"No thanks, Mom."

Wrong answer! Catalina Quinones wheeled around, surprised by the unexpected reply from the daughter with the usually healthy appetite.

"*Que?*" Her mother's eyes narrowed. "Lucy, what's that on your face?"

Busted!

"Nothing; I got to use the bathroom, Ma." Lucy wriggled past Journey and made a break for the bathroom, but her little sister gave her away.

"Lucy has a black eye!"

"What?" The sisters immediately surrounded Lucy. She was more trapped by these little girls than she had been during her sparring match with Shantel.

"Lucy!" Her mother exclaimed loudly.

Eduardo looked up from his paper, frowned and sprang to his feet. He put his paper down and approached his daughter, looking like a referee judging a hurt fighter. The younger girls sensed there was trouble brewing and immediately reclaimed their seats around the kitchen table. Silence reigned while he touched the swollen area of her eye lightly. Lucy tried not to wince from the pain during her father's brief examination. He did not speak but signaled Lucy to go into the living room as if he were sending her to the showers. Shoulders slumped, Lucy threw in the proverbial towel, admitting defeat to herself.

Her father joined her on the couch.

Lucy immediately began to talk, but Eduardo Quinones silenced her with the raising of a hand.

He began softly. "Lucy, when we started this program, it was because we wanted you, after all these years, to have your own time, *mi hija*. It didn't happen the right way, us being called into the school and all, but it happened. It did turn out to be a good thing."

"Dad," Lucy tried to interject, but with a look he silenced her again.

Her father paused, took a deep breath and continued. "I know this training has been good for you. I know how hard you are working. I can see the change in you. You are making yourself very strong. I see you growing stronger in your mind and your body. I see your friendship with Nancy. I see your smile in the morning after your run, the way you glow. I have never seen you so happy, not since you were a little one."

Lucy leaned forward and grabbed her father's hand. "Because I am happy! I am happy, *Papi*."

Eduardo held his daughter's hand in the tiny living room. "Lucy, *mi vida*, you know the plan was to complete the punishment time for Dean Rudy, then to find a hobby you can enjoy for the rest of your life."

Lucy stared down at her lap, not knowing what to say. Her father lifted her chin. He smiled a warm, slightly embarrassed smile. "*Mi hija*, because of you, your mother and I want to get back into shape."

When he flexed his muscles and patted his little belly, it made Lucy giggle in spite of herself.

"We bought a family pass to the YMCA, and we are going to take the girls there. We can go as a family. You can bring Nancy if you would like. They have dance classes and everything. We were going to surprise you and the girls. Let's go today and check it out."

"But Dad, it's not just boxing—it's my team and my coaches; I love it there."

Eduardo loved boxing, too. He had trained with his younger brother when he hadn't been working one of his many jobs, so he knew the draw of a boxing gym. He was aware that boxing was more lifestyle than sport, and he had seen his daughter's dedication. He couldn't help but see the physical change and mental determination she possessed. He also couldn't help the fatherly fear, the protectiveness that he was trying to suppress, but it boiled beneath the surface and now shot out like a geyser.

"God damn it, Lucy! I don't want you hurt; I don't want to see your face beaten. Do you understand me?"

He stopped, suddenly realizing that he had stood up and was now towering over her. He looked down at his daughter who met his eye in shock and sorrow.

Eduardo took a deep breath. He closed his eyes and exhaled again. The din of breakfast and the sound of the girl's laughter in the next room ceased and the little house was silent for a moment that seemed to last a lifetime.

He resumed sitting next to Lucy. Again, he lifted her chin, examining the eye once more.

"How did you get this?"

"Sparring."

"Sparring, huh? Who did you spar? What did she hit you with? How does her face look? Does she have a shiner, too?"

Lucy started telling her father about the match with Shantel. She began the story drenched in sadness and feeling hopeless, fearing that she was describing the last time she would ever see her old gym again, the place that was now her second home. However, the sadness began to evaporate as she described the first round of the battle with Shantel. Her father's interest, signified by a request for more details, began to clear the sadness like a strong summer sun clears mist. By the time she was up to the second round, she was the one on her feet, recreating her movement in the fight, and doing a pretty good impression of Shantel's dancing feet and fluid jab as well. Exuberance flowed through her and spilled over to her father, who couldn't help but take pride in her obvious aptitude for boxing, and secretly wished he had been there. When Lucy got to the end of the match, where the girls had embraced, Eduardo Quinones' wish to get Lucy into dance, or Pilates, or spin, or any other activity had disappeared along with his daughter's sadness, and he knew it. A clear TKO of all his plans for Lucy.

He pulled his beautiful daughter, who had done so much for this family, next to him and dropped an arm over her shoulders. He exhaled as if he himself had just gone five magnificent rounds with Shantel.

"Okay, okay, but today you come to the Y with me, Mom and your sisters; we don't see you much anymore. You can teach us a few things."

Lucy looked at her father with wide eyes. "Does that mean I can keep going to boxing?"

Eduardo's eyes sparkled with love. "Is there any way I could stop you?"

"Daaaadd! Thanks!" was all she could manage to say. Relief mingled with love for her father threatened to overcome her with emotion.

"Wait, *hija*," he cautioned. "No more sparring, for now. You understand? Your mother and I need to talk. She needs to understand and agree, too."

It was not a knockout, although it was a victory. For now Lucy had to be satisfied with that.

"Hey," he pulled his daughter close and whispered as if he had a juicy secret, "with all this working out, just think how hot your Mama will look in a couple of weeks! Yeee haa!" He teased.

"Daaaaaad, gross!"

"Alright, *hija*. *Mis huevos y tortillas* are getting cold."

"Ummmm, Dad," Lucy, patted her father's midsection and teased back, "Maybe you should try some oatmeal."

"Ahh, you want another black eye, huh girl." Eduardo threw a mock right hook before father and daughter joined the rest of the family and the smell of fresh tortillas in the little kitchen, in the little house, in the little suburb by the airport.

The stream of time through the school week raced over bumpy rocks and pooled for moments then raced again. This week had its own special waterfall of excitement for the whole school: the annual prom. Prom, for the seniors, was one more stone to flow over in the stream of high school life. A large, beautiful stone, the kind you put in your pocket and take home and keep for the rest of your life.

For Chuy, what had started as a "work assignment" was turning into his first date with Lucy. The thought was exciting and nerve racking at the same time. It was not how he had pictured their first date. He thought he would be taking her to a movie, or going for pizza, or just coffee and the library, but here he was in a new suit with fourteen of Wolfy's kids included as part of the date.

Now that the hour was at hand, Chuy and four of the other Best Pals junior officers waited at the door of the Rosemont Convention Center, where Layden High had taken over the largest ballroom, as they had done for years. Best Pals parents were among the first to drop off their children, who had been anxious to arrive for hours. Wolfy's kids tumbled out of cars, dressed in their Sunday best, too excited for words. Each kid looked so proud and happy that it sent a surge of emotion and pride through Chuy as well.

Missy, Lynnie, and Salim arrived together, stepping carefully out of the car, looking down at their fancy attire as if they could not believe it was really them wearing such beautiful garments. Chuy and the other officers applauded their entrance as if they were movie stars on the red carpet, while the trio walked gingerly toward them, trying not to not wrinkle their clothes. Once they reached the officers, however, the small group gushed with excitement, unable to contain themselves any longer.

"L-l-l-look, Ch-ch-chuy!" Missy exclaimed. She twirled in her dress of sapphire blue.

Lynnie, not wanting to be outdone, did the same. "Look guys! Do you like my dress? Look at me, too! My mom bought a green dress for me and we had to take it back and get the pink one!"

Salim stood with his arms out from his sides as if his suit were made of paper and his biggest fear was tearing it. "Me, too! Me, too! I got this suit for my aunt's wedding!"

The officers took a few minutes to settle the excited students down and commenced posing with them for the first of the multitude of pictures that would be taken that evening. Ms. Kelly joined the group to check attendance. In a light blue dress, she looked quite different from her usual no-nonsense school wear. Her long hair was curled up and a sparkling necklace and earrings framed her face. She rolled her eyes as the students oohed and aahed over her glamorous look.

"We've got your table set inside, everyone. You all look so wonderful!"

She motioned them to follow her, and the group paraded into the decorated hall. Some students put on noise-reducing headphones, due to the loud, thumping music which blared over the speakers, while Tavo and several others made a beeline for the dance floor.

"Whoaa!" Ms. Kelly called them back. "Let's get settled in first, plenty of time for dancing, party-people."

The Best Pals settled into the seats around their two circular tables. They took turns going to the treat table for cookies, lemonade, and other assorted snacks. Meanwhile, the hall was filling quickly; activity and noise were at a high level. Students usually dressed in T-shirts and jeans, but now looking sharp in new suits and shiny dresses, completed their obligatory photo sessions in one corner. Soon boys discarded their suit jackets and girls tossed aside their heels as they headed to the dance floor.

Chuy walked with Tavo and Paris on their snack run. He was concentrating on his chaperoning duties, and he had not seen Lucy, Nancy and Ulises come in and stand just feet from his table. Nancy was about to call out to Chuy, but Lucy stopped her. She watched a few minutes as Chuy directed the students with a gentleness that made her warm inside. It wasn't long before Ulises had had enough of standing around, so he circled the large table and tapped Chuy's shoulder. Chuy glanced up at him and he nodded his head toward the girls. Lucy and Nancy stood steps away from the table in knee-length dresses, Nancy in teal, with straps that fell off both shoulders. Lucy wore a similar style, but with only one shoulder strap. It was a bright red shade that matched her lipstick. The vision of her took Chuy's breath away. He had planned to be cool and nonchalant that evening, but the plan was out the window. He stood motionless with his mouth open. Wolfy's kids noticed the arrival of the girls and luckily came to his rescue with thunderous applause that sent the girls falling into each other, cracking up, thus breaking the spell on Chuy.

"What do you think?" Lucy directed her question to Chuy, but Missy was the one who replied.

"L-l-lucy, you l-look a-a-awesome!"

Lucy returned the compliment. "Oh, thank you, Missy, so do you."

Unable to contain themselves, the rest of Wolfy's kids got up and rushed the girls, modeling their own fancy prom wear. Chuy was grateful; it gave him time to pull himself together and salvage a tiny portion of coolness. With some effort, the officers brought the students back to their seats to finish their snacks. Chuy walked around the table, finally getting a chance to talk to his date.

"You look AMAZING!"

"Thank you, Jesus," Lucy replied formally, including a slight curtsy. "Nancy made our dresses."

"No way!" Chuy exclaimed, looking at Nancy with new respect.

"I do more than just go to the gym, you know," Nancy informed him.

"Damn! Nance, that's awesome!"

"Well, I would say Lucy fills it out pretty good, wouldn't you agree, Chuy?"

Lucy hit Nancy with a playful punch to the shoulder and the D.J. changed songs.

"Oh, this is my jam!" proclaimed Nancy, raising her hands above her head. "Who's with me?"

The whole table of Best Pals, chomping at the bit to dance, took up her invitation and flooded the dance floor. Ulises and Nancy led the way.

"Go, Nancy! Go, Nancy," Lucy whooped, hands waving in the air. She looked over at Chuy, who had not taken his eyes off her, nor fully closed his mouth since her arrival. She threw her second punch of the evening, this time a little harder.

"Hey!" protested Chuy. "This ain't the gym, take it easy!"

"Snap out of it," she ordered, smiling sweetly.

"Okay, okay!" Chuy rubbed his shoulder, embarrassed that he had been caught staring.

"How about we dance instead of spar?" he asked, still trying to recover his cool.

"Thought you'd never ask," Lucy responded with a grin.

She grabbed Chuy's arm, and he led the way as they waded into the churning pool of Wolfy's kids, who were reaping cheers and applause from the enthusiastic prom crowd for their unusual, undeniably cute dance moves. When the tempo of the music changed to a slow dance, Chuy held Lucy close and she rested her head on his shoulder, feeling content and safe. She gazed up at him and lightly touched under his eye where the remains of the black eye could still be seen.

She touched her own eye. "Make-up," she whispered. "I didn't want matching black eyes for prom."

He chuckled and held her closer, lowered his head and met her lips for one long gentle kiss.

"Lucy," he said quietly, "I think…"

Lucy nuzzled into his shoulder, and he buried his face in her beautiful ringlets, breathing in the aroma.

"Lucy, I think I…la…"

Lucy remained silent but squeezed him tight.

"I think I…like this better than trying to push you around the ring."

They held each other tight as they went into a fit of laughter.

"I think so, too," Lucy admitted and punctuated it with a quick kiss.

The two eventually strolled back to the table, where Lucy gave Chuy a hard nudge with her elbow.

"Hey, you gotta quit beating me up!" Chuy rubbed his arm yet again.

"You're not gonna believe this," Lucy pointed to the entrance.

Walking in was a very dapper Billy Karamitos, dressed in a sharp black tux. He paused in the doorway to adjust the sleeves. Holding on to his arm was the tall, pretty girl from the gym. She had the look of a model as she towered over Billy in her stilettos, but that did not stop the cocky young man from parading her around the room, ending up at the Best Pals' table.

"Hey, guys, what's shakin'?" Billy grinned like the fox in the hen house. "You may know my date…"

"Yes, Billy," Nancy interjected, "we know Crystal. Hey, Crystal, welcome!"

"This prom is much fancier than my schools," Crystal observed, looking around the poshly decorated room.

"Oh, so that answers the question," Chuy smirked.

"What question is that?"

"Why you would ever come to prom with Billy."

The table exploded into laughter at Billy's expense.

"Na, na, na, it's because she's got taste—she knows a good thing when she sees it!" Billy declared loudly above the laughter.

Crystal gracefully draped her arm over Billy's shoulder. "He *was* persistent; and besides, I think he's kind of cute, in a tough little chihuahua kind of way."

The D.J. chose that moment to play the old standard: *Celebrate Good Times*, thus rescuing Billy from further teasing. Tavo and the crew returned to the dance floor in an excited wave with Lucy, Chuy, Nancy and Ulises forming the group into a big circle, in the middle of which each of the Best Pals took turns showing off their dance moves. When his turn came Tavo and his best friend, Jose, demonstrated some breakdancing moves and the prom crowd went wild.

At the chaperone table Wolfy and Kelly whooped it up, while Alvarez looked a little teary-eyed. Wolfy nudged Kelly and nodded toward their friend.

"What?" yelled Alvarez over the music and cheering. "I …got something…"

"Got something in your eye, yeah we know," Coach Wolf finished his friend's overused excuse.

"We are *so* used to it," Kelly informed him.

Outside the limos were still pulling up to the door as more Layden students arrived fashionably late. A black late-model Chevy with tinted windows cruised the street in front of the gala. Packed inside were Armani, his brother, Xavier, and three other friends.

"Check out these losers," Armani's brother, Xavier, sneered as he lowered the passenger side window when he drove slowly past the limos. They slowed to almost a stop and began calling out insults and throwing up gang signs. Armani, slumped in the back seat, did not join in, but sat quietly observing the teenagers dressed in formal wear. It took a moment, but he recognized most of the kids from school. They all looked so different in their tuxedos and fancy dresses. For a moment he was overcome with sadness and envy, but he quickly shook his head to shake off the feelings, the way a dog shakes off water after being caught in a spring shower. The taunts from the car had gotten the attention of security outside the venue. School security officers Norris and Jefferson, led by Dean Rudy, had started walking toward the car.

"Dude, let's go," Armani said to his brother.

"Don't be scared, *hermano*; they school cops. They can't do nothin'."

"I don't need to waste my time watching these kids playin' dress up," Armani argued, trying to appear apathetic.

"Hey, Armani's afraid he's going to get detention," Xavier announced to the others. Armani shrugged and shrunk back low into the seat.

The security trio reached the back of the Chevy.

"Move the vehicle," Norris ordered, slapping his hand down on the top of the car.

At the same time, Dean Rudy's face appeared in Armani's window. Surprised, Armani's only reaction was to look away. The other boys shouted out curses, the cue for Armani's brother to hit the gas pedal. The black Chevy sped off.

Armani looked back, his eyes on Dean Rudy. Instead of the expected look of anger, or at least annoyance, unmistakable disappointment was what he read on the old dean's face.

"Shit..." Armani whispered quietly to himself, then took a hit off the joint someone had just lit. He remained slumped down, staring out into the night, watching the streetlights shooting by like white-capped waves in the ocean. He took another deep hit off the joint and tried not to feel.

CHAPTER 21

The river of time began to flow quickly after prom. Rain had come that weekend, but it was at least a warmer rain, followed by a bright, shiny Monday. After the biting cold of winter, warmth was a relative thing. With the sun shining, the first bike ride of the week was a pleasant one.

"When are you going to fight again, Chuy—I mean a real fight?" Lucy asked.

"Yeah, not sure," replied Chuy. "Big Ces says there is something in Rockford, but he says there may not be anyone for me to fight. How about you? Has your Dad changed his mind about you fighting?"

"I'm not pushing it right now, I'm just glad I get to keep coming to the gym. I'm not sure if he will ever *want* me to fight, but my life is going so well, I don't want to mess it up. I'm just gonna stay patient for now."

"So if everything is going good, does that include me?" Chuy was obviously fishing for a compliment.

"Don't be weird, Jesus." Lucy broke into a sprint on her bike and left him behind, pushing himself to catch up.

When they strolled into practice, Billy and Crystal were already there. Lucy walked up to Billy, grabbed him by the chin and inspected his face.

"What do you think you're doing?" protested Billy, pulling back, with a surprised look on his face.

"Checking to see if Crystal gave you a black eye from prom."

"Get outta here!" Billy scoffed and broke free from her.

"Actually he was a perfect gentleman," Crystal intervened.

"See," said Billy.

Crystal pretended to whisper, saying loud enough for everyone to hear. "I think I am the first girl he ever kissed, but don't tell anyone."

"Wooooo! Billy!" came the jeers from his friends.

"Please," Billy countered, never one to be outdone. "Girls have been kissing on this handsome face since I was in second grade."

"Your mama and aunties don't count," quipped Nancy, who had just walked over to join the group.

"Damn!" exclaimed Billy. "Can we start practice already? I've never wanted to start practice so bad before in my life."

Billy got his wish, and the sounds of laughter and jeers were soon replaced by swinging ropes and the light tapping of feet jumping on mats.

Practice moved at its usual pace. Chuy and Lucy had already run warm-ups and were now in the ring. Big Ces had them taking turns on the mitts and shadow boxing. Lucy was on the mitts when she sensed that something was happening in the gym. However, she kept her focus on the gloves; she would not allow whatever it was to break her concentration. She moved around the ring, slipping and bobbing, working particularly hard on her uppercut as per instructions from Sultan. From the corner of her eye she could see people gathering at the door, finally the round ended, and she looked over. She gasped in surprise when she saw, standing just inside the door at the top of the steps, her father, accompanied by her Uncle Roberto. They were shaking hands, laughing, and talking with Sultan.

"Robbie 'Rockem' Quinones!" the old coach bellowed out. "'Bout time you showed your ugly mug 'round here!"

Sultan finished shaking the handsome young man's hand, slapped him on the back, then stepped back to look him over. "I never could get you in this gym, no matter how I tried," he scolded.

"Sultan, you knew I was a Chi-city boxing kid. I didn't live out here in the fancy suburbs," Robbie Quinones scoffed.

"What ya up to now, boy? I thought you were gonna hit the big time."

"Nah, went as far as I could, but I got me a real job now, working in IT down in Indiana."

"Ha! Y'all moved on. Mark 'The Punisher' is a firefighter now; I am lucky if I can get him over here but once a month."

"What about your boy, the 'Quiet Riot'?"

"Jason? Done joined the Marines, never turned pro."

"Really!" exclaimed Roberto, "He was legit!"

"Oh yeah," Sultan agreed. "You boys had some great sparring sessions, but we always had to come to your gym, if memory serves."

"Hey," Roberto countered, "he was the rookie looking for some good sparring back then; you all needed to take the ride."

Sultan noticed that the gym had gone quiet. The athletes were paying more attention to his conversation than they were to their own training. "Alright, y'all gonna stand around gaping, you might as well come see a real fighter. Come on, gather round."

Alvarez was the first to join the group. Shaking Eduardo Quinones' hand first, he then extended his hand to the former pro as well. Roberto tilted his head and furrowed his brow.

"Yeah I thought I might know you when my brother mentioned your name a while back. You were Louie's boy, right? Out in the country. Depue, Illinois, was it?"

"Wow, good memory! You were just a kid back when I was fighting."

"Yeah, the Depue Boat Races, right? We used to go to all those small-town festivals. Man, they fed us good and treated us right. It almost made that long-ass drive worth it. So you fought with Benny 'The Jet' Henderson? How is he? And what about that good heavyweight you had, 'Big Baby' Hosa?"

"Damn, you remember them all!" Alvarez was surprised. He hadn't realized that he had made that much of an impression in his fighting days.

"Hell, yes! You guys were heroes to us kids,"

"Well, more those other guys than me," Alvarez protested.

"Coach is trying to be modest," chuckled Big Ces. "Look, he's blushing."

"Whatever, Ces." Alvarez gave him a playful push. He turned back to Roberto. "So what brings you around?"

"Yeah," interjected Sultan. "You movin' back to coach for me, or you thinkin' about making a comeback?"

"No, no, nothing like that; I'm out of the game, for sure."

Eduardo Quinones broke into the conversation. "He was working with me, but now he's a big shot with his company."

"Not a big shot," Roberto denied. "But things are good." He slapped his brother on the back. "We didn't come here to talk about me. Actually we want to see how my niece, Lucy, is doing."

Sultan grew instantly serious. He lowered his voice. "She has more natural talent than I've seen since I opened this place up. She went toe-to-toe with one of the toughest female fighters in the state, maybe in the country, and that was the first time she ever stepped in the ring!"

The brothers exchanged surprised glances.

Lucy's father frowned. "When she came home after that one, it looked like she may have taken some hard punches, especially to the left eye."

Lucy had remained in the ring while the other fighters had gathered around her uncle and father. She could not hear the conversation, but she instinctively knew they were now talking about her.

"She's not the kind of fighter who's gonna stay away from a brawl," Sultan confided, still keeping his voice low. "She will definitely take punches to give punches; seems to run in the family." Sultan gave Robbie a wink. "I guess we can talk about it, or you can see what you came here for! Big Ces, you got those mitts?"

Big Ces stepped through the ropes and set Lucy through her regular routine. Lucy tried not to think about her dad and uncle as she bobbed and weaved, popping the mitts with authority and expertise.

Sultan watched her for a few minutes, then commanded, "Glove up, Chuy."

It wasn't long before Chuy was joining Lucy in a controlled spar that, by that time, they had done often.

Roberto and Eduardo Quinones moved to the ring apron to watch. Soon they were ducking and bobbing, matching Lucy's motion. Before they realized it they were shouting out instructions and encouragement along with the coaches. At the sound of the bell, Mr. Quinones let out an unplanned cheer. His brother wasted no time in jumping into the ring to give Lucy some pointers. Meanwhile, Sultan and Alvarez had been watching the fighters, but also had been keeping an eye on Mr. Quinones.

Now they both approached Lucy's father and stood on each side of him, saying nothing.

Mr. Quinones, not taking his eyes off his daughter, was the first to speak. "I don't want my daughter hurt."

Alvarez was about to open his mouth, when Sultan stopped him with a slight shake of his head, his eyes remaining on Lucy as well. The three men watched in silence as uncle and niece worked together in the ring. The obvious joy they were feeling in that moment flowed from the ring and touched the hearts of the observers.

Mr. Quinones broke the silence. The concerned father spoke in a low voice, as if he was talking to himself, or saying a prayer, maybe asking God for forgiveness. "This was going to be temporary. She was supposed to do this for a month, serve her time, clear her name, get a break from being a second mom at home. She was going to go on to dance, or something... just going to the Y and working out. It was going to be a good balance to her studies..." His voice trailed off as he struggled to comprehend how this love of boxing was going to change his little girl. He continued more loudly, addressing Sultan and Alvarez. "My brother, he needed boxing; he was on his way to the pen. He was a gangbanger, a real little asshole." Eduardo paused for a moment, overcome with emotion. Finally, looking at the two coaches, he declared, "My Lucy, she's always been a good girl."

Alvarez saw his opening and he took it. "Lucy's a great kid, Mr. Quinones," he assured him. "Let's just say, she was hanging out with some kids who have not found their way in life yet." Alvarez waited for a response from Mr. Quinones who gave him none, so he pressed on. "I don't have a daughter, but if I did, I'm sure I would feel the same way as you when it comes to a sport like boxing, but let me tell you, I was a 'good kid', too. I always tried my best to never be a problem. My mom was dealing with my alcoholic dad and brother. I figured she had enough problems, but even as a 'good kid', boxing kept me straight, away from drinking, bed early, up early. Any fighting in the streets and we were off the team. That's the way it is here, too!" Alvarez was on a roll: "Boxing taught me to take care of my body, to manage my time. It taught me a disciplined lifestyle I still follow today. Look, Mr. Quinones, boxing is a combat sport, but the safety of kids will always come first." Alvarez exhaled, then completed his pitch. "Just know that we will back up your decision, no matter what it is."

Lucy's father stood, silently staring at the floor. He finally spoke. "Well, Coach Alvarez, Coach Sultan, I appreciate all the work you have put in with my daughter, and with all these kids. I have seen a big change in her. She's... you know...happy, more relaxed than she's ever been." His voice trailed off, as he once again became lost in his thoughts. After a long moment, he stuck out his chin, and nodded his head, making a silent agreement with himself.

"*Vamos a ver*. We will see." He shook hands with both coaches, looking them in the eye with the sincerest of thank yous. Eduardo Quinones was still worried, but he knew this was a battle not worth what it would cost him to win. He resigned himself to the fact that he now had another fighter in the family.

By the time he came to that conclusion, his brother had Lucy, Chuy, and Nancy at the speed bag. Roberto's sleeves were rolled up and he was demonstrating working the bag with an expertise not previously seen at the gym—even by the most veteran of fighters. He stepped aside to let the three novices take turns, periodically stopping the action to give pointers and show them new tricks on the small bag.

Mr. Quinones left the coaches and joined the group at the bag. "*Que Pasa?* You showing off?"

"That's why you brought me, right?" replied Robbie.

"I brought you to see the best fighter in the family, and for once you won't be looking in the mirror, *hermano*."

Lucy was confused, but excited. She would not let herself believe what she just heard.

Father turned to daughter. "Lucy," Eduardo began, "if I let you do this, promise me your education—your college—will always come first."

"Of course, *Papi!*" Lucy replied, feeling joy well up inside her.

"You promise me, you will know the difference between tough and smart. Use some defense, not like this *Payaso*," Mr. Quinones gave his younger brother a loving shove.

Lucy and her friends giggled. "Yes Dad."

"If I allow you to compete, it will be for a limited time. Do you understand? We will figure out a goal, and a time frame."

"That's fair, Dad." Lucy tried not to burst with delight.

"Alright, for now I will allow you to..." Mr Quinones could not finish his sentence, as his daughter threw her arms around his neck and hugged him tightly. The rest of the group erupted in applause.

"Okay, *mi vida*, we will meet you at home. Hurry so you can have some time with your *tio loco*."

Quinones and his brother were heading toward the door, but he stopped short and turned around. "I forgot something."

He walked over to Chuy. "You must be Jesus." Eduardo extended his hand.

Chuy gladly shook the offered hand. "It's a pleasure to meet you, sir."

"Good manners and a firm handshake," Mr. Quinones pronounced, looking at Lucy while still shaking Chuy's hand. "I hear you're a pretty good fighter, too."

"Well, sir, I ..."

"You a good student?"

"Honor roll all year, sir," Chuy said with pride.

"And you work with the special needs kids, I hear," Mr. Quinones continued.

"Yes sir, I am an officer in the Best Pals Club."

"*Bien, bien*." Mr. Quinones still held Chuy's hand in a firm handshake. "You know I love my daughter. Right, Jesus?"

"Yes, sir, I'm sure you do," agreed Chuy, standing straighter.

"Good, Jesus, very good. Lucy, you invite this young man to dinner, *entiendes?*"

"*Si, Papi*," agreed Lucy, struggling not to chuckle at Chuy's nervousness.

The brothers continued their goodbyes as they moved toward the door. They heard Lucy and her friends cheering and shouting even as they headed down the steps outside.

"*No te preoccupies, hermano*," Robbie said, putting his arm around his brother. " Don't worry, bro. She's good; she will be fine."

As they left the gym, Quinones playfully pushed his brother's arm off his shoulder and assumed his best boxing stance.

"I blame you, *cabron*." Eduardo threw a jab in Roberto's direction.

Roberto matched his brother's stance, dancing around the older man.

"*Por que*? What did I do?"

"I never should have brought her around when you were fighting. Now I'm gonna have to knock you out."

"*Si, viejitos,* I may be older now, but I'll never, ever be as old as you!"

The two went into a playful clinch and stood together for a moment.

"She'll be fine, big brother; you did the right thing."

Eduardo did not speak, calming his mind and accepting the words of his younger brother. After a moment they turned, arms still over each other's shoulder, and headed to the car. Time for food and family, for a good home-cooked meal, and, of course, conversation about boxing.

Mother's Day weekend was a big deal at Lucy's house, mostly because of Lucy. She had always started the celebration on Saturday morning when traditionally she prepared breakfast in bed for both her mother and father. She and her sisters (who were usually more work than help) would clean the entire house while her mother stayed in bed and pretended to sleep. Mother's Day is the busiest day of the year for restaurants, which meant her mom worked longer, harder and came home even more tired than usual. By the time she arrived home Lucy would have the house neat as a pin, with the girls dressed in their Sunday best. There were also handcrafted gifts and decorations, and a hot meal waiting.

In the last few years, life had become easier for the family. As a certified mechanic, Eduardo Quinones' paycheck increased significantly. The girls were getting bigger and becoming more helpful on this special day, in fact, every day. Most importantly, Catalina was now a manager at the restaurant, working fewer late nights and only one weekend a month.

Mother's Day weekend was the exception, requiring Catalina Quinones' presence to handle the significant increase in customers. This was, unfortunately, the particular Saturday when Lucy had the opportunity for her first fight. In Lucy's mind the timing could not have been worse. So much so that when she told her parents about the upcoming fight, she told them that she was choosing not to go.

"I'll wait for summer to fight, probably mid-June, Mom." She offered. She was surprised when her mother rejected her plan and told her to go to her fight.

"I know how much you want this, *mi hija.* You know I don't like this boxing, but I know how hard you work. If you are dead set on getting in the ring, we might as well get started with it. Perhaps the sooner we start,

194

the sooner it will be over," she said, shaking her head, not even trying to hide the way she really felt. She added, "Now I celebrate Mother's day every weekend because your dad, your sisters and you all work so hard to keep the house running smoothly. Next weekend we will get dressed up, go to church, and go out for a big meal at *Tres Gallos*. We will celebrate Mother's Day a little late and also a victory for my strong, amazing daughter!"

Lucy could only stare speechless at her mother. This was totally unexpected, but much appreciated. Her heart almost exploded with love for her wonderful, understanding mother.

Catalina pulled her daughter into a hug and asked, "Did you ever think I would be telling my oldest daughter to go beat someone up?"

"Only if it was to beat the customers who are rude to you," Lucy replied, hugging her mom back.

Now Saturday morning arrived. It was still dark when Catalina sat on Lucy's bed and awoke her eldest daughter by gently caressing her cheek. Lucy stretched, yawned, and blinked a few times before she could speak. "Mama, why are you up so early? Do you have to go in already?"

"No, *mi vida*, I just thought it would be nice for someone to take care of you for a change. Can I make you breakfast?"

"Just juice and fruit, Mama, I have weigh-ins."

A short time later Lucy and Catalina sat quietly at the kitchen table watching the sun begin to peak over the horizon.

"Mama, did you sleep well last night?" She suspected from the look on Catalina's face that her mother was having second thoughts about how the weekend should go.

Mrs. Quinones did not answer her question and that was answer enough for Lucy.

She grabbed her mother's hand and held it firmly. "Mama, they do everything to keep us safe. We wear headgear, bigger, softer gloves than Tio Robbie used in the pros. We only box three rounds and they have a doctor at ringside."

Catalina smiled faintly. That information did not make her feel better, but she appreciated Lucy's concern for her fears.

Lucy held her mom's hand even tighter, "Mama, this has been good for me. I know I'm stronger in my body, but much more than that I feel more confident; more confident in school, more confident just being me."

Lucy's mom knew that her daughter was speaking the truth. She had watched her daughter bloom over the last several months.

Lucy continued, "My goal is to win the Gloves—that is really not too far off. After that I think I will be done, and you can relax!"

Catalina let out a big sigh, a mixture of resignation and relief.

"Alright my love, go get' em!" She stood up and struck a boxing pose and threw a left and a right to show she meant business.

At that the two cracked up, then realizing how loud they were, they attempted to muffle their laughter, which only made them laugh harder.

"*Mi vida*," Catalina Quinones held her daughter's face between her hands. "*Cuidado*! Be careful!"

"Yes Mom."

"And win!"

CHAPTER 22

The group of fighters heading out for Chuy's second fight was even smaller than the group attending the first one. This time it was Alvarez, Big Ces, Lucy and Chuy. Ulises was driving Nancy, but they were going to leave much later that morning.

"Alright," Alvarez voiced approval when Lucy and Chuy arrived. "Two fighters, two coaches and two fans to follow later. Sounds about right!"

They piled into Alvarez's roomy SUV and headed north then west to Rockford, Illinois. Big Ces turned to face Chuy and Lucy in the back seat.

"This will be the last indoor show before the summer festival season begins in June. All those fights will be outdoors," he informed them. "Rockford has a lot of fighters, but no one is guaranteed a fight. We won't know until we get there, so don't go getting all nervous before you even know if there is something to be nervous about, right Chuy?" He grinned at his protege.

Chuy, now experienced, could picture the fight scene in his head and felt more at ease than he had on the way to his first fight. As they rolled down the highway he purposely worked to relax his body and his mind. He leaned over to Lucy, who had been quietly lost in her own thoughts.

"Are you nervous?" He whispered in her ear.

"A little," she admitted.

"I think the first fight has got to be the toughest, Luc, 'cause you don't know what to expect."

Chuy went on to tell Lucy the details about the weigh-ins, the physical exam, and the waiting for the fights to begin. He told her how nerves had drained him and how he was trying to avoid that this time.

"Let me show you a technique I'm trying," he offered.

Soon they were breathing deeply, consciously relaxing their bodies with each breath. The coaches noticed the silence in the back seat and glanced back to see Lucy and Chuy asleep.

"I think they're relaxed," Big Ces observed with a grin.

After a fifty-minute drive they reached the arena. The Rockford gym was used for two things: basketball and boxing. The ring had been assembled at center court and was circled by chairs, but the better seats were the permanent stands that rose above, off the floor, surrounding the ring like the seats of a colosseum designed for viewing gladiators below. It was ten in the morning, but it could have been midnight in the gym, which was dimly lit with no natural light allowed in from the sunny spring morning. Upon entering, Lucy was reminded of a church: old, dark, quiet, and full of memories.

The matches were to begin at noon. Lucy and Chuy went to the locker rooms to change, then went through the physical exam and weigh-in process quickly. With those tasks behind them, they found seats in the back and worked on relaxation again. As fight time grew closer, and with all the teams arriving, it was not as easy as it had been on the drive up. Cesar and Alvarez were busy talking to coaches seeking to find matches for their fighters. Lucy and Chuy could only wait and hope they would be successful.

"This is the worst part," declared Chuy. "When it's just a show and not a tourney, you're not always sure you have a match. Big Ces says sometimes you can take a long drive and if there's no one that's at your weight or experience level you are out of luck.

"I'll fight anyone," Lucy stated with a confidence she wasn't quite feeling.

"I know you will," Chuy concurred. "Hell, you took on Shantel. I think you can fight anyone in the state. It's the other girl that won't want to get in the ring with you!"

They were interrupted by Big Ces whose sly smirk gave away his news.

"Okay, we got you matched up. You're both fighting kids from here. Your guy's got quite a few fights already, Jesus, but Lucy, your girl is green. You guys know, we take what we get. Now you've got a couple of hours to wait it out. In the meantime, Alvarez is buying me breakfast."

"Oh, I am?" challenged Alvarez, walking up in time to hear Ces' last words.

"Come on, Coach, just like the old days," coaxed Cesar.

"Yeah, the old days almost broke me; you ate more before a fight than any guy I ever saw," Alvarez reminded him.

"Joys of being a heavyweight, Coach, I didn't have to worry about making weight and I always fought last. Hell, if I didn't eat before a fight, it would've been like five hours without a meal!"

"And you would have wasted away to nothing," Alvarez joked, patting Caesar's ample midsection. "Okay, you two, they've got quite a few young kids fighting, so I'm guessing at least two hours before we even warm-up, but that's how long it takes Ces to eat anyway."

"Damn, Coach," Big Ces protested.

"You two okay while we eat?"

They both nodded. Lucy pulled out a novel: *Pride and Prejudice*. Chuy took out his earbuds and his phone.

Alvarez put two thumbs up. "That's what I like about you guys, always prepared."

The gym had filled with people and was now fully lit up, making it considerably brighter than it had been upon their arrival. The Junior Division fighters had begun with the youngest, the six-year-olds, whose gloves seemed bigger than their bodies. They were fighting only thirty-second rounds. Even so, there were eight more fights before the fight card was up to the fifteen-year-olds, most of whom had already been boxing for years, looking slick and experienced. That signaled the time for Lucy and Chuy to begin warming up. Chuy was up first, fight number fourteen. Lucy was right behind him, with fight number fifteen. Finally Chuy, who had grown antsy with the lengthy wait, stepped eagerly into the ring, Big Ces right behind him. His opponent and trainer were doing the same in the opposite corner.

When he judged that the fighters were ready, the announcer, wearing a sharp blue tuxedo, called out over the microphone: "Ladies and Gentlemen—In the blue corner, from the Maywood Boxing Club, wearing the blue and white, Jesus 'Chuy' Ledesma!"

"We gotta get you a better nickname," Ces whispered in Chuy's ear.

"And from right here in Rockford, Illinois in the red corner, wearing the Rockford red and gray, Bobby 'the Bull' Connors!"

The crowd cheered loudly for their hometown fighter. Chuy vowed not to let his lack of supporters deter him from doing his best. The bell sounded and he moved quickly to the middle of the ring, then began shuffling to his right. Conners came out in a bobbing, crouching style, pawing with his left hand.

Not a southpaw, flashed through Chuy's mind, giving him some relief. Chuy automatically threw his jab, which landed flush on his opponent's face. His was the first good punch of the fight, and he would repeat it throughout the round. Connors ducked and bobbed, each time throwing wild right hooks that Chuy either blocked or ducked, answering back with left-right combinations. The round continued in the same manner until the bell ended it.

Chuy returned to his corner, where Alvarez and Ces were waiting, both wearing smiles that telegraphed to Chuy that they were satisfied with his effort.

"Great job, Chuy! Just right," Big Ces said encouragingly.

"You're throwing the jab and combo real nice," said Alvarez. "Now double the jab and watch out for his right hook."

"He moves like Lucy," Chuy observed between taking drinks of water and deep breaths. "But not as well." It was true. 'The Bull' had Lucy's fighting style, but he was not as smooth, nor as accurate. Sparring with Lucy had more than prepared Chuy for this fight, and his confidence was soaring.

The bell for the second round brought more of the same. Chuy moved, blocking his opponent's right hook, and answering back with his own jab and straight right. Connors tried to clinch with Chuy, or trap him in the corner, but Chuy's double jab stung and allowed him to escape from Conners' assault. 'The Bull' had yet to land a punch, at least an effective one.

At the bell Chuy returned to his corner. This time he was the one smiling.

"Don't get cocky," warned Alvarez. "He can still hurt you."

Chuy had clearly won the first two rounds. Without question, Connors would have to stop Chuy with a knockout to reverse the win, and chances of that happening were looking very slim.

As the third round began, Chuy told himself to be careful. He knew that in the ring anything could happen—and it almost did! When the bell sounded, 'The Bull', true to his name, charged, catching Chuy flat-footed, still in his corner. Connors threw a wild, but lucky, overhand right to the temple. The referee immediately jumped in, giving Chuy an eight-count. Chuy looked to his corner with wide eyes. Both Alvarez and Cesar were waving off the punch.

"No problem, get out of the corner! Fight your fight!" Alvarez called out in a sing-song voice, in an effort to relax his fighter. "Block the right; it's all he has."

"Box!" came the instruction from the referee. Connors charged again, throwing wild punches in bunches. Chuy covered himself, ducking and bobbing as well, moving to his right to get out of the corner. Without throwing a punch, Chuy positioned himself where he wanted to be. Now, it was Connors with his back to the ropes. The effort of his onslaught of punches had him spent. He was left without the energy needed to put up a good defense. It was Chuy's turn to go on the offense, landing jabs and straight hands. Connors utilized his strong upper body to tie up Chuy by clinging to him, receiving two warnings from the official, but saving himself from a knockout. The final bell rang. Chuy raised his arms in anticipated victory. Alvarez and Ces cheered their fighter as the referee took the two combatants to the center of the ring to raise the hand of the winner.

Chuy's hair was wet from sweat, but his face was unmarked and smiling. 'The Bull', on the other hand, held a towel to his bloodied nose and was breathing heavily, his head lowered in acknowledgement of defeat.

"Ladies and gentlemen, the winner of this welterweight novice division battle—in the RED CORNER—Chuy looked to his coaches. They were standing in the blue corner. *It had to be a mistake.* "From Rockford, Illinois," the announcer continued, "Bobby 'The Bull' Connors!"

Even the hometown crowd could not accept the obviously poor decision by the judges. They exploded in boos and jeers, throwing empty paper cups and half-filled bags of popcorn into the ring. Chuy shook hands with his opponent and appearing far more dazed than he had been throughout the entire fight, he retreated to his corner and his equally shocked coaches. The referee made a point of following him.

"You fought well, young man," the ref told him. "All you can ever do is your best."

Big Ces was still shaking his head in disbelief when Alvarez escorted Chuy from the ring. Several fans patted Chuy on the back. "You was robbed, kid," shouted an older gentleman in the second row.

Alvarez walked Chuy behind the rows of ringside seats. "Did you make any mistakes at all during that fight?" he questioned.

Chuy looked up with wide eyes, still in disbelief. "Huh?"

"Did you make a mistake?" Alvarez asked again.

The tired fighter paused for a moment. Alvarez had both hands-on Chuy's shoulders.

"Start of the third round, I got the eight count," Chuy blurted out, coming out of his daze. "I was flat-footed; I got caught in the corner. It shouldn't have cost me the fight, but it did. Shoulda never happened."

Alvarez looked his fighter in the eyes. "Sometimes you can learn more by losing, Jesus."

Chuy conceded the lesson, giving his coach an embarrassed grin.

"Put the loss behind you, but don't forget the lesson. Now it's time to watch our girl!"

Big Ces was escorting Lucy down the aisle and into the blue corner, so Chuy moved back a few steps from the ring. The sick feeling in his stomach was fading and he was ready to heed Alvarez' advice and cheer for his closest friend. Lucy's hair was tightly pulled back and she wore a gold tank top and shiny gold trunks with a black stripe.

Chuy looked at his own blue gym shorts and white tank top. *Damn,* he thought, *this girl looks like a fighter's supposed to look.*

Big Ces and Lucy slipped through ropes with Alvarez trailing them. Chuy knelt down next to the steps.

"Ladies and gentlemen, The next bout features female lightweights both in their very first fight. In the red corner from Rockford, Illinois... 'Electric' Elly Brumhurst and in the blue corner, from the Maywood Boxing Club, Lucy 'Rockem-Sockem' Quinones."

Lucy's opponent was tall and thin. In her corner she moved well, throwing her left jab and right hand to keep warm. Alvarez watched her for a moment, then said quietly into Lucy's ear, "Looks like we got some real 'townie' judges, Luce. Don't leave any doubt on who the winner of this fight is."

Lucy nodded that she understood as she ducked and bobbed in her corner, throwing jabs and hooks into the air. The coaches cleared their corners, and the bell rang. Lucy wasted no time, catching her opponent one step out of her corner. The tall, rangy girl threw one pawing jab and BAM! Lucy ducked the punch, answering back with a vicious hook that sent the girl sprawling and had the crowd on their feet. Lucy stood over the flattened fighter, almost as shocked as was the girl she had just hit. The referee motioned Lucy back to her corner, but she did not understand the direction until she heard the shouts from Chuy and her coaches. The ref picked up the count at five and Lucy's stunned opponent struggled to her feet. Before the referee could signal an end to the fight, a towel from the red corner came flying into the ring. The fight was over with one punch.

Alvarez, Chuy and Big Ces flew up the steps cheering wildly with their hands held high.

Alvarez sent Lucy over to the red corner, to check on her opponent and shake hands with her coaches. They greeted Lucy with raised eyebrows.

"Quite a right hook, you got there, young lady," the Rockford Coach remarked, shaking Lucy's hand. The two fighters moved to center ring when the referee gestured for them to join him. The announcer's voice rang throughout the gym:

"Ladies and Gentlemen, the winner by TKO in the very first round, Lucy 'Rockem-Sockem' Quinones"!

As the team left Rockford to return home the coaches could sense the disappointment radiating outward from Chuy and Lucy.

"Come on you two!" Alvarez tried to cheer them up. "It's all about learning. Did you learn something today?"

"Yeah," answered Chuy, "I learned judges can really suck!"

"Ha! You got that right," Cesar snickered.

"Come on, Jesus," Alvarez prodded, looking for a serious reply.

"I know; I let my guard down," admitted Chuy.

"Again! In your first fight you got caught. You made the same mistake twice now, and you are way too smart for that!"

"You're right, Coach; dumb mistake."

"One more question," Alvarez continued. "Did you have fun?"

Chuy was quiet for a quick moment. "Yeah, yes, I did; I had a lot of fun, I mean, I like practicing, I love fighting, I don't even mind the long drives; I like all of it!"

"*Orale!*" Cesar called out, "Good stuff, *hermano!*"

"What about you, Lucy?"

Lucy narrowed her eyes and thought for a moment,

"I don't know; I guess first, I learned what it's like to drive a long way, to go through the physical and weigh-ins…I guess I learned not to get so nervous before a fight, 'cause it's gonna go the way it goes; no point in thinking too much about it…"

"Ah… that's pretty good," Alvarez raised his eyebrows as he looked at Big Ces. "Anything you want to add to that, Ces?"

"Hell no! " Cesar's thundering voice made everyone crack up.

Chuy and Lucy felt better after the pep talk. By the time the team had hit I-88, Lucy was fast asleep on Chuy's shoulder. Chuy stayed as still as he could, so as not to awaken her. He was content to watch the cornfields go by, smelling her hair and trying not to look like a sappy kid with a crush. He hoped the coaches, talking quietly in the front seat, would not notice how enraptured he was with this beautiful girl who was snuggled up against him. Chuy felt as though he could have stayed like that forever, but as they hit the final expressway and the western suburbs of Chicago, Lucy began to stir. She awakened completely as they turned onto 17th Ave.

"Wow, how long was I sleeping?"

"The whole way," Chuy smirked.

"Was your shoulder getting tired?"

"I didn't think so, but now I'm not sure." Chuy rotated his elbow in small circles as he rubbed his shoulder.

"Here, does it feel better now?" Lucy hit him in the shoulder with a quick, playful hook.

"Okay," Alvarez turned to his fighters when they pulled into the parking area at the gym. "One knockout a day is plenty. End of the road, you two; you've got some peddling to do, if I am not mistaken."

The late afternoon sun was still bright and warm as the tired boxers stretched their legs and unchained their bikes.

Chuy could feel his stomach growl. "Hey, I'm starving! What say we get some pizza; I'm buying!"

"Uh, I have to get home. We celebrate Mother's Day today. We're having a big dinner and everything."

"What time do you have dinner? Seven? Seven-thirty? It's not even four! You're not gonna make it that long without eating something." Chuy was determined to convince her as they began their ride down 17th.

"You said you are buying?" Lucy eventually asked.

"Yep."

"You won't let me eat too much, right?"

"Hey, I can't promise that." Chuy lifted out of his bike seat and picked up the pace. "But I can easily eat over half—I can tell you that for sure!"

The two raced through the streets of Melrose Park, over the 25th Street Bridge and on to Cocino's, and hot, delicious pizza!

"Hey, Mr. LeDesma, how are you?" Mr. Cocino, a short, squat middle-aged man with a heavy accent, looked and sounded every bit the part of the Italian chef. He greeted Chuy as if he were the welterweight champion. "We got the best seat in the house for you."

Chuy and Lucy looked around and laughed, seeing no one else in the place.

"And who is this beautiful young lady?" The owner of the establishment continued.

"Mr Cocino, this is Lucy," Chuy proudly replied.

Their host bowed slightly. "Ms. Lucy, so nice to meet you. How is it that I don't know you? Are you from out of town?"

"No, Mr. Cocino, 102 Marion—you may recognize that address." Lucy shook the warm hand of the jovial man.

"Ah, yes," he replied. "Extra-large with sausage and half jalapeno."

"You got it," Lucy giggled. "My parents like a spicy pizza."

"Well, I can finally put a face with a pizza, ha! Okay, you sit; I make you a wonderful pie. The usual, Mr. Jesus?"

Chuy looked to Lucy for confirmation. "Sausage and mushroom, alright? I mean we can do jalapenos, too, if you want."

"Nah, we can skip the hot stuff today." Lucy headed for a table by the big picture window at the front of the store.

"One Mr. Chuy Special, coming right up. You sit and I get you drinks—on the house for my two favorite customers."

"Wow, Chuy!" Lucy settled into her seat. "Come here often?"

"Ah, that's just Mr. Cocino. He treats everyone like that, but I do come here a lot," Chuy admitted with a wink.

The young couple sat at the window watching the late afternoon sun begin to make tall shadows across Grand Avenue. The day could not have ended any better.

CHAPTER 23

A rmani rode in the passenger seat of the '79 Chevy Impala that somehow his oldest brother possessed. He'd never asked how Daniel had acquired the car. Some things were better left unsaid. Little Louie, one of his brother's many flunky 'soldiers' smoked a cigarette as he drove Armani around to check on their turf. Cocino's Pizza was a place they tended to leave alone for a very good reason. Mr. Cocino was a known hothead. Unlike Old Oscar, the feisty Italian man did not tolerate groups of teens hanging out in front of his pizzeria. Armani seldom gave the place a second look, but this afternoon, as the Chevy waited at the stop light on the corner of Wolf and Grand, Armani noticed the lights inside being turned on as the sun began to set. His eyes focused on the couple sitting just inside the large picture window.

"Pull over there," Armani ordered, pointing at an open spot. Louie followed his directions and pulled into the lot, parking next to the restaurant.

"Leave the engine running," Armani snapped, "Let's go!"

The moment the two gang-bangers appeared at the door Mr. Cocino stepped from behind the counter.

"I told you punks to stay out of my store."

Armani ignored the angry old man and started toward Lucy. In an instant, the cozy little diner turned into a volatile place of danger, as Mr. Cocino grabbed a baseball bat from behind the counter and went for the two boys. Chuy did not have time to even look in their direction as he followed his first instinct and jumped up to block the old man's progress.

"Stop, Mr. Cocino!"

Lucy sprang up also. In two steps she had her hands on Armani's chest, not saying a word, but her eyes pleading for him to stop. Mr. Cocino tried to come at the boys, but Chuy had both of his hands on the older man's chest, trying to calm him and keep him near the counter.

Armani glared at Lucy. He was breathing hard from the excitement of the encounter. Cocino's curses filled the air almost as much as the smell of freshly-baked pizza, but Armani heard nothing and could only smell Lucy's hair. The memory of holding her pierced him and suddenly he was more sad than angry. Shock of the sudden awareness of his own feelings snapped him out of it. He saw that Cocino had pushed Chuy backward, two steps closer to the gang bangers. Armani reached behind his back to his belt loop.

"Armani, NO!" Lucy gasped.

Everyone instantly froze. Armani felt a surge of the power he was looking for, when he first entered the pizzeria, determined to break up the romantic dinner. He smiled malevolently at the old man and Chuy, saying nothing—not needing to say a word. His eyes shifted to Lucy, expecting the same look of fear, but to his surprise a look of pity was all he got from her.

In the battle between anger and sadness that waged war over Armani's soul, anger lost as fast as Lucy's opponent had only hours earlier. The winner, however, was a very different emotion—embarrassment! Shame flooded over Armani, washing away everything else.

"Tell your boyfriend he's lucky," Armani sneered in a harsh whisper, though it did not sound as tough as he intended. He and his companion sprinted to the car and raced out of the lot, tires squealing.

The three abandoned would-be victims stood motionless for a while, breathing heavily as they each silently tried to fathom what had just occurred.

Mr. Cocino eventually broke the silence. "Damn punks! Lucy, do you know that kid?"

"We went to school with him," responded Chuy quickly, saving Lucy from any explanation. "He got kicked out."

"Well, the damn punks ain't allowed in my place. They mess up the whole damn neighborhood; I'm calling the ..."

Mr. Cocino's rant was interrupted by a large family noisily entering the restaurant. He instantly reverted to the jovial owner, welcoming in the new customers. Lucy and Chuy chuckled to themselves at the transformation and returned to their seats. In minutes the pizza was delivered to the table, as if the incident had been nothing but a brief intense nightmare. They dug into the pizza with a vengeance, realizing with the smell of their food that they were starving. Grinning at each other, they ate and drank enthusiastically and without shame. Finally, after the fourth piece of pizza, they slowed their pace. Chuy slumped back in his chair.

"Sooooo, how did you like this date?" He asked, fairly certain that he knew what Lucy's reply would be.

Lucy cracked up and threw her crumpled napkin at Chuy. "You know; now I'm going to expect them all to be this exciting!" She warned him.

While the two chatted and ate in the pizzeria on the corner they both secretly wondered if this was the last they would see of Armani.

The month of May in Chicagoland could be cold and rainy, or warm and sunny, sometimes both on the same day. It was a busy time for teachers and students alike. Teachers were hurrying to finish the remainder of the year's curriculum, while students prepared for finals with extra study.

Chuy and Lucy were now sharing morning runs, as well as meeting in the 250 hallway with Wolfy's kids. Nancy and Billy almost always joined them. They had formed their own little gang, talking, and joking with the students and the teachers. One morning, with only a few days until finals, Alvarez and Kelly stood with the group in the hallway taking part in a discussion concerning everyone's summer plans.

"I've got two little girls, so summer is the toughest time of year for me," Ms. Kelly confided. "Keeping those two busy is a lot of work. I love it, though. Between pool, tee-ball games and all our other running around, summer goes too fast, and I end up missing them like crazy when we come back here in the fall."

"Whoa! Slow down, turbo! We haven't even left yet and you are talking about coming back already!" Alvarez tried to top her with his own list of summertime blues. "I got football practice in the morning, master's classes in the afternoon and boxing at night. I don't get to lounge at the pool everyday getting a tan and calling it 'work'."

Kelly answered back with a push to his chest. "Wait and see when you have kids one of these days. Trust me, you have it easy. What about you guys, what is up for you?"

"I work at the recycling plant," answered Chuy. "Seven-to-three, five days a week."

"Dang, Jesus," said Alvarez. "You're a working man, but it sounds like you'll still have evenings and weekends to box."

"And don't forget about Wolfy's kids," Kelly interjected.

"I managed to play baseball on this schedule," replied Chuy. "And never missed a game or practice. And we already have a few activities planned for Wolfy's Kids, including bringing them to the gym to watch practice."

"And the Layden Days Fest!" added Ms. Kelly, "We are coming to see you fight, right?"

"Yep, I remember," Chuy assured her.

"How about you, Lucy?" Alvarez asked.

"Take care of the house, and I will do some breakfast and lunch shifts at my mom's restaurant, but that is only for spending money."

"And she's got a rich boyfriend, so she will have plenty of free time," Nancy chimed in.

"Huh? Wait! Is she seeing someone I don't know about?" Chuy brought the group to laughter.

"Your turn, Nancy; what's up for you?" Kelly questioned.

"I'm going to keep working at Grand Dry Cleaners, on Grand Avenue. I'm doing all the tailoring there. I started this winter; now they have me almost full time."

"So cool!" exclaimed Kelly, impressed by the girls' ambition.

"And that leaves…Mr. Karamitos." All eyes turned to Billy.

Billy looked sheepish. "Um…well."

"GET A JOB!" The group shouted in unison, roaring over the unplanned joke.

When school finally let out for the summer, work replaced school during the day for Chuy and many of his friends, but boxing filled the late afternoons and weekends. The team had a meet scheduled for the first weekend of Summer, this time with only a short drive to the south side of Chicago. This was the first of several outdoor fights that would take place at some of the neighborhood festivals occurring in or near the city.

Southside Fest featured several blocks crowded with vendors, rides, beer stands, bands and patrons. In the center of the activities a boxing ring was set up. By noon, boxing would be the center of attention for several hours. The team got there at ten o'clock Saturday morning, eager to get the show started. The fights began at noon with the Junior Gloves starting the program.

Big Cesar and Alvarez had led a caravan of five cars, the other four driven by parents chauffeuring the younger kids in the club.

Before they left that morning for the festival Big Ces had informed Chuy and Lucy, who were now unofficially team captains, that Maywood was bringing an usually large group of the junior fighters. "I'm gonna need your help in the corner," he concluded.

Chuy and Lucy grinned at each other. This was a sign that Big Cesar had faith in their ability to do more than just throw punches.

Now, an hour after arriving, the team had found shade on the steps of an old, deserted bank not far from the ring. Parents stayed busy reprimanding the junior fighters for chasing and playing, while Lucy and Chuy sat at the bottom steps lost in their novels. Lucy had suggested *Grapes of Wrath* for Chuy, while she was half-way through Hemmingway's *The Sun Also Rises*. Cesar approached the two with the plan for the day.

"Well, good news and bad news. Chuy, no match. Only three in your weight class and the other two are green. It's the first fight for both of them so you're the odd man out. Tough break, but I can use your help, so the day's not a total loss for you. Lucy, we got a tough kid for you. She's an experienced fighter, so this one's gonna take more than one punch."

Lucy nodded, even though a case of nerves threatened her stomach, but that was exactly what she had wanted to hear.

"Okay, Chuy, you got the corner with me, but right now get these little kids to stop running around and eating cotton candy before their fight."

"Ugh," Chuy groaned, doubting that he would have any more luck at that task than their parents. "This is going to be tougher than sparring 'Combat' Calderon."

"Lucy, you have a long wait. You are closing the show so you can kick back for a while."

Lucy showed Big Ces the current novel she was reading. "I'll be sitting in the shade 'til it's my time."

"Oh, I'm so jelly!" Chuy said with an exaggerated shrug of his shoulders.

"Have fun!" Lucy gave a sarcastic wink to her boyfriend.

The festival was crowded with teenagers, eating greasy carnival food, riding ancient carnival rides, and flirting with boys, but Lucy was more than content to read, relax and rest before her upcoming battle.

The sounds of carnival rides and classic rock shared the air with the aroma of caramel corn and hot dogs. This was the background for Lucy as she fell into her book and after an hour or so, into a peaceful nap. She was awakened by the ringside bell and the announcer who had just stepped into the center of the ring. She guessed the junior fighters were starting. Arising from her comfortable spot under a shady tree, she moved to the last row of chairs surrounding the ring.

Big Ces and Chuy flanked the first young fighter. He was dressed in shiny red with a thick white stripe and white waistband on his shorts. The bell rang and the match began. The two boys, both about ten years old, met in the middle of the ring and threw punches furiously, swinging wide like two old- time cowboys in a bar fight. The pace kept up for the entire two minutes until the bell rang and both fighters returned to their corners. Chuy got out the stool, water, and spit bucket while Big Ces gave the boy instructions to slow down and control the action, but when the bell restarted the bout, it was only more of the same: wild furious punches in the middle of the ring.

Well, thought Lucy, *they may not have great technique, but they certainly are both in shape.* The third round finished the same as the other two and Lucy was glad she did not have to judge that fight. The judges gave the totally even fight to the hometown kid, and so Maywood tallied its first loss. Lucy decided to change into her boxing gear. If all the junior fights went as fast as the first, it wouldn't be long before she would be up.

She strolled to the tent where weigh-ins had taken place. After changing into her boxing uniform, she stepped out from behind the cloth divider and almost bumped into another female fighter.

"Oh, my bad!" the girl exclaimed and stepped aside.

"No worries, I'm done. It's all yours."

The girl was tall and dark, with braids wrapped tightly to her head, much like Lucy. Without another word exchanged, the two each knew they had just met their opponent. They smiled and nodded politely, trying not to be obvious as they surveyed each other. Lucy knew by looking that this girl was a fighter, as Cesar had said. No 'one-punch' knockout this time. A shot of nerves and adrenaline assailed her. She stepped out of the tent to see Big Ces coming her way with tape and gauze. He gestured for her to sit down on a bench near the tent and then proceeded to tape her hands.

"The juniors are finishing up; they are going to take a little break. There are ten fights on the card, and you're tenth. It could be an hour, but it could be much faster, so start warming up after the seventh fight," he instructed. Lucy nodded.

"Did you see your kid?" Ces asked, knowing the answer, having seen the interaction between the two.

Lucy nodded again.

"No pushover," he observed.

Lucy made a face. "Good."

Big Ces winked. "That's my girl!"

The next seven fights were a mixed bag of skills from young fighters. Four went the distance; three were quick stops. Lucy got up to start her warm-ups. She was the last fighter from the club, so Chuy had been waiting patiently for her to begin. He grabbed the mitts and met her outside the circle of chairs. The two did not speak as Chuy held the gloves and Lucy popped them, ducking and bobbing in her usual style. Next, he stretched Lucy's arms and shoulders, then stepped away from her as she shadow-boxed. On the other side of the ring, Lucy could see her opponent warming up, too. The girl threw long, quick jabs as she danced lightly on her feet. She looked fast and experienced. Lucy reminded herself that this was what she wanted.

Finally, the ninth fight ended and opposing fighters and coaches approached the ring from opposite sides.

The announcer got busy. "Ladies and gentlemen; the final fight of the evening. In the red corner, from Moline, Illinois, with a record of ten wins and only one loss, Maria 'The Marauder' Morales! And in the blue corner, fighting in only her second fight, but coming off a seven-second knockout win, from the Maywood Boxing Club, Lucy 'Rockem-Sockem' Quinones."

Big Ces murmured in Lucy's ear, "she's got experience, but you got talent. You need tough fights, and you're gonna have one. But do what YOU do. Stay on her with body shots; don't let her breathe. Fight your fight and just know you can beat anyone."

The seed of doubt that crept into Lucy's head after hearing her opponent's record disappeared with Cesar's instruction. She thought of her uncle, who always said, "Don't let your head beat you; fight hard as hard as you can and no matter what the judges say, it will always be a win."

The bell for the first round sounded. Lucy was ready for it and charged to the middle of the ring, but her opponent moved right, throwing jabs that popped off the top of Lucy's headgear. Lucy stepped hard to cut off the ring and maneuver Morales into the corner the way she had been taught, but the slick fighter was one step ahead. She stepped left, sticking Lucy with a straight right hand. Lucy ducked and bobbed, making Morales miss two jabs before landing one.

"Throw punches!" Big Ces shouted from the corner.

Lucy heard and threw a vicious hook, but Morales leaned back, and the punch went harmlessly past her chin. She answered with a straight right that landed flush on Lucy's face. Lucy lunged forward, ready to throw another hook, but the referee stepped in, sending Maywood's fighter to a neutral corner. He gave Lucy a standing eight count, the same as if she had been knocked down. She looked to her corner with a shocked expression.

"Put your hands up," Cesar motioned. "Tell him you are okay!"

"Are you alright?" the ref asked. "Do you want to keep going?"

"Hell, yeah," Lucy answered, almost pushing the referee aside.

"Easy, easy," the ref let out a slight chuckle in spite of himself.

Again Lucy charged to the middle of the ring, and again Morales moved gracefully out of the way, landing another jab. The bell sounded, ending what had seemed to Lucy like a thirty-second round. She returned to her corner frustrated and angry.

"Chuy, water!" ordered Cesar. "Okay, girl, settle down. You came here to win a fight. You gave that round away, but you are going to come back. How many body shots did you throw?"

"Huh?"

"How many body shots?"

"Umm..."

"None, Lucy! Not one, and that's what you do best! You're trying to knock this girl out, but you got to throw punches—your best punches, body shots! Did she hurt you for that eight count?"

"No!" Lucy answered with disgust.

"Damn right she didn't, she's a pity-pat puncher—all arm punches. No power behind them. She can't hurt you, but she damn sure can win this fight." He continued, breathing almost as hard as his fighter. "Cut off the ring; if she steps right, left hook to the body, if she steps left, right hook. Got it?"

"Got it," she affirmed.

Lucy stood and Chuy whisked the stool out of the way and put her mouthpiece in. He made a funny face, causing her to smile. The bell sounded. Lucy went quickly to the middle of the ring, but then stopped, forcing Morales to come to her. She then began a vicious body attack that lasted the entire round. She crowded and pushed the smooth fighter out of her comfort zone, putting Morales' back to the ropes. The second round came to an end just as Lucy had Morales pinned in her own corner, her forehead in her opponent's chest, digging in hooks. Lucy returned to her corner as Big Ces, and Chuy jumped up to the apron cheering with raised arms.

"Yesss!!!!" Big Ces yelled. "That's it! One round her, one round you. But she got you on the eight count."

Lucy was breathing hard but loving every second. This was a fight, and now she could feel it turning in her direction.

"Don't forget," reminded Big Ces, "she's experienced, she's been roughed up before. She may come out with something different. You got to be ready. *Mira*," he added in Spanish. "Look, now throw some hooks upstairs to the head and mix it up with some straight rights and lefts.

But don't leave your punches hanging out there—she will catch you! You slowed her down, but she's still fast."

The coaches cleared the corners and the fighters stood ready for the final round. The crowd was standing, too. Passers-by and patrons of the beer garden had taken notice of the action in the ring and had gathered to make up a larger than normal audience. The loud, cheering crowd made it difficult to hear when the bell announced the beginning of round three.

This time Morales charged Lucy's corner, surprising her with a right and gaining the early advantage. Morales threw a quick combination that did not phase Lucy but scored points and elicited an early cheer from the crowd. She then danced away with a smile on her face that Lucy was determined to wipe off. The experienced fighter had stolen early points and now was going to use her quickness to make Lucy chase her while she picked Lucy apart. The strategy was a good one, that had worked before and would work again, but not with Lucy Quinones. Lucy immediately channeled her anger into a bull rush that sent the slick opponent off balance, following it up with a vicious left hook to the body, doubling with a hook to the head. Morales was trapped again. The body attack she had suffered during the second round had taken the snap out of her punches.

The beer garden crowd gave its full attention to the female fighters, as the tough, smaller girl with the ducking, bobbing street-fighter style mauled the slim, slick boxer. They cheered Lucy on, the tide turning overwhelmingly in her favor. Morales hung on, but she looked tired and defeated. Chuy and Big Ces celebrated with the audience when the final bell ended the match. Lucy allowed herself a smile of satisfaction. She had gotten what she wanted: a tough fight with a very talented fighter, and somehow she had achieved the win. She slept on Chuy's shoulder on the short ride back to the club and woke up feeling sore as she got out of the car and headed for her bike.

"Pizza to celebrate?" asked Chuy. "You know, our new tradition."

"Yeah, but this time, let's have it at my house. My dad said he's buying if I win!"

"Damn! That was a lot of hard work for a pizza."

Lucy touched the slight swelling under her left eye. "Yep, that pizza is gonna taste good!"

CHAPTER 24

Summer brought a montage of work and boxing, and much of what little free time they had they devoted to Wolfy's kids. If their lives were a movie, the scenes and setting would flash across the screen: Morning runs together, split screen of Chuy at the factory and Lucy in her waitress uniform taking orders and charming customers. Then there were scenes of Nancy at the dry cleaners, measuring fabric and hemming up cuffs and skirts edges. And, of course, Billy in bed, offering comic relief. The screens would all come together for group boxing practice at the gym, or at the pool on Sundays, playing and splashing with Wolfy's kids. Then back to split screen with Chuy on the right, Lucy on the left, fighting outdoors at fests all over the Chicagoland area. The screen would cut to dark and happy; summertime music would come to an abrupt halt.

Cut to a dark cluttered house, shaded from sunlight. Armani sat in the filth and smoked a cigarette with his morning breakfast of warm beer and whatever junk food he could find. His montage would show fights with his older brothers, who he was beginning to despise for bringing him into this life of gangs and drugs. Then there were fights with his younger brother, who began to despise Armani for what he was becoming. The montage included drunken haziness, girls he mistreated and ugly gang fights over which corner belonged to which weed-selling gang.

Finally, the screen would cut back to sunshine and romantic music where Lucy and Chuy were holding hands, walking while she rested her head on his shoulder. Where Chuy would pull Lucy to a secluded corner and steal a kiss. And so the summer went. Chuy and Lucy grew closer, Wolfy's kids grew happier and more confident, Armani grew darker and more lost.

In the ring, by the end of the summer, Chuy had fought five more times, racking up four wins and one loss. He had a couple of tough fights and a couple early knockouts. His only loss had come in what was truly an exhibition, as he fought up a weight class against a tough middleweight, giving the guy all he wanted but losing a close decision to the bigger, older opponent. In that fight, he had learned to use his speed and footwork against big punches, and he was as proud of that fight as he was of those that he had won.

When it came to fighting, Lucy, on the other hand, had a disappointing summer thus far. Not because she had lost fights, but because she had fought very few times. The ones she had fought, she had won easily. She had traveled with Chuy to every meet, but only got two fights. Those were with girls she clearly out-classed, ending in the first and second round respectively to keep her opponents from becoming too battered. Her only reward had been getting to spend time with Chuy and working the corners for the junior fighters. She had a natural ability for coaching of which Big Ces, Alvarez and Sultan all took note. They began letting her take the lead in the corner, while standing back and enjoying her passion for the job. She had a talent for recognizing her fighter's strength and the opposing team's weakness and capitalizing on them. The coaches very seldom had to correct the directions she gave the younger fighters.

Before they knew it, only two more weekends of fighting remained on the schedule. Far away Peoria, Illinois, and the biggest fight for the host Maywood Boxing Team: Airport Days, in downtown Northlake.

Friday afternoon practice was light since two major shows were going to be held the next day. The one Chuy would take part in would be in Peoria during the day. Juan Calderon, the experienced fighter Chuy had first sparred with, was fighting at the other event. It would be his first ten round professional fight in nearby Rosemont, a town of convention centers and hotels that bordered the airport.

Practice ended with Sultan calling Lucy and Chuy over. "You two on those bikes all the time, but I'm gonna guess y'all got a license and know how to drive, right?'

Both looked puzzled but nodded yes.

"Y'all ever been to Peoria?" He asked, already pretty sure of the answer. "Well, you're going now. Ya need two to take three juniors with," He said, throwing keys in Chuy's direction.

"Wait... what?" Chuy looked shocked.

Sultan grinned at the boy's reaction, slowed down a bit and continued his instruction. "Take the van to Peoria, that's the keys. Y'all goin' to Spirit Fest, East Peoria. Here's the directions and address." He handed Chuy a crumpled paper.

"Don't fool around. Go straight there; my people will take care of ya when ya get there. When you're done, make sure to get right back on the interstate. I don't want ya lost there. And don't let'em keep ya too late. Sometimes their hospitality takes over. They'll feed ya, but then you come straight home. Call me when you get there and when you leave. He turned his attention to Lucy. "Listen here, girl! You'll be the coach in the corner for those kids. Chuy, you help; y'all got me?"

"Ummm sure, but why...what about Big Ces?" The sudden onslaught of information and responsibility was a lot for Chuy to take in.

"Boy, ya seen Big Ces here this week? Even he needs a week off once in a while, don't he? Alvarez is coming with me to help Joe in his corner. You two are all grown-up, now time you act like it. Drive there, fight, win, eat, come back home."

Satisfied that his plan would work, and that Chuy and Lucy would follow orders, Sultan nodded. "Okay then, you two know how to work the corners, and the card is already set so you both have fights for sure. You want to do this or what?"

Both fighters were speechless, but managed a adamant nod in return.

Sultan let out a satisfied grunt followed by further instructions. "Meet here tomorrow at 9:00 a.m. sharp. Like I said, call me when you get there."

Again, they nodded.

"What up now? Did you two forget how to talk?" Sultan asked gruffly. "When I was your age I was in the Army. I figure you two can handle this; if you can't, say so now."

"Okay, umm…yeah, we're good." Chuy sounded as if he were trying to convince himself.

"Yeah we got this," added Lucy, with far more confidence.

"Good. The van will be here waiting for you. Go win, and don't eat too much! If you ain't careful those folks cookin' will move you up a weight class."

The next morning the duo were already waiting at the gym when the three junior fighters arrived, early as well. Two had walked and the third was dropped off by a mom in a hurry to get to work. In the back of his mind Chuy wondered if his parents would ever have put his life in the hands of a couple of high schoolers just entering their senior year.

"You alright?" asked Lucy, unable to read the expression of his face.

"Yeah sure," Chuy assured her, even though he was expecting a butterfly to pop out of his stomach at any moment.

Lucy saw through him. "Why so nervous? You know it doesn't help you in the ring. We've got hours until we fight. I've never seen you like…" Lucy stopped short. "Wait! You can drive, can't you? Move over, I got it," she ordered without waiting for an answer.

"Oh, thank God," Chuy exhaled loudly as the butterflies dispersed and the look of fear left his face.

"I swear, Jesus, you are the most un-Mexican Mexican I ever met. First, you know the man always drives. And haven't you been driving your mom around since you were, like, thirteen?"

"I am anti-stereotype," shot back Chuy, trying to sound like an intellectual. "By the way, my mom has her license. All that stuff you're talking about isn't un-Mexican, it's un-old-school-Mexican."

"Well," declared Lucy, adjusting the rear-view mirror then expertly pulling out into the street. "Good thing one of us is old school. Otherwise we would never get there alive!"

The three junior fighters played on their phones and snoozed for the almost three-hour drive on the interstate. Surrounded by scenic cornfields, dotted with farmhouses and barns, Chuy and Lucy enjoyed their easy conversation, talking as usual about everything they could think of. Finally, the road signs to Peoria sent them over the Illinois River. They headed east into the urban area, where stores and homes were boarded up and black men—young and old—hung out on corners. The area resembled Chicago's west side, a place that Lucy and Chuy had both been instructed not to enter ever since they were children. They looked at each other with raised eyebrows.

"Where is Sultan sending us?" Chuy whispered, not wanting to alarm the young fighters in the back, who, luckily, were all asleep by then.

The answer came when Lucy rounded a corner and they saw an old, beautiful church. It stood tall at the end of the block, at the far end of a huge cul de sac. The street was lined with tiny houses and shops, many surrounded with wrought-iron fencing. On this beautiful, sunny Saturday morning the gates were wide open. People darted in and out of the tiny houses toting bowls and over-loaded pans of foods to stands run by volunteers. Additionally, lining the cul de sac were trucks selling various tempting carnival food items.

A makeshift boxing ring filled the middle of the street, with chairs and benches facing it on all four sides. Activities appeared to be in full swing. A man in a traffic vest saw the Maywood Boxing Van and wildly signaled Lucy to a prime parking spot not far from the ring.

"You Sultan's people? Glad to have y'all. Long drive from old Maywood. That's alright, we make it worth the drive round here." He shouted into the van, not waiting for an answer. When the Maywood five had all climbed out of the van the friendly man directed them to the weigh-in tent where they saw a few familiar faces from Aurora, along with some other teams they did not recognize. The Maywood squad was hustled through physical exams and weigh-ins, as the fights were scheduled to start in only a half hour. The Peoria coach approached and welcomed the team, then spoke kindly about his good friend Sultan. He went on to explain the way the event would unfold.

"There are ten junior fights, then we break before we go with the senior fighters. You will have plenty of time to change and warm-up. You two fight last," he nodded to Chuy and Lucy. "We heard good things about you both."

Chuy and Lucy thanked the coach for his kind words, then went to work. First they had to get their fighters ready and coach them to a win. Only then could they think about their own upcoming battles.

The junior fighters were dressed, wrapped and ready for the ring quickly. However, no one was fighting from Maywood until the third fight. Once the juniors were ready, Chuy and Lucy had time to look the ring over. There was no tent or canvas over the top of the ring to block the noon sun. That was unusual in itself, but nothing compared to what they were calling a "ring". A large pad had been set out on the blacktop, thus making the ring level with the street. Worn barge ropes strung through poles cemented into car tires made up the "ring." It looked as if kids had put up a homemade ring in someone's backyard! Chuy and Lucy gave each other a perplexed glance, then dropped their heads for a muffled laugh, not wanting to embarrass their host.

They rounded up their junior fighters, taking them down the aisle toward ringside seats. A shirtless man in his early twenties, wearing cutoff shorts and combat boots, stopped eating his corn dog long enough to wish the team good luck as they passed by. Soon enough the second junior match was over and the fights at Saint Lucas Church, East Peoria, Illinois began for Team Maywood. Lucy was all business as she took the lead in the corner, offering short, helpful instruction.

"Don't wait—be the first to throw punches! Outwork him! Show him who we are! You got me?"

The young fighter acknowledged the advice and followed it to a tee, not letting his opponent catch his breath. He worked hard to earn a unanimous decision.

On the way back down the aisle, the same shirtless young man, who was now eating a burger, congratulated the team.

The early afternoon continued in the same manner. Lucy coached with confidence, while Chuy was a good second, taking care of each fighter before and after every round. Each junior fought hard and well, outlasting the opponent because of skills, and conditioning that Sultan and the other coaches instilled into all their fighters. Every time the team paraded from the ring to the van the same shirtless young man, always eating assorted carnival food, congratulated the team and the fighter.

"I think you got a fan," Chuy said to Lucy with a light jab.

"Funny, I was thinking the same thing about you."

Both shrugged their shoulders. It was time to change clothes and wrap each other's hands with gauze and tape. It was now later in the afternoon and time for the senior fighters to compete. Fights nine and ten would be up quickly. The team would be heading home well before dark.

Lucy, in her gold shorts and top, stood outside the ring of rickety chairs, Chuy by her side, and the three junior fighters nearby. The eighth fight had finished, and the fighters had met in the middle to hear a winner declared. Lucy waited, ducking, and bobbing in the aisle, as the participants from the previous fight cleared the ring. The shirtless young man now stood in the opposite corner. Chuy pointed him out once again to Lucy.

"Told you he was a fan. He's got a good seat for your fight."

Lucy smiled and began the short walk down the aisle to enter the ring. She looked experienced and confident. Her opponent, a slender African-American girl, stepped awkwardly into the ring looking nervous and apprehensive. Lucy continued to duck and bob, shadow-boxing in her corner. She was working up a good sweat while the other girl stood in her own corner, hands hanging by her side, seemingly unaware of what she was doing there.

"I'm not sure how many fights this kid's had," Chuy remarked to Lucy while she warmed up. "But don't let that fool you, be ready to work."

Lucy nodded in agreement.

The announcer introduced the fighters. Lucy received polite applause, while her opponent, Catrina Robbins, got a loud cheer from the hometown crowd.

The bell for the first round sounded. Predictably Lucy charged to the middle of the ring, bobbing left and right and suddenly throwing a tremendous right that landed flush on her opponent's jaw. *Another quick knockout* flashed through Chuy's mind, but he was wrong. The punch seemed to wake Robbins up, as though it had angered her into fighting. After that the two fighters let loose a barrage of furious punches in the middle of the ring that lasted the entire first round. Lucy returned to her corner breathing hard.

Chuy gave her water. "Okay, this kid is no pushover. Get back to fighting your style—make her miss! We know she can fight but, can she box?"

Lucy nodded, but as soon as the bell rang both fighters began where they had left off—assaulting each other with wild roundhouse punches in the center of the ring. Neither fighter was willing to take a step back, but with fifty seconds into the second round Robbins landed a wild shot to Lucy's temple that sent her reeling. The referee jumped in with an eight count. Chuy stood up from where he had been kneeling in the corner and cupped his hands.

"Lucy!" He screamed. "Enough!"

Chuy's passion surprised Lucy, and she felt herself grin in the middle of the action. She caught his eye to let him know she understood and stepped back into the action.

This time she reached her arms around Robbins' body and pulled her close, tying up her slender opponent in the middle of the ring. The referee broke them up. Next, Lucy blocked and ducked the wild punches still being thrown her way. She landed her first body shots of the fight and knocked the wind out of her opponent. Lucy's skills were now fully unleashed, and she was introducing jabs into the mix which snapped Robbins' head back. She reacted with a wide swing at Lucy's bobbing head. Now instead of trying to match the wild looping punches of Robbins, Lucy was using them against her, ducking low and responding with straight, accurate rights and lefts, followed by vicious hooks. Robbins was exhausted and hurt, with no defense against Lucy's skill and conditioning. As the bell ended the second round, Chuy and the junior fighters loudly cheered their feisty teammate. Lucy came back to her corner wearing a tired smile.

"Ummm... yeah, sorry."

Chuy stuck out his tongue and splashed water on her face.

Suddenly the referee approached the corner,

"It's over," he said, taking Lucy by the wrist and guiding her to the center of the ring. In the red corner Robbins was being escorted out of the ring. The heat, the furious pace, and Lucy's body attack had been too much for her. Robbins' coach ended the fight after the second round.

The announcer, a jovial looking African-American man, dressed in white from head to toe, stepped into the ring using a totally unnecessary bull horn, as his baritone voice rang through the cul de sac.

"Ladies and gentlemen, the red corner has stopped the fight after the second round. The winner by TKO: Lucy 'Rockem-Sockem' Quinones."

The crowd applauded a great fight, and just like that it was time for the last fight of the day: Chuy's turn, and a chance for a clean sweep for his team. He took off his Maywood Boxing Club tee-shirt and stepped out of the ring to get gloved. Lucy, still dripping in sweat, removed her gloves and headgear. She threw a fresh towel over her shoulder and grabbed the water bottle. In sixty seconds, coach became fighter and vice-versa. Chuy stepped into the ring and viewed his opponent for the first time, only it was not the first time at all. His opponent was the shirtless man! Still in work boots and cut-off jeans, but now wearing gloves and headgear! Chuy turned toward Lucy, who was standing in his corner.

"You gotta be kidding!" he exclaimed.

"Well it looks like he was your fan after all," Lucy cracked up in their corner. "So much so that he wanted to meet you in the ring!"

Chuy shrugged and went into his shadow boxing routine. He was wearing his usual white tank top, red knee-length basketball shorts and white gym shoes. Compared to most guys he fought, who decked themselves out in silk boxing shorts, matching top and real boxing shoes, Chuy looked like a newbie amateur. Compared to his current opponent, however, Chuy looked like a pro confronting a guy off the street, especially since this guy *was* off the street. He'd had to put down his snacks in order to put on the gloves! Now he stood in the red corner ready for battle.

As if she read Chuy's mind, Lucy shouted, "Hey, don't let looks fool ya, concentrate and fight your fight—that's what you told me, and you were right!"

Chuy put on his game face and stepped into the middle of the ring.

"Break immediately when I tell you and keep the punches up. Let's have a good clean fight, fellas," the referee instructed.

The two fighters touched gloves and retreated to their corners.

"Umm...no pressure," Lucy whispered into Chuy's ear, "but the team is undefeated today, so..."

"Thanks a lot," Chuy grinned sardonically, just as the bell started the fight.

Cautiously both fighters circled each other. Chuy began throwing jabs. His heavily-muscled opponent took the punishment without blinking, then threw a roundhouse. Chuy ducked under it, landing a beautiful left-right combination in the process. Chuy danced and jabbed, while his opponent plodded along, missing Chuy completely with his wild shots. Chuy could feel a rush of air when the right hand whizzed past his head, letting him know that there was power behind those wild punches. Chuy landed thirty punches to none and won the round easily, but just as the bell rang that ended the round the shirtless man caught Chuy with his guard down. The referee jumped in, admonishing the other fighter for the late punch, but the damage had been done. Chuy's head was spinning, and his legs were wobbly. The referee walked him back to his corner.

"We can end this fight on disqualification right now," he advised Chuy and Lucy.

Lucy studied Chuy who was slowly regaining his senses.

"No, I'm good," he assured her and the ref.

"We're okay," Lucy concurred.

"Alright, if you say so." The ref went over to warn the other corner.

"Holy crap, this dude hits like a ton of bricks," Chuy admitted, after he swallowed a gulp of water.

"Then don't get hit," was Lucy's solution.

"Great advice, coach! Don't get hit; I'll try to remember that."

The second round was a repeat of the first. His opponent took jabs, hooks, and straight rights from Chuy, but never slowed down. The street guy threw wild, vicious right hooks directed at the head. He might as well have only had one arm, since he never made a move with his left. As the afternoon sun bore down on the ring, Chuy's opponent was relentless. Sweat dripped from his body and a look of sheer rage came over his face. He had only thrown five punches in the round, all of which Chuy had ducked and returned, beautifully artistic combinations that scored points, but had not slowed down the unrelenting man. The second round was approaching its end when Chuy stepped hard to his left, timing the right hook which was coming at him. He would block this punch instead of ducking it. It was a sound enough strategy—until he felt the force of the punch. It nearly knocked him off his feet, even though he blocked it cleanly. The force of the blow left Chuy off-balance, but his opponent did not take advantage, choosing instead to maintain the same plodding pace he had used during the entire fight. At the bell Chuy headed back to his corner, shaking his head.

Lucy worked hard to hide a smile.

"Um… maybe let's stay with ducking the punch, whatta ya say?"

"Ha! Yeah, good call, coach. I think I saw this guy in a scary movie once. He just keeps coming."

"I'm not sure, Chuy, but you may be fighting a zombie. How' bout you stay away from him, we get through this round and go home. "

"Got it, coach!" Chuy winked.

"Hey, I'm serious Jesus. Don't get in a brawl."

"Lucy, I'm tough—not stupid."

In the final round, Chuy continued to maneuver gracefully around his lumbering opponent. He easily ducked the man's wild right. He threw the left-right-left, landing an uppercut, then a hook and a double-hook. Something shifted near the end of the round when Chuy blocked a faltering right hook one more time. Lucy and the junior fighter assisting her jumped up. They could see that the fight was over. The slugger had lost his power. Chuy's wicked combinations and the afternoon sun had done their damage. His opponent turned out to be human after all, and Chuy was the first to feel it. He pressed hard when the man took his first step backward. The guy had no defense and looked tired and dazed. The referee stepped in as the towel from the red corner came flying into the makeshift ring. Chuy jumped up in victory and ran to his corner to hug Lucy and high-five his junior teammates. The defeated strong man slumped on his stool gulping down water. He gave a respectful wave to Chuy for his boxing skills, which Chuy acknowledged with a bow to the other fighter for his toughness.

"The winner, in the blue corner, from Maywood Boxing Club, Jesus "Chuy" LeDesma!" The man in the white suit announced loudly.

Chuy had his hand raised and he glanced over to his corner where the junior fighters were cheering wildly. Lucy, however, had a look of concentration on her face and her eyebrows were furrowed in thought. Chuy caught her eye, and she sent him a thumbs up and clapped her hands.

With the fights over, Chuy and Lucy speedily changed out of their gear and into street clothes. They hustled to the van, where the junior fighters were already waiting.

"Wait one minute," came a big, familiar voice behind them. It was the ring announcer. "We can't send you out on an empty stomach—Sultan would have our heads!"

Chuy and Lucy tried to protest, but quickly discovered it was pointless. The jovial man in white herded the team to a long table just outside the door of the church, as if afraid they would break and run if he let them out of his sight.

"Forget about a damn trophy! Y'all earned a real prize. Sit down, sit!" he encouraged the team members. "Ladies, our guests of honor are here!"

Chuy and Lucy sat on one side of the table, while the three younger fighters sat across from them. Huge plates of fried catfish, corn-on-the-cob, and potato salad were placed in front of them along with an ice-cold pitcher of lemonade. The team sat shyly around the table for all of thirty seconds, then gave up protocol and politeness and dug in! Chuy had never fried catfish before, and he doubted he would have any this good ever again. The food and drinks were amazing. Peoria fighters filled the rest of the long table. The hometown boxers, being served by moms and aunties, were not shy in any way, and quickly got to the serious business of devouring the food. Chuy was enjoying every bite of his meal when a hand landed on his shoulder and he heard a gravelly voice say, "Good fight, man! You got skills, makes me want to train some." It was his opponent, who appeared to have recovered nicely from defeat. He smiled and snagged a huge piece of catfish from the platter.

"Name's Jamal. Good to meet ya, outside that ring." He offered a hand which Chuy willingly shook.

"Hey," Chuy responded, a little surprised. "Yeah, you sure pack a punch. I blocked a right and you still almost knocked me down."

"Ha! Yeah, I need to get serious. I swear after work I'm so beat I have a tough time going to the gym, but I sure like to fight. You know it's better if I do it in the ring. Keeps me out of trouble, ya know."

The two fighters grinned and dove back into their plates.

"Need to save room for dessert, ya'll," Jamal announced. "Best sweet potato pie this side of the Mississippi."

"Sweet potato pie?" questioned one of the junior fighters. "They put sweet potatoes in pie?"

Mom's and other bystanders within hearing distance all laughed.

"Y'all eat stuff we never heard of, too," Jamal pointed out.

"Yeah," added a young Peoria fighter. "Remember when we were in Aurora, and they had tongue tacos?"

"Damnnn!" Commented a Peoria kid.

"You ain't never tried them," scoffed Jamal. "They was good as hell. I think I had ten of em'."

"*Lengua*," Lucy informed them, adding, "At my mom's restaurant it's one of the specialties."

Warm pies were placed on the table. Pieces were cut and huge scoops of vanilla ice cream were placed on top. The fighters did not hesitate to dig in.

"So what do you think now?" Jamal elbowed the junior fighters.

The three had difficulty smiling with their mouths full of pie and vanilla ice cream. They were too busy enjoying the delicious dessert to take time out for words.

"Um, I think they like it," Chuy noted, making everyone roar with laughter.

The hot Peoria sun began to set behind the tall church steeple as the team savored their last bites and washed down their feast with lemonade. Chuy and Lucy were amused by their young companions, who seemed more exhausted from the meal than from their fights. The kindly announcer and the entire Peoria team, including parents, escorted them to the van and sent them on their way back home, with regards to Sultan, demanding a promise that the Maywood team would return next year.

Jamal put a hand on Chuy's shoulder. "I'm gonna give you a better fight next time, Chuy."

"Jamal, if you work on your skills, no one in the state is gonna want to face you, but I think I'm safe."

"Why's that?"

"Cause you keep eating like today, we will definitely be in separate weight classes!"

The Peoria crowd sent them on their way with resounding laughter as Lucy pulled the van out from under the shadowed parking spot and into the late afternoon sunshine.

CHAPTER 25

"**W**ell," said Chuy, as his girlfriend headed toward the expressway, "that was unexpected."

"Yep, unexpected indeed!" She agreed.

Before long the junior fighters were asleep, while Lucy and Chuy settled in for the long stretch of highway that would take them across the state and back to Chicago.

"Hey, since we got three hours to blow, let me ask you something," said Chuy, making himself comfortable in the passenger seat.

"Oh no," laughed Lucy, "What could this be?"

"Why did you ever date Armani?"

"Armani? I haven't thought of him for a long time..." she paused and seriously considered the question. "Well, I don't know... it was my secret life. I had to be so good in school and I had so much to do at home. It was my chance to be... you know...bad!" She finally concluded with perfect honesty.

"How bad were you?"

"Ha! So now the real question! Not that bad; we were all just kids trying to act like gangbangers. Armani was just a lost little kid. Did you know he took care of his little brother?"

"I find it hard to believe that he took care of anybody but himself. He is such an asshole," Chuy scoffed.

"Mr. LeDesma, such language!" Lucy pushed Chuy, still managing to keep her eyes on the road. "You know, he was jealous of you. Deep down I think, well, I know, he wanted to be like you. He wanted to work hard in school and be an athlete and have a good family. But when you have no dad and your mom leaves you in, like, sixth grade, pretending that your jacked-up older brothers are going to get you and your little brother through high school. I mean, what do you expect?"

"Yeah, I guess you're right. I didn't know all that." Chuy paused, feeling a bit guilty for his long-time hatred of Armani. He exhaled then continued with his real question. "Did you...and he...?"

"Oh my gosh, Chuy, if that's what you want to know, why don't you just ask?"

"Okay, I'm asking."

Lucy snapped her head around to view the passenger seat. "No!" She declared, raising her voice loud enough to cause the junior fighters to rustle in the back seat. She lowered her voice to a whisper. "No, I've never... I mean... I haven't... You're stupid!"

"Okay, okay." Chuy back-pedaled. "I'm sorry I even brought up that guy. I guess I was just a little jealous of anyone who has ever even touched you."

Lucy relented. "Chuy, you are so sweet; you have nothing to worry about. You are my first *real* boyfriend."

"Yessssss!" exclaimed Chuy, sitting up and flexing his biceps then bringing his arms down for a chest-flexing pose.

"Keep it down up there," complained one of the younger fighters.

"You're so weird," whispered Lucy.

"Alright, next question?" Chuy continued

"OMG! Really?" Lucy protested.

"You got someplace to be?" taunted Chuy. "Looks like we got a lot of highway left."

She sighed with mock boredom. "Okay, what now?"

"Well, when they announced my win, you had a strange look on your face. What was that about?

"Did I?"

"Yes, what was going through your head?"

"First, should I be scared of how well you know me?"

"Don't answer a question with a question," Chuy replied.

"Umm... it's when they announce your win, it's always Jesus "Chuy" LeDesma. I mean that's just your name, you need a real nickname, and..."

"And you don't like Stallion?"

Lucy raised her voice again. "NO! Hate it!"

"You got something better?"

"Well..." Lucy tipped her head toward him, "You know one of my favorite books growing up was 'The Outsiders'...how about Ponyboy?"

"Ponyboy? Not very tough, Lucy 'Rockem, Sockem'. Where did you ever come up with that?"

"You know Alvarez was 'The Pony Express,' right? It doesn't bring to mind a tough guy, but I like it. It could be a tribute to him, just like mine is a tribute to my uncle. You heard my uncle talk about Alvarez when he was coming up. Tio sure thought he was cool."

Chuy shook his head. "This is all too funny."

"What?"

"I don't want to tell you,"

"Not fair; you started, you got to finish."

"I can't believe I'm telling you this." Chuy took a deep breath, "Well, I was out in the back of my house, shadow boxing and..."

"Flexing," added Lucy with raised eyebrows and a smirk.

"Maybe you know *me* too well, maybe there was *some* flexing happening ...and I said... no, I can't tell you!"

"You have to!" Lucy almost yelled, then, repeated in a whisper. "You have to..."

"I said... to myself... out loud, 'Stallion', you are one bad MUTHA FU...'"

"Chuy!" Lucy squealed out a warning.

"That's not the bad part—my mom heard me!"

They muffled their howls of laughter in an effort not to wake the kids in the back.

Lucy wiped tears from her eyes. "Way to go, dipwad!"

"Yeah I know," admitted Chuy, covering his face in embarrassment. What's worse..."

"Wait! It gets worse?"

233

"Well, that's the point. Raul heard me too. He said, 'You ain't no stallion, you're a pony'."

"See!" Lucy said excitedly. "It's fate, and it will keep you humble. Chuy 'The Ponyboy' Ledesma!"

"The Ponyboy? PONYBOY! PONYBOY!" Chuy imitated a crowd calling out his name. "You're so Awesome!! Okay, I guess it works. Ponyboy it is!" So I guess now I'm a real fighter."

"Um...yeah... almost."

Chuy groaned. "There's something else?"

"Yeah...next we gotta talk about your uniform."

"Alright, alright, one thing at a time!"

When the van finally turned off onto highway 355, they were still quietly chuckling. The summer sun was setting—a beautiful end to a day that had far exceeded their expectations. Traveling in the Maywood Boxing Club van had been fun and sweetly romantic. Another chapter in the lives of the weary travelers inside had been written.

In early August, summer can be in full swing for most people, but for students and teachers, their minds (if not their hearts) are focused back on school. By August 1st, the school parking lot was already filled with teachers preparing for a new year. Students were finishing summer sports camps, band, and summer theater, and beginning the process of dropping off paperwork and signing up for fall classes. The rest of the world was trudging through day by day, tiring of the relentless summer heat, but students were feeling the excitement of another new beginning.

Chuy, Lucy, and Nancy had finished their summer jobs and were enjoying one week of "vacation" with only registration and, of course, boxing on the 'have-to-do' list. The rest of their time was 'want to'. This week they could do what they wanted to do. Lucy and Chuy kept to their morning routine but jumping back in their respective beds after road work for a nap was a wonderful thing to experience.

By Wednesday they were ready for a visit to the pool. They decided to take their bikes over to Forest Park, about ten miles away. Wolfy's kids would be there attending their day camp. Alvarez and his buddy, Mr. Drobs, the AP Spanish teacher, habitually rode to and from Forest Park, so Chuy and Lucy decided to follow their route. They met at 11:00 and leisurely headed down 24th to Chicago Avenue, which took them through the tidy, square brick houses of Melrose Park and Maywood, passing by tiny Walter Luther High School. They crossed 1st Avenue past old, gigantic Proviso East High School, with its huge practice field and rusty, tattered chain-link fence. Cooler air caressed them as they rode over the Desplaines River and through the forest preserve. At Lathrop Street they passed the unassuming, yet beautifully simplistic and costly pillars that marked River Forest. Preferring to stay on the quiet side streets, they turned onto School Street and marveled at the huge, immaculate houses—houses supposedly once owned by old-time gangsters—mansions with impeccable lawns and ridiculous iron fences.

"Once I turn pro, and of course win it all, I'm buying that one." Chuy pointed to a magnificent house on the corner.

"I'll take that one," said Lucy, singling out a more modest, but unique-looking home, streamlined, and eloquent in design.

"I think it's a Frank Lloyd Wright."

"A Frank Lloyd Who?"

"He's a famous architect, silly. He used space and certain features to… never mind," Lucy snickered. "I'll give you my powerpoint presentation one of these days."

Chuy made a face. "Can't wait," he said sarcastically.

The two biked slowly across Lake Street and into Forest Park, arriving at Madison Street, with its diners, restaurants and antique stores, including an old hardware store that had survived the onslaught of chains and super stores.

Ice cream shops and a railroad-themed diner, loved by kids, caught their attention as they cruised by. New Orleans bars with Irish names, Italian restaurants and a high-end Mexican fusion eatery lined one side of the street, while an ancient bank and a bakery that had opened in the thirties occupied the other side. Though not officially Chicago, Forest Park marked the end of the suburbs and the beginning of the Chicago city neighborhoods, like Austin and Garfield Park that spanned the city all the way to Lake Michigan.

"We're coming back here to eat," Chuy shouted to Lucy,

"Good thing you don't have to worry about your weight," she replied.

"Hey, we'll burn it off on the ride home," Chuy reminded her.

The two headed down Circle Avenue huffing it up the steep incline of the bridge. They could hear the sounds of kids and whistles, letting them know that the pool was near.

"Chuy! Lucy! Hey! Hey!" Wolfy's kids all came running when they saw the pair walking toward the pool.

"L-l-lucy, l-look at my s-s-swim suit!" Missy grabbed Lucy's hand. "Come on, I'll s-show you m-m-my dive!"

The kids could not contain their excitement, and eagerly vied for Lucy's and Chuy's attention.

"Wow, what a surprise!" came a familiar voice from the rear of the pack. It was Ms. Kelly.

"Hey, I guess this is the place to be," Chuy observed happily. "Are you working, Ms. Kelly?"

"No, no, no, my girls are running around here—see them?" She motioned to a pair of girls wearing matching pink swimsuits to get out of the pool. "These are my ladies, Adeline and Madeline."

"Addy and Maddy? So cute!" Lucy grinned and waved at the two little wild-haired girls who were making their way toward their mother.

"Yep, you got it!" Mrs. Kelly gave Lucy a hug.

The two girls came closer to their mother. "Girls, meet Chuy and Lucy."

"So you are seventeen years old, and you must be fifteen years old," teased Chuy. "Did you drive your mom here today?"

The girls both giggled and shook their heads. "No, I'm five." said Madeline.

"I'm free," said Addy, holding up two fingers.

"Almost; Adeline likes to add a year," Mrs. Kelly explained, giving her youngest a quick snuggle.

"That will change," said a blonde lady in shades and a huge sun hat.

"Oh, guys, this is Mrs. Jenn."

The attractive woman took off her sunglasses and put out her hand.

"Hey, I've seen you at Leyden," said Chuy, shaking the offered hand.

"Yep," Mrs. Jenn confirmed. "I'm the speech pathologist, but please, no school talk; I can't believe the summer is almost over! Let's enjoy these last few hours."

"Deal!" Chuy agreed. "Do you live around here, Ms. Kelly."

"I'm over in Addison, but this place has the best facilities for kids, so we come here for the girls *and* I get to watch our students play without having to work, which is really great! Alvarez is the one that introduced me to the place—he lives just over the expressway. I'm sure he's somewhere around here, probably doing laps."

As if on cue, Alvarez strolled up to the group.

"Hey, what a surprise!" He clapped Chuy on the back. "Glad you guys could make it! How was Peoria?"

"It was crazy," Lucy told him, "but so much fun!"

"Did they have the ring right down on the street with barge ropes?"

"Oh, yeah," said Chuy. "At first it seemed really weird, but we both fought tough kids—and won! And the food was so good!"

"The catfish, right? And the…"

"SWEET POTATO PIE," all three exclaimed in unison, cracking up with laughter.

"Alright, you guys go hang out with the kids, they are dying to talk with you! I've got this magnificent body that needs constant maintenance." Alvarez headed for the lap lane, but not before playfully splashing Maddy and Addy, who had already returned to the pool.

Chuy and Lucy jumped into the pool and immediately began splashing back and forth with Wolfy's kids. Next, they went down the water slide with a few of the more adventurous of the special needs group. Afterward everyone headed to the concession stand for pizza. Chuy and Lucy forgot about their diets for one meal. Eventually the tired duo reluctantly left the water park and began the bike ride to the gym for practice. The sun and the bike ride had taken their toll, and getting through practice was especially tough, but with the major hometown fights approaching the two did their best, as always.

After practice, Chuy rode to Lucy's house, which had become part of their new daily ritual. It was the part he loved best. He had been pedaling to Lucy's house for most of the summer, where the two would take over the swing on the back patio, cuddling and watching the stars after the sky turned dark. This night, Lucy playfully kissed Chuy on his neck and then snuggled into his shoulder. Chuy gently cupped Lucy's chin and pulled her face to his. He kissed her deeply, breathing in the ever-present smell of her hair that never failed to stir him inside and make him feel as if he could melt into her.

"I love you," they each said with a sigh, then both sat up.

"Did we just say the world's first same-time 'I love you' in history?" Lucy asked, kissing Chuy again.

"I wanted to say it for a long time." Chuy whispered in her ear.

"Me, too."

"Well, now we never have to argue about who said it first." Lucy sighed, snuggling under Chuy's arm.

Chuy looked out into the night sky dotted with stars and the blinking lights of jet planes going to and from the airport. "I've never said that to anyone before, Lucy."

"Me either, Chuy, because I never felt it before."

They kissed again, long and deep, as if they each were taking in the spirit of the other.

"I love you," they said again at the same time, which caused them to break into laughter.

"We are ridiculous," Chuy whispered.

"Oh, yeah, "Lucy agreed.

Lucy sighed again with quiet contentment and put her head back on Chuy's shoulder. "There'll never be another night exactly like this," she murmured into his neck. "This was the best day of summer—ever!"

Chuy agreed happily. They sat like that for a long time, watching the blinking lights and the twinkling stars.

Airplane Days, the annual home-town festival for Northlake, Illinois, highlighted the last week of vacation. The festival not only marked the end of the summer for all students, but for the fighters the festival meant their first hometown fight. The festivities began on Friday night, but because of their fights the next day Lucy and Chuy had decided not to make it a date night. Lucy was going to spend some time at the festival with Nancy but was planning to be home in bed early. Chuy had decided to skip the whole thing entirely, but then Billy came by his home and used his wiles to entice him to go out.

"Come on, Chewbacca, I haven't seen you all summer," he whined. "You're too busy hangin' with your *girrrrrrl-frieeeeend!*"

"Billy, you have grown so much since fourth grade. It really is amazing," Chuy said sarcastically. "Maybe if you would have made it to the gym we could have hung out all summer. I know you haven't spent much time with Crystal because she told me. What the hell have you been doin'?"

"Why are we talking about the past, Chewbacca? Let's go over to the fest tonight. What if some dudes are hitting on your girl? You will need to show those boxing skills."

"First, we all know Lucy can take care of herself, and I ain't worried. Second, you fight out of the ring, you're off the team, but I guess you got to be on the team in order to get kicked off. Seriously, Billy, at your weight class you could totally kick ass. Why don't you get serious about something? Start with boxing."

"I am serious—I'm serious about going to Airplane Days." Billy replied, not even taking a moment to consider his friend's good advice.

"Wow! That hard head of yours would be perfect for boxing! Tomorrow, after I win, we will hang out. Now see ya," Chuy pushed Billy out the door, noticing a familiar smell mixed with his cologne. "Billy, what the hell?"

"What?" Billy tried to act surprised, but instead looked guilty.

"That's what you been doing all summer?"

"What?"

Chuy shrugged. "Whatever!" He tried not to judge. Plenty of his friends smoked weed, but he had seen that go wrong too many times. A lot of those guys became *'weed fiends,'* caring way too much about getting high, then sitting in the cafeteria, saying stuff like "Dude, I got so high last night," and thinking that was the best thing ever.

"You coming to my fight tomorrow, or what?" Chuy asked curtly.

"What do you think? Of course." Billy assured him.

"Then we will talk tomorrow—we *need* to talk and don't come *high*!"

"Okay, okay, *Dad*, I'll be there; I'll see you tomorrow." With a wave of his hand Billy strolled away.

Chuy closed the door and retreated to his room, thinking about his friend, but trying to push it out of his mind. *Practicing conversations never work; neither do lectures,* he thought. He would win his fight, hang with his friend, and remind him of the good times they'd had. School would start and he would spend more time with Billy, keeping him busy! That was all he could do. Chuy fell asleep early, confident that everything would work the way it should.

The next morning Chuy and Lucy cut their morning run a little short since it was fight day. Then they headed over to the festival early. Activities were already getting started, with vendors laying out their merchandise and ride operators checking their equipment for safety. The aromas of carnival food being prepared hung tantalizingly in the air—onions on the grill, sugar spinning for cotton candy, assorted butter covered treats frying in hot oil. It wasn't easy to focus on fighting when their stomachs were begging for treats. Big Ces, Sultan and Alvarez were setting up the ring when the couple approached them.

"Ready for your hometown debut?" Alvarez asked with a warm smile.

"Hey, Coach Alvarez," Big Cesar motioned to the pair, "they don't need us no more. They went to Peoria and won everything."

"Oh, then I guess we can take the day off," Alvarez exaggerated a stretch. "Good! I could use a nap. Let me know how you guys do."

"Wait! Who's gonna get us water?" joked Chuy.

"Yeah, I need someone to hold the spit bucket," Lucy added.

"You were right, Ces." Alvarez held his hands up. "They are big shooters now—so big shots, we don't have a road trip today. Why so early? What ya' gonna to do 'til fight time?"

Lucy held up her book. "I'm gonna find some shade."

Chuy held up a thick novel also.

"Oh! His girl's been a good influence on Jesus." Cesar elbowed Alvarez as they both tried to look impressed.

"What? I like reading." Chuy insisted.

"Yeah?" Alvarez returned the elbow dig to Big Ces, "Comic book...the back of cereal boxes..."

"Just for that I'm not going to let you hold my spit bucket." Chuy pretended indignation, turning his back on his coaches. He walked away, leaving them chuckling.

At noon the junior fighters began the meet as usual. Chuy and Lucy watched as the younger kids from the gym proceeded to fight very well for their team. When they finished, there was a full hour break before the senior fighters were scheduled to begin at three o'clock, when the fest was in full swing, and the day was at its hottest. Of course, Chuy and Lucy, as the featured fighters, would fight last.

In what seemed like no time at all, it was time for the pair to head to the changing tent. As they approached the entrance Lucy stopped Chuy.

"Hey, I've got a little surprise for you," she grinned.

"Here? Now?" asked Chuy, with a devilish smile.

"Ha! Very funny."

Suddenly, Nancy, Ulises and Billy were surrounding them. Nancy was holding a white box and Billy had a gift bag dangling from one hand.

Chuy was caught totally off guard. "What is all this?"

Billy shoved the gift bag in Chuy's face. Chuy took the bag and reached in, pulling out a pair of new white boxing shoes.

"What the...?"

"That's not all; look what Nancy made," Lucy prompted him to dig further.

"Lucy paid for the material," Nancy added quickly.

"We all pitched in for the shoes," Billy volunteered, with a sheepish smile.

"Yes, let's make sure Billy gets some credit," laughed Ulises. "Billy's mom pitched in on the shoes."

"Whatever," Billy shrugged his shoulders. "Just open the box."

Chuy opened it to reveal shiny, red satin boxing shorts and a white boxing tank top. Nancy had created a boxing uniform using the fine fabric that professional and experienced amateur fighters used. In short, it was the real deal. Chuy could now go to any tournament and look like a legit fighter. He stood there at a loss for words, shocked and touched by the gifts.

Bill couldn't stand the silence. "Don't just stand there with your mouth open, go put them on. You gonna miss your fight if you keep looking at your uniform."

"Oh, yeah! I mean...thanks, all of you! Thanks so much!" Chuy gushed, snapping out of it. He gave a quick, grateful hug to each of his friends and went back to change, fighting the urge to wipe his tear-filled eyes in front of them.

When Chuy walked out of the tent a few minutes later, he looked and felt like a different fighter. He couldn't help but feel cool and invincible— and he looked it. Lucy emerged from the tent a couple of minutes later. She delayed her usual ducking and bobbing to take a good look at Chuy.

"That's what I'm talking about!" She hit him in the shoulder with a gentle right hook.

"Let's go, 'Rockem Sockem'!"

"Let's go, 'Ponyboy'!"

The two strolled down the aisle together, Nancy, Billy and Ulises following. The three coaches were already waiting in the blue corner.

"Damn, son, not only do you look like a fighter, you two got yourselves an entourage these days," Sultan joked, putting his hands on the shoulders of his fighters. "Okay, you both have tough kids, but they green and they wild. These are the best we could get at the end of the season, then we got a break 'til the Gloves tourney. I figure better easy fights than no fights at all. You both should be skilled enough to get in, work, get a win, impress the hometown crowd. You feel me?"

They both agreed with a nod.

"Make sure you don't get your ass knocked out being careless! Okay, there ain't no room for me in this corner, so I'm gonna sit my old ass right down and have a lemonade. You two go to work—Lucy, ladies first."

Sultan sauntered over to the nearest folding chair which happened to be occupied by one of the junior fighters. He handed the boy a fistful of change.

"Move, boy, and go get your coach a lemonade."

The boy ran off to complete his mission and Sultan settled in. "Okay, youngsters, let's put on a show."

Lucy stepped into the ring with Alvarez and Big Ces. Ulises grabbed the bucket and the water, while Chuy positioned himself behind the folding chairs to warm-up, where he could still keep an eye on the on-going fight.

In the ring, Lucy and her opponent were facing each other, listening to the instructions from the ref. Sultan wore a look of satisfaction on his face, knowing he had done his job. Lucy was poised and ready in her shimmering, gold uniform with her neatly braided hair, well-contained under fitted headgear. She moved smoothly and rhythmically. Her opponent, on the contrary, appeared nervous and jittery. She was athletically built, with sinewy arms and thighs like tree trunks. Already heavily perspiring from the afternoon sun, strings of blonde hair shot from her headgear and clung to her face and neck.

The fighters returned to their corners for final instructions from their managers. Alvarez looked Lucy in the face, offering her a swig of water.

"Luce, listen to me—I want you to treat this like a sparring session. Today I want you disciplined, and you need to get some rounds in because the next time you step in the ring to fight it will be the tourney, and there will be no holding back. You got it?"

Lucy nodded.

"You really got it, Lucy?" Alvarez repeated, knowing Lucy had a hard time holding back, and in all likelihood she would go instinctively for the knockout.

Lucy smiled, showing her mouthpiece. "Yes, I got it."

The bell sounded and, true to her word, Lucy came out circling to her right, not charging immediately to the center as was her usual style. The fighters traded jabs, Lucy landing hers, while slipping past her opponent's. The tall blonde gradually seemed to gain confidence, but Lucy squelched that with double hooks to the body and head, eliciting a cheer from the hometown crowd, and causing Alvarez and Big Ces to jump up, both shouting, "Whoaaa! Easy!!!"

Lucy acknowledged them with a nod and went back to work just as the bell ended the first round.

Big Cesar splashed her with water, while Ulises slipped the stool in under the ropes. Gratefully she sat down.

Alvarez knelt down and sprayed water into her mouth. "That's the way to work, just like that! Let's get two more rounds in the same way."

"It's tough, holding back," Lucy told him between breaths.

Big Ces winked at her and grinned. "It's good for you."

"But it's not fun," Lucy said, standing up, ready for the next round.

"Then let's have some fun; show off a little bit. You have my permission," Alvarez said, gently inserting her mouthpiece.

Lucy continued to follow Alvarez's directions to the letter. By the third round she was working—moving and having fun, but she was careful not to humiliate her over-matched opponent. When the final bell rang both fighters were happy, the corners were happy, and most of all, the fans were happy. They had witnessed their local girl totally outclass her opponent. Lucy 'Rockem Sockem' Quinones was proclaimed the winner and the hometown crowd erupted with applause and cheers.

The cheers continued when Chuy stepped into the ring, cued by the announcer's introduction.

"Ladies and Gentlemen, entering the ring, another local fighter, from the Maywood Boxing Club, hailing from right here in Northlake, Illinois, Jesus 'Ponyboy' LeDesma!"

Chuy whipped around to face Lucy who was still standing in the blue corner.

"You told 'em 'Ponyboy'?" he asked.

"You look like a fighter now; 'bout time you had a cool nickname, don't you think?" she replied.

Chuy began shadow boxing in his corner. "You are full of surprises."

"Ponyboy, huh…" said Alvarez. "I like it; tribute to your hero?."

"Sure, Alvarez," Chuy grinned slyly. "Aren't you everybody's hero?"

Chuy winked and headed to center ring for the instruction. He took a moment to look over his opponent, a guy about His own age, but much shorter and with a thick middle. The boy looked nervous, surrounded by Chuy's hometown crowd. He was facing an impressive-looking fighter and he knew it. Chuy knew better than to let looks deceive, however, he couldn't help but feel confident. He returned to his corner to hear Alvarez echo the thoughts that had just run through his own head.

"This kid doesn't look like much, but don't let that fool ya'. Watch out for the wild shots; get your work in, stay disciplined."

The starting bell rang and just as Chuy had guessed, a wild right hook came flying at him. He stepped back and threw a picture-perfect straight right. The blow stunned the short, squat fighter and the ref jumped into the middle for an eight-count. Chuy glanced to his corner and received the same response that Lucy had gotten from Ces and Alvarez, "Whoaaa! Slow down!"

The rest of the round Chuy danced and jabbed. He ducked wide, wild punches, making his opponent seem slow and clumsy. By the second round the referee called a merciful end to the fight, thanks to the overwhelming skill shown by Chuy and the obvious exhaustion of the other fighter.

Chuy returned to his corner with a shrug. He'd done the best he could to keep the fight going. Back in the blue corner, he received another one of Lucy's surprises: she had gathered Wolfy's kids, Ms. Kelly and her daughters, Chuy's mom and dad and Raul, and finally Coach Wolf. They were all waiting to meet Chuy as he climbed out of the ring and down the steps. The cheers from the crew, along with those of other classmates and locals, was deafening. Chuy bounced down the steps, grabbed Lucy and pulled her back up into the ring. Her family, including her Uncle Ricardo, joined the loudly cheering crowd. The clamor could be heard throughout the fest, even drowning out the classic rock music that blared out from the carnival rides. People stopped in their tracks, trying to figure out what all the racket was about.

Back in the ring Lucy and Chuy laughed and hugged each other tightly, causing the crowd to erupt yet again.

"We got the most 'cred' for the easiest fights we've ever had," Chuy whispered in Lucy's ear, bringing laughter from her one more time.

The two victorious fighters stepped down into the mass of their waiting fans. Of course, Wolfy's kids jumped out in front of everyone, grabbing them by both hands then escorting them to the concession stand, where Coaches Wolf and Alvarez bought pizza for the fan club.

Wolf nudged Chuy. "I guess boxing has paid off for you, Jesus," He observed with a proud smile.

"It seems like things are paying off for you, too, Coach. You guys are going to the state tournament for summer baseball, right?"

"Yep," Wolf responded proudly. "One of eight best teams in the state. That is the best ever for Layden baseball, but it's only the summer tournament. Even if we win, it won't be an *official* state title. We have to wait until spring to see if we can really bring home a title. From what I've seen and heard, it looks like you'll have a chance at a state championship before we do!"

Chuy shrugged. "We'll see; In the meantime, I'm going to knock out this pizza. Thanks, Coach!"

The whole group enjoyed the late afternoon party, along with family and friends who had become like family. Eventually the sun set on the fest and delivered a beautiful summer night. The sound of carnival rides, screaming kids and classic rock, the smell of popcorn and funnel cakes, the desperate push to enjoy the end of summer filled the air and would long live in the memories of all. Chuy and Lucy wandered among the people they loved, giving each other secret glances, showing each other their love with every step. Another amazing night in what had been an amazing summer.

CHAPTER 26

One by one the parents of Wofly's kids drifted in to claim their children. Some headed home, while others stayed to enjoy the festivities. Ms. Kelly and her daughters made their way to the rides, leaving Alvarez to announce to Chuy and Lucy, "Okay, you two, great job; be careful tonight. I'm taking Coach Wolf and Ces over to the beer tent, so you're on your own. You think you guys have fans, wait 'til I get Wolfy over there with all his old players! It'll be a mob scene."

"Sounds like you better be careful, too," Lucy noted with a twinkle in her eye.

"And don't drink too much!" added Chuy with mock seriousness.

"Listen, bro, at my age, you can't drink and have a bod like this, and I've never seen Wolfy have more than two beers in all the time I've known him. It's this guy I got to keep in check." Alvarez pointed a thumb at Cesar.

"Yeah, right! " scoffed Big Ces, with a playful push that sent Alvarez flying. "With you two old ladies, I've *got* to behave myself. It's like drinking with two moms!"

After the three coaches headed out Lucy snuggled into Chuy for a moment.

"Nancy and I are going to take my little sisters on the rides, so I'll see you tomorrow, right?" she questioned softly, looking into his eyes. He missed her before she was even gone.

"You bet," he spoke quietly in return, adding, "hey, you did good today."

"You too, babe," she whispered in his ear.

He held her tightly for a short time, then took a deep breath, drawing into himself her special scent.

Reluctantly Lucy ended the moment with a peck on the cheek before running off with her sisters and Nancy.

"Bye, see you tomorrow. Love you!"

Chuy stood motionless for another stretch of time, intoxicated by this young, amazing woman who seemed to care for him almost as much as he cared for her.

"Eww, Chuy's got a guurrrlfriend!!"

Chuy's moment was interrupted by Raul, who suddenly loomed over his shoulder.

Chuy rolled his eyes. "You and Billy need to hang out. You both have the same stupid sense of humor."

"Ha! Naw, I've had enough fest for today. Besides, you ain't the only one killing it; I got a little hottie of my own."

"Ewww, Raul's got a guurlfriend!!" mimicked Chuy, unable to resist.

"Okay, I got to take your parents' home," Raul announced, after Chuy's mother and father had hugged and congratulated their younger son one more time.

"Listen, Ponyboy," Raul hugged Chuy. "Be safe tonight, see you tomorrow. Hey little brother, ya did good," he called out over his shoulder.

That left Billy and Chuy alone to continue the celebration by themselves. Of course, Billy got himself another slice of pizza.

Chuy was in awe of how much his little buddy could eat. "Dude, slow down! How many slices you gonna have?"

"I'm a growing boy," mumbled Billy, around a huge bite that filled his cheeks.

The boys meandered through the fest, pausing to watch several cover bands, stopping at food stands as they searched out more drinks and sweets for Billy.

"So Crystal's not coming to boxing much anymore. I heard she got a night job," Chuy mentioned as they walked.

"Yeah, I guess," replied Billy sheepishly.

"What? You don't see her? I thought that's what you've been doing—I mean, I never see you anymore."

A group of grade schoolboys interrupted, pointing at Chuy,

"Hey, it's Ponyboy! Hey good fight today, man!"

Chuy acknowledged them with a wave. "Thanks fellas."

"I'm gonna join the club when I go to high school," announced a baby-faced boy.

"Me, too," his friend echoed.

"Hey, you don't have to wait," Chuy told them. "It's Maywood Boxing Club on 17th. Have your mom or dad bring you, even if it's just to get a good workout."

"Cool!" the boys answered in unison, shadow boxing with pretzels and hot dogs in their hands. "Thanks, Ponyboy."

Chuy grinned at his new-found popularity, but he did not let Billy off the hook. "So... if you haven't been spending time with Crystal, and you haven't been boxing, and if you aren't working, then what...?"

Billy remained silent, but a moment later two young girls caught sight of Chuy before he could continue interrogating his suddenly quiet friend.

"Come on, he was in my study hall last year," One whispered to the other, loud enough for the boys to hear.

"Hi, Chuy, remember me? A cute young girl wearing too much make-up came running toward Chuy. "We saw your fight."

"Yeah, we saw your fight," echoed her friend, a slightly chubby girl with a pretty smile.

"You're really good, Chuy, or do we call you Ponyboy?" Both girls giggled.

"No, Chuy's fine," he told them.

"When do you fight again?" asked the first girl, stepping in front of her friend in a bid for Chuy's full attention.

"Not 'til the state tournament."

"I bet you win," she stated, trying desperately to flirt.

"Thanks," Chuy replied, "but the competition is going to be much stronger than today."

"I still bet you win," the young girl gushed. Unable to think of anything more to say, she blurted out, "See you at school."

"Yeah," seconded her friend. "See you at school!"

"Oh my god, he's so cute!" The girls ran away laughing, again talking loud enough for Chuy to hear.

"Dude, I guess you think you're pretty cool now," Billy stared at the ground shaking his head.

Chuy recognized jealousy when he saw it. He tried to brush away Billy's fear that he was being left behind.

"What? They're just kids."

"You love it," Billy accused angrily.

"Wait, you think I take any of this seriously? What's your problem?"

"Whatever," Billy scoffed, turning, and walking away.

"Whoa! You think because some kids, who don't know anything about boxing, were a little impressed today, that I think I'm all that?"

"Exactly!" Billy shot back, his sudden irrational anger perplexing Chuy even more.

"Dude! Stop!" Chuy took two giant steps catching up with his friend. He put his hand on Billy's shoulder. Billy wheeled around, spitting fire.

"You think it's a piece of cake being your friend? Everything comes easy to you; you want to box. You win every time. You like a girl? Lucy's in love with you. Best Pals President. A-plus student. Mr. Perfect!"

"Whoa, I started boxing because I couldn't play baseball, remember? You were there! So I won a fight at the fest. You know that means nothing. If you would come to practice once in a while, with your talent at your weight class, you would have a better chance at a title than me. When it comes to Lucy, if she would have even looked at me last year I would have crapped my pants! Hell, you took Crystal to the freakin' *prom!* Where the hell is this coming from?"

"It's coming from you being a stuck-up A-hole!" Billy stormed off past the lights of the fest and into the night, flipping up his middle finger as he went.

Chuy stood shaking his head in disbelief. He had very seldom seen his friend in a bad mood, let alone this angry. Billy seemed to have been changing over the summer—not seeing friends, not going out, not coming to practice, not seeing Crystal. Before he could consider Bill's state of mind any further, Chuy was pulled out of his contemplation by Billy's own voice. It sounded like his friend was now calling out to him. From the sound of his voice something was very wrong.

Chuy raced to a point just outside of the festival lighting and stepped into the shadows leading to the parking lots. Billy's voice cried out again. He searched the dark shadows, and finally made out what appeared to be two bodies piled on top of a third. Getting closer, Chuy could see Billy was on the bottom of the pile, punching, kicking, and swearing as fists were furiously pummeling him.

Chuy shouted, *"Hey!"* thinking it would stop the beating, but the assault on Billy did not even slow down. Chuy, who by then had reached the scene, threw himself at the two, through pure luck catching his knee near the temple of the closest attacker. The two attackers plowed into each other and knocked Billy free. Chuy used his momentum to roll quickly to his feet. If he were to use his boxing skills, the last place Chuy wanted to be, was on the ground. The two guys who were beating Billy jumped to their feet as well. Chuy instinctively went into his boxing stance.

"Ha, look at Mayweather!" one sneered. They had no idea Chuy had fought earlier that day.

The two were about Chuy's age, maybe younger. Chuy thought they were probably gangbangers waiting outside the fest to jump kids and steal their money, or get a thrill out of beating someone up, or both. Smaller kids were prime targets. An anger raged in Chuy that he never felt in the ring.

"Yeah, look, he thinks he's..."

The gang banger did not get the next word out. Chuy caught him with a straight right that sent him flying. His partner grabbed Chuy by his collar. Chuy swiped his arm away, but not before he heard the tearing of his own shirt. He had another right ready to launch, but suddenly he was grabbed from all directions. A punch to the back of the head sent Chuy flying forward. He should have known cowards like these always traveled in packs, never fighting one-on-one, or even two-on-one. Kicks came flying in. In a split second the gang bangers had Chuy down. He could have been hurt badly, but despite taking a beating himself, Billy used a good old-fashioned double leg take-down, a move he had done a hundred times as a junior high and freshman wrestler. The gutsy move sent one of the gang bangers down on top of Chuy. The kicks stopped as the group realized they had begun to kick their own man. Chuy, and now Billy, were still on the ground and resigned to taking a beating. They were surrounded by at least eight of the bad guys when distant voices came from the fest. The shouting moved rapidly in their direction.

"Hey what the…? Come on, guys!"

What sounded like a stampede of feet came running to the rescue.

"Let's go, we outta here!"

The voice sounded strangely familiar to Chuy. He rolled onto his back in time to see the attackers running through the lot. He recognized one guy for sure—Armani!

Behind Chuy the group that had scared away the gang bangers came to a halt. It was the baseball guys. Lucky for Chuy and Billy they had decided to go to the fest together before their summer state quarter-final game coming up on Monday. Leading the charge was Chuy's old buddy, Ricky Ramirez, who now looked and sounded like a grown man. The gang bangers, who did not want the attention or a fair fight, were already halfway to the street. Ricky reached down, giving Chuy and Billy each a hand. Billy was bloody from several cuts and scrapes and one eye was swollen closed. Chuy was unmarked, but his white tee-shirt was torn, dirty and bloody.

"Hey, bro, you okay?" asked Ramirez, breathing hard.

"Yeah," wheezed Chuy, "Thanks to you guys." The team gathered around Chuy, shaking his hand.

"I think you're still undefeated there, Ponyboy. Not a mark on ya, but you got somebody's blood on that thing that used to be a shirt."

Chuy shook his head, clearing the cobwebs from the cheap shot by the guy who had hit him from behind—the guy that he was sure was Armani.

"Gutless cowards, man," Chuy growled.

Ricky put his arm around Chuy's shoulder. "Of course; if they'd seen what we saw, none of those cowards gonna take on Ponyboy by themselves."

A large figure stepped forward to face Chuy.

"Glad we got here when we did."

The voice belonged to soon-to-be sophomore sensation Manny Ochoa. It took Chuy a moment to recognize him as he was now taller and thicker than he had been a year ago.

"Wow! you got huge, bro!"

Ricky slapped Manny on the shoulder. "Yeah, his power numbers are better than mine," he confided to Chuy, continuing, "he's finally straighten' em out and put 'em outta the yard!"

Chuy shook Manny's large hand. "Man, those bangers are lucky you didn't catch any of them. Funny how things go. You know, I'd still be playing ball if it weren't for you."

"Well, then you can thank me," The large sophomore replied. "You look great in the ring, Chuy!"

Ochoa continued to shake Chuy's hand with a strong grip. "We're gonna go to State this Monday for summer ball. When is state for you and Lucy?"

"Ours is called the Gloves Tourney. We'll lay off 'til fall, then it's our turn, so you guys gotta win one first."

"Deal!" agreed Ricky. "We'll get the ball rolling!"

"Deal!" Chuy returned. "And thanks for saving our asses."

"They ought to be the ones to say thank you. I had 'em right where I wanted them," insisted Billy with a sneer, wiping the blood from his nose.

"Yeah, right!" Manny and his teammates turned back toward the parking lot. "Billy, you were kickin' the crap out of their feet with your face."

After the laughter died down, Manny continued, "Hey, we're all heading' to Cocino's for some real pizza, none of this carnival crap—you guys wanna come?"

Chuy answered for both of them. "No, I think we had enough action for one day. Seriously, Ricky, Manny—all you fellas. Thanks, and good luck on Monday! Get a win!"

"Hell, yeah! Remember, we win at state, and you win at state; that's our deal. Right, Ponyboy?"

"Yep, that's the deal, 'Rocket'!"

CHAPTER 27

Armani awakened just after twelve noon with an aching head, dry mouth and sore throat from beer and weed. It was a feeling he was growing used to. He dragged himself out to the kitchen, where, despite the beautiful, sunny late-summer day, it was still dark as night. He switched on the kitchen light, sending cockroaches scattering back toward some form of darkness.

"Shit," Armani grumbled to himself. *How had things gotten so bad?* He toyed with the idea of opening the drapes and throwing out furniture, really cleaning the place like it used to be, but instead he wandered back to his room and lit a cigarette and smoked it. Achieving no satisfaction, he then lit a joint. He was hungry, but the thought of eating in the filthy house made his stomach turn, producing a sick feeling in the back of his throat. He finally decided to pick up a burger, then meet his boys on their corner. Grabbing a pile of cash that he had stolen the night before at the fest, he stuffed it in his pocket, took a last hit on the dwindling joint and made a stop at the bathroom. Semi-groomed, he emerged from the bathroom and was immediately grabbed by his t-shirt and thrown against the wall. His brother, Xavier, pushed him hard, his face inches from Armani. The smell of cigarettes and booze on his breath caused Armani to recoil. Xavier reached into Armani's pocket and pulled out the wad of crumpled bills.

"What the hell ya think ya doin', stupid little *cabron*?" snarled the older brother.

"What the f...? Get off me!" Armani snapped back.

"*Basta!*" came a deep-voiced command from down the hall. The oldest of the Rodriguez brothers, Daniel, was clearly the alpha. A "Let him go."

Xavier reluctantly released Armani's shirt and gave him a shove down the hall toward the shabby, cluttered living room. Warily, Armani kept his eyes on his brother, preparing a defense in his mind in case he should be attacked again. Xavier was tall and thin, with movie star good looks. His long greasy hair and a pronounced scar on his left cheek only made him look cooler and more dangerous. It was no wonder he was always surrounded by high school girls rebelling against their parents, competing to be the girl of a real "bad boy" gangbanger. It was a good bet one of those types was in his room, still asleep from too much late-night partying.

Daniel, on the other hand, had the same body type as Armani—short, thick, and muscular. Daniel had already done a stint in Joliet Maximum Security Prison, where he had spent his free hours lifting weights and it showed. One look at his physique made other tough guys think twice. He was dark and serious, looking closer to thirty-three than his actual age of twenty-three.

"Sit down, Armani," Daniel ordered.

"What's all this bullshit?" demanded Armani, slouching down on the couch.

"The bullshit is you, *cabron*!" screamed Xavier, kicking the sofa. "What the hell ya think you're doing? Jumpin' little kids at the fest for their lunch money, ya think you a big man, *vato*? That's punk-ass bullshit!"

"So, I got some extra spending money, what's the big deal?" Armani lit another cigarette.

"You stupid muthaf…" Xavier slapped the cigarette out of Armani's mouth.

"Xavier," Daniel said in a calm voice, "*tienes una cerveza y calmete.*" He motioned Xavier to the kitchen to get a beer and to calm himself.

X straightened up, glaring at Armani before reluctantly leaving the room.

"*Hermano*," Daniel began in his deep whisper. He paused, lighting two cigarettes and handing one to Armani. "This is business. You have a job, and it ain't jumping little *vatos* at the fest."

"Who cares about those little *cabrones*? They just rich white kids. Since when does X give a shit about them? Where do you think I learned it from? X and his boys always got money from the fest."

"He gives a shit, little brother, because things have changed. Those kids you jumpin' are buying weed from us now."

"So now we got their money and our weed; win, win," argued Armani with a shrug.

Daniel blew out a large puff of smoke, leaned forward and took a deep breath, trying to be patient with his younger brother. "Armani, we ain't dealin' with no pocket change no more. Those white kids sell for us. Think about it, *hermano*, where are all our customers?"

Armani sat silently, not knowing what his brother expected him to say.

Daniel answered his own question. "In the high school. *You* gonna sell weed at that school? How 'bout your homies? You and most of your boys been kicked out, and even if we got our own people there, they're bein' watched. These rich white boys you talkin' bout, they're our best dealers. You messin' with your own family, and you don't even know it, *cabron*."

"Come on, how much could they be bringing in?" Armani asked with a smirk.

"A shit lot more than you're bringing in", interrupted Xavier, yelling from the kitchen. He stepped back in the living room and handed his older brother a beer, then glared again at Armani. He continued his tirade.

"This *pinche cabron* thinks he knows the business. How about the shit you supposed to be doin'? Last night there was Cobras on Ozzie's corner, and where the hell was you and your boys? Out jackin things up; time you grew up, son!"

"Me grow up?" Armani arose from the sofa. "Listen to you, big man, bangin' sophomores in high school 'cause girls your age want nothin' to do with a loser like you!"

"Loser? You want to see a loser? Bitch!"

Xavier leaped over the coffee table that separated the two and grabbed Armani by the throat. Armani desperately swept his hand down to break the grip, but before he could do anything else Xavier punched him full in the face, fattening his lip instantly. With one hand on Armani's throat, the older brother cocked his arm back to hit him again, but luckily for Armani, Daniel grabbed the arm and flung X back. Daniel stood between the two fighting brothers, arms stretched out, with a restraining hand on each brother's chest. He said nothing, but his action and authority stopped Armani and Xavier in their tracks. The sound of heavy breathing seemed to last for minutes, broken only by the creaking of a bedroom door.

"Xavier," a timid female voice came from behind the door. "I'm scared; I want to go home now."

"Do your job or you're out of here," Xavier snarled at Armani, then turned to the bedroom.

"It's not your house, asshole; it's Mom's," Armani weakly argued.

"You see Mom here? Do your damn job, or you're gonna see what happens," X threatened.

Armani was about to respond, but Daniel stopped him.

"ENOUGH!" He raised his voice, causing Armani and Xavier both to step back in fear. Un Daniel almost never spoke louder than a scary whisper.

Daniel exhaled deeply, putting both hands to his lips almost as if he were praying. The younger brothers held their collective breath. They had witnessed the quiet, muscular man when he was angry. Fear welled up inside each as they took another backward step. The room was silent again.

"Xavier?" whined the voice from behind the door, now sounding as if the girl were crying.

Daniel exhaled again then shook his head, suddenly amused by the situation. He grabbed his brother's beer and handed it to him. "Get that little bitch out here," he commanded.

He then turned to Armani, drawing his little brother to him with a muscular arm.

"*Escucha*, listen to me," he said quietly. "You don't remember this, but we had to fight hard for that street corner, back in the day. You need to watch your corner, *hermano*. I got plans for you, but this is supposed to be the easy stuff. If you can't handle it like a man, how can I trust you with anything more? Now, go clean yourself up and go to work."

Armani knew better than to say anything. He just nodded in agreement. Daniel escorted him as far as the bathroom. Armani stepped inside the dingy, dirty little room. He turned on the light and looked into the mirror. His lip was swollen. He splashed water on his face, then shook his head and looked away, not liking what he had seen. A cockroach scurried across the sink and he slammed his hand down, but missed the roach. He looked in the mirror again and ignored the pain in his hand. Suddenly he wanted to climb back in his bed. Instead, he switched out the light and left the house.

The bright light of the midday sun hurt his eyes. Armani dropped his head and began the walk to his corner. When he got to his front gate, he noticed a card tucked next to the mailbox. 'Armani' was written in unmistakably feminine handwriting. He grabbed the card and ripped in open, his heart beating fast, thinking it was from Lucy. He was disappointed to see it was signed by Mrs. Eldridge, who had helped him with his reading. Without reading its contents, Armani crumpled the card and tossed it to the ground, continuing his walk, but something told him to turn back and retrieve the crushed note. He smoothed it out and read it. This crazy teacher was checking on him, even though Layden seemed like two lifetimes ago. An ever so slight smile came over Armani's lips. *Crazy lady,* he thought to himself. He folded the card carefully and placed it in his front pocket. Armani dropped his head again and returned to his walk. *Crazy lady.*

All too soon the first day back to school was about to arrive. Only one more day of vacation. Chuy and Lucy started that day with their ritual trip to the gym.

Although they both secretly loved school, they shared a mutual reluctance of returning to the same old grind. Biking to the gym, they passed the time reminding each other of how fast their high school years had gone by. This, after all, was Senior Year! They were on the precipice of adulthood, with just nine months between high school and the rest of their lives. They told each other they could easily do this with the end so close at hand.

After pulling up to the gym, they locked up their bikes and climbed up the stairs, where they were greeted with unusual sounds and smells. The back doors leading to the fire escape were wide open. People were talking and music was blaring from the outside, replacing the usual sounds of ropes tapping and bags popping within the gym.

Nearing the doors, they detected the unmistakable smell of fried chicken wafting up from the back yard. They gave each other a questioning look, then dropped their gym bags and hurried to the door which opened onto the fire escape. At the bottom of the steps a picnic table loaded with food and drink, and surrounded by coaches and teammates, awaited them.

Sultan spotted the pair first and yelled up (mouth full of chicken), "Don't stand there drooling, you two. Come on down here and get you some."

Lucy and Chuy raced each other down the steps.

"Okay, don't get hurt getting your food—there's plenty for everyone."

Chuy loaded a paper plate with chicken thighs and coleslaw. "What's going on?"

"We hit a full season, guys," Big Ces informed him, walking over to add more food to his own plate. "We got us a little break, then it's tourney time."

"Break?" asked Lucy.

Sultan grinned at her. "Yep, even I need a break and so do y'all, 'cause when we come back in two weeks, it will be to get ready for state. Me and Big Ces gonna take our vacations. Alvarez is starting football, and you two characters, along with all the other students, need to get school off on the right foot."

"No boxing for two weeks?" Lucy was dismayed.

Sultan corrected her. "That's not what I said, young lady, no boxing practice *here*. Once you start this sport, you are a fighter 'til you done, like your uncle. Yes indeed! You still have to do your road work in the morning, shadow box, pushups, but you need to get out of this place for a couple weeks; miss it for a little while. And you will miss it. No hitting bags, no sparring, you need to let your hands heal, 'cause when we come back, you will work like you never have before. We will be trainin' for the tournament and let me tell you somethin'; we don't play!"

"I know," interrupted Chuy, "You laugh, and you joke but you generally..."

"DO NOT PLAY!" Lucy, Chuy, Alvarez and Big Ces all completed the sentence in unison.

Sultan grinned then unexpectedly turned his attention to Chuy. "And speaking of playin', boy, I heard you had a little ruckus outside my ring. You know how I feel about that, Jesus."

Big Ces began to speak up for Chuy, but Sultan silenced him with a raised hand.

"You can be in the wrong place at the wrong time, but that usually means you're out too late or with the wrong people. Which one was it, Ponyboy?"

"It was still early; Coach and I was just with…"

A loud voice came roaring down from the diminutive figure at the top of the fire escape. "Hey, it's a party!" It was Billy, almost falling down the steps in his eagerness to get at the food.

"It was just him." Chuy pointed a thumb in his direction.

"Were you guys talking about me again?" asked Billy, breezing past the group as he sped toward the table. "I know I'm everyone's favorite subject."

"Whoa! Slow down!" Sultan stopped Billy cold, blocking his view of the table. "Where you think you goin,' boy? This food is for the fighters, and I ain't seen you all summer."

"You saw me on Saturday, Coach. I was workin' the corner."

"Workin' your jaw—just like always."

The fighters laughed as Sultan reached out and pulled Billy close to inspect the bruises on his face. "You workin' your jaw after the fight got you in some trouble, boy?"

"Nah, Coach—you can ask Chuy. I was just heading home. Bunch of wannabe gangbanger punks jumped me. You know coach, they like to jump the little white guy, but I showed 'em."

"Humm…," Sultan growled. "You showed 'em how to take a beat down, huh? If you eatin' boy you better be showin' up for practice!"

"Of course, Coach. That's why I'm here. You know it was a busy summer and all," Billy concluded, relieved that Sultan appeared to be letting him off the hook.

Sultan released Billy and turned his attention back to Chuy.

"Punks is punks, Jesus," he said in a low, serious tone. "They got no purpose; they got no heart; they got no drive. You stay away from them, you hear? If I get news of one of my fighters retaliating, that fighter will be outta the club. You understand me, Jesus?"

"I do, Coach," Chuy assured him.

"You worked too hard to blow it on punks. You understand?" Sultan reminded him one more time.

"Yes sir...I mean, yes, Coach," Chuy answered again.

"Okay! Good! Now y'all eat. This is your last cheat meal for a while. After this, road work, shadow box, rest and get your school squared away. The tourney will be here before you know it, and I want everybody ready!"

The whole team proceeded to eat well, laugh, and enjoy the rare day off. They lingered around the table for more than an hour, reluctant to let the party end. Eventually an impromptu kickball game broke out on the back field and before too long it began getting dark. Lucy and Chuy ended the party by thanking Sultan for the great food and fun, and they thanked the other coaches for a good season. They headed back home on their bikes, fully energized and eager to practice and prepare for the State Tournament.

The sun had almost set by the time Chuy walked Lucy to her door.

"Hey Luce, um... I was wondering, you know, since we don't have practice on Friday, if umm, maybe..."

"Why, Jesus, are you nervous asking me out on a date?" Lucy teased.

"Ha! I guess it's silly, but you know, we are always with Wolfy's kids, or with Nancy and Ulises. I thought it could just be us—you know, a real date."

Lucy smiled up at him. "You mean a car and everything? You won't pick me up on your bike?"

"Well, let's not get carried away," joked Chuy, "but, yeah, something like that."

"Well, Mr. LeDesma, I would be honored. So, I'm sure I will see you at least one hundred times before that, but I'm looking forward to Friday and our *real* date."

"Yes, one hundred times first and then Friday night." He suddenly—and unexpectedly—grabbed Lucy and kissed her long and deep, taking her breath away.

"By the way," he called out to the flustered Lucy as he jumped on his bike, "You can call me Ponyboy."

CHAPTER 28

Lucy and Chuy didn't see each other one hundred times, but they gave it their best shot. They ran together in the morning, met each other after classes, and attended the after school 'Welcome Back Party' for Wolfy's kids. They also jumped rope and shadow-boxed and in the early evenings they relaxed on the swinging bench in Chuy's backyard. So when Chuy knocked on Lucy's door at 6:30 Friday evening (on the dot) things shouldn't have seemed different, but they did.

Chuy didn't come riding up on his old bike; instead he pulled up in Raul's shiny-red classic Oldsmobile, clean as a whistle inside and out. He wasn't wearing his usual workout gear; instead he wore a freshly-pressed dark-blue button-down shirt, dark pants, and polished dress shoes. He had come to Lucy's house hundreds of times, but this time he had a case of butterflies, as though he were getting ready to get in the ring. He tried to figure out why he was so nervous. After all, they had gone to prom together; they had been spending so much time together; they had seen each other sweat and sleep and be silly. But that was different. After all this time, it was just him and his beautiful girl. Of course, Lucy would not feel the same way. She would just laugh, punch him, and think he was being a dork. With that in mind, Chuy exhaled and rang the doorbell. The door opened. As if he had taken a surprise left hook to the jaw, Chuy took an eight count, with eyes open wide and mouth gaping.

Lucy stood before him in a tight-fitting, mid-length shimmering silver dress with matching heels. She wore light make-up and her naturally pink lips were augmented by lipstick just a shade darker than natural. Her thick curls, pulled up on one side by a silver barrette, spilled down her bare shoulder.

"Chuuuuuuyyyy!!" The shrieking voices of Lucy's little sisters snapped him out of his trance.

"Hello, Mr. Ledesma," she said, smiling and adding a slight bow.

"Umm, ummmm, wow!"

With that, Lucy slowly and deliberately moved her clutch purse to her left hand and then, in a flash, popped Chuy in the shoulder with a solid right.

"Ow! Okay, that's the girl I know," Chuy exclaimed, rubbing his shoulder. "I did not recognize you there for a minute."

Lucy grabbed his arm and prepared to be escorted to the car.

"*Espera!* Wait a minute, you two," commanded a voice from behind them. Mr. Quinones and the whole family suddenly appeared in the doorway. "Let's get some pictures!"

Several minutes later, after the family took turns taking and posing in pictures, Chuy and Lucy finally made their departure.

Lucy looked around, as though something was missing. "Where's Raul?" She asked.

Chuy grinned broadly. "Home resting after all the hours he put in this summer making me a decent driver."

"You never told me!" Lucy scolded.

Chuy shrugged and gave her a look of love. "I've been planning this for a while and wanted to surprise you."

Lucy gave him a light kiss, not wanting to smear him with lipstick. "Mission accomplished."

"I guess this is our real prom," remarked Lucy as they got into the car. "So, where to?"

Chuy glanced at his girl, wearing a sly grin. "Awwh, the night is full of surprises," was all he would say.

"Does that mean you didn't plan anything," Lucy teased.

"Well, let's just say I took the advice of a very wise man. I've got my fingers crossed."

Chuy drove just beyond the 25th street bridge and headed east. In a few blocks he made a turn.

"Dom's Steak House?" Lucy guessed, amazed.

"Well, I'm not taking you to Olive Garden dressed like that."

"But, Chuy, isn't this place expensive?"

"I worked all summer, Luce. Besides, I was told it's the best deal in town."

They pulled into the parking lot of the old-school steakhouse, distinguished from the neighboring buildings by the canopy over the entrance. On this clear evening the two walked arm in arm through the doors of the establishment, which made them instantly feel sophisticated beyond their years. Chuy noticed that the place was filled with a much older crowd, and for a moment he wondered if he had taken the right advice.

"Hello, young sir and hello, young miss," greeted a smiling man with a thick European accent. "Will there be two for dinner tonight? We have a little bit of a wait."

"Hello," responded Chuy, trying not to appear timid. He cleared his throat, but his voice came out in a bit of a whisper. "Coach Gary Wolf said to mention his name."

"WELL! Why didn't you say so? If you are a friend of Coach Wolf, you are a friend of mine. Right this way. How is Coach Wolf these days?"

The host gushed as he guided Chuy and Lucy to a horseshoe-shaped booth with plush, red-leather seats. "That man got my boy, Tony, to college. Oh yes! He played baseball." The gregarious maitre'd put his arm around Chuy's shoulder, lowering his voice as if he were telling the couple a deep dark secret. "My boy Tony, he was a wild one! You know, baseball; it kept him in line. Okay thanks Oh, I don't know what I would have done without Coach." He paused, thinking back on those days, then continued. "Now, my Tony is an engineer. Oh yeah, a real big-shot, my boy!"

The attention Chuy was receiving was noticed by nearby diners who looked up, favorably impressed by the striking young couple. The looks of approval and the over-the-top service they were experiencing left the young couple a bit embarrassed, but also more than a bit flattered.

Lucy slid close to Chuy and whispered in his ear. "I think we are the youngest people in this place; I mean, that have *ever* been in this place, but I love it! You did good!"

Within minutes a waitress arrived with salad on a rolling cart accompanied by a silver tray with an array of dressings.

"Steaks for you tonight, folks?"

"Ummh," said Lucy, I was thinking about the chicken."

"Yes, please," interrupted Chuy, knowing how much Lucy enjoyed a good meal. "We'll have the filets tonight, please."

"King or petite?" asked the waitress.

"I'll have the…

Chuy cut her off again. "King for both of us. I'll have medium rare and you, Lucy?"

"Well, since you have taken over, you can tell her I'll do medium rare as well."

Chuy grinned and the amused waitress chuckled.

"Sounds good folks, be back shortly."

Lucy gave Chuy a questioning look, "Okay! Who are you and what have you done with Chuy?"

"Hey, we didn't come to a steak place for chicken, and I didn't work all summer for my girl to get the little steak."

Lucy relented. "Well, okay; I guess you can be in charge tonight."

The two ate and chatted, falling easily into their normal comfort level, enjoying the old-fashioned 60's charm of the renowned establishment, and the most amazing steaks either had ever eaten.

When they finished their meal, the waitress returned with two large pieces of a decadent-looking chocolate cake. "Compliments of Jorge," the waitress informed them, motioning towards the maitre'd.

Lucy finished her dessert, then sighed with contentment. "Officially, the best meal I've ever had, but don't tell my mom," she informed the waitress, who had discreetly deposited the leather-enclosed bill next to Chuy.

"That was amazing, Chuy," she reaffirmed a few minutes later when they settled into the car.

"Oh, there's more," announced Chuy. "We are right on schedule. We're going to see a show."

"Great," replied Lucy. "What movie are we going to see?"

"Who said anything about a movie?" Chuy's sly grin returned.

They hit the expressway and within minutes they pulled up to the Dyer's Lane Theater. The marquee read: 'A Chorus Line.' A small crowd was already gathering in the brightly-lit lobby. Chuy handed the keys over to the valet and walked around to open the car door for Lucy. She stepped out into the lights of the marquee, turning heads as Chuy escorted her. Chuy's chest puffed out with pride when he noticed the admiration his girl was attracting.

"I think you are the star tonight; people can't stop looking at you," he whispered in her ear.

"Am I going to have to punch you again," she giggled, snuggling against his arm, and trying not to blush.

They strolled around the theater lobby, admiring the huge chandelier centered above them, the lighted stairway, and the luxurious red carpeting throughout. An usher escorted them to seats not far from the stage. Waiting for the play to begin, Lucy rested her head on Chuy's shoulder and sighed with satisfaction. He inhaled the familiar smell of her hair with long deep breaths and was equally content. Since the first time they had met he had been intoxicated by her scent. He always would be, he thought.

Eventually the curtain went up and they were taken for a behind-the-scenes look at young background dancers working desperately to make it on Broadway. The show was breathtaking for the young couple, and they both instantly fell in love with live, professional theatre.

"So, was that Wolfy's idea, too?" asked Lucy on the ride home.

"Nope, all mine. Okay, that's a lie—it was Ms. Kelly's," Chuy admitted.

"Wow, how many people did you collaborate with on this date?"

"Did you have a good time?"

"Don't answer a question with a question."

"Did you?"

"Yes, the best!"

"Then let's just say I was smart enough to ask the right people."

They drove over the bridge, past the turn to Lucy's house.

"Um, I live there in case you forgot that Chuy," Lucy noted.

"One more stop."

"Are you sure you don't want to quit while you're ahead?"

"Am I ahead?" inquired Chuy, wearing the familiar sly grin.

"Well, I don't think you can top the dinner and the show, but I'm curious what you have up your sleeve," she admitted.

Chuy pulled up in front of his own house, which was unusually dark that night.

"Are you thinking about ending this fantastic date with some jump rope and shadow boxing?" Lucy joked.

"Well, you know me; I'm going for the knockout."

Chuy escorted Lucy to the backyard and motioned her to sit in the back porch swing. Before joining her, he walked over to a cord near the garage, plugged it in and instantly lit up the backyard with twinkling white lights. He pulled a lighter out of his pocket and lit several tiki torches, which had been strategically placed around the dark corners of the yard, adding the finishing touch to what was now a romantic cozy getaway.

"Oh...Chuy!" Lucy gazed at him, her eyes glittering in the gentle light. Emotion took her for a moment, and she threw her arms around his neck and squeezed. Chuy held her close, with his face buried in her curls, thinking it was his favorite place to be in all the world. The two melted into a deep, long breathless kiss.

"Knockout," Lucy murmured into Chuy's ear.

Chuy sat next to his beautiful girlfriend, a girl to whom six short months ago he was afraid to talk. Now he was sitting next to her and she was snuggling up to his shoulder. He lowered his head and the two kissed again with tongues entwined. Chuy lowered his hand, slipping it inside Lucy's dress.

"Chuy, I'm not ready for that yet."

"Okay, that's fine." Chuy quickly pulled away. Lucy snuggled back into him, resting her head against his chest. She could feel his heart beating. After a couple of minutes, she stretched up to kiss him lightly on the cheek. "Are you alright, Chuy?"

" Umh...Lucy...can I tell you something and you promise you won't make fun of me?"

"No promises." Lucy smiled softly. "Tell me."

Chuy hesitated, then exhaled loudly.

"Chuy, you can tell me anything. What's going on in that head of yours?"

"Well, it's just…I mean…I've never been with a woman before. I mean I've made out…"

"Are you trying to make me jealous?" Lucy interrupted, pushing him lightly.

"Seriously," continued Chuy, not meeting her eyes. "I mean I have never *been* with a woman."

"So why is that a bad thing, Chuy? That doesn't make you less of a man. I have seen in so many ways what a good man you are."

"But you and Armani, I know you never went all the way but I'm sure you two…"

Lucy cut him off. "Chuy! We were just kids. Armani was a screwed-up little boy who wanted to be a bad-ass. I mean, I was screwed-up, too. We were both trying to look bad-ass, but I knew better. The truth is Armani just wanted a girl on his arm, and I was dumb enough to think that made me a cool, tough chick. Ha!" She paused at the thought and felt a moment of gratitude that she was no longer that girl. "Chuy, I don't know who I will be with one day," she continued, "but I do it won't be now when I'm only seventeen—not even close. I've seen too many of my friends make the wrong choice when it comes to sex."

Chuy nodded. "Lucy, I like what we have. It's enough for me right now, and since you're my best friend, I'm gonna be totally honest…I'm kinda relieved."

They melted into a long, sweet kiss and relaxed into each other's arms.

"Wait a minute, Chuy," Lucy sat upright. "What was the 'move' you were trying."

"I have no idea! I was making it up as I went along."

The two fell into each other in muffled laughter, then returned to a comfortable silence.

"I don't really know where to touch a girl to make her, you know, feel good," Chuy eventually confessed.

"Chuy," Lucy spoke with quiet emotion in her voice, "you are a real man, and the sweetest man I have ever met. I'm not sure who will be my 'first' but you are truly my first love."

She reached down and took Chuy's hand. "You touch a woman here."

She rubbed his open hand on her soft cheek, then kissed his hand softly. "And you touch a woman here." She brought his hand to her chest.

Chuy eyes widened.

"Easy, Ponyboy, I mean here, in her heart." She placed his hand in the middle of her chest.

They gazed deeply into each other's eyes, with his hand surrounded by both of hers. He could feel her heart beating rhythmically. She raised her hands to his face and pulled him close for another long, wonderful kiss. They leaned back in the swing and watched the stars twinkling above and the landing lights of jets as they streaked across the night sky. The perfect end to the perfect night. A knockout.

CHAPTER 29

The first two weeks of their senior year seemed to fly by. Chuy and Lucy were glad to get back to the gym at the end of those two weeks. Just as Sultan had predicted, the hiatus had left them refreshed, missing the gym, and ready to get back to work. Following their magical date, the two had concentrated on settling into the new school year. They attended the welcome meeting and party for Wolfy's kids and found time to hang out with Nancy, Ulises, and Billy in spots other than the gym.

Billy seemed to be returning to his old, carefree self. As the cuts on his face slowly healed it became easier to forget about his 'disappearing act' during the summer. This Thursday morning, however, Billy was obviously anxious. His normal goofy demeanor was replaced by obvious worry and anxiety. Chuy stepped down out of the school bus to see Billy standing silently by the door.

"What up, Eminem?" Chuy greeted him. Billy did not answer.

"Dude, what's up with you?" Chuy repeated.

"I need to talk to you, man, I...umm..." Billy's voice faded.

Chuy stopped in mid-stride, turning to stare at his friend, "What's going on with you, Bill?" He demanded.

"I can't go this way, not today. I'll have to talk to you later, but it will be before lunch, I promise. Just don't... I mean stick to the schedule 'til I can..." Billy looked as though he were about to cry.

"Bill, what the hell? You're talking gibberish." Chuy's concern became anger as his patience wore thin.

Billy rubbed his hands on his face. "I need to talk to you before lunch; if I don't find you, you find me. Just...I got to go... I got to think." Billy turned and ran up the back steps. Chuy called out to him, but he did not stop.

That was so weird, Chuy thought to himself. *Why is he so messed up?* He shrugged and continued up to room 250, passing the area where Armani and his boys used to hang out. Chuy smiled with satisfaction when he saw the leftover gangbanger wannabes. The group that used to be a menacing presence in the school was now nothing more than a few pathetic stragglers. Armani and the majority of his crew were gone, and without a leader, these remaining kids weren't idolized or feared. They were still a black mark on the school, and they still answered to Armani, but they were more to be pitied than feared. Before he could give the matter another thought, he was interrupted by Wolfy's kids who came rushing toward him in a wave of joy and innocence.

"Ccchuy!" Missy was, of course, first. "Look at my new dress, Ccchuy," she demanded, twirling in front of him.

By then the rest of the crew had him surrounded. He greeted them one by one as he worked his way toward Ms. Kelly's room. By the time Chuy made it inside the door, the Thursday morning Best Pals meeting was ready to begin. Chuy approached Lucy and gave her a quick peck on the cheek. Nancy and the other officers of the club were all there, but Billy's absence caused Chuy to worry again about his strange behavior. By the time the meeting ended he decided not to mention Billy's weirdness to his other friends, but just go on with his day. Billy would be Billy again by the afternoon he assured himself.

This year Chuy had gym class smack dab in the middle of the day. He left his morning books in his gym locker and planned to grab his afternoon books from his upstairs locker, which would give him even more time for lunch. Another joy of this year's schedule, lunch was the same time for him, Lucy, Nancy, and Billy. Senior year was starting off to be far more satisfying than he had dared dreamed of back when he had been a scared freshman with reading difficulties, whose only goal had been to make the baseball team. Eagerly he dressed for gym class, catching up with classmates, who were also changing jeans for gym shorts. They headed on into the gym, ready to enjoy another workout.

As a senior PE leader, Chuy got the class started with warm-ups, an agility run, then stretches. They had just finished and were taking a quick water break when Coach Stark called out Chuy's name.

"Jesus, you got a pass from the dean here," he shouted loudly enough for everyone to hear. "They finally caught up with ya!" he kidded, cueing the class to send out jeers of "Busted, Chuy!"

Chuy rolled his eyes. "Sorry Coach, looks like you are actually gonna have to do some work and run your own class for once."

"Get outta here, you!" Stark playfully pushed the pass into Chuy's chest.

Chuy hurried back into the locker room to change clothes once again. Going to the dean usually struck dread in the hearts of students, but Chuy knew he had not done anything deserving of punishment. It was most likely Dean Rudy needed help getting a kid into the boxing program, or he was looking for an idea for Wolfy's kids. Chuy approached the Dean's office already planning out what he would do with the rare extra time he would have after this meeting. A quick stop at the cafe for sure, then maybe a surprise visit to Coach Wolf or Alvarez. He probably had time for both.

When Chuy got to the office he was immediately struck by the feeling that something was off. The normally smiling administrative assistant looked serious as she directed Chuy to take a seat. In fact, the entire office gave out a very serious vibe. Chuy began to internally question what was going on. Instantly the realization that Billy was in trouble came to him. It could be why he had been acting so strangely this morning. Chuy's stomach started churning. He waited anxiously, watching security guard Mr. Norris, then Police Liaison Officer Nick go in and out of Dean Rudy's office. They both avoided eye contact. Chuy's gut continued to churn.

What is going on here? screamed the voice in his head.

Finally, Dean Rudy stepped out of his office and signaled for Chuy to come in. Before Dean Rudy could return to his seat, Chuy spoke out.

"Is it Billy? Is he alright?"

Dean Rudy appeared confused for a moment, then he slowly sat down in his chair, motioning for Chuy to take a chair also. He took a long, deep breath before he finally replied.

"Chuy, we have a situation, but I'm sure we can get it all worked out. As you can see we are meeting here in my office—just you and me. We are not in the conference room with Officer Nick; it's just you and me."

Now it was Chuy's turn to look confused. "Billy's okay," he said, half statement, half question.

"Jesus, let me get to the point. You know that we are trying to clean up this school. This year we have decided to do unannounced sweeps of the building using drug dogs."

Chuy listened, still looking, and feeling completely bewildered.

The dean cleared his throat and continued. "We found a significant amount of marijuana in your locker."

Chuy jumped out of his chair, "What the f...?"

Dean Rudy stood up to meet him face to face. "Whooa! Relax, Chuy! We all know you better than this. First I'm going to ask you a question, but you need to sit and calm down."

Anger burned at Chuy's face, but he followed the Dean's direction.

"Before I begin, I'm going to tell you two things. First, I have no doubt that you did NOTHING wrong. Do you understand me, Chuy? It's students like you who have made a big difference here."

Anger flowed through Chuy's body like a volcano, keeping him from hearing and absorbing the dean's words.

"Chuy!" Dean Rudy raised his voice. "Do you understand me? We will get through this."

Chuy exhaled, trying to extinguish the flames of anger. Biting his lip and looking away, he nodded his head yes.

"Number two: I have to follow protocol. I have certain guidelines I need to follow in this situation, no matter who it is, do you understand that?"

Chuy nodded again, still fighting the flames.

"Alright, first question: was the marijuana in your locker yours?"

"NO!" Chuy shouted.

"Okay, okay. That's good; I believe you, Chuy." Dean Rudy maintained a calm voice. "I believe this is not yours, but again, I have to ask these questions."

Rudy paused and gave the young man time to gather his thoughts before continuing. When he judged that Chuy would at least be able to understand him the dean continued: "Now, do you know how weed would have ended up in your locker? When was the last time you were there?"

"It wasn't there yesterday. I used it after lunch. In the mornings I always use my gym locker."

Dean Rudy nodded and paused to jot down a note. "Good. Now we are getting some info. So it could have been put in there this morning. Does anyone else have the combination to your locker?"

Billy's face flashed into Chuy's mind, but he dismissed that picture and replaced it with the picture of the gangbangers in training who had been hanging out by the stairwell.

Chuy suddenly stood up. "It was Armani Ramirez. Well, not him, but those punks of his. They somehow got into my locker; maybe I left it open, I don't know, but that asshole and his punk friends..."

"Okay, okay, Jesus, settle down. That could be it; it makes sense to me." The dean gently put his hands on Chuy's shoulder, pushing him back down into the chair.

"Now, you have got to let me do my job. I told you I have to follow protocol, so I need to call your parents before we go any further."

Chuy sat up straight, but before he could speak, Dean Rudy stopped him. "You can sit right here while I talk to them, and I will tell them the same thing I told you. I believe you are innocent. I believe this is some kind of set-up. I believe we will find out what happened. You have to trust me, Chuy."

Chuy doubled over in his chair and put his head in his hands for a moment. He rubbed his face, trying to erase the feelings of anger and hate. Dean Rudy picked up the phone and began dialing.

Chuy didn't hear a word that Dean Rudy said to his mom. He wasn't even angry that the dean was calling her with such bullshit. He trusted the dean and knew that he was only doing his job. Chuy was innocent; soon the whole school would know he was innocent. He wasn't angry about any of that. What made Chuy so damn angry was that face—the face of Armani. That smirk! Chuy could see it now. One of his little minions telling Armani how he somehow got into Chuy's locker and planted the weed. All of them laughing, thinking they really jacked up Chuy's life.

Armani was gutless—a punk, and his little gutless punk friends still had their dirty, gutless hands all over this school. They could still pull off something like this.

It didn't matter that people like Wolfy, Alvarez, Kelly, Norris, and Dean Rudy worked so hard to clean up the school. It didn't matter that Big Ces had turned his life around all those years ago and started the change in this school, that Ulises had continued fighting for. It didn't matter that Lucy and Nancy were walking examples of what it looked like to grow up and shun that stupid life. Still these damn gangbangers and their little punk wannabes were like cockroaches. You couldn't kill them; they just kept on coming back. This situation was proof of that, and it caused Chuy's blood to boil.

Without warning, even to himself, the anger boiled over him like a molten eruption. He jumped up from his seat. Chuy didn't think about breaking Dean Rudy's trust. He didn't think at all. Anger had replaced judgement. He reacted to the smirking face in his head, to the injustice and the damage done to him and his school. He shot out of the office, past the administrative assistant and out the door. Every part of his training came into play and gave him the endurance and speed to help him bolt out the side door and down Wolf Road toward Grand Avenue. He would pummel the smirk off Armani's face.

Neither Chuy nor Dean Rudy had any idea that Alvarez and Billy were waiting in the office, a fact that made no difference in Chuy's furious brain, but, in truth, made all the difference in the world. In the dean's office chaos had taken over. Dean Rudy had moved quickly from behind his desk, but he was no match for Chuy's dash out of the building. Rudy was not even sure which direction Chuy had taken. As he attempted to follow after him he was met by Officer Nick.

"Chuy ran," he shouted out as he passed Alvarez and Billy. "I don't have time for either of you right now!"

"Wait," Alvarez yelled back, but the dean was already one foot out of entrance five, checking all directions to see if he could spot the angry young man.

"It was me!" screamed Billy. "I had the weed."

The dean stopped in his tracks.

He turned to face the teacher and student. "Do you have any idea where Chuy went? Home? To see Lucy?"

"I know," said Billy without hesitation. "Let's go, we don't need a car."

In a time that may have shattered the Layden half mile track record of two minutes, Chuy had reached his destination. As soon as his breath returned he screamed out, "Armani, you punk, where are you? Come on tough guy, show your face."

Chuy had made an easy guess that he would find Armani at his usual spot, and he was right. It was slightly past noon. Armani was parked in front of the empty storefront just behind Oscar's. It was far enough off Grand not to be seen by the cops, or to bother Old Man Oscar, but in the path to attract the spill off of high school kids passing by. Itr was the perfect place to sell weed and flirt with adventurous girls looking to hang with the 'bad boys'.

Armani was sitting in the passenger seat of a beater Chevy, smoking a cigarette, and drinking a forty-ounce *Colt 45* wrapped in a paper bag. From the way he dressed, to what he drank and the Newports he smoked, he had become the stereotypical Latino gangbanger without even realizing it. Now his most hated enemy was shouting his name. Out of nowhere this *pinche* goody-two-shoes was looking for a fight. Maybe he had finally got up the nerve after Armani and his boys had kicked the shit of him and his little buddy at the fest. Armani didn't really care why; he was up for some action, and he wasn't scared of this so-called 'boxer'. He stepped out of the car and walked toward Chuy.

"Let's go, punk," shouted Chuy. "Let's go, you puss!".

"Sure," growled Armani, discarding his half-smoked cigarette. "I don't know what finally brought you here, but I'm glad you came to get your ass kicked."

"What brought me here? You got your little punk wannabe's to put weed in my locker. Now how about you be man enough to fight me alone without your little bitches to get in my way!"

Chuy was expecting a look of satisfaction but instead Armani looked puzzled. For a moment, Chuy's rage gave way to the same puzzlement.

"What ya talkin' about, *cabron*? Weed? Maybe you should ask your little buddy about weed," Armani sneered, pointing a finger over Chuy's shoulder.

A call came from behind. "Chuy, stop!" It was Alvarez. "Chuy, you need to stop, now!"

Alvarez had reached the busy corner by dangerously cutting across traffic. Behind him Billy was fighting for breath, struggling to keep up. Alvarez crossed the street but stopped, giving Chuy room. "You are making a big mistake."

Billy caught up with Alvarez, but bent over, working to catch his breath. "It was me," he wheezed. "It was me." When he could breathe again he straightened upright, facing his consequences. "It was me, Chuy," Billy admitted, a sick look on his face. "That was my weed. I'm sorry, I'm so sorry, Chuy."

Armani had been listening long enough; he was itching for a fight. "You think I give a shit about you?" He taunted Chuy. "You think you're a big shot boxer? Ha! I don't give a shit about you, or your slut girlfriend. I had her first, *pendejo!*"

Chuy raised his fists. Armani had already put his hands up for battle.

"No, Chuy!" screamed Alvarez. "You fight on the street, you lose everything! Chuy please, listen to me!"

Chuy held his position, locking eyes with Armani.

"You better listen to your babysitter, LeDesma. This ain't no boxing ring, we fight for real out here." Armani continued to push for the fight.

"Chuy, don't! You will lose everything because of me, please, man!" Billy pleaded.

Time stood still while the two enemies stood toe to toe, eyes locked. Finally, Chuy dropped his arms and stepped backward. "You ain't worth it." Chuy spat out with disgust, then turned to walk away.

"That's it, walk away. You ain't such a big man out here, huh! This is my turf, and don't come back! I won't give you the chance to back down next time!"

Chuy kept walking, but Armani's words had put a grin on his face. Now he didn't even hear what Armani was saying. Alvarez reached out his hand, and Chuy took it and squeezed it for a moment, then Chuy looked at Billy and noted the fear and sadness displayed on his faced. "You need help, Billy."

"I know," Billy mumbled, dropping his head. "Will you help me?"

Chuy put his arm around Billy and the three headed back toward the school. They could still hear Armani yelling. Chuy looked at Alvarez and pointed his thumb behind him at the screaming gangbanger.

"I think he may have anger issues."

Alvarez laughed and nodded. "God bless him, Chuy. I'm just glad you made the right decision back there. Any fight, for any reason outside the ring and Sultan would have to kick you off the team. You know that, right?"

"Yeah, but that's not why I stopped."

"Really?"

"For a minute there I just kind of felt sorry for him."

"Yeah, agreed Alvarez quietly. "I know what you mean."

CHAPTER 30

"I blew it." Billy spoke with his head down, his voice barely a whisper. "I jacked up everything. I mean, I guess some guys can handle weed, but man! I became a fiend. I spent the summer getting high; I didn't go out with Chuy and the guys…I mean, Crystal, she just went on with her life…it got to where I didn't care that much about anything else but getting high. I figured I would sell, then, I'd get an extra quarter and that would be it. I mean it was just weed. It wasn't like I was doing the hard stuff."

"How did that work out for you, Billy?" Mr. VanRoyen spoke calmly and quietly. He was a gentle man, near retirement, wearing glasses that rested on the end of his nose. He had seen too many situations like this, (and too many much worse) in his thirty plus years working as the veteran social worker at Layden. He, Billy, and Billy's closest friends filled the office, sitting on a big, fluffy sofa and assorted chairs. Weekly meetings with the social worker was only part of the program Billy needed to complete before he would be allowed back into Layden.

"When school started I was going to cut way back, you know, maybe just on the weekends, or whatever." Billy exhaled loudly, paused, then began again. His friends could hear the emotion in his voice. "Then when

281

I went to buy, there was Armani's brother. He was like; 'Dude, you can make some real money.' Truth was I was too scared to say no. He wanted me to sell here, at school. I didn't know if they were watching me, so I brought it here…Chuy, I'm sorry, man." Billy lowered his head while tears dropped, sinking into the well-worn carpeting.

"Billy, you're supposed to be my best friend." Chuy's voice was cold and angry; he was not letting his friend off the hook.

Billy sat up and pulled himself together, wiping his face. The time for tears was over. It was time to accept the consequences of his actions. If that meant losing his friend, so be it. He was ready to start his own fight back to being himself.

"I panicked; I mean, anybody could smell the stuff. I was by your locker, and I've known your combo since freshman year. I know you don't go there 'til the afternoon. I figured no one would check you since everybody knows you don't smoke weed."

"So you used me and our friendship so you wouldn't get busted."

Billy bit his bottom lip as he looked his friend straight in the eye. His voice trembled, but he kept eye contact with Chuy. If this was the last chance he had to talk with his closest friend, he was going to make it count.

"When I left you that morning, it took me awhile. I knew you would go to your locker in the afternoon, so I figured I had a few hours to work up the courage to turn myself in. I needed help, so I finally went to Alvarez. I told him everything. If we would have been there five minutes sooner…"

"But you weren't." Chuy did not give an inch.

"Chuy," Lucy whispered with pleading eyes.

"No, Lucy, he's right," Billy asserted.

Nancy and Lucy shifted to the sofa, one on each side of the grieving boy, whose head rested in his hands. Feeling the girls' support, Billy sat up and gave them each a look of thanks before returning his gaze to Chuy.

"Why don't you tell your friends what is next for you, Billy," Mr. VanRoyen prompted.

Billy cleared his throat and continued, "Since this is my first offense— and because Alvarez spoke up for me—I'm out of school for a week. I have to be in an after-school program. I can't go to boxing, or Best Pals until I finish the whole program—and I'm on final warning for the rest of the year. If I screw up again, I'll be kicked out for good."

"Would you like to tell your friends about some of the positives that may come out of this, the ones we talked about," Mr. VanRoyen calmly suggested.

"Mr. VanRoyen thinks it's better if I stay busy, so I'm going to join the wrestling team. I did it my freshman year and I think I may be a better wrestler than boxer. It's right after school, so I won't have time to get lazy. Who knows? I may surprise some people. I also got a job!"

"What?" Chuy exclaimed with exaggerated surprise, breaking the tension in the room.

Billy was relieved to see his friend smiling again. "Yeah," he continued, still speaking quietly. "I've started working at my Uncle's body shop. Right now I'm just sweeping up, but he said if I keep coming on time and showing interest he'll start teaching me how to work on cars."

Chuy stood and faced his friend. "Well, if someone told me that Billy Karamitos had a job I would say that *they* must be high."

Billy chuckled, feeling slightly relieved. He allowed himself to think that just maybe Chuy was going to forgive him.

Chuy continued with a warning. "Right now, Billy, it's all talk. I need to see you step up before I can trust you again. I'm gonna check in on you and if you aren't doing the things you say, we are through as friends."

Billy exhaled once again, looking a little more like his old self. "Fair enough," he replied.

"I believe that wraps it up for now. Billy and I will keep meeting on an individual basis, but this was a very important part of our process. Thank you all for coming," said Mr. VanRoyen, signaling Chuy, Lucy, and Nancy out of the office, then closing the door behind them.

Chuy put his arm around both girls as they paraded down the hall and back to class.

Lucy nudged Chuy. "You forgave him already, didn't you?"

"Hell, yes! He's an idiot, but I knew that from day one."

"But you gotta make him earn it, right?" Nancy already knew the answer.

"Girls, we can't make it too easy on our son, or he will never learn," Chuy unnecessarily informed them.

They strolled down the hall feeling a lot happier than they had felt before the meeting. All three knew in their hearts that Billy was going to be okay.

The next few weeks without Billy hanging with him seemed strange to Chuy, so getting back to the gym made life at least feel a little more normal. Roadwork, school, boxing practice and time with Lucy made up the wonderful routine that Chuy had grown to love. After completing his assorted assignments, the old Billy returned to the crew, resuming his place beside Chuy, and that particular drama became nothing but a sad memory.

Soon Chuy felt as if they had never had summer break. He had to remind himself from time to time that this was his senior and final year. There was a big difference this year, however. The added notoriety from boxing created a reaction he had never experienced in his earlier years at Layden High. Virtually everyone had read about Lucy and Chuy in the sports section of the local paper, and many students had watched the fights at the fest. Even teachers and custodians stopped Chuy to ask him about his next fight and congratulate him on his victories. Between boxing and their work with Wolfy's kids Chuy and Lucy had become mini-celebrities.

Having lunch almost daily with his best friends was an added pleasure in what was shaping up to be a memorable senior year. One day in early October, the discussion at the lunch table was about that very subject:

"Ladies and Gentlemen, here he comes, wearing the white t-shirt, blue jeans and what may have been at one time white Chuckie's... Jesus, 'Ponyboy' LeDesma! Billy's foghorn voice encouraged a few kids to applaud, including Lucy and Nancy.

"For a kid that almost got us kicked out of school, you aren't keeping much of a low profile, are ya!" Chuy teased, sliding in next to Lucy at their lunch table.

"Hey, I did my time and I'm keeping my promises," answered Billy. "Got pre-season wrestling today after school, and I'm coming to boxing practice tomorrow."

"Welcome back," said Nancy. She couldn't help but add, "'Pothead Billy was a real a-hole."

"Nice mouth, young lady!" Billy stuck his chin in the air and spoke with a bad English accent. "You see, as a reformed man, I would never use such language, only the King's English."

"The King's English?" Lucy almost spit out her lunch. "Who is this kid? Did you actually learn something in class?"

"Indubitably," Bill replied, giving her a look of mock superiority.

He continued with the bad accent. "Now, how are my two pugilists doing? What shall I expect to see when I attend practice next fortnight?"

"Umm, I thought you said you were coming tomorrow; fortnight means two weeks." Lucy took a bite of her sandwich.

"I actually thought it was just a video game, but it sounded like the King's English," Billy responded, dropping the accent.

"Give it up!" Chuy and Nancy exclaimed in unison. They teased and chatted for the rest of the lunch period. Just as they got up to leave Ricky Ramirez and a few of his boys made a stop by the table.

"Hey, Ricky," greeted Chuy, who was the first to notice their arrival. "You know, I've seen you a hundred times, but I never ever said congratulations on the summer tourney—fourth in the state, not too bad."

"Yeah, should have won it," Ricky grumbled modestly. "Now you two need to win a couple of titles since we let you down."

"You didn't let us down, bro. Wolfy said it was the best summer he ever had!" Chuy protested.

"I guess, but it's the spring season that really counts in baseball, you know that. You guys go to Gloves next month, right? You two ready?"

"Gettin', there," replied Chuy.

"Hey," Ricky continued, pointing a thumb at Billy. "How's your boy doin?"

"Umm, you got it backward; he's *my* boy," Billy instantly protested.

"Yeah? Well, next time you're gonna bring weed to my school, tell me and we won't save your ass."

Billy's expression changed instantly from triumphant to sheepish.

"Easy, killer," Ricky relented, "I didn't come by to give you shit. Actually, my mom said you did good work at Family Services."

"Your mom?" Billy looked shocked.

"Yeah, Einstein—Mrs. Ramirez."

"Mrs. R is your ma? She's so cool, but how was I supposed to know that's your mom? All you Mexicans are named Ramirez."

"Dammnn! Yeah and all you white people are named Smith, or Jones," Ricky retorted. His baseball buddies cracked up over that observation.

"Yeah? Well I'm not white, I'm Greek." Billy stood up, sticking out his chest.

"Okay, you Greeks are all named Kristopolopolos!"

"Dammnnnn!" now it was Chuy and his crew's turn to bust out laughing at Billy.

Billy began to respond, but Ricky cut him off. "Nah, nah, enough; I just came over here to tell you what my mom said to tell you. You're lucky though; lucky you got out at a good time, that shit just got real, right?"

"What ya mean?" asked Nancy.

"You ain't heard?" Ricky continued, "Those gangbangers who were selling you weed got shot up for real. Your boy Armani's house got torn up!"

Surprised, Lucy jumped up. "What? When?"

"The news came out about a half-hour ago. It's all over the school. You know shit like this travels fast. Armani's house got shot up good. Word is, it was a kid named Javi from Eastside. My boy here knew him." Ricky, pointed his thumb at one of his teammates. "Tell'em, Abouchar."

Ricky's teammate stepped forward. "Yeah, I went to grade school with that kid. He was special needs—dude couldn't even read. I guess his dad was iced by some Kings back in the day. He always used to talk about it. The little dude had revenge tattooed on his fingers—I mean for real—and that was in 8th grade."

"You say he was a little guy, right?" Ricky asked.

"Man, he looked like a 4th grader when we was in 8th grade," Abouchar affirmed. "Haven't seen him in a while, but I'm sure he still looks like a baby, but he knows how to get a legit A-K47, and he knows how to pull a trigger. I'm guessing some older Cobras set up the drive-by and let this little dude take the hit. Now he'll spend the rest of his days in lock-up. That kid won't last a week in Joliet," Abouchar concluded.

"What happened to Armani?" Chuy asked, shocked by the news.

Ricky shrugged. "Word on the street is the oldest brother is toast and the other one is messed up in the hospital. They say if he lives he ain't ever gonna walk. I didn't hear anything about Armani."

"Are you sure about all this?" Lucy asked, as disturbed as Chuy.

"Dude, it's all over the news. Ms. Gonzales showed us in her class. I'm sure it's legit. See, you sit around eatin' lunch, ya miss all the action. Ask Alvarez or Wolfy; they'll know."

Chuy shook his head. "I don't even want to know about that shit. It makes us all look bad. Man, I'm just gonna train hard and try to bring some good pub to this school."

"That sounds good, bro," Ricky agreed, grabbing Chuy's hand for a quick shake. "We'll do the same."

"Bet," said Chuy.

Ricky went on to give each member of Chuy's group a handshake and a quick hug, until he came to Billy, he held out his hand and then snatched it away as Billy reached for air.

"Ahhh, just kidding Kristopolopolos." He laughed and offered a real handshake.

The news spread fast and was covered and analyzed by every news service in the Chicago area. Javier Gomez was a special needs student from Eastside High School, a neighboring suburb. Intellectually, he was not much higher on the scale than Wolfy's kids. He was a sophomore who could not read. His father had been a gang member who had been killed, but no one remembered who his killer was, or if the killer had ever been found.

Armani's oldest brother, Daniel, would have been a toddler at the time of the original killing and his middle brother had been years from being born, but that's the way it works with gang violence; it never has to make sense. In the most likely scenario, Javier had been given a weapon, a driver and some weed by a Cobra leader who wanted Armani and his family out of the way. They easily convinced Javier that the bad guys lived in the run-down house in Melrose Park.

Javi did the dirty work, resulting in one, possibly two, less rivals for the Cobras. They knew there would be little retaliation if the job was done right—and it was. What the Cobras did not expect was the retaliation they received from the school and the community.

Layden High School had slowly, yet effectively crushed the gang problem in the school. Dean Rudy had led the fight along with Officer Nick and security officers Norris and Jefferson. Layden had become a safe place to attend, to grow, and to learn. Teachers like Wolfy, Kelly, Alvarez—the whole faculty, in fact—had made the school a more fun, productive, positive place. Of course, students like Nancy and Lucy, who once had a foot in that gang world, but now had publicly turned their lives around, were huge influences on the other girls in the school. Athletes like Ricky and Chuy were an equal influence on the young men. When such a dramatic change of culture happens the list of factors involved is endless, but the real turning point at Layden was simple: the good kids were now the cool kids. Lost freshmen looking for an identity and a place to fit in were now taken under the wings of great young people with empathy, who knew what it felt like to want to fit in. Those previously confused souls were no longer prime recruits for gangs.

Fall at Layden became a magical time for some of the kindest kids in any school anywhere. However, when it came to the gangs, and the black mark they had put on the community with the vicious attack on Armani's family, students and leaders stopped being kind and became very angry. As history has shown, few beings are more passionate than students embracing a cause.

The news media covering Chicago took notice. The incident itself became secondary to the reaction of the community, especially the school. Groups of students took to the hallways and the streets, peacefully demonstrating against such violence. A silent prayer vigil was held in the Center Court. Athletic teams took moments of silence before games to encourage recognition and support. Posters promoting peace and a march through the community were other strategies that were put in place, all insisting on a crime-free educational environment. Even Wolfy's kids, with the guidance of Ms. Kelly, made a peace video for the morning announcements. "Give Peace a Chance" left a lot of students and educators moved to tears. A prime example was Alvarez, who, of course, on several occasions nearly created a puddle of tears in his classroom, much to the delight of his students, who loved to make fun of his crybaby ways.

During all the upheaval Lucy and Chuy were training for the fight of their lives. The Gloves Championship title meant more to them than a personal victory. Their community needed to be shown in a positive light, and the two-star fighters were committed to being that light.

Several days after the incident, as the two completed their morning workout, they talked about the buzz from the murder.

"You feel any pressure, Luce?" Chuy asked.

"Pressure? Nobody's paying attention to us," she responded.

"That's what you think! I hear channel nine is sending a truck to the gym sometime this week."

"Well, I guess Northlake and the club could use some good publicity. Let people know that good things happen here as well." Lucy never stopped throwing punches as they ran side by side.

"Alvarez said the big talk ain't about the shooting, but how we are all trying to clean things up."

"Really?" Lucy responded skeptically. "I'm not sure that's what the news is all about. Remember, if it bleeds it leads."

"Huh?"

"Ha," Lucy chuckled. "That's an old news saying, they get higher ratings with killings than with peace marches."

"Why are you so smart? Or is it that I'm that dumb?" Chuy threw a few punches of his own.

"Umm... a little of both?"

"Hey!"

They turned the corner towards Lucy's house. The day was already sunny after an early sunrise. Though school had begun, it was still very much summer. Chuy fake-sparred with Lucy, payback for her comment. After their shadow boxing session the two sat on Lucy's back stoop to rest a while.

"So are we going?" Chuy asked.

"Where?"

"You know where, the wake."

Lucy sighed. "Yeah, I need to go. Do you want to go with?"

"Do you think I should?" asked Chuy. "The last time I saw Armani I was accusing him of setting me up, and I was this close to kicking his ass. I don't think he wants me there."

"But I want you there." Lucy leaned against her man. "I was going to ask Billy, Ulises, Nancy and you."

"Okay, if it's what you really want. I don't want to kick Armani when he's down; I mean, he's an asshole, but nobody deserves to have his house and his brothers shot up."

"There's a lot of people that think that's exactly what they deserved," Lucy pointed out.

"Well, my mom and dad taught me not to judge, so yes I'll go with."

Lucy rested her head on Chuy's shoulder. "Ponyboy, you are a kind person. One of the many reasons why I love you."

Chuy looked down into Lucy's luminous brown eyes. "That and, of course, because I'm devastatingly handsome."

Lucy rolled her eyes. "And modest, so, you ask Billy and I'll ask Nancy and Ulises. It's Friday afternoon at Reynolds Funeral Home. Ms. Kelly said the student council is going to sponsor a prayer vigil. I guess some of Wolfy's kids will be there, too."

"Prayer vigil?" Chuy asked with concern. "Is that really a good idea? I'm not sure Armani will like the idea of a group from the school he got kicked out of being at his brother's wake."

"Well," Lucy answered, still leaning against his shoulder, "the school is about promoting peace. They are serious about getting rid of this gang problem. It will bring something positive, showing the rest of Chicago we meet violence with peace..."

"You said that well. Maybe you could be our Latina Martina Luther King."

"Or Cesar Chavez," Lucy added.

"Who? Ha, just kidding."

"Get out of here," Lucy ordered, with a push for emphasis. "You got to get ready for school."

"Damn! You're right." Chuy began to sprint down the driveway, "See you in the 250 hall!" He shouted over his shoulder.

CHAPTER 31

F riday at four o'clock Chuy and Lucy met their other friends in the parking lot of Reynold's Funeral Home. They walked as a group around the corner to the front entrance, noticing a significant number of police officers making their presence known. Police had been in front of Armani's house ever since the attack had occurred. Chuy surmised that Armani would need protection for a lot longer than it would be provided.

Nancy nodded toward the impressive crowd across the street. A group of students and adults, all dressed in black, holding candles, solemnly stood in the parking lot. "Looks like a big turnout," she observed.

"Let's stop over there first. Maybe a few kids who know Armani may want to join us," Lucy suggested.

The group crossed the street, heading directly for Sara Erl, the president of the student council. She was a cute girl with a round face, bright blue eyes and an ever-present smile. Today, however, she looked very serious, but she couldn't help but smile when Chuy and his friends approached.

"Hey, Sara," Billy called out, "this is really something."

"Yeah, a lot of people showed up. We're trying to bring a message of peace. I hope the people in the wake know that."

"Anybody going in?" asked Ulises. "They can come with us."

Sara shook her head. "To tell you the truth, not too many kids here knew Armani that well. Dean Rudy, Mr. Norris and Mrs. Ethridge are the only people that I know who went inside." She leaned toward the group, lowering her voice. "I've seen some pretty rough looking characters go in, too. A few didn't look happy that we are here. Do you think you could tell Armani that we mean no disrespect? We're just trying to spread a message. I hope he and his family understand."

"I'm not sure he wants any of us here," said Lucy. "But if I can talk to him, I will."

The conversation was interrupted by a familiar squeal. "Ccchuy! Hey, Cccchuy!" The crowd parted, revealing Wolfy's kids, led by Missy with Ms. Kelly bringing up the rear.

"Hey, Chuy!" The new arrivals began to yell.

Mrs. Kelly hushed them with a "Shhhhhh!" Guys, remember what we talked about."

Chuy, Lucy, Nancy, Ulises, and Billy took a minute to greet each of the Best Pals.

"Lucy!" Missy grinned widely. "Guess what! We get to hold candles if we promise to be careful."

"Yes," echoed Salim. "We promise."

Ms. Kelly looked a little frazzled. "Okay, guys, Chuy and his friends have to go now." She gathered up her charges and called out, "Good luck," to Chuy and the others.

"Thanks, Kelly," replied Nancy, "but you may need it more than us."

Kelly smiled and gave them an over-the-shoulder wave.

The wake was not well-attended. There were far more people across the street than within the funeral home. Those inside included a few tough-looking older guys, but the assemblage at the wake was comprised of mostly little kids and old people. Chuy and his friends entered the building and proceeded to a row of chairs near the back. There was no reception line, only two middle-aged women dressed in black who sat to the right of a closed coffin. They leaned against each other, not talking, but looking blankly into space. After taking in the scene for a couple of minutes, Lucy took the lead and motioned her friends to follow her to the front. Pictures of Armani's family on large white boards had been placed on easels around the outer perimeter of the sparsely lit room. The small procession paused before each one to observe Armani's family during happier times. Four clowning boys and a smiling, but tired-looking mother. More pictures showed the boys growing older and harder looking and the beautiful mother aging, appearing sadder with each passing year.

Lucy approached the two despondent women, introducing herself.

"I'm so sorry for your loss," she said quietly. "I'm Lucy, a friend of Armani, and these are a few of his former classmates."

Her friends followed Lucy's lead and introduced themselves, solemnly offering their condolences.

"I'm Rita, Armani's mother." The woman was barely recognizable from the pictures of her as a young beauty. "This is my sister, Connie. Thank you so much for coming. Not very many of Armani's friends are here. I'm sure he will appreciate it. I think he stepped out to smoke a cigarette." The statement seemed to embarrass her. "I'm sure he will be glad to see you," She concluded, looking down at her hands as her eyes filled with tears.

Chuy spoke up with a confidence that surprised him. "Ma'am, the truth is Armani hasn't been in school for a while, and the last time we saw each other it wasn't on very good terms. But it was actually a misunderstanding, not Armani's fault—right, Billy?"

"Yes, right," Billy mumbled, looking down at his freshly polished shoes.

"We just came to tell him, umm..." Chuy faltered.

Nancy jumped in. "That we can put the past behind us. If he needs someone to talk to, or hang out with, we are here. I mean...well...maybe something good can come out of this."

During a long silence Rita Rivera stared at the small group who seemed to care about her son, even though apparently he had not been very kind to them.

"I left my boys alone," She stated haltingly. "I ran away; I put Armani and Joey in the hands of the two older boys who I could not control." Rita began shaking but continued confessing her shame to these young people she didn't even know. "I pretended I was doing the right thing because I was so tired all the time. Now Daniel is dead and Xavier is in the hospital. If he lives he won't walk again. Joey's living with a family I don't even know, and Armani is an angry, silent stranger to me. If you can, please help my Armani." She ended when tears spilled over and began streaming down her cheeks.

Her sister had just calmed her and settled her back down into the chair when Armani appeared. While time stood still, Mrs. Rivera's muffled sobs were the only sound. Armani stared at the group for what seemed an eternity, then motioned for them to follow him to the front door.

"Armani," Lucy began, as they reached the door, "we told your mom and we are telling you, we can all start again. We all want to start over, Armani." Armani stopped and stood frozen, staring directly at Lucy, but seeming as though he was looking through her.

Lucy kept advancing toward him. "Armani, everyone deserves a second chance—a chance to begin again; I mean, Nancy and I did it. You can, too!"

"And the kids outside, they want you to know they mean no disrespect," Interjected Ulises. "It's a peace rally, that's all."

Caught up in the moment, Chuy felt overwhelming pity for his old enemy. Maybe this was the wake-up call Armani and his gangbangers needed. Without thinking, he spoke up, "Man, I know things have been jacked up between us for a long time, but who knows? Maybe we change all that, Armani; maybe we can make *something* positive. You can come back to school—you know—finish your senior year. You don't want this to happen to..."

Armani lifted his hand, stopping Chuy in mid-sentence. He looked at each member of the group with such a strong, unflinching stare no one could meet his eyes. Silence filled the dark lobby. Armani turned and walked away. "Fuck you" were his only words as he went out the door.

No one in the group had anything to say as they walked quietly out of Reynolds Funeral Home. The sun had set and the flickering of nearly one hundred candles brightened the darkness. Chuy and his friends walked across the street to the rally, each one of them lighting and holding a candle. The five took their place among the others, united in silence. Chuy felt heavy and sick and sad, and the candles flickered in the autumn breeze.

As Summer had flowed smoothly into autumn, the start of the school year flowed smoothly into a daily routine. Lucy and Chuy worked steadily through their training regimen to make ready for the first—and most important— tournament of the year. The peace rally at the wake of Armani's brother had received significant favorable publicity for the community, as well as for the school. A week later it seemed to be old news, archived, and forgotten. The media had moved onto the next guaranteed-to-sell story of the day. That's why Chuy and Lucy were surprised when they saw that one local news station was still interested.

A Channel Nine news van was parked outside the gym when the two approached on their bicycles. A stunning African American woman, probably in her mid-30's, dressed in a gold Channel Nine blazer, rousted her cameraman who was taking a smoke break by the side of the van.

"Oh, we missed it!" she announced loudly, looking slightly aggravated. She waved at Chuy and Lucy and called out, "Hi guys. Hey, would you mind riding up here again? Oh! I'm Cynthia Taylor, by the way. Ha! I'm all flustered. We are doing a story on your wonderful gym and especially focusing on you two. Do you mind?"

Lucy and Chuy exchanged embarrassed grins, shrugged and circled back down the street. The cameraman jumped to position, then gave a thumbs up. Chuy and Lucy rode toward the gym again, trying to look casual, but exchanging awkward glances.

"We can use that," the cameraman called out.

The two fighters led the way up the stairs into the gym and proceeded to get ready for practice. Alvarez, Big Ces and Sultan were gathered by the ring. The news crew spotted them and headed in that direction to talk to the coaches. It became apparent to Chuy that Ms. Taylor had obviously been there before and had come back only to film the two local fighters on their bike ride to the gym.

"Alright, movie stars," Sultan boomed out, "let's show these people what the party is about!"

Cesar and Alvarez jumped to begin their daily work with the fighters. Chuy and Lucy, along with Nancy and Ulises, took the captains' role facing the line of fighters and started the workout, acting as normally as possible under the circumstances. As the boxers began, Billy, who had been attending wrestling pre-season practice, came running in.

"He must have known he could get on TV," Chuy remarked loudly, and the team busted out with shouts of "Billeeee!"

"Whatever!" Billy snapped back, never to be outdone. "I'm a two-sport athlete. Besides, I can't help it if the camera loves me!"

The rest of the practice continued smoothly. Sultan and Big Ces took time out for a quick interview with Cynthia Taylor. Lucy and Chuy were in the ring sparring when it was Alvarez's turn. Between rounds the two leaned over the ropes to listen to part of the interview.

"So, you are also a teacher at the local high school. Do you think this club has made a difference in the school as well as in the community?" the beautiful reporter asked.

"Definitely," replied Alvarez. "There was a point back when I first began teaching at Layden when younger students, or my special needs students, didn't have great examples to look up to. Over the last four years, however, our student leaders, our athletes—like these fighters here—our club leaders, just all the upperclassmen have made all the difference. Kids like Chuy and Lucy not only represent us in the ring but are also officers in our Best Pals Club. I…I just can't say enough about them; I mean, they will never know the difference they are making."

At that moment the bell rang for them to begin sparring. Chuy grabbed Lucy into a clinch.

"Oh, my God, Luce, Alvarez is going to cry on TV!"

Lucy pushed him away but nodded vigorously, showing her mouthpiece along with a huge smile.

Practice was coming to an end when Cynthia Taylor called over the two fighters. "Ladies and gentlemen, let me introduce you to two of the stars of the Maywood Boxing Club: Jesus 'Chuy' LeDesma and Lucy Quinones. Guys, how have you made such a big difference in your community?"

"Ummm," Chuy began, trying not to look at the camera, "I'm not sure about that. We haven't won any titles yet."

"Yet you both have been successful in the ring and out. From what we hear, you and students like you are making a difference here. She directed the microphone to Lucy. "Tell us a little about you, being a female in the ring."

"Well, I can't say I was always hanging around with the right crowd, but once I got involved with boxing I think it really helped me. Boxing is showing me how to focus on a goal and work to achieve it. I want to win Gloves, but my ultimate goal is to get my law degree and come back to help this community, especially Spanish speakers immigrating here for a better life, like my parents."

"And I bet they are very proud of you! Would you like to add to that Chuy?"

"I want to thank my coaches, and Layden baseball coach, Mr. Wolf, for pointing me in this direction. Boxing has definitely helped my confidence. I never thought I could be president of a club like Best Pals. I never thought younger kids would be looking up to me, but, like I said, I think coaches, teachers, teammates, and my family, of course, led me here."

"Well said by two young people who are *making a difference* in Chicago. For Making a Difference, this is Cynthia Taylor, Channel Nine News."

With that the camera turned off and a round of applause ensued from the team and coaches who had all gathered around during the interview.

"Great job guys! I bet we can use most of this," Cynthia informed them, handing her mic to the cameraman.

"Oh, man, two movie stars!" shouted Sultan. "Well, I guess that's all for practice today; everyone gotta get home and watch themselves on TV since we all sooo pretty and all."

"Wait! Wait!" yelled Billy. "Where's my interview?"

"Come back on Sunday; we'll do a whole hour on you." The camera man spoke his first words of the night and sent the gym into a roar of laughter.

Billy just shook his head, waving off the crowd.

"You nervous about the tournament?" Chuy asked Lucy on their bike ride home. They were hurrying along, as the fall sky had already darkened.

"I guess. We gotta win now, right?"

After a thoughtful silence Chuy continued, "do you think we did all that—made a difference like Alvarez said?"

Lucy stopped at her corner. "I know you made a difference in my life." She looked deeply into Chuy's eyes and gave him a gentle kiss. "Now go home!"

"What, aren't we going to hang out?"

You mean, *make out?*... *NO!* I have a test tomorrow, and I got to tell my mom and dad about all this publicity. So GO HOME!"

"Rejected," complained Chuy, clutching his chest in fake heartbreak. "You are blowing your big opportunity to be with a TV star!"

"Yeah, I'll take my chances. See you tomorrow." She sped away toward her house, looking back once to blow him a kiss.

Chuy watched as she rode away. Lucy Quinones—*his girlfriend!* It was hard to believe that he had gotten so lucky. On the last stretch home Chuy thought how maybe they were making a big difference, maybe not, but one thing was for sure; his life was now very different. Pride and satisfaction flowed through him. He had to call his dad and tell his mom and Raul. They would never guess what happened at boxing practice today; that part, too, was for sure!

CHAPTER 32

Gangs don't die; they simply fade to the point where no one cares. Two days later Channel Nine aired the piece during both the morning and evening news programs. Sitting in the lonely, quiet house with boarded-up windows, riddled with bullet holes, Armani was in the dark, but for the light of the television. He had flipped to the morning news to see if the courts had done anything to convict his brother's killer, but instead happened on to the piece about boxers helping to make a difference in their community. Armani was instantly jealous and angry, then empty and sad, followed by alone and hopeless. But in the end all he felt was lost.

He looked at the ashtray filled with cigarette butts, then around the house that had not been cleaned since way before the police had removed the yellow tape from the shooting. He remembered how he used to clean every day when Joey lived there. He thought back to when he was younger than his little brother was now, and Joey had been just a toddler. Earlier that day he had chastised his mother for leaving him and Joey with the older brothers. Even as she cried and begged for forgiveness at her oldest son's funeral he had cursed her. It had felt good, so good at the time. He had felt empowered hurting her—justified. At the time, he had felt vindicated as he watched her crumble into her sister's arms, his mother and his aunt looking broken and ashamed.

Now Armani began to remember the little birthday parties and Christmas mornings and the single mom who held four boys together by a shoestring. She had magically prepared dinners with a budget of pennies, and she had created special occasions out of nothing. They might not have meant much in the eyes of the world, but Armani had known what love was in the old days. She had bought their modest house on her own, only to be pushed out by her eldest sons following a battle over their anger and greed.

The more the memories filled his head, the larger the hole grew in his heart. It was as though a dull spade were digging deeply into his chest, then pulled out and pushed back in deep again. After a few minutes, he went to his room. It was messy and dirty, but untouched by the police. He lay his head on the dirty sheets and began to cry. A little whimper at first, that grew through his body until unleashed sobs shook him to his core. Overwhelmed by emotion, Armani, scared at first, gradually let go and allowed the current of pain to envelop him. Gradually he started to feel cleansed, and his heart grew lighter.

Armani had no idea how long it took to free his mind and body of the pain, but when it was over he arose from the bed, went to his closet to grab a sweatshirt. Upon hearing rain falling on the roof this dark Tuesday morning he reached for his warmer coat instead. He stuffed his keys into the front pocket and was surprised to feel a piece of paper. He pulled it out and read it by the light of the television.

Armani dashed over to the far end of the room behind the beat-up sofa. He stomped down on the floor, listening and moving about until he detected a hollow sound. He tugged at the board using his bare hands, but finally gave up and hastened to the kitchen for a screwdriver. After working at the crack in the board for a few minutes he managed to pry up a slat. He peered in, using his phone's flashlight to see better. After studying what he found stashed under the floor, he left it where he had found it and replaced the board.

Armani sat on the dirty floor for a very long moment, finally he shook his head as if waking himself from a dream. Quickly, he went to his room and shuffled through the top drawer of his dresser until he found the card that Mrs. Ethridge had left him, in what seemed like years ago. He smoothed the card where he had crumpled it initially, opened it and read the immaculate handwriting—*we are thinking of you, hope you are well.* He pulled up his hood and plunged out into the October rain. When Armani reached his old corner, two young boys were standing there. They had been waiting daily for nearly a week to see him, like two good soldiers holding their post.

"*Hermano!*" they called out to Armani, "You okay, man? What's next? We gonna waste some Cobra's, or what boss?"

Armani hurried past them with his head down. "Go home, get outta' here!" he told them gruffly.

The two boys looked blankly at Armani, then at each other.

"Hey, dude, we got ya..."

"I said GET THE HELL OUT OF HERE!" Armani stopped and glared at both young men. "Beat it!"

"Man, what are we supposed to do?" one of them whined.

"I don't give a shit." Armani's voice trailed off as he dropped his head and crossed Grand Avenue. "Go back to school," he finished in almost a whisper.

The two boys stood unmoving, struggling to comprehend what they had just heard. After several minutes they sprinted across Grand, keeping a safe distance behind Armani as they followed him toward the school. When he reached the main entrance Armani climbed the stairs up to the double doors. The smell of Layden High School came rushing to greet him as he entered. He turned to the entrance booth to come face to face with Mr. Norris, who appeared slightly shocked to see him there. Although suffering from heaviness and despair, Armani couldn't help but smile slightly.

Norris stood motionless. "Uh, Armani, I don't think you can be here."

"I know." Armani tried to look Norris in the eye but could not quite handle it. "I guess I should have called...I'd liked to see Dean Rudy, Mr. Norris; I mean, if I can."

Norris had never seen Armani look anything but smug and distant, but the sincerity written on the boy's face was all it took for the security officer to pick up the phone.

"Come on in, Armani," Norris invited with a gesture.

"Thanks, Norris," Armani said quietly. "Um… I think I got a couple other guys with me, I mean they followed…"

"I got them." Norris motioned the boys toward the entrance booth. "I'll take care of these characters. Let me call Jefferson; you can walk down with him."

Armani just nodded. Sadness and shame suddenly overtook him. He shook his head as if he were shaking off a solid hook to the chin.

Security guard Jefferson came to the door, meeting Armani as he stepped inside. He reached out his hand. "I'm sorry about your brothers, but I'm glad to see you, Armani."

Armani felt his bottom lip tremble. He steeled himself, took a deep breath and nodded again. Without saying more he followed the security guard to Dean Rudy's office, where Rudy was waiting for them at the door.

"Armani, I'm glad to see you again."

"Yeah, Dean Rudy, thanks for coming to the wake."

"You know, Armani, I can't let you back here unless you follow the correct procedure. I mean, we can…"

Armani interrupted the Dean. "I will do what I have to do," he said. "I need help, Dean Rudy. I need help with a lot of things. I'm not sure what to do…" He paused. "I just know what I *don't* want to do."

He took the note that he had found out of his front pocket and placed it in front of the dean. Rudy read the note silently then leaned back in his chair and exhaled heavily.

"So he knew they were coming after him, and he wanted you to have this information."

"I guess," Armani replied in a broken voice, with one tear rolling down his cheek. "Daniel put the note in my winter coat, maybe so I wouldn't find it right away, but he still wanted me to have it. I guess he knew they were gonna try to take him down."

"Armani, I can help you get your life back on track when it comes to your education. It really isn't hard, if you do the right things; I mean, that's up to you. I cannot *officially* tell you what to do when it comes to this other situation. I mean, I am not allowed, but um…give me a minute." Dean Rudy picked up the phone. "Please tell Dave I won't be at the admin. meeting; thanks, Joan." He ended the call and looked Armani in the eye.

"As I was saying, I can't advise students on certain things, especially when that info came from a note *I've never laid eyes on*," he winked at Armani. "But...strangely enough, someone was just telling me about a young man who suddenly came into some money. That someone had a few good, solid ways for the young man to make the most of it."

Dean Rudy picked up the phone again. "Joan, please hold all my calls."

The next three weeks at the gym were extremely busy for all the fighters, but Chuy and Lucy took the time even more seriously than the others. It was the final push before the tournament. They would need to win three fights to capture the crown in their division. During the last two weeks of training sparring took place at a record pace: girls versus guys, heavy versus lighter, younger versus experienced. All of them pushed to peak at tournament time. Fighting lightweights helped the heavier fighters to work on speed, while heavier fighters helped the lighter ones learn to handle heavy hitters. "Bull in the Ring" was an exercise that set one veteran fighter against several younger fighters, who each sparred every other round against the veteran. In theory the novice would get better, while the experienced fighter could work on his conditioning, facing a fresh opponent every other round, sometimes for as many as ten rounds in a row.

Several fighters from the club, who had moved on to the pros, came back to help Sultan and his current team, just as they had been helped years earlier. Both Chuy and Lucy benefited greatly from this experience, taking part in battles that Sultan, Alvarez, or Big Ces carefully monitored by controlling the action, as the sessions could have become full-out brawls, with tough, proud Maywood athletes refusing to take a backward step. The coaches especially had to be wary of cuts and knockouts that could derail any championship hopes.

It was a fine line between being ready and at their best for the tournament or overdoing it and peaking too soon. It was a line that Sultan had treaded for many years. His expert coaching found his two headline fighters ready by the time that the intense sparring ended the week before the tournament. Now, one week of conditioning was all that was left to accomplish. They completed the week exactly the way their coaches instructed them: nothing more, nothing less.

Finally, THE weekend arrived. Lucy and Chuy were ready. Everything that could have been done had been done. Whether they won or lost, they could not be faulted for lack of preparation. All that remained was the car ride down to Springfield and the weigh-ins on Friday morning. The first fight of the Gloves Tournament was set for Friday night.

The team headed South on Interstate 55, a straight shot to the capital city of Springfield. Sultan and Alvarez led the way in Alvarez's car. Big Ces drove the van, chauffeuring Nancy, Chuy, Lucy, Ulises, and Billy. They passed the time talking, snoozing, and listening to music. Even though they had a day off from school, the team members had to get up earlier than usual. It was more than a three-hour drive and they planned to be one of the first groups to weigh-in, then have a light practice, breakfast, then rest for much of the day. The team arrived well before the nine o'clock check-in time, glad to have completed the long, monotonous drive of boring highway bordered with boring cornfields.

As they pulled up to their destination, Chuy and Lucy could plainly see this was much grander than anything they had taken part in before. The lot was already filling up with vans, cars and even a few buses. The team from Maywood walked as a group from the parking lot to the convention center, in awe of the huge building sprawled out before them. This was the venue for the biggest music stars in the world when they swept through Central Illinois on nation-wide tours. But for this weekend the Land of Lincoln Convention Center was the temporary home to amateur boxers from all over the state. Fighters of all shapes and sizes lined up for physicals and weigh-ins. Some fighters wore plastic suits, designed to drop the last few pounds of water weight before the weigh-ins.

Sultan, seeing the awe-struck look on his fighters' faces, guided them to the side of the entrance for a brief talk.

"The place is a hell of a lot bigger than any place y'all fought before, but the ring is the same size, so I don't need you to poop in your pants," he said in his usual gruff voice. "Y'all go change, then get in line and keep them mouths from gapin' open or ya gonna get a fly in your throat and get to chokin' before you even step in the ring!"

Chuy and Lucy grinned at each other, then shook out the butterflies and tried to look cool. This was already more than they had expected but having a coach who had seen it all so many times put them at ease.

The long drive was over. Soon physical exams and weigh-ins would be finished as well and they could check into the hotel, leaving only one box left to check off: the actual fights. They had worked so hard and came all this way for the chance to fight and win. The next few hours would drag by but fight time would surely arrive; Chuy and Lucy could hardly wait.

Light workout, breakfast, sleep. The two fighters reported to the Convention Center not really knowing what to expect, but happy for their experienced coaches who had laid out the day's schedule and prepared them in the best way possible. Sultan and his coaches had instilled confidence into their fighters, and so in the late afternoon Lucy and Chuy reported back to the Convention Center confident—they were ready to fight and win!

Before they headed into locker rooms to change clothes, Alvarez took them over to the bracket board. Chuy had three fights to make it into the championship round on Sunday. Lucy's division had fewer fighters. Her record and reputation had earned her a bye in the first round. Two wins would get her to Sunday night and a championship fight.

Alvarez gave them more good news. "Check it out, Chuy, if you face the number one seed, it won't be until championship night."

"Is that the good news?" Chuy looked doubtful.

"You tell me. You both have returning champs in your brackets. They are the favorites, of course. If you win, you will see them in the finals and you'll be fighting the best of the best for sure. That's what you both wanted, right?"

Chuy and Lucy looked at each other and grinned.

"I'm good with that, but I think Sultan was right; she is gonna poop her pants." Chuy teased.

"Get outta here!" Lucy gave Chuy a healthy push.

"Lucy's got a tough kid for sure," Alvarez agreed. "But Chuy, you'll be fightin' Willie "Guns" Gundersen. He's number five in the nation. So…"

The smile disappeared from Chuy's face.

"Ha! What's that smell!" Lucy and Alvarez both cracked up at her comment and the look on Chuy's face.

"Bring him on." In spite of his brave words a little shot of nerves punched Chuy in the stomach.

"Alright now," Alvarez put his hand on the young fighter's shoulder, "let's not get ahead of ourselves; let's just win the next one up! Chuy, you got two fights tonight you gotta win, then one Saturday night, and it's on to Championship Sunday. Lucy, one tonight, one tomorrow, one Sunday. Chuy, you're up pretty soon. You might as well get ready to go now."

A version of a three-ring circus was starting to take shape behind them. Three rings had been set-up and fighters who had already changed out of street clothes were beginning to gather. Warm-up had begun with coaches barking out orders. The familiar sound of ropes rhythmically whirring and tapping, the smack of gloves on paddle mitts, and the murmur of the gathering crowd added to the growing roar that was filling the arena. When 80's stadium rock began blaring from the state-of-the-art sound system everyone knew the boxing circus was about to begin. Chuy would be one of the first to get the show started, and that made him happy. He was ready to compete in his first-ever tournament, ready to become part of the circus. He was ready to fight.

CHAPTER 33

A stout man in a white tuxedo stood in the center ring. "Ladies and Gentlemen..."

It took a few seconds, but Chuy soon recognized the man as the announcer from the Peoria fights. "In the Red corner from Danville, Illinois, in the red shirt and white trunks, with a record of 11 wins and 5 losses, Justin 'Justice' McCabe!"

A heavily muscled opponent with reddish-white skin and dishwater blonde hair acknowledged the crowd or swatted at a fly. Chuy couldn't tell which. McCabe was considerably shorter than Chuy though much thicker.

"And in the blue corner, wearing blue trunks with the white top, from Maywood Boxing Club, Jesus 'Ponyboy' LeDesma."

Chuy stepped forward and bowed slightly to the crowd and his opponent. He then stepped back, ready to go.

"Keep your distance, Chuy, use the jab," Big Ces instructed.

"Don't brawl with this kid," added Alvarez. "Use your reach!"

Chuy nodded. His training had taught him to jab, move and counter with the right. He intended to keep busy in the first round, but not get into an all-out war while he gauged the strengths and weaknesses of his opponent, who definitely looked like a slugger.

As Chuy and his coaches had predicted, McCabe came out throwing hooks, ducking, and bobbing. It was basically Lucy's style, but less compact, less refined, and far less effective. Chuy peppered him back with accurate jabs, bothering McCabe and causing him to become even more wild. As the fight continued, McCabe gradually, then clearly, ran out of gas, allowing Chuy to land lefts and rights at will. The referee eventually gave the exhausted opponent an eight-count. It put a pause to Chuy's onslaught, thus allowing the fight to continue for another one-sided minute. By the end of the second round Chuy's opponent was frustrated and bloody. Just when Chuy stood for the beginning of the third round, a white towel came floating down in the middle of the ring. With that, Chuy had won his first fight in the state tournament. Elated, he jumped high in the air, and let out an audible sigh of relief. One down, two more to go—just to get to the championship. One of those fights would be later that very night.

Jesus "Ponyboy" LeDesma stepped out of the ring to the cheers of his team. Ulises, Billy, Nancy, and Lucy surrounded him, giving him pats on the back and sweaty hugs. A few fans at ring-side shouting, "Good fight, Ponyboy!" earned chuckles from both Chuy and Lucy.

Lucy's fight was scheduled for eight o'clock, but as the evening wore on, it became clear the times listed for fights were optimistic estimates at best. Despite three rings going at once, the fight card was backed up, hours behind schedule. The night would drag on, well past midnight. For Chuy, especially, this was going to be a test of patience and mental endurance, as much as boxing skill. He eventually went up to the deserted balcony to read "The Sun Also Rises," Lucy's suggestion for the weekend. He planned to come back down to watch Lucy's fight, then wait again for his final fight of this long, grueling evening.

Chuy was fast asleep in the balcony with his novel on his chest when Lucy finally began her warm-up. It was well past nine o'clock. Lucy in her gold and black uniform, with matching gold shoes, looked as impressive as any of the more experienced fighters in the tournament. Her tightly braided hair, covered by her perfectly fitting headgear, rhythmical bobbing movement, ferocious hooks to the paddle mitts all made her look every bit a champ, just waiting to be crowned. If anyone doubted her deserving the privilege of the first-round bye, watching her prepare would put that doubt to rest. She made her way to the ring looking as though she were born to be there.

Meanwhile, Billy had raced upstairs to awaken Chuy when he failed to put in an appearance ringside. The two decided to watch the fight from the balcony, which gave the ring below an added sense of grandeur. The stadium which had been about a quarter full at the beginning of the tournament, when Chuy fought, had now filled to capacity. Lucy's striking figure and professional demeanor soon brought much of the crowd to focus on the middle ring. The charismatic announcer from Peoria attracted the attention of the rest of the spectators with his booming introduction.

"Ladies and Gentlemen! Welcome to one of the most anticipated fights of the evening: in the blue corner, wearing gold, the undefeated sensation from Maywood Boxing Club, Lucy 'Rockem Sockem' Quinones. And in the red corner, it's the 'lady in black,' from the Boys and Girls Club, right here in Springfield, Illinois, with a record of 12 wins and no losses, 'Stone-Cold' Sonja Ortega. A huge cheer erupted for the hometown favorite. Neither she nor Lucy reacted to the applause. Both fighters had their eyes firmly fixed on their opponent.

In the balcony, Billy nudged Chuy. "Dude, everybody is watching these two."

Chuy raised his eyebrows. "Holy crap! I'm sweating bullets for her!"

When the starting bell sounded, the two tough fighters did not disappoint the crowd. They met in the middle of the ring and proceeded to throw bombs at each other.

Lucy's crouching style served her well in the opening seconds of the first round. While her opponent stood tall, firing looping hooks, Lucy ducked and bobbed, delivering shots that were more compact and far more accurate.

After taking two big shots in the opening minute, Ortega backed up one of her jabs with a straight right, catching Lucy, but not slowing her down. Lucy responded by going to the body of the taller fighter. It was evident that Ortega was not used to fighting when moving backward and Lucy took advantage and poured on the punishment.

The bell ending the first round brought a small cheer from Lucy's corner and from many nonpartisan members of the crowd, while the

Springfield fans were understandably silent. They knew their hometown favorite had just lost the first round.

Lucy returned to her corner, to receive water and a few instructions. In the opposite corner coaches were screaming, flinging water in the face of their fighter to convey their sense of urgency and concern.

This was not Ortega's first tournament. She was ranked as one of the best fighters in the tournament for a reason. The name 'Stone-Cold' was a name she had earned for being a stoic fighter, showing no emotion as she had walked through twelve victories, without losing a round. She sat in her corner, without expression, staring at Lucy from across the ring. She meant to turn the tables on this new sensation. Having lost the first round she needed to dig her way out of a hole, and it began with the bell sounding the second round.

Ortega darted out quickly to the middle of the ring, but this time firing straight jabs followed by straight rights. She was not going to trade hooks with Lucy, and she was not moving backward. She threw deadly straight hands, then attempted to smother Lucy in a quick clinch, pushing her backward, throwing punches and clenching alternately. She took Lucy out of her rhythm and used her size and strength to push her backward, then Pop! Pop! Left! Right! Clinch! Push! Pop! Pop again. The referee finally gave her a warning for pushing and the crowd sent up a thunderous BOOOOOOO!! When she was given a warning for clinching, the crowd responded the same way. The wily fighter and her corner were using her skill, strength, the hometown crowd plus a timid official against the talented, but less tournament-savvy Lucy. It was working.

Lucy was frustrated, but as Ortega clinched again, in spite of the warning, Lucy turned the tables and pushed her opponent away, landing a vicious hook to Ortega's rib which appeared to hurt her. Just as Lucy was about to follow up her best punch of the round, the referee jumped in, with a warning for the push that gave Ortega time to catch her breath. Lucy shook her head in amazement and looked helplessly at Big Ces in her corner. He gave a "hey, deal with it" shrug which was no help or consolation.

The second round ended, and the momentum had clearly shifted, magnified by the huge roar of the partisan crowd. It looked as if whoever won the next round would be moving on in the tournament. The referee, the crowd and the odds all seemed to be stacked against the scrappy Mexican girl from Northlake.

Lucy went to her corner and sat down hard on the wooden stool. She was frustrated and angry and, for the first time in a boxing ring, she felt like crying. Across the ring the other corner was celebrating.

"Give me your mouthpiece, Lucy." Alvarez spoke gently, almost a whisper.

He handed the mouthpiece to Big Ces to rinse.

"Take a big deep breath," he told her.

Lucy looked at him with pleading eyes. Alvarez lowered himself to his knees, placing his hands on her cheeks.

"Next round tighten up your stance to the max and aim your head to the middle of her chest. When she clinches you, you are going to throw hooks to both sides and up the middle; she will not stop you from throwing. You are gonna double-dig to the left side where you hurt her. When she pushes you, you're gonna step hard against it so she can't get any distance. You are going to throw, throw, throw! And you are going to win this fight. Do you understand me?

Lucy nodded her head weakly. Her frustration began to wane with Alvarez's calm instructions. He could see his fighter regaining her confidence. "This is no different than..."

"Clinch drills at the gym," Lucy finished his sentence.

Alvarez continued. "She will take a step back, you need to..."

"Go upstairs," Lucy completed the sentence for him again. With that said, Big Ces replaced her mouthpiece.

"You are so much smarter than Cesar looks," Alvarez joked, breaking the tension, and getting a brief chuckle from his fighter.

The coaches grabbed the stool, water and bucket and cleared the ring. Chuy and Billy had taken advantage of the break and they were both breathing hard as they rushed from the balcony down to Lucy's corner. They arrived in time to hear Big Ces say, "This is her house, Lucy; if you want to win you can't leave any doubt that you deserve it."

Lucy signaled her understanding, then gave a quick wink to Chuy who was looking concerned. He broke out into a big smile. The bell sounded and the warriors met in the middle of the ring. Ortega threw a straight right-left combination which Lucy ducked, landing two hooks in return, and sticking her head in the middle of her opponent's chest. The taller fighter clinched Lucy as she had done before, but this time Lucy, in a stance even more compact than usual, threw short but strong hooks into her ribs. Ortega pushed, but Lucy was ready for it, going back into the clinch that had worked so effectively against her in the previous round.

It was not pretty. Neither the crowd nor the judges could see the toll Lucy's body shots were taking on the hometown fighter. What appeared to be a wrestling match to the crowd was working in Lucy's favor. She could hear her opponent groan with every shot. Lucy turned her hips hard, making the compact hook thud against Ortega's ribs. The strategy was working for Lucy even though the crowd voiced their displeasure with boos and catcalls.

Alvarez turned to Big Ces. "She's gotta get the knockout; they ain't gonna give her this one!" He pointed toward the judges. Just then Lucy sprang upright from a tightly crouched position, threw two double hooks to Ortega's left side, then stepped back when her opponent crumpled.

"Well, that might do it," Cesar observed, visibly cheered.

Ortega bravely got up and took an eight-count. She nodded her head yes when the ref asked if she wanted to continue.

Lucy bee-lined toward the hurt girl, sticking her forehead into Ortega's chest. A right hook to the bruised rib caused the backward step that Lucy had been waiting for. Okay It was the same right hook she had used to end the first round. This time it put Ortega down to the mat. The referee jumped in, stopping the fight and the crowd sent out an OOH!!

The first fight of the tourney for Lucy had been a war. The team from Maywood sent out collective cheers and sighs of relief. The Friday night battle with the hometown favorite was over. Against the odds, Lucy had won!

Later Chuy and Lucy retired to the balcony to eat and rest. Lucy was chowing down on a huge burger and a mound of fries. Chuy, who was limited to slowly eating a salad, watched with envious eyes as Lucy stuffed a huge bite into her mouth.

"Sorry," she mumbled, mouth full of burger.

He rolled his eyes. "Sure you are."

"Poor baby, after the next fight you can eat all you want," she reminded him after swallowing.

"Yeah, whenever the hell that is." He continued to pick at the salad.

"Hey, with this next win, we will both be one win from fighting in the championship our very first year, so stop your pouting, Ponyboy, or should I call you Crybaby boy?"

"Not clever," grumbled an impatient Chuy. "Not clever at all."

Down below the fights dragged on. It was past midnight before Chuy even went down to warm-up.

By the time that Chuy completed his warm-up and stood ready to enter the ring, the crowd had dwindled down to teammates and their families. Not realizing it, Chuy had a look on his face that caused Sultan some concern. He put an arm around the young fighter and spoke quietly into his ear.

"Sometimes it ain't the other fighter that gets ya, son. Just like in life, it ain't always what you expect that trips you up. You been sittin' a long time; it's late, you are tired. You got all day tomorrow to rest and fight again. That is, if you win! You lose, you be watchin', boy. So tell me, you been doin all this work so you can watch? You wanna watch your girl fight tomorrow while you sit? You pissed 'cause you been waitin' around, boy?"

Chuy felt the anger and frustration that had been building up inside him rise toward the surface.

"Yeah, I'm pissed," he admitted from between clenched teeth.

"Good, son! Now you take it out on that boy over there. He da one that done made you wait. He da one between you fightin' or sittin'."

Chuy's body became energized. The frustration and anger that had fatigued him now motivated him. The wise old coach had turned on the right switch at the right time.

Alvarez and Big Ces escorted their fighter down the aisle and into the ring. Directly across from them, Chuy's opponent and his coaches entered as well. The other fighter was tall, with a spectacular physique and the face of a movie star. His shoulders were very broad, and his torso tapered down to a small, tight waist. He was obviously older than Chuy by several years. Chuy appeared to be completely outgunned.

Immediately, as though he were a mind reader, Alvarez got in Chuy's ear. "Don't let this guy intimidate you, Chuy. Me and Cesar scouted his first fight. He looks like Tarzan, but he moves like Frankenstein."

Chuy could hear the announcer in the background.

"...with a record of six wins, three losses in the red corner, from Chi-town Boxing Club, Rocky Matarazzo."

"Oh, and by the way, his name is Rocky, of course!" Cesar slapped his fighter on the back.

Alvarez stood directly in front of Chuy, forcing eye contact. "Okay, Jesus, this kid is not a serious fighter. We see this all the time. He played football at a dinky little college and boxing is just a hobby. He's been doing it for a while, but that don't make him a real boxer. He's got athletic ability, but he doesn't put in the time like you do. He was chasing girls and partying with his boys while you were doing road work. He had to cut weight big time to make this division, so the more you make him move, the better. You understand?"

Chuy gestured yes, renewing the anger in his belly.

Alvarez continued his pep talk. "This kid just started a year or two ago. He's never sparred with pros. He's never had a coach, or a gym like yours. This one is yours to win. He's going to move slow, so use your speed! AND STAY AWAY FROM THE RIGHT HAND!" Alvarez shouted over his shoulder as he stepped out of the ropes.

The bell sounded at one in the morning for Chuy's second fight of the evening. 'Ponyboy' surprised the big fighter by coming out firing. He jabbed, snapping back the head of his older opponent. Matarazzo pawed the air with a jab, but Chuy ducked it, throwing double hooks in return. He moved smoothly and gracefully, while his opponent plodded after him, holding his right hand high, waiting to throw it. He would have to wait until the next round, as the bell sounded before an opportunity presented itself. Matarazzo had not thrown a right, or any other effective punch, throughout the whole round. The coaches had scouted this guy perfectly and Chuy had dominated the round. He returned to his corner bursting with confidence.

"Great job, Jesus! But don't get cocky." Alvarez poured water into Chuy's mouth.

"He's going to want to tie you up and work inside," Big Ces advised, as he rinsed the mouthpiece. "Don't let him catch you. If you stick and move he won't be able to; his feet are too slow."

"STAY AWAY FROM THE RIGHT HAND!" Alvarez shouted again as he left the ring.

The second round was more of the same. Chuy made his opponent look slow and one-dimensional as he peppered him with lefts, landed solid straight-hand rights, and then danced back out of danger. Matarazzo threw the powerful right, but Chuy was well out of his reach. As the second round came to an end Chuy had his opponent in a corner. He had just stepped in to land a body punch when Matarazzo threw a wild right hook that landed on Chuy's shoulder but knocked him into the ropes. Fortunately for Chuy, Matarazzo was too spent to follow-up. Chuy regained his balance and danced back to the middle of the ring, wisely staying out of the corner.

When the round ended, Chuy returned to his corner rubbing his left shoulder. Billy, Nancy, Ulises, and Lucy were all loudly cheering Chuy's one-sided performance against the impressive looking, but underwhelming, challenger.

Alvarez seemed a little more relaxed. "Okay Ponyboy, I vote we stay out of the corner with this kid."

Chuy nodded his agreement and rubbed his left shoulder while Big Ces took out his mouthpiece.

"You won the first two rounds, Chuy. The only way you can lose is with a knockout. You get that?" Alvarez asked.

Chuy nodded again.

Alvarez clapped him on the back. "Alright, let's get a win and go to bed! What do you say, Ponyboy?"

"Deal," He answered, spitting out his final a mouthful of water and taking his mouthpiece back from Ces.

"And..." Alvarez started.

"STAY AWAY FROM THE RIGHT HAND," Big Ces and the rest of the team shouted in unison.

Chuy grinned for a moment, in spite of the mouthpiece, then turned to focus on his opponent and assumed his boxing stance.

The bell for the final round sounded, cueing the sparse crowd to cheer the skinny Mexican kid who was schooling the Adonis.

Matarazzo raced across the ring, right hand cocked to fire. The Ponyboy danced to his right, landing a beautiful jab over the top of his opponent's guarding left hand. The referee gave the stunned fighter an eight-count. Chuy could sense the fatigue and frustration in his opponent. His growing confidence told him to pursue the bigger fighter and go for a knockout. The skilled, young fighter threw big, looping punches, backing Matarazzo into the Maywood team's corner. Below him Alvarez and Big Ces shouted their protest at the move. Chuy's punches were getting wider and wider, no longer straight, and accurate as they had been throughout the entire fight.

Suddenly the fatigued Matarazzo turned and threw one wild, but powerful hook, catching Chuy on the top of the head and sending him to one knee. He popped up, but it was too late—the referee sent the bigger fighter to a neutral corner and counted Chuy to eight.

Below him, Alvarez and Big Ces screamed, "Go back to fighting your fight!" More embarrassed than hurt, Chuy heeded his coaches' advice. For the remaining minute of the fight Chuy popped the jab and moved, landing more shots as Matarazzo barely hung on until the ending bell. Chuy's corner let out a big cheer in the nearly empty stadium. Alvarez and Big Ces stood with arms folded, wearing half-smiles, half-smirks.

"Okay, I won, don't yell at me. I learned my lesson." Chuy grumbled.

Alvarez put his arm around his fighter. "I sure as hell hope so."

All that was left was for the referee to raise Chuy's hand in victory to the cheers of the few die-hard spectators.

The building was almost empty when Chuy walked down the steps of the ring. Once Ces had removed his headgear, he turned to Alvarez. "How did you know that guy?"

"I never met that kid before," replied Alvarez, giving Chuy a puzzled look. "We just saw him fight earlier tonight."

"But how did you know he played football, and that he cut that weight and that this was a hobby?"

"Ha! Chuy, you forget I've been around this game for a long time. He's in his twenties and only had nine fights. He's big and athletic, so I'm sure he played at least high school ball. To get down to your weight, he had to cut. It just makes sense."

Now it was Chuy's turn to look puzzled.

Alvarez continued after they reached the van and started for the hotel. "The truth is, Chuy, that you and Lucy have great coaches and you come from a great gym. You haven't been doing this very long, but you've sparred with some of the best. You and Lucy both have a load of natural talent. You also got heart, my young friend, and that's something you are born with.

I've seen kids like that Rocky character since I was your age, so I knew him. I also know you, Ponyboy. You two can make some real noise down here. I mean, you kind of already are!"

The van pulled up to the hotel. Sultan and Big Ces, having arrived a few minutes earlier, were waiting at the entrance for them.

"Sleep now, down here at nine for breakfast, stretches, back to the room for more sleep. Semi-finals start at seven p.m. tomorrow. We will be there at six." Sultan laid out the next day's schedule as he walked them through the lobby and to their rooms. "What say we get a couple of more wins?"

"Sounds like a plan," agreed Lucy, giving Chuy a tired kiss on the cheek, and turning toward her room. A hot shower and a soft bed would be their reward tonight. A championship title would be the reward for a win on Saturday.

Sleep would have been wonderful, and Chuy was really looking forward to it, but his internal five o'clock alarm went off and would not let him let him go. He sent Lucy a text on the off chance she wanted to run with him. He thought that it was more than likely that he would get no response, but "Let's go!" came back in seconds. The two ran quietly through Springfield's downtown, which looked almost deserted in the Saturday morning dawn. They spoke very little, comfortable in their silence.

"You nervous?" asked Chuy eventually.

"Nah, not yet" Lucy answered with a little laugh, "You?"

"Hell, yeah!" admitted Chuy. "I guess this kid I'm fighting was a junior division champ. He's had a ton of fights, but he just moved up this year."

"That means he's sixteen. You gonna get beat up by a freshman?" teased Lucy.

"Um, first of all sixteen would make him a sophomore; second, you know that doesn't matter. He's experienced and used to winning championships. What about your kid?"

"She won a close fight in the opener and got a walk over 'cause the winner in the other bracket damaged her hand. She hasn't had many fights. Sultan says my style should be perfect against her."

"I think you are getting cocky, Luce," warned Chuy.

"And I think you need more confidence. You got everything it takes to get to the championship and to beat that defending champ, even though he's supposed to be some Superman. We worked hard, Chuy. We got the best gym in the state, the best coaches and we are good. Why *not* us?"

They stopped in the hotel's lobby. Chuy wrapped his arms around his girl. "Thanks for the pep talk, Luce, but to tell you the truth, I was lying; I ain't nervous at all—I'm ready to win this thing. I just remember how you fell for me because I was humble and shy."

Lucy cracked up. "Yeah, where did that guy go?"

"Hey," Chuy shrugged, "I blame you; look what you have created."

Chuy went into his announcer's voice. "Ladies and Gentlemen, from Maywood, Illinois: your welter-weight champion, 'Ponyboy' LeDesma!" He finished his imaginary reenactment with his imitation of a cheering crowd.

"Okay, champ, enough of that. Let's get breakfast, even though I'm not sure I can keep it down after this act." The two headed into the lobby, both happy, proud, and excited by their progress, but still nervous over the upcoming night of fighting.

CHAPTER 34

The Convention Center floor had only two rings in operation on this Saturday night, but the crowd was larger and more rowdy than the previous day. The semi-finals in all divisions were taking place that evening. There would be no long wait nor early morning fight like he had had to deal with the night before. The fights were scheduled to start at seven, with Chuy scheduled at eight and Lucy at nine. The day of eating and napping passed quickly, and Chuy was dressed, hands wrapped and warming up, feeling confident and ready to go. He was aware of the talented younger fighter he was facing, but when he saw the baby-faced opponent, he couldn't help but relax a little. As they stood outside the ring waiting for the current fight to end, Chuy moved and jabbed the air while listening to Big Ces give him instructions.

"This kid has been fighting since he could walk. He's legit, fast, and experienced. You learned last night not to let looks fool you. This kid is the real deal. The good news: he was scheduled to fight in at one thirty-nine division and couldn't make the weight, plus he fought a brawler last night who gave his body a pretty good beating. He had a tough intro to the Senior Division. The bad news is, he's lightning fast, but you've sparred guys this fast before. If you don't rough him up and fight tight, he *will* out-point you, so don't let that happen!"

By the time Ces finished talking, the ring was cleared and ready for the next match. Now Chuy and his coaches stepped into the ring. Billy, Ulises, Nancy, and Lucy were sitting in chairs right below Chuy's corner.

Sultan sat with them, looking cool and calm. His work preparing his fighters had been completed the minute they showed up for the tournament. Now he could relax and allow his coaches to coach, his team to cheer and his fighters to fight. He sat, observed, and did not speak a word.

Across the ring, the baby-faced fighter, dressed in red, white, and blue, shadow-boxed, throwing punches with blinding speed.

The announcer came to the center ring. "In the red corner, former Junior Division Champion with forty-seven wins and only three losses as a junior, and adding two wins with no defeats in this, his first Senior Division tournament...ladies and gentlemen, from Aurora, Illinois, 'Coolio' Julio Alvarado!"

Pausing for a moment, the announcer introduced Chuy with almost equal enthusiasm. The bell rang and the fight was on.

Alvarado attacked immediately, throwing jabs and right crosses, bouncing in and out of Chuy's reach. Chuy blocked the majority of the punches, and the jabs that did land bounced off his forehead with very little effect. The younger fighter was fast, but the punches he landed were so light that they surprised Chuy. The round ended with a left hook from Chuy to Alvarado's body that had to have hurt. Chuy returned to his corner happy with his performance. That changed in a moment when Chuy received the most punishment of the fight thus far. Alvarez and Big Ces were both screaming at him, their voices mixing together in such disharmony that Chuy had no idea what they were saying. He only knew they were furious!

"What do you think you're doing, Chuy? We talked about this," shouted Alvarez.

"You can't give away rounds, Chuy—he's too good!" screamed Cesar.

Chuy's look of dismayed confusion led Alvarez to silence Big Ces with a wave of his hand. He then continued in a slightly calmer voice.

"Chuy, you've got to throw punches! You've got to crowd him. Take out the body—muscle him!"

"I did," Chuy pointed out.

"One shot!" Alvarez stuck his index finger in Chuy's face. "You are getting out-pointed."

"He can't hurt me," Chuy protested.

"Right, he's a patty-cake puncher, but he can out-point you, and he just did." Alvarez continued, "You can't count on a knockout; take him to the body, slow him down, make him cover up so you can attack. YOU ARE LOSING!"

The last word rang in Chuy's ears. He sat up high, retrieved his mouthpiece and nodded acknowledgment to his coaches. The bell for the second round sounded.

Immediately, Chuy went on the attack, demonstrating why he was quickly becoming a crowd favorite. He threw quick punches meant to punish, but to his surprise he missed most of them as his slick young opponent dodged and slipped, dancing away. 'Coolio' was not allowing himself to get caught in the corner. Alvarado scored points when Chuy started to get wild. The only points for Chuy were earned by vicious hooks to the smaller fighter's body. They slowed Alvarado only for a second before he moved backwards, shooting jabs that did not hurt Chuy, but did score points for the crafty kid. Finally, at the end of the second round Chuy trapped Alvarado in a corner, stepping hard to his left when the junior champ tried to escape. Still Chuy was throwing wildly, missing big hooks that his opponent avoided by ducking them. The bell sounded and Chuy slouched back to his corner. Now he was angry; he felt the fight slipping away from him. There was no doubt in his mind he was down two rounds to none, and he was in the desperate position of needing a knockout, or at least a huge one-sided round to even have a chance at winning.

Alvarez sensed Chuy's frustration. He placed his hands on the back of Chuy's head and pulled him close to his face as he knelt in front of his seated fighter.

"This thing is not over, Chuy. You hurt him to the body, but you are missing him upstairs. Stay downstairs; keep your stance compact, tight hooks—not wild. Turn on the hips, just like you were taught. Hit him in the body. If he blocks with his arms, pound his arms! Don't waste a shot! Remember, he tried to cut weight, and in the juniors they only fight two-minute rounds. You still have plenty on your side."

Alvarez's talk took the edge off the hopelessness and frustration Chuy was feeling.

"If you are going to go down, Chuy," Alvarez said slowly and clearly in his ear, "go down swinging!"

The coaches cleared the ring, and the Saturday night crowd cheered the slick junior champ versus the tough, hard-charging kid who had come from nowhere to make this an exciting fight of contrasting styles.

Chuy shot out of his corner at the sound of the bell. He unleashed a brutal body attack, pummeling his opponent, who appeared to have no answer to the barrage. Chuy kept a compact stance, not bothered by the harmless jabs coming his way. Alvarado still landed a few blows, but Chuy threw hard to his body. Even the punches which landed on the arms made such a noise that the crowd 'oohed' and 'aahed' at Chuy's power. From 'Ponyboys' corner, coaches and friends howled. Chuy might not win the fight, but he was giving it all he had, while staying controlled and focused at the same time. Two straight minutes of the punishing body attack had taken its toll and slowed Alvarado, but Chuy, even with his strong conditioning, was beginning to tire as well. The crowd cheered to encourage the gritty fighters in the final minute. Then, just as Alvarado landed a pretty jab and began to dance away, Chuy reached out, stepping long with his right foot, and threw a hard right hook to the jaw that caught the former junior champ and sent him stumbling into the ropes— and down to the canvas!

Alvarado knew how to handle the knockdown, and he remained one knee on the canvas, catching his breath, then stood up by the count of eight. He positioned both hands up to signal he was ready, while Chuy waited in the neutral corner, ready to pounce on the hurt fighter and resume the attack. Suddenly, the referee grabbed Alvarado by the wrist and walked him over to his corner.

The ring doctor came forward and examined the injured fighter, while the referee whispered something into the ear of Alvarado's coach. Whatever the referee had said caused the Aurora coach to throw a white towel in the middle of the ring. Just like that the fight was over and Chuy had won.

Chuy jumped into the air, as his corner exploded with joyful emotion. The crowd roar was a deafening mixture of cheers and boos. Alvarado stamped his foot and walked over to his coach, with his hands out, looking for an explanation.

The referee came over to Alvarez, whispered in his ear, then held Chuy's hand up in victory. In the middle of the ring, the two valiant fighters met for a brief hug. Chuy lifted Alvarado's hand in a show of sportsmanship, but when he saw the younger fighter wince in pain, he dropped the hand and gave him a pat on the back. Alvarez ran over to the opposite corner and talked briefly with Alvarado's coach. After the ring had been cleared Chuy questioned his coaches.

"Did I hurt him in the ribs?"

Alvarez laid it out for Chuy. "Oh yeah, you hurt him, but that's not why they stopped it. He could've finished and he probably would have won the decision."

"Why then?" Chuy asked, not understanding.

"The coach from Aurora is Julio's dad, Carlos Alvarado. I remember him from back in the day. He was a pretty good fighter—smart, too! Tonight he was smart enough to know not to let his boy fight 'Guns' Gundersen tomorrow. Not when he's undersized, and not for his first senior tourney. I'm sure that ref reminded Coach Alvarado of what Gundersen could do to his boy."

"So if someone's gonna take a beating, tomorrow..." Big Ces shrugged his shoulders as he put his arm around his fighter.

"Great!" Chuy groaned as understanding sank in, "Is this my pep talk?"

"Scared?" Alvarez questioned.

"Should I be?"

Alvarez exhaled deeply, then put on an ear-to-ear grin. "Chuy, my boy, some of us are too crazy to be scared. Looks to me like you're turning into one of us!" Alvarez gave his tired fighter a wink.

"Got nothing to lose now, right?" Chuy concluded.

"Nope, not a damn thing. You have won the respect of every fighter, coach and fan in this place, Jesus 'Ponyboy' LeDesma. You don't have a damn thing to lose!"

"Oh my God! Are you going to cry, Alvarez?" Chuy and Big Ces asked at the same time.

"What do you think? Of course," admitted the smiling, proud, teary-eyed teacher. "Now let's go watch your girl!"

Chuy got a big hug from Lucy, then he promptly went to work holding the paddle gloves for her warm-up. He resigned himself to no rest until after her fight. Sultan had taped her hands, smiling the whole while, not giving even one piece of advice. After Lucy's warm-ups, the team assembled behind the rows of ringside seats. Alvarez and Big Ces tried to look serious but failed miserably. They seemed loose and confident, almost giddy. Chuy and Lucy exchanged quizzical glances, having noticed the strange demeanor of their coaches.

"Umm...you guys okay?" Lucy asked, ducking and bobbing, continuing her warm-up.

"What?" Big Ces tried to look innocent. "Just get ready, and don't be overconfident."

"Huh," snorted Lucy, "I'm not..."

She didn't finish her sentence, as the crowd erupted loudly, a reaction to a knock down happening in the ring. The downed fighter stumbled to get up, but the fight was over. Lucy was on deck. No more time for questions or banter.

Lucy, coaches, and friends took their places in and around the ring. She ducked and bobbed expertly in her corner, but as her opponent entered the ring, Lucy saw what had caused the light-heartedness of her coaches. Entering the ring was Elly Brumhurst from Rockford—the first girl Lucy had faced, the one she had put down within the first seconds of her fight.

Brumhurst had won her preliminary bout by a split decision, then received a walkover when her next opponent had injured a hand in her own prelim fight. More important than those circumstances, however, ewas the look on the Rockford fighter's face. She had seen Lucy beat the hometown hero in her quarterfinal round. She remembered Lucy's power and skill. Brumhurst looked scared and was defeated before she ever walked into the ring. Lucy's demeanor did not change. *Anything can happen in the ring*, she told herself. She approached Big Ces (still wearing his confident smile) and took her mouthpiece from him.

"Hey, Luce, anything can happen in the ring." He echoed her thoughts. She nodded in agreement.

During introductions, Lucy bobbed and shadow-boxed, eyes fixed across the ring, scoping out her opponent as she always did. Brumhurst looked down at the ring mat, barely moving her body. When the bell sounded to start the fight, Lucy came out swinging, opening up with hooks aimed at the body. Brumhurst tried to move away, using an ineffective jab while going backward, but Lucy easily slipped away, backing her opponent into her own corner.

Lucy fired hooks to the body, causing the fighter from Rockford to drop her hands. Out of nowhere Lucy came up top with a vicious, jumping left hook that snapped her opponent's head back. The referee immediately stepped in for an eight count and was met with a white towel to the face, thrown when the Rockford coach had seen enough. He would let his fighter take her preliminary victory with the knowledge that she needed a lot of work to make it to a future championship night.

Thirty seconds into her semi-final match Lucy won by a TKO. The two person Maywood team would have two fighters in the finals.

That night the team celebrated with pizza from a take-out around the corner from the hotel and a movie on TV. The coaches each grabbed a couple of slices and said an early good night, leaving the younger crowd in Chuy's room. They settled in to eat and watch the car racing action film Billy had insisted on. Billy, of course, was the first to ignore the movie in favor of reliving the fights.

"Chuy, dude! You beat up that big Rocky dude last night, and then that little Coolio kid almost whipped you." Billy laughed in his too-loud-for-the room voice.

"No joke, man," said Chuy, navigating the words around a mouthful of pizza. "I couldn't catch that kid. He was slick. I guess he's been fighting since he was eight years old. I know he'd win at 139, but he was a pound and a half too heavy for that division."

"How about Lucy!" Nancy joined in. "I thought that little girl was going to crap her pants before she even threw a punch."

Everyone laughed. "But you know what?" Nancy continued, "she had the guts to get in the ring. Hell, the girls I'd be against are big as tanks! No thanks, not for me!"

"I usually don't like an easy fight," Lucy said after swallowing her own mouthful of pizza, "But I'm kind of spent; I'm glad I had an easy one and I'm glad we can sleep tomorrow. Chuy, you must be beat."

Chuy nodded. "This pizza, shower and another good night's sleep is all I need. I think we should run at nine tomorrow, cool with you?"

Lucy smiled. "Totally cool with me!"

As Lucy got up to leave, Ulises spoke up. "Hey, Chuy, Lucy, I fought in this tournament twice. I never made it to Sunday night. If I had, I would probably still be boxing. You guys are doing amazing, no matter what happens tomorrow. I do have an idea, though."

"What's that?" asked Lucy.

"FREAKING WIN!" Exclaimed Ulises. "Come on, I'll walk you ladies to your room."

"Oh, my guy is a gentleman," declared Nancy.

"Too tired, can't move," yawned Chuy, dropping back onto his bed, arms outstretched.

"I'll give you a pass this time," said Lucy. She bent over and gave Chuy a quick kiss on the cheek. "You earned it. See you tomorrow, Ponyboy."

Billy did a quick pick-up of the room while Chuy dragged himself into the shower. Soon both boys climbed into their beds and switched off the light. Settling in, Chuy let out a deep exhalation. How far this adventure had come! Tomorrow he would fight one of the best boxers in the nation. As if Billy was reading his mind, he spoke to Chuy in an unusually serious voice, slightly surprising the tired fighter.

"Hey, bro, I want to thank you."

"Thank me?"

"Yeah, I know you could've brought anyone, or no one, and had the whole room to yourself."

"Yeah and pizza to myself, too!" Chuy chuckled.

The room went silent, strange since the silence was coming from Billy. "Hey, Chuy," he eventually said. "I'm really sorry man; I almost jacked it up for you."

"For you, too," Chuy reminded his friend. "What was so great about gettin' high man? I mean, I smoked before; it just gave me a headache and munchies, and then all I wanted to do was sleep."

"Ha, hell I don't know." Billy thought for a minute. "I guess at first I felt like I was getting away with something; you know, like I was a little kid being bad. I mean my parents didn't know. You guys didn't know. I guess it was a little bit of a thrill. Then it became like an escape."

"Escape from what, Billy? You don't do shit," laughed Chuy, trying to lighten the mood.

Billy laughed, too. "Yeah, I know right? But that was it; I'd smoke, chow, play Fortnite. Do nothing, but when I was high, that was fine. When I'd wake up, I would feel like shit, but then I'd get high again, and it was all good. It sounds stupid now, especially to someone like you, Mr. Perfect."

"Perfect? Ha! Me? Come on, Billy, you have known me better than anyone. Perfect? Dude, I suck at reading; I was in Special Ed. I couldn't make the baseball team. Lucy is my first girlfriend and I almost shit my pants when I first tried to make out with her."

"And now you are the president of Best Pals, you got a smokin' hot girlfriend, freshman kids want to be like you, and tomorrow you are fighting for a state championship."

"And you're my best friend," Chuy concluded, smiling in the dark. "Face it, my brother, we came a long way. In a couple of months, I could be watching you in the state wrestling tournament, but that doesn't even matter, Bill. You bounced back—you were on the mat. Hell, you could have let me take the fall. You could have blamed Armani and his brothers. You could have left and never come back, like Armani did. I know it's hard to walk through the halls after you F'd up, but you did, Billy."

"So.... I almost F'd up everything and you are telling me how cool I am?"

"Yep!" Chuy said adamantly.

"Ha, Well, Chewbacca, at last you are seeing things my way."

Chuy let out a deep breath. "Go to sleep, Karamitos."

They lay silently in their beds for a long while, both grinning in the dark.

"Billy?" Chuy whispered, as if they were at a childhood slumber party. "You still awake?"

"Yes," Billy whispered back.

"Do you think I got a chance tomorrow? Do you think I can win?"

Billy let out a quiet laugh followed by a noisy yawn. "The way I see it, Chuy, you already did."

"Ha!" Chuy closed his eyes. *For once the little guy with the big mouth was right. Now he just had to show William "Guns" Gundersen.*

CHAPTER 35

Championship night! One ring, a huge crowd, and bright lights. Nancy had forced her friends to hand over their uniforms in the morning so she could have them cleaned and neatly pressed. Now she was proud of her attention to detail as the Maywood team stood out among all the finalists. Lucy was decked out in her solid gold uniform, while Chuy looked sharp in his satin-blue shorts and white top. Both fighters stood outside the dressing rooms, ready to line up for the opening ceremony.

"Looking good," Nancy pronounced with pride. "I almost hate to cover them up."

Chuy and Lucy, both nervously bouncing up and down, gave Nancy a questioning look.

"What do you mean 'cover them up'?" Lucy inquired.

Right on cue, Ulises and Billy approached the fighters, each of them holding a square white box.

Chuy and Lucy did not speak but stopped bouncing to watch their friends simultaneously open the boxes and unfold shiny satin robes.

'**Ponyboy**' in big, white blocked letters was on the back of a blue robe. In the other box was a gold robe embellished with '**Rockem Sockem**' in black script writing.

"What the...?" "Are you kidding?" The two fighters' voices mingled together in excitement.

Nancy beamed at both of them.

"You...these are..." The two still could not create a full sentence between them.

"Put them on—you guys have got to go now!" Nancy draped the robe around Lucy.

Lucy and Chuy hurriedly slipped into their new robes and jumped into the forming line of finalists. They both tried to look tough and serious, but neither could hide their smiles. The Maywood fighters looked and felt like champs.

Two fighters from each weight division were the only boxers left after three days and two nights of boxing. The arena went dark and silent for a moment, during which the fighters prepared to march to the center. The crowd responded to the march with deafening cheers. Music cued, two lines walked down each side of the venue turning to line up facing each other, separated by the ring. Soon each fighter would be face-to-face in a battle for a State Championship title.

"Ladies and Gentlemen!" The now familiar voice of the announcer rang out. "Your Illinois State Finalists! Now it's time tooooo THROW DOWN!"

The crowd went wild. Thunderous cheering and foot-stomping halted the proceedings for several minutes. Chuy felt the goosebumps of excitement. He looked down the line at Lucy, looking every bit a champ herself. He raised his glove, and she did the same. The time was here at last.

After a few matches into the fight card, the crowd was warmed up and eager for more. It was Lucy's turn and she stood ready to enter the ring. Having taken down one of the hometown heroes, her sharp look, no-nonsense style and punching power had turned her into a crowd favorite. She strode into the ring to thunderous applause. In the red corner, receiving an equally loud ovation was her opponent—the reigning state champions

The announcer began the introduction: "Fighting for the Women's Lightweight Division Illinois State Championship: In the blue corner, wearing gold trunks with gold top, hailing from Northlake, Illinois, and fighting for the Maywood Boxing Club, Lucy 'Rockem Sockem' Quinones. And in the red corner, with a record of twenty-seven wins with only three losses, wearing the green trunks, from Park Forest, Illinois, fighting for the Fighting Southside Irish Boxing Club, the defending female lightweight Champion: Ladies and Gentlemen- Justine 'the Queen' Murphy!"

After the pre-fight instructions, the combatants, both ducking and bobbing, stared each other down. They backed up to their respective corners, the stares remaining fixed, as if breaking eye contact was a sign of weakness. Neither would willingly show any sign of surrender. Big Ces rinsed Lucy's mouthpiece and stuck it in her mouth, not saying a word. The time for talk was over. The bell sounded and both fighters sprinted to the middle of the ring. The champ wasted no time, throwing sharp jabs. Lucy ducked and bobbed, answering with a double jab, which caught Murphy in the jaw, sending her back a step. Recovering quickly, she threw a lightning-fast right cross which landed squarely on Lucy's forehead.

So it began, an epic battle that had the crowd on their feet from the opening bell. Lucy continued ducking and bobbing, but always moving forward with double hooks and jabs thrown from a crouch, followed by powerful jumping hooks that snapped the head of the champ backward. Murphy responded with stiff jabs and crosses, also thrown with blinding speed and pinpoint accuracy. The crowd "oohed" and "aahed" with each expertly thrown punch. When the first round ended the loudest cheer of the night resounded. The spectators were in for a treat—and they knew it!

In the corners the coaches splashed water, toweled off their fighters and rinsed mouthpieces, but spoke very little. The two young women were each fighting their best fight, and their coaches could ask for nothing more. Now it was up to styles, conditioning and, ultimately, the judges to pick the winner.

The second round was more of the same. Lucy landed a stunning hooking jab, but as she loaded up for another, Murphy countered with a right that momentarily stopped Lucy in her tracks. Lucy responded with rights and lefts to the body. Murphy came back with a right-left-right. The crowd was ecstatic with the action. After the second break, the fury continued to the third round. At this point it was anybody's guess as to who was winning. The two warriors arose from their stools and danced in their corners, each breathing hard, waiting impatiently to finish the battle. The bell sounded for the third and final round. Both fighters moved to the middle of the ring to touch gloves as a sign of respect. That marked the last time that a punch was *not* being thrown that third round! Like sprinters to the finish line, both boxers threw leather as if their lives depended on it.

Lucy was catching her opponent with right hooks to the head and body, doubling up with the left whenever Murphy tried to avoid the right. The champ was finally getting a feel for the timing of Lucy's bobbing motion and landing more significant rights than she had in previous rounds. By the time the round approached the end both fighters were exhausted. Using all her finesse, Lucy managed to maneuver Murphy into a corner where she landed a right to the body that finally allowed the champ an opportunity to pull Lucy into a clinch, the crowd roaring all the while. Lucy struggled to push out to freedom, but the deceptively strong opponent held her long enough to catch her own breath and dance herself out of the corner. The champ had sought to escape, but Lucy bobbed and flew to her left, landing a hook that sent the champ back to the corner.

Chuy and Billy jumped up out of their seats, as did most of the crowd. The entire center section remained standing as the bell sounded that ended the fight! The rafters shook as the two exhausted combatants embraced in the middle of the ring. After their lengthy hug, the referee grabbed Murphy and Lucy by the wrists and raised their hands in the air to the delight of the crowd.

"I wouldn't want to score this fight," he announced loudly, still holding both their wrists. "Best fight I've seen in a long time, ladies! Congratulations to both of you."

Lucy ran back to her corner and jumped into the arms of Big Ces.

"You did it girl! You're a state champ!"

"Ladies and Gentlemen," the announcer shouted over the still cheering crowd. "Please give it up for these two valiant warriors!"

The applause washed over the two fighters like a tidal wave as they each bowed to the other.

Beaming, Lucy returned to the center of the ring.

"Judge Number One scores the bout thirty to twenty-nine in favor of Murphy. Judge Number Two scores the bout thirty to twenty-nine Quinones, and Judge Number Three scores the bout thirty-twenty-nine for the winner …and still Illinois Female Lightweight Champion, Justine 'The Queen' Murphy."

A mixture of boos, cheers and murmurs ensued. Murphy jumped high in the air, surprised at her own victory. Lucy stood motionless. She had won the crowd, but somehow lost the fight in the eyes of the judges. She dropped her head for a moment, swallowed, then stepped past the referee to congratulate the victor. The girls hugged one last time. The referee stopped Lucy as she headed back to her corner, shouting over the tremendous crowd noise, "Young lady, you are a champ. No one should ever tell you differently."

Lucy looked up with a fragile smile and tears in her eyes.

"Thank you, sir," she said. "Thank you."

Lucy returned to Big Cesar waiting in her corner. Alvarez had left the ring at the decision, not congratulating the opponent or her corner. For the first time in his long life of sporting contests he was not going to be a good sportsman. He needed to leave. He rushed past the ringside seats, through the lobby and out a side door to the parking lot.

"NO!" He screamed, ready to punch the closest object. "DAMN IT! BULLSHIT!!" He sat down on a concrete stoop and dropped his head into his hands.

"Okay," he eventually muttered to himself, exhaling, "Okay."

He grimaced at his inability to cope with his own anguish and stood up. "Okay!" he declared one more time, then went inside to congratulate his fighter and her opponent for one of the best fights he had ever seen.

Alvarez found the crew by the table where Lucy had just returned her gloves and was in the process of removing the gauze from her wrapped hands. Even though another fight was going on, the crowd was still buzzing about the fight they had just seen.

Murphy and her coaches were still gathered near the ring. Alvarez stopped, giving them a quick congratulations before joining up with his team. When he drew near he saw that Lucy was covered in sweat, which seemed to make her glow. She was beaming a bright contagious smile.

"My girl," Alvarez grinned, giving Lucy a hug. "That smile is what I want to see."

"I came down here and fought as hard as I could, Coach Alvarez. That's all I could do, and that's all I wanted to do," Lucy said as people from the crowd left their seats to show their support for her with an encouraging word, or a light pat on the back.

"You was robbed, young lady," an older man decreed as he patted Lucy on the shoulder.

Another man approached with his young daughter, around the age of Lucy's youngest sister.

"Can my girl get a pic with you?" the man asked politely.

"In every close fight, a fighter has got to dig deep. When they got nothing left, that's when they throw the last big punches," said Alvarez. "That's what you did, Lucy. That gold trophy should be yours."

Lucy shrugged her shoulders. "Well, this one will do just fine!" she held up the second-place silver trophy, "For *this* year!" she added with a grin.

Alvarez and Lucy exchanged a high five, then prepared to watch the next fight, after which Chuy would be up against one of the best young boxers in the nation. It was almost time to see if the tough Mexican underdog from Northlake, Illinois could even last three rounds against the three-time Illinois state champion, national quarter-finalist, and Olympic hopeful.

The safe bet was absolutely not!

Chuy was gloved up, loosened up, and ready to fight. Big Ces and Alvarez stood apart, next to Sultan while the rest of the team sat beside him at ringside. Suddenly Sultan arose and walked over to Chuy.

"You—Billy boy, come here; time for you to earn your keep."

Billy's eyes opened wide in surprise. "Me?"

"No, the other little white boy," Sultan teased. "Yeah you! Get up here!"

Alvarez and Big Ces stretched out and reclined on Billy and Sultan's now open seats. Chuy's teammates were waving and giving thumbs up to him.

Sultan was right behind Chuy when he stepped up to the ring. "I'm in your corner today," he announced with his usual gruffness. "Boy, don't look so shocked, Who do you think was in Big Ces' corner when he won the Gloves? Who do you think was across from Alvarez and his coach, Louie, when they robbed us of the middleweight championship all those years ago?"

"Please! Lucky we had fair judges that day!" shouted Alvarez through cupped hands in response to Sultan and his booming voice.

"What you waitin' for, Billy boy? Get up here with your fighter."

"But... but..." Billy stammered.

"Lookie, here!" Sultan shouted to the team, "I finally said somethin' to shut him up."

"I can't …" Billy started but was cut off by the coach.

"Can you hold a bucket, boy?"

Billy nodded yes.

"Then you can do this! Let's go!"

The look on Chuy's face spoke volumes, but the veteran coach answered before his fighter could give voice to the question. Sultan placed his hands on each side of Chuy's face and spoke slowly and calmly.

"I brought your guy Billy in here to show you, this ain't no damn Cesar's Palace and you ain't fighting for the heavyweight championship of the world. This is just another fight where two guys get in a ring. You understand?"

Chuy nodded slowly.

Sultan continued calmly. "A kid with less than twenty fights who's been fightin' for little less than a year ain't got a chance against this guy. He's gonna win Nationals—or turn pro—probablyds both. I'm here to make sure you don't get hurt, boy. You feel me?"

The wise coach studied the look on his fighter's face.

"Listen here, boy; I didn't say we throwin' in the towel before we start. You and Lucy are two of the hardest working, toughest, most naturally gifted fighters that've come my way in a long time. Maybe ever! You have an opportunity here. YOU GOT NOTHIN' TO LOSE! EVERY SECOND YOU STAY WITH THIS GUY MAKES YOU A BETTER FIGHTER! Nerves are out the window right now! You fightin' in front of a crowd like this, in this place, for a championship and you know YOU GOT NOTHIN' TO LOSE! I want you to take a deep breath, look around and take it all in."

Chuy felt the anxiety drain from his body as he looked around; the excited crowd, the muscular, athletic man standing across from him, the huge venue filled with the booming music, the smiling announcer in the white tuxedo, his friends and coaches at ringside, and his best friend holding a bucket, looking more nervous than any fighter in the tournament. Chuy let out a laugh in spite of all that was going on around him. His old coach gave his fighter a knowing look of confidence and pride.

"Now, you be careful," Sultan advised in a serious tone. "But you have fun. This is a moment you will remember for the rest of your life."

The announcer began: "Ladies and Gentlemen: for the Men's Division Welterweight Championship of Illinois. First, in the blue corner wearing the blue and white, a talented new fighter making his mark in his first State Tournament, the Maywood sensation, Jesus 'Ponyboy' LeDesma. And in the red corner, wearing red trunks, a fighter that needs no introduction, one of the most decorated boxers in the Illinois fight game, fighting for his fourth state title, a national quarter-finalist, ranked number two in the nation, Ladies and Gentlemen... William "Guns" Gundersen!"

The crowd roared for the popular champ, but their support did not bother Chuy. He felt strangely calm as he met Gundersen in the middle of the ring. The champ was imposing. He was clearly older than Chuy, with pronounced muscles glistening in the strong lights above the ring. He looked Chuy straight in the eye as Chuy struggled to maintain his relaxed composure, but as he returned to his corner, the confident demeanor of his veteran coach, as opposed to the utter fear on the face of his boyhood friend, sent the young fighter back into a peaceful state of mind.

"Nothin' to lose," he said to Sultan.

"Nothin' to lose," the coach echoed.

The bell sounded, and the battle began.

CHAPTER 36

'**G**uns' came out confident, almost cocky, holding his hands low. He threw lightning quick jabs, measuring Chuy. They popped off Chuy's gloves with such power that his hands were forced back into his own face. Chuy's attempted jabs were blocked by Gunderson, or he slipped the punches and returned with jabs and long strong body shots to Chuy's stomach and ribs, but for some reason he did not go in for the kill.

Chicago fighter, Lance "The Hawk" Hawkins was the only fighter Gunderson and his coaches believed could give him a fight in this tournament. Gundersen had defeated Hawkins in a one-sided unanimous decision in the semifinals. The reigning champion cruised through the first round, sure that this new kid from the tiny team in Maywood could not challenge him. When the bell sounded the crowd offered little response for the lackluster round.

Chuy slouched back to his corner. He could feel the effects from the body shots that Gundersen had thrown. His body had never taken such damage before; it was a strange feeling.

"You havin' fun out there, Chuy?" Sultan mocked, throwing water into his fighter's face. "You havin' fun being his moving punching bag? He just working on body shots—he's practicing, Chuy!" Sultan began to shout.

"You can let him get his work in, or you can go after him. You wanna be a sparring partner, or you wanna fight this guy?"

"I came to fight!' Chuy shouted back.

"Alright boy, that's a lot more fun. Stop being conservative! Mix it up with this boy—slick fighters hate it when you get'em dirty. Crowd him, and for Lord's sake, throw the right hand! Throw hooks, uppercuts, and MORE THAN JUST ONE PUNCH!" Chuy nodded and arose so Billy could remove the bucket and the stool from the ring.

"Go show him something!" encouraged Billy.

"He's dangerous," Sultan warned, with both hands-on Chuy's headgear. "But you ain't gonna know nothin' if you don't really fight him."

Chuy nodded. He was going after Gundersen, and he would rather get knocked out as a fighter than go the distance as a practice dummy.

In the second round Chuy came out quickly, surprising Gundersen in his corner. The expert fighter moved out rapidly, but Chuy followed him throwing hooks and straights that were dodged or caught. Though he was not scoring, Chuy followed his coach's advice and kept the pressure on. At least he was not getting hit. Chuy crowded the champ, attempting to clinch, but Gunderson had fought many guys who had tried to push and clinch. He clinched Chuy instead and spun him, landing a right and left that stunned the challenger. Gundersen turned to dance away, but instead of falling back as expected, Chuy kept the pressure on. His conditioning helped him shake off the shots, and answer with the first good straight right of his own. The crowd was awakened by the feisty underdog and began to cheer for Chuy. Unexpectedly, Chuy charged the Champ full on, wrestling with him as they both fell into the ropes. The referee immediately tried to break the two, but Chuy refused to let go.

"What ya doin, man?" Gundersen was angry. He glared at the ref and pointed at Chuy, who then received a warning for holding. The crowd booed the call. Hungry for action, they were now firmly on the side of the underdog, who was apparently determined to turn this match into a real fight.

Chuy could have taken the easy way, letting the Champ cruise to another victory, but instead he poked the sleeping tiger. Gundersen was angry now; he threw a left-right-left combination as he danced backwards. Showing a tough chin, the Ponyboy stepped through, ignoring the punches. He then threw an overhand hook that caught the champ with his hands down.

The crowd jumped to their feet. William 'Guns' Gundersen had not become a three time state champ by letting some unknown kid take his crown. Far more embarrassed than hurt, he danced to the middle of the ring with Chuy following. The wily champion began sharp-shooting, sending stinging blows over, through and around Chuy's defense.

In his corner, Sultan grabbed a towel. His fighter had shown spirit and landed some good shots, but the coach was not going to let Chuy get hurt in his first tournament. The crowd was still cheering Chuy on, but Gundersen was sensing a knockout. He began to lose his focus on Chuy to play to the crowd. Dropping his hands, shaking his head, dancing, and showboating, Gundersen lifted both arms high in the air for a moment then threw a left-right-left. Pop! Pop! Pop! Sounded off Chuy's forehead. Gundersen raised his hands for a crowd response, expecting Chuy to fall, or at least take a step backward. Instead, LeDesma, mimicking his girlfriend's style, bobbed down, his glove almost touching the mat, and sprung up, copying Lucy's special jumping hook which landed flush on Gundersen's chin as he was moving away. The blow caused the champ to trip on his own feet, and he landed flat on his rear. The crowd blew up! 'Guns' jumped to his feet and made a pushing motion to the ref to indicate that Chuy had shoved him. The referee was not buying it; he had clearly seen the punch and he began an eight count. Chuy had captured the crowd's support and pissed off one of the most dangerous fighters in the country.

In the corner, Alvarez, Big Ces and the whole group jumped to their feet, calling Chuy's name. Chuy hustled to a neutral corner and glanced over at Sultan who was grinning and shaking his head. He motioned for Chuy to keep his hands up. The next minute saw Gunderson retaliate with everything he had. Chuy covered and clinched in the corner, protecting himself enough to keep the coach and official from calling the fight. Chuy was deceptively strong; he had had enough work sparring bigger pros that he could clinch and hold. The round came to an end just as he turned Gundersen, pushing him against the ropes and digging in two vicious body shots underneath the Champ's defense. Chuy returned to his corner feeling a little shocked at his success and looking surprisingly fresh. It was Gundersen in the red corner who was breathing hard.

"Great Job, Chuy!" Billy screamed.

"You fogettin' the bucket, boy?" Sultan looked a little shocked himself. "He don't like gettin dirty, Chuy. Oh! And by the way, wherever that hook came from, you can throw it again. I think you can muscle this guy—keep wrestlin' with him. You just may have stronger legs than him so remember, the more you throw, the less he can throw. Stay with one-two, one-two, one-two-three and mix in the uppercut and that big hook. You went and got yourself in a fight, Jesus!"

Chuy listened to the instructions intently, nodding his understanding throughout.

"You know you done pissed him off, boy; you know that, right?"

Chuy got off his stool and stood in his corner, looking around at everything and everyone. "I got nothin to lose Coach," he declared.

"Nothin to lose, son!" Sultan echoed.

His breath was coming back, just like it always did, after all the miles, the practices, the sparring. After all the work, his breath was coming back. Sweat burned his eyes as it always did, while his legs screamed for oxygen. There was that familiar weakness and fatigue from the top of his hips to the bottom of his feet. But now there were new feelings, new parts that hurt. His left eye had never been swollen like this. Most of all, his body had never hurt like this before. He had never been hit in the ribs and abs like this. That pain was new, as new as the noise, the lights, huge crowd, and the enormous stadium.

The Land of Lincoln Arena, with its glaring lights and cavernous hallways, was large enough to hold every concert that ever played in Central Illinois. Now on Championship night, with the ring at the center of the huge venue, all the attention from the hordes of attendees was on Chuy and one of the best middleweights in the nation. For Chuy, William 'Guns' Gundersen added one more element of unfamiliarity. The guy Chuy had seen in the sports pages, and heard about in every boxing gym in Illinois, now stood across the ring from him. He was in the blue corner and Gunderson was in the red corner, and now Chuy had a chance to win. 'Ponyboy' LeDesma over William 'Guns' Gundersen! Three more minutes and that long shot of long shots could come true!

The minute between the second and this last round was frantic with action, but time froze for Chuy. All the thoughts that ran through his head: his mother and father, the divorce, literacy class, the first talk with Coach Wolf, sappy Coach Alvarez, tough-ass Coach Sultan, Ms. Kelly and Best Pals Club, Armani and his gangbanger wannabe buddies, Billy and the weed, but most of all, Lucy. The way Lucy looked after practice, all glowing with sweat made him feel like he never had before. Her smile left him weak and nervous and so happy he felt like he would burst. Lucy fought so well. It had been the fight of the night. At least that's what he thought until the announcer stepped into the ring to jolt him from the thoughts racing through his head. Chuy came back to the present moment as the man with the huge voice and white tuxedo grabbed the mic and said, "Ladies and Gentlemen: Please give it up for these two amazing warriors!"

The crowd was on their feet at the sound of the third-round bell. Gundersen immediately came out, landing a double jab and a straight hand that rocked Chuy. A collective gasp came from the audience and those in the blue corner. The referee took a step toward Chuy, but in a split second the tough kid from Northlake answered back with a left-right combo of his own.

Now it was Gundersen's turn to step back while a deafening roar rocked the Convention Center. It was at that point in the fight when an amazing thing happened, a moment that turned the fight totally around. Chuy realized that he had taken the best that Gundersen had to offer and he was not going to be knocked down. Perhaps Gundersen had not trained as hard for State, wanting to wait and peak at the Nationals. Perhaps his semi-finals fight had taken more of a toll than he had realized. Perhaps his anger and frustration with the (now partisan) crowd sapped some of his strength. Or maybe—just maybe—the kid in front of him had trained with enough big strong fast fighters to be accustomed to the kind of power that Gundersen had, so much so that the champ had punched himself out in the second round. The reason was immaterial. Chuy could now walk through Gundersen's punches with little fear. The contender from Maywood walked straight ahead. Throwing right-left-right. Gundersen slipped punches and answered with slick hooks, but Chuy countered them with straight, no-nonsense rights and lefts of his own.

Now it was Gundersen clinching. Chuy worked furiously to gain punching room. Gundersen shot jabs while going backward, scoring, but not slowing his hungry young opponent. Chuy now had the champ on the run, much to the delight of the crowd. Below his corner, Lucy and Nancy, arm-in-arm jumped up and down with excitement and pride. Cesar and Alvarez screamed their approval, their voices blending with those of the crowd.

As the round came to an end Gundersen dug deep into his reserve, showing the heart of a champion by peppering Chuy with double jabs that sent the tough Mexican kid's head snapping back. Chuy rolled his body, looking as if the champ had doubled him over, but then exploded from the mat with the same borrowed Lucy 'Rockem, Sockem' Quinones' jump hook from the mat. It knocked Gundersen to his left against the rope. Chuy followed, but the bell ended the battle. The building vibrated from the roars of the cheering crowd.

Chuy had not won this fight. He was outpointed, winning only one round, but he had won the crowd. "Pony! Pony!" rang through the arena. Chuy and Gundersen stood face to face for a moment but Gundersen skipped the customary embrace, turning his back on Chuy then heading to his corner. Chuy followed him to where the champ's coaches extended congratulations to the kid who had given their fighter a run. Gundersen slumped on his stool and stared forward.

Chuy retreated to his own corner with the crowd calling his name. Billy was the first to hug his friend enthusiastically. The Maywood team stood below Chuy, screaming for him, with joy shining from each of their faces. Lucy and Nancy were in the forefront. Lucy's eyes told Chuy how proud of him she was.

"Ladies and Gentlemen, please give it up for these two great fighters," the announcer urged the crowd once again. When the cheers finally died down, he continued: "The winner in the red corner and still Illinois State Welterweight Champion, William 'Guns' Gundersen."

No one was surprised by the decision. Gundersen had dominated the first round, despite the knockdown. He also won the second and probably the third. The surprise of the night wasn't the scoring or the decision; it was simply the guts, toughness, and conditioning of the skinny kid from Maywood Boxing Club.

"Pony! Pony!" The cheer went up again. When Chuy bowed to the crowd the applause continued. As he was about to step out of the ring, he felt a hand on his shoulder. Gundersen had hustled over to open the ropes for Chuy, an immense sign of respect. As the two walked down the steps, Gundersen, who had received a lesson in humility that would keep him grounded and help him in Nationals, bumped gloves with Chuy.

"Respect, bro," were the only words he said, then he turned and walked away.

The team was still elated when the van left Springfield that Sunday evening. Although they were leaving with only two second place trophies, they had won the hearts of the boxing community. Maywood Boxing Club was a force to be reckoned with and *everyone* in the state knew it.

"I am sleeping all day tomorrow," declared Billy.

"Me, too!" said Lucy.

"Like the sound of it," Nancy agreed.

"Dude, I can't miss a day like you kids. I gotta work, I got a real job, can't miss another day," Ulises added.

Everyone in the van waited for Chuy's response.

" I'm sleepin' already. I might sleep for a week," he finally told them, then settled back and closed his eyes.

"Oh, you rookies, you know nothing," Big Ces spoke up from the front. "Tell'em, Alvarez."

Without turning his head, Alvarez corrected the plan, "You *do not* miss tomorrow, my children."

"Yeah? Coming from a teacher, what do you expect? We won't even get home 'til midnight, and that's if we're lucky," Billy grumbled.

"Of course we won't," Alvarez continued, still facing forward. "But, Billy Big Mouth, you shut up for once. You sleep in the van, you get home, tell your parents all about the weekend…Lucy, how you got robbed, Chuy, how you gave a bad ass a run for his money. Billy, how you worked Chuy's corner. Nancy, how you surprised everyone with the coolest robes in the state, etc. etc. And don't forget to mention how Billy ate more than humanly possible without spending a cent."

The crew laughed.

Alvarez continued, "Then… you tell mommy to call the school, tell them you will be in late tomorrow. Then…you take a beautiful warm shower, snuggle up in the blankets and set that alarm for 9:30 or so. You get up, look in the mirror to see how cool you are, have a nice little breakfast. Then...you come into school!"

"Why come in at all?" asked Billy.

"Because, my loud friend, you will be the talk of the school tomorrow. You got to come in and get your props! Hell, by Tuesday they'll be on to the next thing. All your names will be on the announcements—I already called it in! You might as well be a star while you can. It's good for the club, and you know I never mind a little attention thrown my way! That's the way you do it, children. No practice tomorrow, go home, go to sleep again."

"Is that what you're doing, Alvarez?"

"Just the part about looking in the mirror." Alvarez turned to face the team. "That's the way I should do it, but I'm so used to waking up at five, I'll probably just stick with my normal routine, but no weight room tomorrow. I'm leaving work right at three-thirty, I'll probably be asleep by seven tomorrow night."

The team van headed up Interstate 55, through the corn fields of Central Illinois. Soon the van was quiet on the inside as the teenagers passed out one by one from the excitement of the weekend. Alvarez and Big Ces talked quietly, recalling their first tournament, reliving high school days and then bringing up any topic they could think of to keep them awake until the drive was finished.

CHAPTER 37

The next morning Lucy and Chuy arrived at school on time. They had skipped their morning run but were still operating on pure adrenaline from the weekend. Neither had slept past six o'clock. Billy, in fact, was the only one who took Alvarez's advice, arriving at 10:30, but still finding plenty of people to tell all about how he had "worked" Chuy's corner for the big fight.

When the morning announcements reported that the Layden fighters had made it to the finals, losing tough fights to the reigning champions, cheers could be heard throughout the school. In PE class, Coach Stark brought Chuy in front of the entire gym where he received a standing ovation. Lucy was interviewed by her Advanced Placement Psychology classmates and teacher on the mindset of a combat sport versus other high school sports: what motivated her to begin, what continued to motivate her.

In her fashion class, the teacher projected pictures of the robes and uniforms that Nancy had created for her friends. Ms. Foss said that she had never been so proud of a student for using skills learned in the class in such a unique and important way. Nancy gracefully accepted applause from her impressed classmates, while she gleefully thought about the "A" she was certain to get.

Of course, Wolf and Kelly brought the special needs kids into the cafeteria to present Chuy and Lucy with crowns and belts the students had made for the fighting pair. Mr. Wolf silenced the whole cafeteria, then Missy presented the items. The cafeteria was immediately ringing with applause!

"Gosh, Chuy," Lucy exclaimed as Missy placed the crown on her head, "just think what it would be like if we would have won!"

Chuy tried to look regal under his paper crown. "Yeah, Salim and the rest of the kids would have come in on the Goodyear Blimp!"

As Alvarez had predicted, the crew was the talk of the school for a couple of days. Chuy noticed a few whispering freshmen pointing at him and looking awed. He smiled to himself, though he knew his time as a celebrity was going to be short-lived. As Alvarez had predicted, everything was back to normal by the end of the week. Still, Chuy couldn't help but feel proud.

The next week, Lucy, Chuy, Nancy, and Ulises were back at the gym. Billy was wrestling and doing very well; he was 3-0 in the young season. Chuy and Lucy, now solidly the leaders at the gym, were just about ready to start warm-ups when they spotted a pair of unexpected visitors. At the top of the stairs, peering in the doorway stood Armani!

The sight surprised Chuy. His immediate thought was that his old enemy was looking for trouble. *What balls he's got showing up here*, he thought angrily.

Chuy took a step toward the door, but he was redirected by the sarcastic booming voice of Sultan!

"You two big shots need a formal invitation to begin practice now that y'all had a decent tournament? Well then, Mr. Jesus and Ms. Lucy, if you would be so kind as to get your butts moving, it would be greatly appreciated."

Sultan gave them a look that caused both athletes to respond with haste. Chuy began leading the warm-ups and calisthenics. Out of the corner of his eye he saw Alvarez talking to Armani. Armani soon left, returning seconds later with a boy who appeared to be about twelve years old. Alvarez talked to the pair for a while, then led the young man to a spot on the floor and assisted him in the warm-ups. Chuy looked over at Lucy, eyes wide with surprise. Lucy grinned and kept working. She recognized that Armani had brought his little brother Joey to the gym!

Armani stood quietly by the door, watching the workout, at times talking with Big Ces or Sultan. Joey tried his best to keep up with the group, getting instructions from Ulises and Nancy. When it came time for stations, Lucy showed the boy how to hit the heavy bag and how to shadowbox. Chuy instructed him on the tricks of the speed bag and the two-handled bag. The best advice Joey received from all his coaches: be patient, it takes practice, the more often you come, the quicker you will pick up.

"I'm not very good at any of this stuff," a frustrated Joey confessed to Chuy as he desperately tried to time up the speed bag.

Chuy encouraged the young man. "Hey, man you're catching on fast. You should've seen me when I first started. Truthfully, you're better at the rope than my friend Billy, and he's been coming here for almost a year."

Joey wasn't convinced, "Really? Is that true?"

"Cross my heart and hope to win Gloves," Chuy declared. He patted the boy on the shoulder, "Listen, little dude, there are a ton of people that don't make it through their first practice. You are doing great, just remember ..."

"I know," interrupted Joey. "Just keep coming; the more you come, the quicker you'll get it, the better you'll be."

"See you're a smart kid.

"I don't know about that, I just heard it fifty times already."

"Because it's true! Now less talking and more working!"

When practice ended, Chuy and Lucy went to their usual area to remove their hand wraps and towel off. Armani approached with his hand extended. Chuy shook the outstretched hand. Armani stepped over to give Lucy a hug.

"How surprised are you guys to see me?"

"Won't lie to you, I would have lost the bet." Lucy admitted.

"Ha!" Exclaimed Armani. "A lot has happened since… well, you know. And I wanted to say…"

"Stop, Armani!" Lucy held up her hand. "You don't have to say a thing. Just tell us what made you decide to get your little brother into boxing."

"You did Lucy; you and Chuy. Joey's a good kid. He's always been interested in boxing. I don't want him to end up like..." Armani dropped his head for a long moment, "Well, I guess this will keep him busy and out of trouble, and maybe... well, I have no right to ask... but... I was wondering if maybe you could keep an eye on him for me? You know, make sure he's showing up and doing alright."

"Yes!" both fighters exclaimed in unison.

"Are you going somewhere?" asked Lucy.

"I guess I got another surprise for you. Yeah, I'm going into the Army."

"Armani, really?" Lucy was excited for him. "That's... something I never expected."

"Yeah, I guess I never expected to be saying it. " Armani looked happier and more hopeful than the two had ever seen him, "Well, first I gotta finish my school stuff. Dean Rudy helped me out with this credit recovery program. I'm gonna stay with my mom and aunt in Puerto Rico and I can do the program on-line there. I joined an Army training program with a recruiter there. They tell me I should be able to go in this summer."

"What about Joey?" Lucy inquired.

"Well, that's the thing. He's doing so well staying with his friend Miguel's family that he's going to keep living with them. We sold the house and made enough to pay for Joey's expenses and then some. Let's say they are getting rewarded for their kindness to my little brother."

"Wow, you did alright, huh?" said Chuy, surprised but glad to hear it.

Armani shrugged, "Yeah, turns out people want to buy in Northlake because of the school—I guess because of students like you two. The price of homes has gone up, even one that comes with bullet holes!"

The three laughed together in a way they never could have guessed would ever happen.

Armani leaned in as if he was telling a secret, "Between us, my older brother Daniel had a lot of cash he had stashed over the years. I didn't know what to do with it, but a wise man told me to do something good with it, so Joey and Manny are going to get a pretty good down payment on college.

"Armani!" Lucy clapped her hands. "That is so great. I am so proud of you."

"See Lucy, If you stuck with me you could have a man with tall cash!" Armani said with a wink.

Lucy gave him a quick hug, "Sorry, Armani, but when it comes to my heart, Chuy wins."

"You know when it comes to a lot of things, I think you are right, Lucy. Chuy wins." Armani gave Chuy one last handshake and a wistful smile. "Yep, Chuy wins!"

The End